The Phantom Church and
Other Stories from Romania

Pitt Series in Russian and East European Studies

The Phantom Church and Other Stories from Romania

Edited and translated by
Georgiana Farnoaga & Sharon King

Selection, introduction, chronology,
and biographical notes by
Florin Manolescu

University of Pittsburgh Press

Published by the University of Pittsburgh Press, Pittsburgh, Pa. 15260

Copyright © 1996, University of Pittsburgh Press

All rights reserved

Manufactured in the United States of America

Printed on acid-free paper

10 9 8 7 6 5 4 3 2 1

Library of Congress Cataloging-in-Publication Data

The phantom church and other short stories from Romania / edited
and translated by Georgiana Farnoaga and Sharon King; with an
introduction, chronology, and biographical notes by Florin Manolescu.
        p.   cm.—(Pitt series in Russian and East European studies)
    ISBN 0-8229-3951-7 (alk. paper). —ISBN 0-8229-5608-x
(pbk. :alk. paper)
    1. Short stories, Romanian—Translations into English.
I. Farnoaga, Georgiana.   II. King, Sharon, 1958–
III. Manolescu, Florin.   IV. Series: Series in Russian and East
European studies
PC871.E8P48   1996
859'.30108—dc20.   96-25237
                                                      CIP

A CIP catalogue record for this book is available from the British Library.

❧ Contents

〜〇〜 *Gender and Society*

〜〇〜 *Voices of the City*

❦ *Introduction* Florin Manolescu

The beginnings of Romanian short fiction coincide with those of
written Romanian literature. More precisely, the Romanian short
story has its roots in the intersecting of oral with written literature: on the one hand, folk tales, legends, and epic ballads; on the
other, popular books on the life of Alexander the Great and similar heroes, Old and New Testament stories, saints' lives, and historical writings.[1] All these genres and forms constitute a heritage
of tremendous epic force, which most Romanian writers have
drawn on. Indeed it is evident in the very first works of short fiction: Costache Negruzzi's historical short story "Alexandru
Lăpușneanul," published in 1840, was a masterpiece of the genre.[2]

The beginnings of modern Romanian literature date from the
1830s, when the pressure of the Ottoman Empire upon the
Romanian Principalities had started to ease, thus allowing for
greater freedom in national and cultural expression. This trend
gained momentum during the second half of the nineteenth century when, in a few short decades, Romanian literature caught up
with genres that had taken several centuries to develop in Western European countries. For instance, novel writing evolved from
the modest attempts of the 1848 generation to the enduring
works of Nicolae Filimon (*The Old Gentry and the Nouveaux
Riches,* 1863) and Ioan Slavici (*Mara,* 1906). At the same time,
progress in disseminating literature (through the rise of magazines and newspapers as well as books), translations, borrowings
from various genres, and the rediscovery of earlier Romanian

---

1. *Alexandria* was first translated in the early seventeenth century. Metropoli-
tan Dosoftei translated *Saints' Lives* in 1682. The narrative legends opening Ion
Neculce's 1743 Moldavian Chronicle are considered the beginnings of the short
story genre in Romania.
2. In his *History of the Romanian Literature from its Beginnings to the Present*
(1941), G. Călinescu, one of the most important Romanian literary historians,
states that "Alexandru Lăpușneanul" would have become as famous as Shakespeare's *Hamlet* had it been written in a language of world circulation like English.

writings, neglected under foreign rule (from around 1711 to 1821), all enriched the existing heritage.[3]

These developments took place against a background of ever increasing cultural self-awareness. The first national theaters were established in Iaşi and Bucharest in the mid-1800s. Medieval historical chronicles and collections of folklore began to be published around the same time.[4] After the 1859 unification of the Romanian Principalities—Moldavia in the north and Wallachia in the south—institutions of higher education were founded in Iaşi and Bucharest, and the Romanian language shed its Cyrillic alphabet in favor of the Latin, which better reflected its Romance origins.

Romanian literature came to full maturity on the very eve of the country's formal independence from the Ottoman Empire (1877). The last three decades of the century saw the emergence of the classical Romanian writers: Ion Creangă and Mihai Eminescu in the province of Moldavia, Ioan Slavici in Transylvania (which was part of the Austro-Hungarian Empire until 1918), and Ion Luca Caragiale in the province of Wallachia. Ion Creangă, the first great Romanian storyteller, drew his inspiration from Romanian folklore to write fairy tales and short stories that have been compared to works by Charles Perrault, François Rabelais, and Laurence Sterne. Mihai Eminescu, inspired by Romanian folklore as well as German philosophy and Romantic literature, is the father of modern Romanian poetry and author of stories of the fantastic that recall Novalis and E. T. A. Hoffmann. The short stories of Ioan Slavici describe the rural universe of Transylvania, with its religious and ethnic concerns, in a manner reminiscent of the *Heimatkunst* of late nineteenth-century German authors. The playwright and prose writer Ion Luca Caragiale focused on the universe of the city, which he satirized with Voltairean wit. Some of the best-known stories by Ion Luca Caragiale (whom the Romanians have often compared to Mark Twain) appeared in the widely circulated gazette *Universul* (1899–1901), underlining the close connection between short fiction and the daily newspaper.

The press in fact served as the main vehicle for the development and diversification of the Romanian short story. In the pages of newspapers, almanacs, and popular calendars, short fiction flourished as a blend of the

3. Literary landmarks like the allegorical *Hieroglyphic History* (1705), by ruling prince Dimitrie Cantemir, and Ion Budai Deleanu's epic poem *The Gypsiad* (1801–1812), were first published in the late 1800s, having lain virtually forgotten until then.
4. They were published by Mihail Kogălniceanu and Vasile Alecsandri, respectively.

local tradition (to which one must add the larger Eastern European or "Balkan" features of sociability, inventiveness, and humor) with Western influences (conveyed mainly through translations). The press also became a support for the "popular" story. This type of short fiction was generally rejected by the representatives of elitist or "high" culture, who labeled it vulgar and immoral.[5] However, it enjoyed great popularity with the general public. The first stories of this type were tales of adventure about daring Romanian outlaws (N. D. Popescu) and science fiction novellas, either set in the future (Take Ionescu, Alexandru Macedonski) or dealing with interplanetary travel (Victor Anestin).

Thus, during the second half of the nineteenth century, the canon of Romanian short fiction developed in two distinct directions: writings of high artistic merit, addressing the elite, and works with popular appeal, aimed at the masses. Most twentieth-century prose writers would relate to one or another of these poles, so widely different in structural, thematic, and stylistic registers, as well as in outlook and audience. Mihail Sadoveanu, one of the greatest prose writers of the twentieth century, and the interwar novelists and short story authors Liviu Rebreanu and Hortensia Papadat-Bengescu were the most prominent representatives of the elitist trend. Cezar Petrescu, who wrote short stories of the fantastic and adventure and espionage stories, as well as H. Stahl, Victor Eftimiu, Felix Aderca, and Gib Mihăescu (who all wrote science fiction in the first half of the twentieth century) had a less sophisticated readership in mind.

After World War II this clearly delineated bipolar system broke down under the pressure of the Communist dogma enforced by the Stalinist regime. For the first time in its history, Romanian literature was completely cut off from its traditions. "Socialist Realism," the new, Soviet-imposed aesthetic—mandatory until the mid-1950s—was an artificial, arbitrary set of literary dictates to which every Romanian writer had to conform. After a short period of transition (1945–1947) in which Romania was still able to maintain some of its prewar political and aesthetic pluralism, literature became a tool in the service of the new society, its purpose to glorify the achievements of the workers and peasants in carrying out the Communist Revolution. The only possible heroes in poetry, prose, or theater were the formerly exploited masses, now representatives of the "dictatorship of the proletariat" and victors in the "class struggle" against the former bour-

---

5. A virulent critic of the genre was Nicolae Iorga (1871–1940), a prominent Romanian literary historian.

geoisie and landowners. Language was simplified; the number of themes permitted severely curtailed; and many literary forms and trends (fantasy, erotica, surrealism) disappeared under the ban. Certain genres, such as detective stories, science fiction, and children's literature, were allowed to express only the most outrageous clichés of Cold War propaganda. In accordance with Lenin's theory of "two cultures," the "old" (prewar) literature was portrayed as bourgeois, decadent, false, and degenerate; the "new" proletarian literature of the Soviet type was heralded as genuine, authentic, objective, and vivid. Most of the short prose works published during this decade (later referred to as the period of "vulgar sociologism" or "proletcultism") were journalistic rather than imaginative in nature and were signed by the opportunists and party activists of the moment, turned writers overnight, or by "fellow travelers," many of whom were, in fact, talented writers.[6]

Faced with this brutal attack on their personal and creative freedom, some writers capitulated; others stopped publishing; a few committed suicide; many emigrated. A gulf thus opened between the writers of the diaspora and those left behind, with any direct communication between the two groups forbidden for nearly half a century.

The authors who stayed in Romania and chose to ignore the official proletcultist dogma either faced attacks for writing decadent bourgeois prose or resigned themselves to writing clandestinely and postponing publication. Marin Preda, for instance, though still able to publish a volume "deviating" from Socialist Realism in the late 1940s (*Encounter in the Fields*, 1948), was accused of "violent language" and "literary naturalism" by the emerging Communist critics.[7] Vasile Voiculescu wrote his short stories of the fantastic in secret in a desperate attempt to recover the neglected sources of Romanian folk mythology. Mircea Horia Simionescu, an inventive political parodist, and other writers of the Târgovişte School (Radu Petrescu, Costache Olăreanu) were able to publish their volumes only in the more liberal 1960s. The generation of writers of the 1960s and 1970s returned to the humiliating restrictions and taboos of the 1950s, satirizing

6. Vulgar sociologism refers to the reductionist application of Marxist-Leninist principles to the analysis of art and literature. "The Proletcult" was an organization that promoted the development of a distinct proletarian literature and art in Soviet Russia immediately after the October Revolution. The term "fellow traveler," originated by Leon Trotsky in his book *Literature and Revolution*, designates a writer who supported the tenets and program of the Communist Party without actually belonging to it (or necessarily believing in it).

7. Regrettably, we were unable to obtain the rights to any of Preda's works. (Editors' note.)

them in their work. Some, like Radu Cosașu, had at first adhered to the Socialist Realist style, only to turn away and ridicule it ingeniously in their later prose.

But the relative freedom of the 1960s meant more than simply the rejection of Socialist Realism as the only possible aesthetic doctrine and its replacement by a more vaguely defined "Socialist Humanism." It also meant the rediscovery of Romanian literary tradition by an entire new generation of writers: Fănuș Neagu, Nicolae Velea, Sorin Titel, D. R. Popescu, Ștefan Bănulescu, Ana Blandiana. Although unable to rid themselves completely of previous proletcultist taboos, these writers refocused their work on the individual and his or her subjective world. This, in turn, led to a rehabilitation of some of the formerly banned genres: fantasy (Ștefan Bănulescu, A. E. Bakonsky), detective stories (Ion Băieșu), and science fiction (Ov. S. Crohmălniceanu). Finally, the 1960s made possible the appearance of literary experiments and avant-garde movements. The most important of them, "aesthetic oneirism," exploited dreams as a literary technique. Its principal spokesman was Dumitru Țepeneag; other representatives included Leonid Dimov, Virgil Mazilescu, Daniel Turcea, and Vintilă Ivănceanu.

This period of cultural liberalization was short-lived, however. Following his visit to China and North Korea (1971), the Romanian president Nicolae Ceaușescu launched his own mini "cultural revolution," attempting to regulate ideologically all forms of intellectual and cultural activity. As institutional control on literature began to reassert itself, writers opposing the restrictions put upon them turned dissident or were forced to emigrate. Among them was Dumitru Țepeneag, who had been successfully publishing his innovative stories of the fantastic until 1971–72, when they became incompatible with the new ideology. He started publishing in France in 1972, and settled in Paris three years later, after Ceaușescu withdrew his Romanian citizenship, in a scenario similar to the one the Russians had enacted for Alexandr Solzhenitsyn. An earlier member of the Romanian literary diaspora was Petru Dumitriu, who had left for Germany in 1960. In exile, his literary output shifted from conformity to the doctrine of Socialist Realism to a biting satire of the totalitarian system he had intimately known. Ioan Petru Culianu, who emigrated in 1972, settled in the United States, where, like his mentor Mircea Eliade, he taught the history of religion at the University of Chicago. Culianu shared Eliade's fascination with the mysterious world of the Far East, esoteric doctrines, and the relationship between the sacred and the profane. His untimely death in 1991 cut short a literary output that bears comparison to that of Jorge Luis Borges or Umberto Eco.

The major problem the writers of the diaspora encountered, besides being cut off from their native soil and culture, was deciding which language to write in. Some chose to adopt the language of their new country: French for dramatist Eugène Ionesco and essayist Emil Cioran; Spanish for the novelist Vintilă Horia; or, for the prose writer Ioan Petru Culianu (an erudite polyglot and cosmopolitan), Italian, French, and English. None used both his native *and* adopted languages, as did Vladimir Nabokov (Russian and English) and Samuel Beckett (English and French). When the writings of most Romanian exiles appeared abroad, they appeared in translation.

The great exception among emigré authors was the writer and historian of religion Mircea Eliade. A member of the diaspora from 1945 to his death in 1986, he wrote and published all his literary works abroad in Romanian. Widely translated (particularly into French, English, and German) and partly published in Romania in the late 1960s, his works reveal him as a prominent representative of the Romanian school of the fantastic. Extensive publication of his writings did not occur until the early 1990s.

Unlike writers of the diaspora, who freely chose their themes, language, and means of expression, prose writers of the 1970s and 1980s who remained in Romania—Gabriela Adameşteanu, Mircea Nedelciu, Cristian Teodorescu, Gheorghe Crăciun, Bedros Horasangian—took refuge in a literature of photographic realism. On the pretext of maintaining the realist nature of the narrative, they exposed the social misery of everyday life during a period that Ceauşescu's propaganda machine cynically called the "Age of Light." At the same time some authors—especially Mircea Nedelciu and Gheorghe Crăciun—continued the literary experiment inaugurated in the late 1960s by Ţepeneag. This was possible because of the interest shown by the new Romanian school of literary criticism in the theory of the text and in narratology.

The 1970s and 1980s also saw a growing radicalization of the Romanian short story and novel (especially in the "political" novel). More and more writers expressed their opposition to the system, thus creating a political discourse otherwise impossible to achieve in a totalitarian regime. As political pressure on literary creation increased once more, censorship, which had been formally dismantled at the end of the 1960s, came to be exerted by agencies like the Central Committee of the Communist Party, the Council of Socialist Culture and Education (a sinister realization of Orwell's "Ministry of Truth"), and by the publishing houses themselves. As a result, the works of writers such as Paul Goma, Dorin Tudoran, Ana Blandiana, and Mircea Dinescu were banned outright. Other writers were able to publish only parts of their works, the rest being "shelved" indefinitely. For instance, the short stories of Mircea Cărtărescu, the principal representative of the 1980s generation, did not reach the public until 1989, and then only in an abridged and altered edition acceptable to the censor. The full text of his works did not come out until the 1990s.

Almost identical was the situation of the young authors who appeared on the literary scene after 1989. Authors such as Ion Manolescu honed their writing skills in university literary clubs in almost total secrecy. Most of their stories written before 1989 used photographic realism, parable, allegory, satire, or travesty, techniques Romanian writers resorted to so as to indict their oppressive regime obliquely. These young writers also consciously endeavored to connect its two disparate branches: elitist and popular. They combined "serious" literature with traditional adventure and science fiction, even comic strips and cybernetic fiction, these last two specifically because they were rejected by the official culture. Furthermore, in their desire to counteract the harmful effects of "protochronism"—the government-supported theory that all Western artistic and literary innovations had been preceded by Romanian efforts in those fields—they experimented with postmodernism and textualism, thus reestablishing the link between Romanian literature and European and world literatures.

The course of Romanian postwar literature, especially from the mid-1960s until 1989 (the year that marked the end of Communist dictatorships in Eastern Europe), was thus characterized by a continuous struggle between the representatives of official culture (party activists, political propagandists, and "Party writers") and the representatives of a free and authentic culture. What direction Romanian literature will take remains to be seen. For now, at least, it has returned to the past to recuperate previously forbidden themes (as in the stories of Cristian Teodorescu) or has expressed anxiety over a present still ravaged by the sins of the past (as in the works of Răzvan Petrescu).

The present anthology, which contains stories written between 1949 and 1996, puts forward the notion of a genuine Romanian literature, one that flourished despite the political dogmatism of those who tried to control and therefore destroy it. The variety of stories included demonstrates the extent to which the policy of conformity and control typical of all dictatorships failed both culturally and spiritually. This anthology is also the first to present the writers of the Romanian diaspora as an integral part of Romanian literature. Without them, the Romanians would not only be poorer, they would also be fewer.

True, the selection could be expanded to encompass more names and titles, but its principal purpose would remain the same: to give a new audience samples of a literature that reached its readers in spite of great obstacles, providing them with a space to find themselves with all their fears, nostalgia, phantoms, and joys.

❋❋❋ 1940–1990: A Chronology

1940	June 26	Following the Ribbentrop-Molotov Pact of August 23, 1939, Romania yields its northeastern provinces, Bessarabia and Northern Bucovina, to the USSR.
1940	August 30	Following the Diktat of Vienna, issued by the Axis powers of Germany and Italy, Romania is forced to cede the northwestern part of Transylvania to Hungary.
1940	September 6	King Carol II abdicates; his son Mihai I takes over the Romanian throne. General Ion Antonescu is designated as head of state.
1941	June 22	Together with Germany, Romania attacks the USSR. Its goal is to regain the territories occupied by Soviet forces in 1940.
1944	August 23	Marshal Ion Antonescu is arrested on the orders of King Mihai I; Romania switches allegiance and joins the Allies against Germany.
1944–1945		Between August and May 9, the Romanian army liberates northwestern Romania from Hungarian occupation and helps liberate Hungary and Czechoslovakia from Nazi domination.
1944	September 12	Romania signs the Armistice in Moscow. The Soviets, with one million troops on the territory of Romania, start to exert pressure on the country's political and economic structures.

In late September, the Society of Romanian Writers and the Union of Professional Journalists are reorganized in Bucharest. Restructuring is preceded by attacks in the press on major prewar Romanian writers, literary journals, and publishers. At the end of the month, the society adopts a platform stressing the need to follow Soviet models and develop a culture for the masses. This paves the way for Socialist Realism, the only artistic doctrine permitted until the mid-1960s. The first victims of this dogma are the surrealist school; their poetry will disappear from the scene for two decades.

1944   October 3   An article in *Scânteia*, the Communist newspaper, calls for a purge of authors. Many writers are arrested; others commit suicide. Some become expatriates (in France, Germany, Italy, Spain, and the United States).

1945   March 6   Under Soviet pressure, a government entirely controlled by the Communists takes power. It is headed by Prime Minister Petru Groza.

1945   March 22   The government implements an agrarian reform, limiting private ownership to fifty hectares.

1946   Drought and the deliberate disorganization of Romania's administration lead to famine in Moldavia, the country's northeastern province. 120,000 die.

1946–1948   In July 1946 approximately two thousand book and magazine titles are banned. By 1948 the number reaches eight thousand. Nearly all important Romanian writers are affected.

1946   November 19   Parliamentary elections take place in an atmosphere of terror and intimidation. Communists, using the slogan "Vote for the Sun," win elections by voter fraud.

1946–1954   Hundreds of thousands of people—politicians, army officers, priests, professionals, farmers—are relocated, thrown into prison, sent to forced labor camps in Romania or the USSR, or executed for opposing Communism. Marshal Ion Antonescu is executed on June 1, 1946; Iuliu Maniu, the leader of the National Peasant Party, dies in prison in 1953 at age seventy-five; Lucrețiu Pătrășcanu, an anti-Russian Communist leader, is executed in 1954, after a six-year imprisonment.

1947 June	General George Marshall, United States Secretary of State, delivers "Marshall Plan" speech at Harvard. The United States offers European countries financial support to reconstruct economies destroyed in World War II. Stalin forbids countries in the Soviet sphere of influence (Iron Curtain countries) to accept the aid.
1947 September 22–27	Communist delegations from nine European countries meet in Poland and establish the "Cominform," an international agency granting Moscow control over European Communist parties. The cold war begins.
1947 December 30	King Mihai I is forced to abdicate and leave the country. The People's Republic of Romania is proclaimed. The Communist Party remains the only political party allowed in the country.
1948–1949	Nationalization of the principal industrial, mining, banking, insurance, and transport enterprises and of health centers, pharmacies, and theaters takes place.
1948 August 3	The new law of education forbids the teaching of religion in schools. Private schools are abolished.
1949–1953	Construction of the Danube–Black Sea Canal, a forced-labor project imposed by Stalin, begins. Over two hundred thousand political prisoners, primarily intellectuals, are sent to work there.
1949–1962	Private farmers are forced to surrender their lands, animals, and equipment to large farming cooperatives on the Soviet model. Tens of thousands are beaten, arrested, imprisoned, or murdered for resisting collectivization.
1950	Numerous private dwellings are nationalized. Communist Party leaders and various government officials move into the newly nationalized residences.
1956–1959	Massive arrests and imprisonments follow the 1956 revolution in Hungary, protests and demonstrations in Romania, and the 1958 withdrawal of Soviet troops from Romania. Vasile Voiculescu is one of the writers arrested to prevent anticommunist uprisings.

1965	March 19	After the death of Gheorghe Gheorghiu-Dej, the Communist premier of Romania, Nicolae Ceaușescu assumes leadership of the country.

The National Convention of the Writers' Union removes its president, the poet Mihai Beniuc, a fanatical adherent of Socialist Realism, from office. A period of relative liberalization in literary and artistic expression follows: new genres and styles develop; new literary journals flourish. Ceaușescu promotes a new artistic doctrine, "Socialist Humanism."

1966   October 1   A government decree forbids interrupting the course of a pregnancy in the interest of increasing the birthrate. From this date to December 1989, Romanian women can have abortions only if their health is threatened, if they have brought up four children, or if they are past the age of forty.

1968   August 21   Romania alone among Eastern European countries condemns the Soviet invasion of Czechoslovakia.

1971   Following visits to China and North Korea, Ceaușescu launches a mini "cultural revolution" directed against liberalization, Western cosmopolitanism, professional competence, and intellectuals. Book publication decreases; the Communist Party decides exclusively which titles may appear. In protest, some writers publish abroad: Dumitru Țepeneag in France, Paul Goma in Germany, A. E. Baconsky in Austria.

1971   December   A new law on "state secrets" controls and limits contacts between Romanian citizens and foreigners.

1971–1989   Writers and artists resist official attempts at politicizing culture by organizing acts of open protest and dissidence. The government responds by banning writers from publishing (e.g., Ana Blandiana, Paul Goma) or withdrawing their Romanian citizenship (e.g., Dumitru Țepeneag).

1974   Ceaușescu proclaims himself president of Romania. The cult of personality flourishes; Ceaușescu is compared to Alexander the Great, Pericles, Cromwell, Napoleon, Peter the Great, and Abraham Lincoln. More and more artists emigrate from Romania.

1977 March 4	A 7.2-magnitude earthquake strikes Bucharest and its environs, devastating the city and leaving 1,570 dead and 11,300 wounded. A national state of emergency is declared.
1977 August 1	335,000 miners in the Jiul Valley go on strike, demanding better working and living conditions. 4,000 workers are dismissed and another several thousand are relocated.
1977	A protest movement led by writer Paul Goma involves two hundred people.
1977–1978	At national conventions in Bucharest, Cluj, and Iaşi, numerous Romanian writers oppose the official attempts at re-Stalinizing culture.
1979	An attempt to set up a Free Workers' Union of Romania, with over two thousand members, is brutally repressed by the Secret Police.
1983 March	By government decree, private typewriters must be registered and licensed annually at the local police station.
1985	Dorin Tudoran, a dissident poet since 1979, is obliged to leave the country. He emigrates to the United States.
	Over seven thousand buildings in the old city center of Bucharest are destroyed to make room for the "People's Palace" (a colossal administration building), as well as a residential area for political VIPs. Forty thousand people lose their dwellings. Văcăreşti Monastery, the most important example of eighteenth-century religious architecture in southeastern Europe, is demolished on Ceauşescu's orders.
1985 September 11	After Ceauşescu announces the Village Planning Program, five villages in the vicinity of Bucharest are razed to the ground.
1987	The Crângaşi Cemetery in Bucharest, with approximately six thousand graves and funeral monuments, is leveled in preparation for the Dâmboviţa-Danube canal.
	The number of book and magazine titles published returns to the postwar level: 1950—2,921; 1975—3,877; 1987—3,000.

1987	November 15	Several thousand factory workers attack the Communist Party headquarters in the city of Braşov. Their revolt is an expression of the population's despair with the austerity measures imposed by Ceauşescu to repay the country's foreign debt (lowering of salaries, loss of jobs, food rationing, shortages of electricity, water, and fuel).
1989	December	Ceauşescu is removed from power as a result of the popular revolt beginning in Timişoara and continuing in Bucharest. On December 25, after a brief trial, he and his wife are executed.
1990	May 20	Ion Iliescu, a former Communist official, is elected president of Romania.
1990		In a climate of conflict between irreconcilable political forces, efforts are made to create a pluralist government. Censorship is abolished, and restrictions on foreign contacts and travel are removed. The first steps toward establishing a market economy are taken.

Private publishing houses emerge in Bucharest and other major cities. Volumes that could not be published under the Communist regime see the light of day. Works by writers from the diaspora (Mircea Eliade, Vintilă Horia, Dumitru Ţepeneag, Ioan Petru Culianu) appear in large editions. Former political prisoners publish their memoirs.

✖✖✖ *Note on Romanian Pronunciation*

Romanian spelling is virtually phonetic, each letter representing a sound. Here are the Romanian letters and sounds, with similar English pronunciations, and English and Romanian examples.
Pronounce:

a—like *a* in *garden,* only a little shorter: Ana Blandiana, Albac, Matei Basarab

ă—like *a* in *alone:* mămăligă, Cărtărescu, Costică

â—like *i* in *evil:* Brânduş, Scânteia

b—like *b* in *bell:* Belu, Berevoi, Buzău

c before consonants and vowels other than e and i—like *c* in *call:* colivă, Calu, Cuca

ce and ci—like *che* in *chest* and *chi* in *cheap:* Cega, Rece, Crăciun, Nedelciu, Luciosu

che and chi—like *ke* in *skeleton* and *ki* in *ski:* Tache, Prunache, Mihalache; Chinezu, Paraschiv

d—like *d* in *dean:* Adina, Dionisie, Claudiu, Dania

e—like *e* in *entry:* Ene, Eliade, Eleonora, Petrescu

f—like *f* in *feast:* Fieraru, Fănuş, Florică Florescu

g before consonants or vowels other than e and i—like *g* in *gun:* Gane, Gabriela, Baltag, Fulga

ge and gi—like *ge* in *gem* and *gi* in *gist*

ghe and ghi—like *ge* in *together* and *gi* in *gimmick:* Gheorghe, ghid

h—like *h* in *hurry:* Harieta, horă, Mihai, Prahova
(The h is silent in the *che, chi* and *ghe, ghi* groups.)

i—like *ee* in *meet,* in all but final unstressed position, where i is very short: palincă, Cristian; but Buşteni, Călimăneşti î—the same as â. Spelling used in initial position

j—like *s* in *pleasure:* Cluj, Mirajului, Joia

k—like *k* in *kilometer:* kilometru

l—like *l* in *loll:* Lola, Lică, Leu, Iolanda

m—like *m* in *market:* Marin, Maria, Manolescu, Manoilă

n—like *n* in *nick:* Nicolae, Neagu, Duminică, Dan

o—like *o* in *sorry:* Sorin, Obor, Cosașu, Solomonică

p—like *p* in *part:* Lopată, Pană, Panait, Popescu

r—similar to Spanish or Italian *r:* Radu, Nicușor, Ursu

s—like *s* in *seen:* Sinaia, Silviu, Simionescu, Sena

ș—like *sh* in *crush:* Criș, Băieșu, Șușteru, Ștei

t—like *t* in *tell:* Titel, Tulea, Teodorescu, Tăchioaia

ț—like *ts* in *mats:* Luță, Vița, Țepeneag

u—like *oo* in *cool:* Culianu, Lupu, Sandu, Săuca

v—like *v* in *victor:* Victor, Valentin, Voiculescu

x—like *x* in *ax:* Axenie

z—like *z* in *zone:* Groza, Răzvan, Lăzărescu

ᘓᘓᘓ Acknowledgments

Before anything else, we would like to express our heartfelt gratitude to the authors of the stories. Through their writings, they helped 22 million Romanians survive spiritually under Communism. We feel honored by the opportunity they have given us to make their work known to an international audience.

Our work on the anthology has benefited from the love and dedication of many people on both sides of the Atlantic. We owe them all an immense debt of gratitude. Professor Florin Manolescu of the University of Bucharest and the University of the Ruhr at Bochum generously cooperated with us from the beginning to the end of the project. We are indebted to him for his unerring judgment in selecting stories, his pertinent introduction, enlightening chronology, and concise yet comprehensive biographical notes. Our thanks go to him for his unfailing patience, team spirit, and support.

Professor Michael Heim of the University of California, Los Angeles, offered us invaluable assistance in editing the translations. A wonderful mentor and friend, he has our deepest thanks and gratitude.

Professors Ştefan Stoenescu (Cornell University) and Mircea Martin (University of Bucharest), together with Angela Martin, editor at Cartea Românească, kindly helped us clarify certain cultural points.

Laurenţiu Ulici, president of the Romanian Writers' Union, Ioana Ieronim, poet and cultural attaché at the United States Romanian embassy, author Gabriela Adameşteanu, Professors Petre Nicolau and Mihai Pop of the University of Bucharest, Traian Iancu and Cecilia Popescu of the Fondul literar al schiitorilor din România, Dan Fârnoagă, Nicoleta Dascălu, Anastasia Luca, and Cristina Popa facilitated our access to Romanian sources.

Noted author and radio commentator Andrei Codrescu encouraged us in our project, as did Agota Kuperman, former cultural attaché at the United States Embassy in Romania, Professors Gail Kligman and Ronald Vroon of UCLA, and Muriel Joffe of the Council for the International Exchange of Scholars.

Alan Hanson, director of UCLA's Office of Residential Life, and Cheryl Sims, assistant director, offered us constant support, while their office provided us with optimum working conditions.

Sarah Adams, Walter Anderson, Ken Burkett, Janet Chennault, Maya Edlis, Corrine Hatton, Priscilla Heim, Jeff Hertzig, Karolyn Holler, Marcia Kurtz, Ernest Latham, Kelly Quinn, Patty Rajman-Anderson, Robert Roberts, Curt Steindler, Ronald Vroon, and Jules Zentner read parts of the volume and made useful suggestions. Robert Agajeenian, Marc Ballon, Cristina and Gabriela Butu, Bob Levy, Teresa Masear, Nicola McGee, Anita Reetz, and Simmi Singh graciously helped with the final editing.

Costin Neamțu designed a poignant cover illustration, while Paul Merrill lent us artistic support.

Toni Cole from the Office of Academic Computing at UCLA, together with Jody Cohn, Julie Gerst, Stacey Gomez Chaleff, David Lam, David Leonard, and Alex Lozano, from the Office of Residential Life at UCLA, demystified the secrets of the computer for us.

Finally, we would like to express our deep gratitude to Catherine Marshall, editor-in-chief, and Jane Flanders, senior editor, of the University of Pittsburgh Press, Ronald Linden, director of the Center for Russian and East European Studies at the University of Pittsburgh, and Jonathan Harris, editor for Eastern Europe at the University of Pittsburgh Press for their commitment to our work.

Georgiana Farnoaga and Sharon King

I dedicate my work on this translation to the memory of my parents, Dr. Clyde R. King and Mrs. Lillian I. King.

Sharon King

*Rural Traditions*

ꙮ V. Voiculescu (1884–1963)

V. Voiculescu studied literature and philosophy at the University of Bucharest (1902–1903), then transferred to the School of Medicine, where he received his M.D. (1910). Chief of staff in a military hospital during World War I, he made his literary debut in 1916, with *Poems*. In 1927 a second volume, *Poems with Angels,* came out; it was followed by several others. In 1940, Voiculescu was appointed director of the literary program on Romanian radio. In 1941 his work received the National Poetry Award.

During the interwar period, when he did most of his writing, Voiculescu was a major representative of Romanian traditionalism. However, at the end of his life, after a long term in prison for his supposedly anticommunist views, he finished work on two volumes of short stories with fantastic themes. Magic, totems, and archaic folklore became his major sources of inspiration, as if in defiance of the official cultural trends of the time. Published posthumously in 1966, his collected short stories, *The Bison's Head: Stories I* and *The Last of the Berevois: Stories II,* are considered by many critics to be his best work. Other writings that appeared after his death include the poems *The Last Imaginary Sonnets of William Shakespeare in Fictitious Translation* (1964), the novel *Blind Zahei* (1970), a collection of *Plays* (1972), and the anthology *Magic Love* (1975).

"The Last of the Berevois," the title story of *The Last of the Berevois: Stories II* (1966), was written in 1949.

The Last of the Berevois

It had rained a lot of blood and the times came in red and whirling.

In the turbulence of change the great hunters yearning for vain dangers, who once climbed into the bowels of mountains to chase beasts, had all but vanished. The landowners who once felt it their duty to protect woods and fields from wild animals, had perished too, to the last generation. The local peasants had been relieved of their weapons, down to the last gun barrel and shabby pistol, and in the confusion of an age's beginning, creatures were breeding undisturbed.

The mountains swarmed with wild beasts. Frenzied wolves besieged sheepfolds; bears leaped at herds of cattle, dodging the herdsmen's clubs, nabbing calves, and leaving without so much as a greeting.

In the absence of weapons, ancient practices and primitive techniques of defense began sprouting from beneath the snowdrifts of the ages.

They sprang up ever faster as horrors multiplied. Fantastic apparitions gleamed through the mists on the peaks. Shadows of giants trod on the Babel of sickly, puffy clouds. In the blinding darkness that hurled masses of snow into the valleys, walls of snow swirled down, enveloping herds, dazing cowherds, and—swirling back up—taking two or three stray cattle as prey.

Ultimately, spirits would have to be summoned for assistance and occult powers set in motion.

Seven villages at the foot of Mount Stur anxiously took counsel, fanning their recollections.

Bad news kept coming from high up, from the summer pastures. Not a week passed that there was not a heifer stolen or a bull torn to pieces. Worst of all was a monstrous thief of a bear whose impious taste for meat was driving the cattle herders wild. This surely was the Unclean One. It sniffed out the humans' tricks, evaded their traps, crept unseen, and charged just when it was least expected, as if having seen it all in a crystal ball. It fell upon the men when the fog lay heavy, just as they were sitting down to eat, while they were fast asleep. It impassively seized the cattle from under the noses of the dumbfounded cowherds and then vanished into the wilderness, followed by a chorus of impotent hoots and barks.

Even the boyars from Bucharest would have had trouble with such a beast, let alone a few herdsmen armed with nothing but clubs and courage.

A different way, different means, had to be found. As always during times of great danger, layers of elders were sifted through, huts with patriarchs were pored over, until in a corner of a remote hamlet an ancient man emerged, ageless, nameless, the magic of yore still alive in his mind. He had cut himself off from the world. Harassed by priests, persecuted by teachers, dragged into court by doctors, and scorned by the young, he had fled and buried himself alive in his hovel. There, his name long forgotten, his art a well-guarded secret, he lived a hermit's existence, with only a cow, a few sheep, and a flock of hens for company.

The few men who still remembered him called him "The Old Man with the Knit Cap." That was all they knew about him: be it summer or winter, he wore a long pointed cap, knit from thick wool yarn, like a crocheted sock.

"I inherited it from my forefathers," he would say to anyone who addressed him as "Knit-Cap." "In olden times, when I was young, only people of renown wore such things. Now I'm the only one left." And he would don the magic hat as if it were a limber coif of chain mail, unaware that originally it had been the sacred headpiece over which pagan priests—the ancient magicians—would lay their miters, and kings their crowns. It was the famous headpiece of those entitled to wear hats, the mark of the freemen and the highborn from among whom rulers of the common folk were chosen.

The messengers found the old man doing chores and gathered around him humbly.

The old man, confident that Fortune's wheel had turned and his time had come again, listened to their complaints. Then, full once more of the old pride of being knowing and wise, he emerged from his protective shell of silence. Without considering what he would do or how he would do it, he promised them then and there to rid the mountain of the vile creatures. His magic was like a title of nobility that charged him with obligation. The humble throng knelt in supplication for help and succor, their obeisance investing him with an authority that had long been smoldering in him.

All at once he was a different man. The change occurred without warning, in full view of the cowherds, like a transfiguration. His faded eyes grew young again, their pale blue glinting like dark steel. His cheeks reddened, his face grew smooth. He shook off his cap and his gray locks tumbled down his neck. His hunched body straightened, revealing a muscular chest that thrust forward like a balcony above his belt.

A deeply hidden power flared in his eyes, his gestures, his voice. Out of the shrunken old man arose a stern master, demanding submission and obedience.

The villagers blinked in amazement and glanced away against their will. Passion had so ignited the old man that he seemed to blaze from within.

The metamorphosis did not last long, however. It flickered, then went out.

Diffidently, the villagers inquired what he might need from them. They feared he would demand their souls.

"Nothing," the old man replied. He only asked how many cowmen there were with the herds.

"Seven."

"Good," he murmured. "More will be needed." But he would choose his own helpers.

"Are there womenfolk up there?"

"No, none."

"That's good, too." None might dare go up as long as he was there.

As a lord would, he dismissed the men. They departed full of doubt: if the old man took no money, how could he do good work?

The mage set about his tasks. After rummaging through his hut, he slung a cloth bag full of tools over his shoulder, stuck his flute in his belt, flung his two-reeded bagpipe over his back, and started on his way.

He stopped to call at a few isolated houses, where he spoke to the people through the fence. Then he went on.

One hour behind him, a creature dressed in such a way that no one would recognize it sneaked out and stealthily headed for the mountain. An hour later another creature crept out, taking a different trail. This was in accordance with the old man's instructions that they would not know of each other and could not meet. Each had received orders for a different waiting place where the old man could find him when the time came.

The magician's arrival roused the cattle and the men from their torpor.

His first task was to put out the herdsmen's fire—the fire of modern times, sparked with a tinderbox or matches.

Then he kindled the fire of yore, the living fire, the only one that could influence the spirits. The spark that engendered it—as if it were a child—had to spring like a living seed from a hardwood stick rubbed against a hollow in a piece of softer wood.

Carefully, the mage gathered all the objects and tools in the herders' household that were made of iron or other kinds of metal: axes, knives, pails. He even picked up the tripods. Milk now had to be heated in wooden casks on hearths with stone corners. He took the cowbells from the necks of the cattle but left in place the smaller bells whose silver alloy was useful to magic. He seized the men's army knives and flintsteel, tore off their brass-buckled belts and stripped the rings from their fingers. He nearly ripped a cowherd's earlobe when pulling out the earring the herd's mother had placed there at birth, to protect his life. All of these things he hid far away, in a hollow under a mound of toppled boulders.

The world of the mountains was returning to the epoch of wood and the age of stone.

Then he went after the herdsmen—big dull-witted men, worthless and lazy, like most people nowadays. They would eat and sleep all day long if they could and think only of the women in the village, for whom they sometimes left their jobs. Since they were shameless and disobedient and always at loggerheads with one another, it was only with the greatest trouble that the old man made them obey him and start working magic with him.

At first they jokingly agreed to go along with the old man's plan, seeing it as an occasion for games and merriment, unaware of or not trusting in the significance of the enterprise. Gradually, however, the magician's powers vanquished them, molding them into one body and one soul. They were to follow his commands like a troop of soldiers. After ordering them to wash themselves thoroughly, he gave each of them a clean change of clothes. Then he began a sort of initiation with each herdsman, instructing him privately what to do and how to behave. He was to keep himself clean, was not to swear or use the devil's name, was forbidden to touch liquor or tobacco or profane himself with cattle flesh and above all, was to refrain from speaking. No matter what might happen, he must not say a word while in the grip of magic.

In the meantime the old man gathered weeds and roots from the mountainside: dragon's blood, bear's claw, wolfsbane. Out of them he concocted the magic potion which imparts valor and ensures victory. Then he stored the brew away in a tub hidden behind the door of the herders' hut.

When everything was ready, he summoned the men to rehearse the ritual, to envision how the magic was to proceed.

But as luck would have it, never had the bear done so much harm as during the time the mage was busy with his preparations. One might have thought the beast knew what was in store for it and was bidding farewell to the herds.

One moonless night, which was propitious for the bear, the old man released his spells. In the dark, he entered the wattle-and-daub hut, which was forbidden to everyone else: the cowherds ate and slept outside. To the left of the door lay the hearth, where he built a fire from the embers. Against the back wall lay a manger he had constructed in secret. It was covered with a white cowskin, underneath which something moved. The old man rearranged the skin so that the horns pointed out.

Then he brought in the seven herders, one by one. Silently they did his bidding, lining up, three on one side of the door and three on the other, the two wings flanking the seventh man, their leader.

At a signal the young men wheeled around and thrust their staffs into the ground along the walls. Then they wheeled back and lay down, their heads aligned with the clubs behind them. Stretched out on the earth, they now formed a half circle whose opening faced the manger at the back. They were guarded by the seven staffs as if by spears.

From the pen outside came the snorting of restless cattle. A bell at the neck of a cow rang as if in warning. The quivering sound rippled against the whiteness of the herds in ever broadening circles of tinkling bells. And the countless silvery bells resounded in the night without.

Inside, the fire dozed. The herdsmen pretended to be sleeping heavily, with snores and moans. The magician, knit cap on his head, stood reciting spells. Through the door, open to the stars twinkling in the vault of the sky, a huge black creature crept in on all fours, warily, noiselessly, as if on shoes of felt. It turned to the right, glided stealthily past the arc of men lying on the floor, and stole over to the manger. There it stood up, stretched out its paws and charged at its prey. Terrified bellows came from under the writhing hide. Roused, the cowherds sat up and rubbed their eyes dazedly. The fire flared; the spellcaster had poured a concoction over it that made it leap into startled flames. The men jumped to their feet, leaving their clubs behind. The beast, discovered, tried to withdraw. Now they could see it was a man in a bearskin, his arms covered by shaggy fur. The bear's head, its fangs grinning, rested on his forehead; the lower part of his face was covered by a black mask.

The mage drew the flute from his belt and started to play. The men circled the creature in a leaping dance, holding thin reeds in their hands. As they went round the beast, they narrowed, then widened the circle to the rhythm of the flute, now charging boldly at the bear, now dropping back, afraid. The wild being in their midst rushed at each of them in turn. The cowherd under attack struck the creature with the reed, breaking it. The purpose of the game was to postpone defeating the bear. And the fierce beast not only defended itself but struck down the frail stick, assailed the men, and even caught one or two in its claws, into which it had thrust its hands. The bear was allowed to tear at whatever it caught, while the cowherds could only dodge the attacks. Their powerless reeds symbolized the clubs that had not yet been enchanted. Blood spurted from one man's thigh. A deep gash oozed red in another's arm. The man hiding under the bear's skin had to remain unknown; otherwise, once he was back in the village, revenge would pursue him.

The blood was the signal for the dance's end. The old man with the knit cap raised his head. The flute grew silent. The circle broke. The cowherds ran out through the door, leaving their staffs in place. The fight with the as yet uncharmed men was over. The victorious bear gazed around proudly, bellowed fiercely, sniffed the tracks of the fleeing men, and went out in pursuit of them.

The spellcaster threw another mixture of butter and spices onto the fire, then covered the glowing coals with heaps of dry birch bark and fir twigs, which crackled and burst like fireworks set ablaze.

Enveloped by sparks, the old man invoked the spirit of the great mountain bull, the old archbull, patriarch of the bulls of the present, to give strength to his descendants.

In the meantime the huge black creature had reentered the room. It lifted its head in pride, shook itself, then went down on all fours. Fearlessly approaching the manger, it grabbed at it with its claws. Terrified roars again broke out from under the mysterious hide. Hearing them, seven horned beasts rushed in from outside, wrapped in large cattle skins.

Six of them had tufts of grass in their belts and hooves swaying at their sides. Their tails beat the air with each movement. The seventh, the strongest of them all, had a bull's member hanging from under its belly, a wooden rod painted red; two black woolen balls swung behind it.

As they entered, they guzzled like cattle, slurping in turn from the bucket with the magic potion, three on one side, three on the other, the bull in front of them, ready for the fray.

The old man had thrown tufts of bear and wolf hair into the flames to banish fear and make the heart brave. He uttered the final spell, placed the bagpipe reed to his mouth, and burst forth into a wild gurgling, as if inspired by another Orpheus. The beasts, motionless until then, began to stir, and the magic dance started. The bull advanced, nosing the ground and snorting. Its six companions kept close to it. The bear, as before, tried to head back toward the door, but the pack of magic cattle rushed at it furiously. They cornered it on all sides and rhythmically pushed it into their midst. The circle of beasts, now widening, now narrowing, teased the bear with syncopated bellows, as the magician guided them from the pouches of his bagpipe, which he inflated and deflated in turn.

Pierced by horns, kicked by hooves, and shoved in all directions, the bear roared as the monstrous circle charged at it menacingly.

When at last the bagpipe fell silent, the bull thrust its horns into the hips of the bear. The bear hurled itself to the ground. The man in the mask crawled out from under the skin and in an instant vanished through the door. The huge skin—a black pool in the ever changing light of the restless flames—lay lifeless in the middle of the room, its paws tossed back.

Another dance, this time in celebration, began around the trophy. The mock cattle trod over the bear's corpse to the beat of the dance, pounding it again and again, parading around it. They took turns goring it rhythmically, their heads bent as if in penitence, their horns brushing the ground. Then they broke from the circle, howling and running around the room, only to return and close in on the beast, stomping on it amid triumphant roars and bellows.

Finally the bull lifted the bearskin with its horns and flung it at the wizard's feet.

The men panted, dazed by the magic potion and by their wild twisting and leaping.

The old man motioned them to stop. Obediently, they again lined up, in a circle of six, this time with their backs to the manger. The seventh, the bull who had led the fight and killed the bear, stood in their midst, facing the mysterious manger.

The old man let them rest briefly while he gathered the clubs lined along the walls, bundled them together, and leaned them against the door. Then he started another tune, this time a gentle invocation.

The bull moved away from its motionless companions, sniffed the air, and gave a long roar. Muffled roars came in response from the manger. Then, from amid the thrashing hay sprang the image of a white heifer, a woman swathed in gauzy white scarves, her face hidden by a bridal veil. The cattle skin under which she had lain, unseen, quivered on her back. Two small horns, like new moons, glittered on her forehead.

A heady smoke permeated the room, the smell of burned hair together with a wild scent of rawhide, blood, and sex, the odors found in boarding school dormitories, barracks, and monks' cells.

The mage swiftly changed the song of lament into a wedding song, and the bagpipe squealed merrily. The bull and the heifer approached, facing each other; they stretched out their necks and brushed against each other. The bull nuzzled the heifer and licked her neck caressingly.

Suddenly the fire went out. Startled, the heifer rushed out through the opening the bull had created in the circle. With a bellow it followed her. They both disappeared into the night. As it ran, the bull seized the bundle of staffs leaning against the door and took them with it.

The ritual required the conqueror bull to mate with the rescued heifer somewhere in the wilds where the old man had prepared their bed. The mating was to take place silently and secretly, after which the couple was to part at once and forever. Neither was allowed to shed the cattle skin or the mask under which they hid their faces. The woman would remain unknown, as would the man who had acted as the bear. Death awaited the man who tried to uncover the mystery.

The pursuing bull laid down the seven herders' clubs on the marriage bed so that they would harden like its own virile member. The child engendered that night was destined to become a great beast-killer, impervious to fang or claw.

Exhausted, the remaining six men stripped off their skins, unstrapped the horns from their heads, and fell asleep, ignorant of the reason their leader had left them and of the role the bull had yet to play. Each knew only what concerned him, only what the old man had taught him. And the magician had vanished when the couple did, but only after locking the six men up inside the hut.

Just as day was breaking, and the cows in their stalls were mooing to be milked, the magician returned accompanied by the head herdsman, who was carrying the enchanted staffs.

The sleepers reluctantly awakened to their shouts.

"Get up, get up," the old man urged, breaking the spell of silence. "Only devils and boyars rise so late. Good men, like angels, get up early in the morning to set about their tasks."

The final scene of the ceremony unfolded outdoors, in the light of day, amid cheers of joy.

The spellcaster handed the cowherds the enchanted clubs, which he had rubbed with a magic salve. Each man in turn raised his club in the pale morning light, which reflected like a candle off the shiny wood. Then, arms outstretched, they shook their staffs to the four horizons—saluting the mountain, cursing the dark places—and surged forward to strike the bearskin spread out on the earth.

The time had come for the bull's spirit and strength to pass into a real bull. The herders walked in among the cattle. Some of them lifted up the wooden beams of the animals' pen; others drove them out with shouts. The cattle split into two groups. A stream of bulls and barren cows poured into the pasture; the milk cows headed toward the mountain.

In accordance with the old man's instructions, the strongest bull was driven away from the herd, along with half a dozen white cows separated from their calves, their udders unmilked and swollen. Chased with hoots and sticks, they were led to the neck of a narrow gully and pushed in. The gully ran straight into the mountain, where it ended in a broad semicircle surrounded by stone walls. There was no water, no grass, only boulders that had toppled into the parched creek bed that thrust up to the sky.

Beset on all sides, the seven bewildered cattle ran blindly into the trap. Turning their heads to the men beleaguering them, they bellowed to the rest of the herd.

The mage thrust a pole in the ground at the bottom of the ravine, where the riverbed was only a few steps wide. He had wrapped the bearskin around it beforehand, placing the bear's head at its tip and stretching the paws out on two pitchforks that pointed threateningly at the throng of stunned cattle.

In order to eat and drink they would have to confront the bear, who blocked their way back to the corral. From atop the rocky crags surrounding the gully, the cowherds peered down at the trapped beasts.

Slowly, the cattle regained their calm. They stood motionless for a long time. Then the cows lay down, resting their feverish udders on the cool stones, damp with dew. From a distance they looked like white statues ruminating in solitude. They lay peacefully, as if merely in a different pen, waiting to be taken out and milked as on any other day.

The bull alone remained upright, uneasily watching the lower end of the gully, in anticipation of the danger. The men were no longer visible; only the scarecrow was. Impatient, the bull turned around and roared several times to the bottom of the ravine, whose walls shone like clear glass. Newly roused echoes answered him. He paced with heavy steps around the inside of the enclosure, inhaling the air of the heights through his nostrils, puffing and snorting at the slippery crags, shaking his horns at the blue horizon as if to an enemy. He lifted his bulging eyes, their whites crisscrossed with blood-red veins, to a vulture above him, which was flying slowly, in ever lower circles, in search of carrion.

Time passed.

Perhaps the wind had failed to blow the bear's scent in the direction of the bull; perhaps the worn-out fur had relinquished its smell.

One herdsman strode along the mountain ridge to the back of the ravine and pushed some boulders over, hoping to urge the cattle forward. The rocks thundered down the steep slopes, crashing behind the beasts. Numb, they did not budge. They did not understand what was happening. The herdsman stopped, afraid the rebounding stones might crush the animals.

The old man resorted to another trick. Bellows now resounded enticingly from the mouth of the gully. He had placed a wooden cask between his knees, a piece of hide stretched tautly across it, a tuft of horsetail stuck in the middle. He slid his salve-anointed fingers over the tuft, stroking it skillfully. The cask gave out now the wailing moan of a hungry calf, now the bellicose roar of a mighty bull.

The cows rose, pricking up their ears. The bull stepped forward and listened intently, his neck thrust out, his eyes fixed on the immobile scarecrow. Then stepped back. He had seen through the deception. He would not be taken in.

At midday the cowmen rounded up their herds at the narrow end of the ravine. They began hooting, yelling, calling out, and cracking their whips, as if they were bringing in the cattle from the pastures. Their cries crisscrossed and collided against the stone walls of the valleys, which churned madly, as if in a great battle.

Yet this only made the seven stubborn beasts draw back even further.

The old man had patience. He knew that hunger and thirst can vanquish anything. In the early afternoon the captive herd moved of its own accord. The hour for the second milking had come, the time when the cows longed for the herdsmen's hands to soothe their full painful udders. From below one could hear the cowbells clanging and the calves mooing softly for their mothers. The loose bulls lowed to their captive companion. The trapped cattle set off, slowly and hesitantly, toward the narrow passage, where the monster barred their way. The cows, stung by hunger, were the first to descend. The bull lingered behind, bellowing fiercely, his eyes flaming at the herder who stood watching on the crest of the mountain.

The cows went halfway down the riverbed, stopped for a moment to stare at the creature, then rushed back to the guardian bull, their goggling eyes riveted on the place of danger. Prodded by his terrified consorts, the bull started forward proudly. After taking a few steps toward the motionless bear, he gave a ferocious roar from deep in his chest, inhaled with a snort, pawed the ground with his hoof, and bellowed menacingly, the folds of his throat shaking like a war banner. Then he lifted his head and faced his enemy. But the enemy did not respond to the challenge. It stood like a dead tree trunk. Again the bull gave forth the battle cry, his mane standing up on his neck. He pawed stones to heighten his fury, shook his horns, and slapped his sides with his tail in great wrath. The phantom image remained as still as stone.

The bull repeated his challenge several times.

Perplexed, he returned to the cows and stood before them protectively. Nothing would rouse him. His only duty was to defend the females in his care. Let the adversary come to him.

Other ways would have to be found.

A young cow in heat, driven toward the bear, bellowed out her yearning for a bull. Her scent tickled the nostrils of the bulls in the herd. They roared back to her.

Yet the bull in the ravine remained indifferent to the bait. He merely wrinkled up his damp muzzle, flared his nostrils, and curled his upper lip, revealing broad teeth in a sinister grin.

They would have to awaken his prowess with the enchanted potion, which the warrior bull and its companion fighters had drunk the night before.

The old man straightened his knit cap, crept past the bear with a full bucket, and swiftly laid it down in plain sight of the bull. Before the animal, frozen with fury, could react, the old man was gone.

The magician was sure that the bull, thirsty and hoarse from so much bellowing, would drink the magic potion, which would stir up his courage, dispel his caution, and goad him to attack.

If the bull charged the phantom, knocked it over, and trod on it, he would never again draw back when a real bear crossed his path. He would assail the bear fearlessly. This was the ironclad law of magic.

So the old man and his companions waited expectantly for the concoction to succeed where none of their previous attempts had.

The bull strode with measured steps toward the bucket. He eyed it suspiciously, sniffed at it noisily, then lowered his sinewy neck as if to drink, and with the tip of one horn hurled it against the rocks. Like myriad feathers, the bucket's staves flew in all directions, big drops of the potion splattering over the parched stones and drying up instantly. Only the strong, heady scent remained.

Grimmer than ever, the bull returned to the cows.

Evening was falling. All ploys had been exhausted. There was nothing more they could do. Confused, the herdsmen stared at the mage and waited anxiously.

Disheartened, the mage kept his eyes lowered. Then, searching for support, he glanced up at the peak of the mountain.

Harsh, pitiless, the mountain glared down at him from all its sharp crevices, which seemed to be bleeding in the sunset. The old man discerned a command in its fierce clarity. Was it a rebuke?

Had he made a mistake? He searched deep within his mind. Narrowing like a shaft of light through a keyhole, he passed through to his most secret core. His trade had been handed down to him from generation to generation, along with the hatred and the envy of the commoners, for this was the destiny of all who rose even a head above ordinary mortals.

Had he forgotten something? He descended to his father, Berevoi the Younger, a well-known healer and spellcaster, who for the numerous complaints heaped against him—that he had driven away the rains, made the cattle barren, and put a knife to his enemies—had been forced into exile to Transylvania, where he had died.

Had he neglected a custom? He went down even further, down to his grandfather, Berevoi the Great, master of the zodiac, reader of the stars, who kept genies stopped up in bottles as servants, and who had been killed by the ruling prince because he had foretold a boyar's rise to the throne.

Had he omitted some part of the ritual? He slipped back even further. Along the trail left by the burning of the ancient spirit, he sank to the nethermost depths, invoking the names of the dead. Sliding down the chain of his lineage, he reached his most ancient forebears.

Had he overlooked some task? In his passion he shook awake his ancestors, likewise coiffed in knit caps, the bravest of whom had hurled themselves bare-chested onto naked spears to bear living witness to the gods about the misfortunes befallen their people. What had he left out? What had he failed to do?

But the Berevois of yore, all martyrs of magic, passed by sadly without answering him. And their sorrow wrenched his soul.

Suddenly the doors of his inner darkness were thrust aside, and the great bull of olden days appeared, not lured by an image but with his horns reddened with blood. Then the tragic bear of ancient times, the one who had died gored by a bull, came forth to impart his secret. Magic had deserted man. Its power had been bestowed upon iron and steel. What the mountain was waiting for were hunters with dreaded weapons, not an old man left over from bygone centuries. And all these spirits summoned him to them.

The interior blackness closed in upon him once more.

He awakened. Now he knew. The magic bull demanded true manliness, a living enemy, not a lifeless scarecrow. He glanced around him. The cowherds were leaving. He had permitted the man who had acted the part of the bear to go. He alone remained.

The code of magic prevented him from actually touching the beasts. Like a lord, he was meant to guide their destiny from above. But nothing could stop him now. He had made up his mind. He felt free, as if dozens of chains he had been dragging had suddenly fallen from his wrists and ankles.

At peace with himself, the mage emerged from behind the rocks. He glanced up at the mountain, as if to size up his opponent, then strode resolutely toward the bear's image. Hastily he stripped the skin from the pole, pulled it over his arms, and stepped out boldly above the neck of the ravine. There he stopped. The bull had seen him. He pivoted, flexed his muscles, bent his forelegs, hunched his back, lowered his head and, immobile, stared at the apparition with evil, demonic eyes.

Several minutes passed. The old man held his ground. The bull shook his head as if putting a shadow to flight, then softened the sinister fury in his eyes. Yet his tail continued to flick snakelike against his flanks, and the arches of his knees remained tense.

Displeased, the old man made another move forward, crawling on all fours. Then, incensed by the animal's passivity, he rose up several times, roaring like a bear and waving his outstretched paws. Trembling, the bull crouched even lower, ready to charge. The magician retreated back to the pole and leaned against it: a peaceful bear rising to look at the huge honeycomb of the mountain, from which light was trickling like stone honey.

And he waited.

But the bull did not budge. He stayed as if glued to his herd.

The man fidgeted in the heavy fur, queried the spirit of the depths, and made up his mind. This time the mountain smiled to him coaxingly and approvingly. Calmly, he took off the bearskin, all the while keeping his eyes fixed on the bull. He dropped the skin at his feet and stood with his arms outstretched, crucified against the arms of the pole.

The herders on top of the cliffs stood as if turned to stone. Only their eyes moved, shifting from the man to the bull and back. Horror had stifled their cries in their throats. What was the old man waiting for? What was he planning to do?

The mage was daydreaming, his thoughts in another realm. He was biding his time. Was it true that magic had died, both in man and beast? Perhaps it was. Nevertheless, his magic here, the last magic of all, demanded to be fulfilled. The bull had to win at any cost. Then he, a useless magician, would die too, along with his useless magic.

He summoned all his strength, set his will, and cast another spell, not with smoke or voice but with his mind, directing it straight between the bull's horns.

Once again something kindled in him, its heat making him radiant. The bull moaned softly. The magician's spark went out, and the old man in him again began spinning a thread backwards. Was it his fault that he was not succeeding?

There he stood, ready to give account. But he would bear living testimony, when and where he was called to, of all that was lacking, of all that had been lost, a spokesman for all those abandoned here below. And taking the bearskin in his hands, he rolled it into a ball and hurled it at the bull, whose horns challenged him like the tips of two lances.

The beast could stand it no longer.

He flashed like a bolt of lightning over the few steps separating them and kicked the fur to dust between his legs. Reaching the old man, he caught him and, with a terrifying roar, raised him up on the spears of his horns, then plunged down the gully like a whirlwind.

The furious cattle rushed like torrents after him.

The next moment the horde had surged out of the ravine and were madly racing across the open field. There the bull flung the old man to the ground from the height of his horns. The pent-up herds, roused to blood lust, trampled him as they stomped after their chief.

The charging throng stopped only when it reached the edge of the precipice. Trimphant, the bull waved on one of his horns the knit cap snatched from the magician's head, proudly displaying it to the mountain and proclaiming that thenceforward no one could stand against him.

And, majestic, he trumpeted forth from his steely throat to the four horizons that he, the bull of Mount Stur, had killed the most awesome beast, the bear-man, the last defender of cattle, the last of the Berevois.

Bucharest, October 27, 1949

枢 Fănuş Neagu (1932–)

Fănuş Neagu graduated from a teacher training college and the Mihai Eminescu School of Literature before enrolling at the University of Bucharest. While a student, he worked as editor of the national youth newspaper, *Scânteia Tineretului* (1954–1956). Later he served as deputy head editor of the *Luceafărul* literary magazine and secretary of the Bucharest Writers' Association. In the early 1990s Neagu became director of the National Theater in Bucharest.

It Was Snowing in the Bărăgan (1959), Neagu's first published collection of sketches and short stories, was influenced by the violent romanticism and folkloric realism of his predecessors Mihail Sadoveanu and Panait Istrati. The novel *The Angel Has Shouted* (1968) showed Neagu's mastery of narrative techniques and his uncanny ability to depict stark human dramas while using opulent Balkan forms of expression. *The Angel Has Shouted* and several other of Neagu's works, among them *The Deserted Railway Station* (1964), a collection of short stories, and the play *The Team of Noises* (1970) received Writers' Union Prizes. Other works include collections of short fiction, *The Afternoon Nap* (1960) and *Beyond the Sands* (1962), and two collections of fictitious sports reviews-cum-essays.

"Beyond the Sands" was first published in *Beyond the Sands* (1962).

Beyond the Sands

—*to my father, who waited for the waters to come*

It was 1946, a year of terrible drought. Şuşteru hadn't seen a leaf of tobacco in four days. That afternoon, needing a smoke badly, he pulled a bunch of leaves from the ivy vines creeping up the front of his house, crumbled them between his fingers, and filled his pipe. His eyelids drooped with sleepiness; although it was only just past noon, he had just gotten up. "Damn it," he thought.

"You spend one night keeping vigil, and it takes you two days to recover." His wife, mother-in-law, and children were not at home. "Out getting food," he said to himself. "Scattered about the village like flour in the hands of the blind."

Şuşteru walked out onto the road, his body short and thin, his shirt hanging over his pants. He craved a head of lettuce to eat. During the night he had dreamed it had rained and his kitchen garden had turned green again, the way it had been in good years. Since the drought had begun a summer ago, he always woke up with a desire to eat something he couldn't have. "That makes sense," he thought. "Dreams are born in the stomach and die up in the mouth. It would be good if man could have no dreams at all."

"Give me your pipe, Şuşteru. Please. Just one puff."

It was the village cantor.[1] People said the cantor had lost his mind from hunger. All day long he sat by the side of the ditch, legs tucked under him, eyes fixed on the cloudless sky, chewing sorrel, if he could find any, and mumbling a line from his prayer book, "Thou, Lord, who art sleeping in the laurel grove."

"It's not tobacco, man," Şuşteru replied. "It's a weed. It stinks, and it burns your throat."

He looked down the village street. In front of the town hall a woman was gathering manure in a wheelbarrow to plaster the porch of her house. Under the acacia by the whitewashed bridge a dog was shaking off his fleas. A horse was being shod at the blacksmith's; he could smell the hoof singeing.

Şuşteru turned slowly round the end of the fence and walked towards the river. He stopped by the ditches that once had brought water to his kitchen garden. They were empty; the silt on the bottom had dried and cracked. The riverbed wound its way along like a gray caterpillar, the patches of sand and hardened yellow clay shining desolate in the sunlight. Withered roots hung from the bank on the village side. The milkweed in the village pasture had shriveled from the heat. A field mouse hissed on a mound of earth next to a black briar bush. A rider appeared in the distance, on the top of a low hill.

Şuşteru made the sign of the cross in the dust with his toe and burst out laughing. As a child he believed this would make a spring gurgle up. How stupid he had been! Every year, in the first week of spring, he would go to the village pasture with a short wooden stake and dig up the spring crocuses. He could still see them, white, with two fronds, like drops from a milk pail. As he rushed off to pick them, his mother's words would sound in his ears, "As many crocuses as you bring home, that's how many chickens our brooding hens will lay."

And he had believed her.

The rider he had seen earlier on the little hill was approaching the village at high speed. "He's crazy," Şuşteru thought, waving his hands. "He'll kill the horse if he keeps it up all the way to the bridge." Catching sight of Şuşteru, the rider pointed back toward the hill and called out that the stream would soon be flowing again. It had rained in the mountains; soon the Buzău would be full.

At first Şuşteru didn't understand—his mind had gone blank—and by the time he came out of his stupor the man was far away, vanishing beneath the red arches of the bridge like a ghost across the River Styx. Şuşteru stood still for a moment, his eyes frantically searching the riverbed. He seemed to feel the coolness of the mountain water touching his face. An urge came over him; he jumped over the ditch and ran up the bridge, clawing, scrambling on all fours, panting. One of his shirtsleeves, drenched with sweat, hung from his arm like a loose bandage. He tore it off and flung it away.

Suddenly the cantor appeared before him, fanning flies with an acacia branch.

"Cantor," Şuşteru called out, "the water's coming. I have to take the boat down to the river and clean the ditches. We'll be eating lettuce in a week."

It took Şuşteru half an hour to get his boat out of the shed and drag it through the dusty street to the riverbank.

In the meantime the church bells had begun to chime. "Dong-dong," the big bell tolled; "ding-ding," went the small one. The *toaca*² did not sound; it was sounded only when the priests congregated for the holy days.

Now the whole village converged on the banks of the stream, the men rushing with hoes and pickaxes to break up the mounds of dirt clogging the openings to the ditches, the women gathering their children under a sumac tree on higher ground, afraid the waves might seize them and whirl them away to their deaths. For some reason they believed that when the water came it would flow down from the mountains accompanied by a harsh, evil blizzard, and they shivered in advance, like feeble beasts sensing a hard winter coming. Two of them rolled a large stone—a stone as big as a tree stump—to the shallowest place in the stream in preparation for their washing. In a hole in the riverbed an old man was lining up fishhooks on a string he had fastened to a stake thrust into the bank. Half of a worm hung from each hook as bait. A girl was combing her chestnut hair, fanning it out in the sunlight, and singing a sad song that sounded like a dirge. At the height of the digging, the men stopped for a moment and rolled their trouser legs above their knees to keep them dry. The only clothes they had left were what they had on; the rest had been traded for corn with the rich land- and millowners in the villages above the plains.

After the ditches were cleared, Şuşteru walked over to his neighbors and asked for tobacco. They gave him enough to fill his pipe twice. The cantor followed a step behind. Şuşteru offered him a smoke. Then he walked on slowly, keeping close to the riverbed, pulling at the tatters of his shirtsleeve in an effort to cover his bare arm, reddened by the sun. Seeing the man with the fishhooks, he flew into a rage and yelled at him to remove them, so as not to scare the fish off on the first day.

"All right, all right," the old man said, unruffled. "I'll take them out. But it won't make any difference. Don't you know that fish swim upstream? Once the Buzău gets to the Siret, the fish will come too."

"Right," Şuşteru admitted. "I'd forgotten. Leave them in."

"Who knows?" said the old man. "Maybe I'll catch a few perch. Once I caught a sheatfish here as big as a pig."

Suddenly enraged again, Şuşteru screamed, "No! Take them out! And don't say I didn't warn you!"

It was getting dark. The sun was sinking below the horizon. The villagers, still crowded on the riverbank, would not budge, but were losing patience. Here and there the women had kindled fires. Night was falling. The men went up to Şuşteru to ask him what was wrong with the stream. The water wasn't coming; there was no water in sight.

"If you can't see it," Şuşteru told them, perched on the edge of his boat, "try and hear it. Put your ears to the ground and listen."

Five men immediately hurled themselves to the dust on their stomachs. Şuşteru called out to the women on the bank to stop their chattering and joined the five men in the sand. Nothing. The ground, dry about six feet down, was silent. Clods of earth have no voice. The men who were still standing waited tensely, their eyes glittering in their sockets, their beards, blue-black as prune paste, giving them a fierce look. Şuşteru picked himself up clumsily.

"I could hear it a moment ago," he said. "It was like a faraway clap of thunder." An idea flashed through his mind. "Wait a minute. Maybe the millowners in the hill villages have cut off our water. Those thieves have dug large ditches. What if the water is running into their ponds? It will take a week to get here if we don't go and nail them."

The men looked at one another in silence. Şuşteru could be right. The millowners had made it hard for them to get water in the past.

"They got our clothes for nothing. They left us naked," said Şuşteru. "Now they're cutting off our water too."

They dropped their tools and rushed back to the village for their horses. They had to bring water or the village would perish.

Within a quarter of an hour a group of some twenty riders had formed. The men on the bank shouted to them to pick up their axes and spades. They were certain there would be a fight.

Şuşteru spurred his horse with his heels and the posse set off, spread out at first, then closing ranks like a cavalry unit preparing for the signal to charge. Their progress was slow. The horses' hooves kept sinking in the sand. A horse stumbled and neighed. His master struck him in the head with his fist. The moon had risen in front of them. It was yellow and wrinkled like the cheek of an old woman. The sand glittered, its ivory-white edge rising up to the moon or perhaps its whiteness flowing from up there down into the riverbed. Şuşteru rode out in front. The hill villages were far ahead. The nearest of them was an hour away across the fields. The posse, however, kept to the winding riverbank. They had hardly covered half the distance when two horses, weakened by fatigue and hunger, dropped in the dirt and rolled their eyes backwards. The men stopped and dragged them to the bank.

"Skin them here," Şuşteru told their owners. "And don't let the carcasses slide into the riverbed, or they'll foul the water."

Its ranks thinned, the posse ambled on under the towering dark blue sky. The moon's face lay resting on the ridge of a barren hill that rose ahead of them. There was no trace of light either to their right or to their left. After the burning heat of the day, the fields blew hot breaths at them. The horses were covered with sweat; you could gather the foam from their hips with your hand. The men urged them forward, sometimes gently, tapping them lightly on their muzzles, sometimes roughly, with the handles of their spades, harsh words rumbling in their throats.

They reached the first mill. It stood on a barren bank. The pond in front of it was dry. The riders drove their horses on, telling themselves the water had been cut off higher up. Seven of them dismounted and started walking alongside their horses. The men in front, realizing the others were trailing behind, set off at a trot along the narrow bank. When they reached a bend in the river by a poplar forest, Şuşteru pivoted his small, hairy horse and counted the riders. Half of the group was still with him. It was an hour to the next village, he thought, if not more.

A little before midnight the posse reached the second mill. They had seen it in the distance, hidden among old willow trees, its roof steep and covered with tin. Not far away, on higher ground, stood a house with boarded-up windows. A flock of ducks flew above them, honking, then disappeared over the fields.

"They're coming from the pond," said Şuşteru. "They've been in the water all this time."

The men brought their horses in close together and clutched their axes to their chests. The riverbed made a sudden turn to the right but a few hundred steps further on it changed its mind, turned again to the left, and cut across the pasture. They galloped between the steep banks toward the dam. There they dismounted. The pond, like the one before it, was dry, and the ditches feeding into it were half full of earth—no trace of water anywhere.

The men couldn't believe it. Staggering, they crossed the bridge that led to the mill. A calf lying on the path bellowed in its sleep. A dog barked inside the mill.

They heard a cough, hoarse and muffled, and the sound of someone bolting the door. The miller was frightened; he thought they were thieves. They returned to their horses without a word.

Şuşteru was the first one to break the silence. "They didn't collect the water here," he said. "We need to go higher up, to the other mills."

Four men left the posse and headed back to the valley, their axes hanging from their belts. The others followed Şuşteru until they could see the riverbed stretching ahead—an endless straight swath of chalk. Then they too left him.

Şuşteru did not call them back. He looked at the moon withering above the ridge of the hill. He raised his bare arm and struck his horse on the neck with the reins. Before him he could feel the coolness of the waves.

⚮ Nicolae Velea   (1936–1987)

Nicolae Velea studied forestry at the University of Braşov before obtaining a degree in philology from the University of Bucharest (1958). In the 1960s he served as editor for such literary magazines as *Gazeta literară* and *Viaţa nouă;* later he worked as a journalist and as a script writer for the *Bucureşti* Film Company. His first literary work, *The Gate* (1960), was awarded the Academy Prize. In this and subsequent collections of short stories, Velea focused on the psychological and behavioral changes brought about in rural Romania by the social and political upheaval following World War II.

A keen analyst of the southern Romanian peasant, Velea enjoyed telling stories whose moral he knew in advance. His characters follow tortuous paths, naive yet subtle in their search for a different reality. Thus Velea's work is suffused with paradox and irony.

Other works include the collections *Eight Stories* (1963), *Watchman of Harmonies* (1965), *Flying Low* (1968), and the novel *An Acre of Flowers at War* (1972).

"Carefree" first appeared in *Eight Stories* (1963).

Carefree

It dawned on Duminică[1] that he had always been in a hurry. He told himself that he didn't need to be so anxious, that not much time had passed, that there was plenty of time left. He could afford to relax now, to indulge himself. All his life he had lived quickly, maybe too quickly.

Duminică was the best driver in the district. He worked for the most prosperous cooperative farm, and for the past two years had been in charge of driving the parade float down the main street of the provincial capital on official holidays.

In the past the village of Lupoaia, where Duminică worked, had been poor and backward. But for many years now, the village and the people had shaken off their poverty. They had built themselves large houses and had surrounded them with ornate cement fences, which alone cost over five thousand *lei*.[2] It was a long time since anyone had tried to settle a quarrel with a knife. And Sandu, the militia[3] officer, who had been recognized for his courage when he stayed in Lupoaia some years back, could now be seen kneading dough for cakes on his porch in the evenings.

These days Costică, the head of the collective farm, Nanu, the clerk in the village store, and Marin Rece, the man in charge of the cattle, would reject all offers to drop by for a drink after work. They would refuse firmly, proudly, insisting that they had to attend their evening classes.[4] The reverence with which they held their notebooks under their arms made Duminică feel that he had all the time in the world. The hurry of these people twice his age to get to a place where he had already been gave him the impression that he still had time to relax, to indulge himself. He could postpone making serious decisions for a long while yet.

Duminică was young; he was not yet twenty. But in his mind's eye there still burned the image of the canister of golden corn their rich neighbor had given his family during the drought of 1946. In exchange, his family had handed over their saw, a pair of tongs, a hammer, and the inner tube Duminică used to play with.

When the rains came, the ditches filled with water, and corncobs and twigs would drift along with the current. On such days Duminică would be overcome with sadness. As a child, he had not been allowed to follow along the ditches to see where the cobs would go, which ones went the furthest, which ones got stuck in the mud or were swallowed by the whirling waters. He could not race after them for kilometers or bet on them as the other children did. He and his brother had only one pair of shoes between them. Duminică had to rush home and give them to his brother, who had classes in the afternoon.

At first Duminică befriended Şoalcă, a young mechanic from the hydroelectric mill. Şoalcă lived with his parents but had his own room, and Duminică spent many nights there playing backgammon. After Şoalcă's parents had made the plum brandy for the year, the two youths would go down into the cool cellar and play the game among the barrels. One Friday they began early in the morning and played all day long. Around lunchtime old Tăchioaia stopped by. She had been homeless since her son-in-law chased her out of the house. She always spoke out against him, calling him a stubborn capitalist and a hooligan. She did so for a good reason:

her son-in-law was still pursuing personal wealth and had not joined the collective farm. Tăchioaia asked Șoalcă for a mug of brandy, saying she had roundworms in her belly and wanted to drown them. She sipped at the brandy and watched the boys play. Șoalcă kept winning. Annoyed, Duminică turned to the woman just as Șoalcă was picking up the last pieces on the board:

"See? He's lost again! He's got nothing left."

"Be careful, dearie," Tăchioaia advised Șoalcă. She was on his side; she was drinking *his* brandy, after all.

Șoalcă laughed and promptly won the next four games. Duminică, his face green with envy, laughed the whole time and told the old woman that his friend was losing. Șoalcă lost his patience and explained to Tăchioaia that the winner of the game was the first player to get rid of all of his pieces. Tăchioaia, who did not know the game, found it hard to believe him. "How can you win if you're left with nothing?" she asked. Șoalcă continued to win and Duminică continued to laugh maliciously, repeating that Șoalcă was losing.

"You've lost again," Duminică said.

"How can you say that? Can't you see that I've won?" Șoalcă replied.

"You don't have any pieces left."

"That's right. And what do the rules say?"

"Rules or no rules, you have nothing left."

"Careful how you play, dearie," Tăchioaia sighed.

After a few more games, Duminică motioned to the old woman.

"See? He's lost them all again."

"What are we playing here, dammit?" Șoalcă cried.

"Backgammon, of course."

"And the one who finishes first is the winner. Right?"

"No!" Duminică repeated obstinately. Tăchioaia went on encouraging Șoalcă, advising him to throw the dice toward this corner or that, whichever seemed more lucky to her. Frustrated, Șoalcă was now trying hard to lose. But he kept winning instead.

They played on until evening, one endeavoring to lose, the other to win, both failing miserably. Upset at seeing Șoalcă finish first every time, Tăchioaia started to cry. Incensed, the two young men started trembling from head to toe.

All of a sudden their noses began to bleed. They stopped playing, wiped the blood off their faces, and calmed down.

"It's good that we had a bloodletting," Duminică said quietly.

"We had reached an impasse," Şoalcă agreed.

Sometimes, at night, Duminică could be seen racing his car across the Frumoasei fields, attempting to startle the jackrabbits with his headlights. And when he needed cigarettes, he never walked to the village store, though it was less than a kilometer away; he drove his truck or a tractor.

Duminică did these outrageous things with both diffidence and curiosity. And he went through many stages. At first he was angry with himself; then he was surprised that nothing bad happened to him, as he thought it would. And when people scolded him for being wasteful, he received their rebuffs with the same curiosity, wondering which of his deeds, if indeed any, would have consequences on his life.

And he proceeded to do things just as he liked.

Seeing Duminică's face constantly creased with lack of sleep, the head of the collective farm decided to protect him from his own negligence. And so it came to pass that Duminică was assigned to transport the cooperative's milk and eggs; the load would force him to drive slowly.

But before this new assignment, something else had occurred.

During a holiday hike, Duminică met a girl named Adina Gheorghe, a farming technician in the neighboring village of Cuca. They met at the top of the mountain, where the mist hung very low and the hikers could see one another only from the waist up. They almost seemed to be floating as they walked along. When Duminică first caught a glimpse of Adina, his cheerfulness vanished. He was shaken to the core, as if by a premonition. He became quiet, almost bashful.

On the way back, Duminică invited Adina to ride with him in the truck. After a while, he turned to her in an attempt to regain his cheerfulness:

"We've only gotten to know the top half of each other."

"What do you mean, only the top half?" she exclaimed.

"Because of the fog, I mean. It came up to our waists."

"But there isn't any fog now."

Adina was a proud girl, and her pride made her appear aloof and distant.

Duminică would have liked to make a witty retort to the effect that the first impression was always the strongest and that to him she would always seem only half a person. But her condescending tone intimidated him. His response seemed clumsy; it died in his throat.

A few days later Duminică found himself in Cuca, just as Adina was finishing her day's work. Seeing her come out of the town hall, he stopped his car nearby, in front of the village store. He went inside and looked around without buying anything, then emerged just as Adina was passing by.

"Hello, there!" He tried to sound indifferent but only managed to sound sullen.

"Good afternoon," she replied.

"How have you been doing?"

"Fine, of course. Why do you ask?"

She was condescending again, so he said, irritated:

"Well, I mean, what are you doing after work?"

"What's it to you?"

"I'd like to know, that's all."

"I'm going home. Is that all right?"

"I'll give you a ride."

"I have my bike with me."

"Well, I'll take you and your bike as well!" he burst out with a kind of desperation.

His outburst surprised Adina, confused her. Duminică did not fail to notice this. He grabbed the bicycle, put it in the back of the truck, and opened the passenger door.

"Go ahead, get in," he said.

As they rode along, Duminică grew more confident, believing he had overcome the girl's resistance.

"Up there on the mountain, I saw only the top half of you," he said tersely, forcefully.

"You've told me this before."

"I don't want to know only half of you."

"Why not?"

"You'll be more beautiful to me once I see all of you," he said, almost casually.

"How would you know?" she replied, her face curving into a smile.

"You will be, take my word for it," Duminică insisted, as if his soul depended on it.

"I sincerely doubt it. A cousin of mine got married once. I looked at her the day after the wedding, and she looked no different at all, no uglier but definitely no more beautiful, either!" And Adina burst out laughing.

Duminică felt she was being condescending again. Realizing he had lost the battle, he blew the horn loudly to cover up her laughter.

The next day he looked for her once more, and found her. This time, Adina did not get into the truck. They walked instead. When they came to a deserted area, he took her in his arms and kissed her. She fought him until he pressed his lips against hers. Her arms flailed once or twice, then dropped at her sides, weary and accepting. She closed her eyes.

After the kiss, she took him gently by the ears and pulled his face toward hers. She stared at his face as if trying to remember something. Then she pushed him away, almost angrily. Then she turned around and started home.

Duminică walked silently along the path on the opposite side of the road. He accompanied her for a while, coughed twice discreetly, then turned back without a word.

He didn't look for her again for nearly a week. They had just assigned him to transport the collective farm's milk and eggs, and he was sick with rage.

Adina thought that he had taken her for easy prey, that she had been nothing more than a moment's enjoyment by the side of the road. She went to see him, to tell him he was wrong.

She found Duminică in the yard of the farm, waiting for the milk to be loaded onto his truck. He was leaning against a fir tree, beneath a placard with uneven lettering that urged the workers to take good care of their tractors.

Furious, Adina opened her mouth to speak, then stopped abruptly. He looked weary, defeated. Her anger vanished.

"Has something happened at home?" She was frightened, and startled by her own fear.

Duminică rubbed his eyes and stared at her as if she were far away.

After they finished loading the milk canisters onto the truck, Duminică placed her bicycle on top, closed the back door, and opened the passenger door for her. Adina got into the truck, and he drove her home in silence.

They began seeing each other in the evenings, as if it were the most natural thing in the world. They never set a place or a time, but they always found each other. Duminică now smoked a lot, but after being with Adina, his breath and his body did not smell of tobacco.

Duminică soon got used to transporting the milk and the eggs, and became cheerful once again. Adina noticed the change when one evening he asked her teasingly:

"Do you ever dream of me?"

"No, I don't."

"You don't? Why not?"

"If I did, it would end with me killing you."

Adina was both ashamed and angry when any man sneaked his way into her dreams. None of them escaped unscathed. If she awoke halfway through the dream, and the man was still alive, she would turn over, piece the dream together, and end up destroying him.

"What are you talking about?" Duminică asked.

Adina told him about her nocturnal murders.

"So if you don't dream about me, it must mean you are fond of me," he laughed.

"Yes," she said, simply and defenselessly.

They both laughed awkwardly. From then on they tried to talk about other things. It seemed too early and too trivial to bare their true feelings to each other, as they were.

They started to send each other melancholy letters, laughing all the while. When one would make too overt a confession, the other would mock it in the same laughing tone.

The two felt protected by something that allowed them to play at being one thing and yet be something else altogether. Something that allowed them to linger outside of themselves, their real selves. Something that allowed them—or so they thought—to reconstruct what should have been there in the first place.

They wanted to be carefree a little longer, not for good, not forever. They had no idea of the dangers their game was fraught with.

One day, Duminică showed up at their date tired and upset, having wasted the whole night playing backgammon with Şoalcă. Adina had not slept well either. The day before, the cooperative farmers in Cuca had killed a beautiful horse, a horse she had loved, and then fed the horsemeat to the farm chickens. A careless tractor driver had later run over some of the chickens with his machine, burying them beneath the huge treads. Adina was angered and dismayed by the senselessness of the slaughter. The tractors had come, making horses superfluous; the horsemeat had ended up in the stomachs of the chickens, and the chickens had been crushed under the tractor's wheels.

Duminică had come to Cuca in his truck. He had to go to the village of Săuca to pick up the milk and eggs from their farm because their truck had broken down. Cuca was on the way.

Adina climbed into the passenger seat. Duminică tossed out a sentence carelessly.

"I don't know if I've told you before, but I'm married. . . ."

And, either because his voice was hoarse or because of the heavy stress he put on the words, Adina (who may have been too tired to notice) heard only the words and not the jest underneath them.

"Are you really?" She stressed her words as heavily as he did.

"Yes, really. May lightning strike me down if I'm lying!"

"You're joking, I hope." Her voice was now thin, anxious.

"No, I'm not. I'm really married. Have been for two years now." Duminică's voice was casual, his thoughts elsewhere.

"Well, then . . ."

Adina opened the door and jumped out of the truck.

For a long moment Duminică drove on. Then he turned back. At the bend in the road he found her body outstretched, impaled on one of the wooden posts that had replaced the concrete barriers that had vanished long ago. Adina's arms hung out limply from her shoulders, as if she had been crucified.

Duminică grabbed the girl under the arms and attempted to lift her up.

"Easy," she said, almost sleepily. Then her body jerked twice, relaxed, and froze.

Duminică knew only this: that something real had finally happened. But it had happened too quickly, too easily, for it to seem truly real.

He pulled Adina into the truck and leaned her stiffening body against the passenger door. He continued on toward Săuca. In front of the clinic, he stopped the truck, took the girl in his arms, and carried her inside. A woman passed him on the stairs.

"Can't you see that she's dead?"

Duminică returned to the truck without a word. When he arrived at Săuca, he couldn't remember where the collective farm was. He took a side road and drove for a long time. When he came to his senses, he found himself trying to drive up a steep slope. It had now grown dark, and he had great difficulty finding the farm. The only person around was the night watchman, who pointed him to the canisters of milk. Duminică loaded some of them onto the truck, and left others on the ground. Then he drove off.

On his way back, Duminică did not stop in Lupoaia. He kept driving. He only knew that he could keep on driving for a long time because he had a full tank of gas. Then he heard Adina's head banging against the window. He tried to remember who it was that was sitting next to him. When he realized it was Adina, he turned off the engine. He started it again, trying to recall her last name. At first his mind refused. He tried not to think about it any more, but her temple kept striking the door, and it suddenly came to him.

Duminică refilled his tank from his spare canister of gas, then threw the canister away. He was now driving very fast, trying to get to a place, a piece of ground, where things could be a little unreal again, where things could still be carefree.

The lids on the milk canisters bounced up and down; milk streamed from the truck. Duminică drove a long way, he did not know how long, until he reached a riverbank. He saw a river in front of him but did not realize how wide it was. He had no idea it was the Danube.

He did not stop. He told himself that there was no time to lose, as he drove over the riverbank. The truck immediately began to fill with water and sink. Around him everything was white. The truck was enveloped in milk. The intense whiteness dazed Duminică, frightened him at first; then it filled him with joy. He told himself that he had found that place, the place where everything was unreal and reparable. And once you were there, you couldn't drown in rivers of milk! "That's enough now. You can stop the game," he said quietly, as if talking to someone.

Duminică frantically turned the wheel to the right, toward something he believed could be started anew, begun as it should have been.

The truck continued to sink.

Both of them had believed that they were truly protected by the ease of the times and sheltered by the people around them. They had believed they could play at their lives as long as they wanted, however they pleased, with no consequences.

Adina Gheorghe and Duminică.

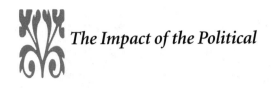 *The Impact of the Political*

⚜ *Petru Dumitriu* (1924–)

Petru Dumitriu studied philosophy in Bucharest and Munich. After a short story collection (*Eurydice*, 1947), which relied heavily on parable, he went on to adopt the official style of Socialist Realism. In 1950, for instance, he published *Road without Dust*, in which he presented the Danube–Black Sea Canal, a forced-labor project, as a grandiose achievement of Romanian Communism. Later however, Dumitriu attempted to strike a balance between his own vision of literature and the accepted Communist ideology (with the novel *Family Chronicle*, 1956).

In 1960 Dumitriu emigrated to the West, where he continued to write and publish in Romanian and French. In *Appointment with the Last Judgement* (1961) and *Incognito* (1962), he satirized Romanian themes; in *The Far West* and *The Initiated* (both published in 1966), he extended his satire to Western culture.

Other works include *The Man with Gray Eyes* (1968), *The Fine Journey* (1969), *To the Unknown God* (1979), *Zero, or Point of Departure* (essays, 1982), and *The Harvest* (1989), all published in Paris.

"The Best-Cared-For Horses" was first published in *Revista scriitorilor români* No. 1 (Munich, 1962).

The Best-Cared-For Horses

The village winds along the road that cuts through its middle. The houses seem to cling to each other. Some are whitewashed and painted blue, with white stucco crosses and flowers. They are the houses of the Romanian peasants. Others are whitewashed and painted light brown and pinkish yellow. They are the houses of the Saxon[1] peasants. At one end of the village there are more blue houses; at the other end there are more brown and pinkish yellow houses. Otherwise they look the same. The Saxons' houses may be a little larger and more prosperous. The Romanians' daughters dress in white and black. The Saxons' daughters dress in blue and black and wear long ribbons in their braids, which fall

35

down their backs to the hem of their skirts. The men wear boots. The women also wear boots, but with heels. In the village there is a Romanian Orthodox church and a Lutheran church. Where the pub once stood the cooperative store now stands. Where the town hall used to be now stands the People's Council.[2] Where there once was the police station, there is now the militia headquarters. The villagers don't talk much to each other. They belong to different nations, and then, that's how things are in these times. People withdraw behind their large gates, behind their high garden walls covered with tiles and rising higher than the roofs of their houses. No one can see you when you're in your yard. Maybe just one of your neighbors, from over the wall or over the fence. (On the other side lies the stable, the grain barn, and one part of the L-shaped house.) The village doesn't yet have a collective farm. But it will soon.

Overhead stretches the enormous sky. Down below, the village lies motionless. Only on Sundays does it stir, when the bells toll and the peasants, clad in white homespun and small black hats, stream toward the two churches. The two nations dress similarly, but not identically. Otherwise, it is quiet in the village. Large trucks move down the road incessantly, but they don't stop there. Sometimes trucks full of convicts pass through on their way to the prison fortress at Făgăraș or the penitentiary at Aiud.[3] They don't stop either. Perhaps the son of Uncle So-and-So is in one of those trucks. He went to many schools, then to the university. He became an engineer, then got involved in politics. Then they heard from him no more. He came one time, at night, to see his parents. Then he left again. Maybe he's not even in the country any longer.

Uncle So-and-So is a bony, wrinkled peasant, who, like all peasants, looks older than his age. His wife, because she has a son of thirty-odd years, is an old woman. They both till the land. They have two horses, no more. They have a neighbor on one side, but they never see him. Their house, their stable, and their grain barn all stand with their back to his farm. They have another neighbor on the other side. He's a calm, silent, even brooding man. He never glances over the wall. He hardly ever sees them, and speaks to them rarely. His wife, however, her face white, her eyes keen and restless, says good morning, good afternoon, and good evening to Uncle So-and-So and his wife and talks to them about one thing or another. She's a lively, bustling woman. Her husband is not good enough for her. He's too dull and weak for her liking. Yet she doesn't play around on him. Instead she talks all the time, pokes her nose everywhere, looks into everything, sniffs out every detail. She doesn't like her neighbors. They are too quiet. She says hello to them, and they say hello back. But nothing more. She asks them a question, they give a brief answer. They never volunteer a word. They look away when they speak to her. They are always in the house or the stable. Especially the old man. And the horses are always well brushed, well groomed, well curried. Uncle So-and-So spends hours in the stable. He talks to his horses, mumbles to them. The neighbor woman finds work to do in the yard, loiters by the wall, eavesdrops. But she doesn't understand what he says. In any event, she is puzzled. The old man has the best-cared-for horses in the village. But why? What for?

One day the old man falls ill. The horses are still groomed, are still the best-cared-for horses in the village. But why? Why should they be? The old woman stays out in the stable for hours. Her husband is dying and yet she remains in the stable, brushing and currying the horses.

Early in the morning, while the mist still hangs in the air, the old woman takes the horses out to the fields. Their coats shine with all the combing and brushing.

Finally the old man dies. The doctor comes, but it's too late. The old man has passed on. The old woman summons the priest. She asks him a favor. The priest does not understand her wish. It cannot be done. It goes against custom. No one does it that way. Anywhere. The old woman pleads with him. She weeps. The priest relents. If that's how she wants it, so be it. They carry the dead man out of the house into the stable and place him on a makeshift table of sawhorses topped by planks. The horses, their coats shining, their eyes gentle and innocent, snort and nibble at the oats in the manger, crunching noisily on the grains. The family members stand shoulder to shoulder in the candlelight. The neighbors from both sides as well, together with their wives. The stable smells of hay, candle wax, incense. The dead man is small and thin, his face the color of earth. There is a candle by his head, a cross in his hands, and flowers around him in the coffin. The priest reads the prayers for the dead while the cantor intones nasally, "I shall be as the hyssop flower. I shall be cleansed by thy mercy, O Lord." The priest and the cantor sing, the old woman weeps quietly, the women dab their red eyes, the men stand impassively. Some think of nothing, others think of their own death, whenever it may come. Forgive us, O Lord. Have mercy on us, O Lord.

The horses snort again. From up above, through the beams of the loft where the hay lies stacked, a straw of hay drifts down onto the dead man's sunken face.

They take the dead man to the graveyard. The old woman is left all alone. The horses are still the most beautiful, the most glossy, the best-cared-for horses in the village. The neighbor woman stares over the wall, bids the old woman good morning. At night she sees lights in the stable and hears the old woman talking. After a while the neighbor woman goes to the militia headquarters and speaks with the captain. A few nights later the captain comes to her house and stands in her yard watching the lights flicker in the old woman's stable. The night is damp and silent. Suddenly there is the sound of dogs barking, their growls echoed by baying from neighboring villages. Then it is quiet again. The only sounds are those of water dripping from rotting leaves and the creek murmuring at the edge of the village, as it runs under the slumbering wheel of the mill. "Yes, I think so, too," the officer says, and departs in his long overcoat and heavy boots.

The next morning a truck full of soldiers stops in front of the old woman's house. They jump out in their heavy boots, clutching their automatic pistols to their chests. They pound their fists on the gate. The old woman opens it; they burst in. Others climb into her yard from over the neighbor's wall. They surround the stable, aim at the door. The old woman tries to hide the truth. But the lieutenant is from the village too. He knows the old woman. "Forget it. We know," he tells her. He stops in front of the stable and shouts, calling the old woman's son by name. "Come out! Hey, you, come out! Give yourself up! You're surrounded! You can't get away. Come out with your hands up!" The two of them were schoolmates. Then they took different paths. The lieutenant knows that he himself is an officer. He represents the power of the state, the power of the people. The other is a man who has strayed. He is lost, weak, alone. He is a fool. "Come out with your hands up!" The old woman's son comes out, blinking his eyes like an owl. He is not used to sunlight. His face is yellow and his beard is long. His mother rushes to embrace him but two soldiers grab her hands. She shrieks, "My child! My son! I gave you away! Don't take him away from me! My child, oh, my son!" She falls to her knees; her knees have given way. Drool pours from her mouth; she moans softly. Her cries are almost inaudible, so vast is the sky above.

They take her son away. Now only the deserted house and yard are left, and the horses, who snort and nibble oats in the stable, in the dark.

The old woman's son had been the one who had curried and cared for the horses, for he had had nothing else to do day and night, year after year. It was *he* who had lain on his stomach on the beams of the loft, gazing between them at the face of his dead father while the priest was chanting the funeral prayers.

The neighbor woman feels something is wrong, though she can't quite say what it is. She talks to a villager who answers yes or no, but says no more. Then the villager leaves and goes about his business. Romanians or Saxons, they all act the same. It's as if I can't talk to anyone anymore! Dimly, she feels very lonely, yet she can do nothing to escape from her loneliness.

And now the old woman's horses are not cared for at all.

❧ *Dumitru Radu Popescu*   (1935–)

Dumitru Radu Popescu studied medicine before turning to literature. He made his debut in 1958, with *The Flight,* a volume of stories in the tradition of Romanian rural prose. Later, however, his writing became original and profound. For example, his political novels, *F* (1969) and *The Royal Hunt* (1973), create a realm of fantasy and abnormality within a detective story structure, combining direct and indirect discourse with interior monologue to suggest that we live in a world in which everybody is guilty and truth is undiscernible.

From 1981 to 1989 Popescu was president of the Romanian Writers' Union.

Other works include plays, movie scripts, collections of short stories—*The Parasol* (1962) and *The Sleep of the Earth* (1965)—as well as the novellas *The Blue Lion* (1965) and *Anastasia Passed By Sadly* (1966). Popescu has also written several other novels, among them *A Beer for My Horse* (1974), *The Rains Beyond the Century* (1976), and *The Cloud King* (1976).

Several of Popescu's works have won Writers' Union Prizes. His novel *The Royal Hunt* was translated into English in 1985 and published by the Ohio State University Press.

"The Tin Can" first appeared in *The Flight* (1958).

The Tin Can

All forests have their mysteries. Amidst the trees and the grasses, creatures are born and die at every moment, creatures that pass through the world unknown to humankind. Silence reigns over tree and bush, devouring with equal indifference the laughter of those who are happy and the cries of those in despair. Clad in green, gilded with the tones of autumn, or buried in snow, the forest maintains its unique beauty regardless of season or weather. The ancient trees with their hollow trunks resemble strange giant violins that have lost their voice. On stormy days and nights the wind glides with countless unseen bows across them, bringing forth heartrending music. Thunder booms in accompaniment, like broken drums beaten by drunken gods, and the rare witnesses who have ventured among the trees listen in wonder to this masterful symphony of pain. On calm summer nights, when the sky looks like a huge tunnel of blue marble studded with thousands of tiny flickering yellow stars, the forest breathes quietly through its unstirring leaves, heavy with verdure. The beasts recline on the soft warm moss, listening to the simple sweet concert of the night: skylarks performing their trills to the familiar rhythm of the tireless crickets.

That morning János Kovács's pigeons kept circling indifferently above the forest. The three bells of the Romanian church in Sănceni tolled at regular intervals, their distinct timbres calling the faithful to service with a ceaseless prayer. Alone on the porch, János Kovács crossed himself three times, begging the Almighty to forgive his sins and excuse his absence from the holy service. His real name was Ion Fieraru,[1] his faith Romanian Orthodox, and he had always been a God-fearing man. But the times had changed, and the new rule[2] had obliged him to change his name. In fact, he himself wasn't quite sure whether he was Hungarian or Romanian, Orthodox or Catholic. When his parents and grandparents had joined their Rives, they hadn't paid much attention to nation or religion. His own wife, Floarea, a Romanian woman from the village of Feretău, had departed for church with their daughter, leaving János behind to look after the house. (They had dismissed their old servant, a nephew of Floarea's, and had little trust in their new servant, a Hungarian from Sănceni.) But in truth, János didn't want the new mayor or one of the village policemen to see him attending the Romanian church. "I'm Hungarian," he would say whenever the occasion arose to show that he was not opposed to the new rule. He had grown accustomed to not speaking a word of Romanian even in his own home with his own family.

A chicken hawk appeared above the forest and fell like an arrow on the flocks of pigeons flapping heedlessly in the blue morning sky. Sensing the danger, the birds scattered into the air. János Kovács cupped his hands before his mouth and hooted at the hawk to drive it away.

"Hey, there! Shoo! Shoo!"

But the hawk continued its pursuit, determined either to sate its hunger or spite the man with his harmless hoots and threats. It jabbed its claws into a dove's back and, after circling János Kovács's yard twice, flew over the trees, heading for a place only it knew.

A gunshot split the air near the border patrol barracks. Kovács jumped, startled, then smiled. Maybe the thief of a hawk had gotten its just deserts. At the same moment he glimpsed a man at the edge of the forest. He held something black in his hand which looked like an old-style revolver. János Kovács saw the stranger slip behind an oak tree, then cautiously leap over the ditch by the beet patch and disappear into the mayor's cornfield. Who could it be? A spy from Romania who had crossed the border during the night? The thought frightened him. What if the spy came and asked him for lodging, reminding him of his previous name and identity? What then? No, he could never give him lodging. He was Hungarian now. And even if he did have Romanian blood in his veins, there was very little left. If the authorities found out he was hiding a spy in his house, it would be the end of him. They would shoot him, take away everything he had. No. Ten times no. But what if the spy threatened to kill him? Spies have no laws to stop them and no God to believe in. What then? He would hide him for two or three days. Too long. Only one. He would keep the man talking while his servant ran to fetch the Hungarian border patrol or a German officer quartered in the village. What if the spy managed to escape?

"Oh, God, what have I done for you to punish me so?" János Kovács cried, his fingers tugging at the few tufts of hair remaining on the top of his head. He felt miserable. Fate had ordained that the new border between Romanians and Hungarians was one kilometer from his door. Many in the village looked at him askance: the Hungarians hated him because he had been a Romanian, the Romanians because he had become a Hungarian. But what could he do? Was it his fault there had been both Hungarians and Romanians among his ancestors?

The stranger rounded the corner of the barn. Kovács froze. What could the spy want from him? What if the Romanians came to power again? He started to run past the house, hoping to hide in the vineyard. But the stranger kept advancing cautiously, barring his path. There was no way he could reach the vineyard. What could he do? He crept into the shed and hid behind the new flour mill. His dog Lupu[3] (whose name he had changed to Farkas), sensing a stranger near, barked furiously and strained against his chain to show his master he was earning his keep. Feeling a wave of coldness course through his body, Kovács tightened his shirt collar around his neck. The icy sensation rose to his head, descended once more, then rose yet again.

The stranger now stood by the front gate. Kovács could see him through a crack in the wall. He had no revolver in his hand, only a water flask. He was about forty, unshaven, with purple circles beneath his eyes from lack of sleep, and a searching, distrustful glance. He did not look like a spy. Kovács felt less afraid. No, the stranger could not be a spy. He came out from behind the flour mill and walked calmly toward the gate. The stranger inclined his head in greeting.

"Good afternoon, citizen," Kovács said in Hungarian, opening the gate.

"I've come for some water, if you don't mind," said the stranger.

"Of course I don't mind."

While the man lifted the bucket from the well, Kovács eyed him thoughtfully. The man was clearly a Jew. Since the Germans had started taking them from their homes and sending them God knows where, many Jews from the city of Oradea had hidden in villages or forests. Some had even crossed the border into Romania so that all trace of them would be lost.

"You're a Jew, aren't you?"

"Me? No. Why do you ask? You see, I . . ."

"Don't be afraid. I can keep my mouth shut."

The Jews had lots of gold, were stinking rich. János Kovács was sure of that. Ferencz Vass had become rich off them. Whenever he came across Jews, whether he knew them or not, he would take them into his house, promising to help them cross the border. He would tell them he paid no attention to differences in nationality. It was the man who counted! He never asked for much money, just a few *pengo*,[4] thus winning their confidence. At night he would lead them to the border down paths only he knew. And since the paths were twisted and steep, the Jews would leave their luggage behind, in the wagon, covered with hay. Vass's son Ghiuri would follow them later in his wagon, taking another road and meeting them at an appointed place and time. Once inside the Romanian border, they were more concerned about the fate of Ferencz Vass's boy—since he never showed up at the place they had agreed upon—than about the loss of their belongings. No one but János Kovács knew the truth about Ferencz Vass's shady dealings. Some suspected it, to be sure, but the new mayor had so much power and wealth that anyone who dared speak ill of him ended up gnawing his nails in a basement prison cell.

The stranger drank half of the water he had poured into his flask. He refilled it and let the bucket fall back into the well. János Kovács stared at him, trying to guess which pocket held his gold and money.

"What were you doing in the forest, mister?"

The stranger didn't respond. He glanced down, as if the answer might emerge from the water drops he let fall from the bucket, drops which mingled with the black earth.

"Please don't give me away," he suddenly blurted out, his voice almost inaudible, as if his fingers and not his mouth had emitted the sounds. "I'll give you anything you want. Please don't give me away."

"So the Jew has money," Kovács thought. Out loud he said, "I have no quarrel with you. I don't know you, you don't know me. It's true that the border patrol questions me every morning and every night if I've seen anything suspicious. Lots of Jews have been caught around here. Some were shot on the spot; others, who had money to pay. . . ."

He almost added "were shot later on," but stopped just in time and waited for the Jew to unlace the strings of his purse. Then he continued, "A purse opened at the right time will keep mouths shut. That's the way it is. If you have money, even hell will let you go."

The Jew took his wallet out of his coat pocket and handed his host half of the money he had inside. Kovács accepted it like a debt paid.

"The patrols fall asleep before daybreak. It's easier to cross then," Kovács said. "The border in the forest across the road is practically unguarded. . . ."

Kovács paused. What if they caught the Jew and the Jew told on him? Why had he said so much? He smiled innocently, trying to repair the damage he had done.

"At least that's what I heard," he murmured, "and I . . . I'm not sure. Or . . . the border in the forest. . . ."

The words caught in his throat. Flustered, he stammered even more. Then another thought crossed his mind. What if the patrol saw him talking to a Jew?

"Go now. Go and hide. The patrol's due any minute now."

The Jew asked Kovács for a loaf of bread. Kovács gave him half a loaf and watched him closely until he disappeared into the forest.

Kovács was pleased with the money he had received. He could now buy two fat piglets, or three lean ones, in Oradea next Monday. He decided to buy three. More was always better.

Suddenly Kovács struck his forehead with his palm. He turned and started running toward the forest, cursing himself for not thinking of it earlier. Where could the Jew be? Kovács left the dirt road behind and plunged into the forest depths, heading for the marshes where he hoped the man had hidden. Low bushes rose like hurdles in front of him, forcing him either to go around them or push his way through the branches with his hands. A prickly blackthorn clung to his shirt, tearing it across the back and grazing his skin. Sun rays filtering through the leaves flashed across his sweating face but never reached his small faded-blue eyes, which glittered with the desire to find the band of Jews. He would help them cross the border the way Ferencz Vass did! The money he would earn, God in heaven, the money he would earn! The piglets that would fill his yard! Jews had gold, heaps of gold. If there were only fifteen in the whole band he would still earn a tidy sum. He would help them cross the border into Romania and promised to deliver their belongings the next day.

Just as he neared the trail, Kovács heard a male voice singing loudly:

"My pretty lass, my darling one,
Pum-pa-ra-rum, pum-pum,
Oh, my darling pum-pa-rum,
My fair lass, darling one. . . ."

János Kovács froze in his tracks. He recognized the voice of Dorog, a sublieutenant in the border guard. Just yesterday Dorog and Marlock, a German lieutenant, had stopped at his house. Now they were drunk again. Were they coming for another swig of *palinca*?[5] What could he do? What if they didn't find him at home? Should he run back and greet them? What would they do to him if they found him in the forest? What could he tell them?

"Hey, you, you stinking Romanian! What are you doing standing there like a stick of wood?"

The two men had appeared in front of him, not ten paces away.

"I'm Hungarian, sir! Mr. Marlock, sir!"

"Got any *palinca* left?"

"Yes, sir, Mr. Marlock."

"Lots of it?"

"Yes, sir, Mr. Marlock, sir. Lots."

"Citizen Ion Fieraru, what are you doing here in the forest?" the border sublieutenant asked, poking fun at the man's evident fright. "Trying to go back to your people?"

"I'm Hungarian, sir," he repeated. "My name is János Kovács."

"Kovács? Kovács my foot! You're consorting with spies, I'll bet. Well, are you?"

"I'm Hungarian, sir. I love my country. Hungary. I just happen to live by the border."

"What were you doing in the forest? Put your hands up!" the sublieutenant ordered, greatly amused at Kovács's ashen face. "To the gatehouse! Forward, march!"

Marlock doubled over with laughter.

"Mr. Sublieutenant, sir! I've got children! And *palinca!* I was just coming to tell you I've caught some Jews! That is, I haven't caught them. They're going to cross the border tonight. Over there, on the other side of the road. At dawn. They're in the marshes, sir. I . . ."

The two officers suddenly grew very attentive.

"You're not lying, I hope."

"I swear on . . . anything you want, sir."

Twenty minutes later the officers, led by Kovács, found the Jew who had been looking for water. He had his wife and daughter with him. The girl was about eighteen and shapely, with black eyes now filled with terror.

János Kovács crouched behind a bush so that the Jew couldn't see him. He was afraid the Jew would tell the representatives of the new power that he had given him half a loaf of bread and a flask of water. Marlock, revolver in hand, went up to the girl and stroked her cheeks. Kovács guessed his intention and knew no one would stop him from carrying it out.

After the five left for the gatehouse, Kovács rose to his feet and in two bounds reached the clearing where the Jews had been resting. The grass was trampled. He searched the area carefully, hoping to come across something valuable. He rummaged through the grass and leaves with a dry branch, but found no gold. He searched farther, in the bushes. He glimpsed a piece of colored paper covering something. He removed the paper with his branch. It was a pile of human feces.

Disappointed, János Kovács returned home, clutching an empty tin can and the remaining quarter loaf of bread he had given to the Jew. He would plant flowers in the can, a red geranium or some other shrub, which he would place at the window of his house to make it pretty. The bread he would give to the dog.

Back in his yard, he tore a crust off the loaf and tossed it to the dog. "Eat up, Farkas!"

Two shots rang out in the silence. Kovács looked up at the forest. He closed his eyes and pictured Lieutenant Marlock. The parents must have been in the way.

The bells of the village church tolled the end of the service. János Kovács crossed himself three times out of habit.

"Here, Farkas! Come and get it!" he called, tossing him the rest of the bread.

Suddenly Kovács's face lit up. He remembered there was a geranium blooming in the garden. Picking up the can, he went to transplant the flower.

⚇ *Radu Cosaşu* (1930–)

Radu Cosaşu began to write in secondary school, his poems, film reviews, and editorial commentaries appearing in *Revista elevilor,* the national school magazine (1948–1949). After studies at the University of Bucharest, and at the Mihai Eminescu School of Literature, Cosaşu became a journalist turning out feature articles, columns, and stories that displayed all the features of Socialist Realism—bombastic revolutionary rhetoric, mandatory optimism, regimented aesthetics. In the 1970s, however, with the first volume of the cycle *Survivals* (*Survivals* I, 1973), Cosaşu transformed the clichés of politicized writing into literature by the force of his ridicule. At the same time his short stories reflected the unique world of the Romanian Jew.

Other works include *Survivals* II (1977); *Short Story Writing: The Profession* (*Survivals* III, 1980); *The Fictionalists* (*Survivals* IV, 1983); *Logic* (*Survivals* V, 1985); and *A Clear Head* (*Survivals* VI, 1989). Cosaşu also wrote magazine essays, articles, and reviews collected in: *One August on a Block of Ice* (1971), *Another Two Years on a Block of Ice* (1974), *Five Years with Belfagor* (1975), and *Living with Laurel and Hardy* (1981). Cosaşu twice received the Romanian Writers' Union Prize.

"Burials" was first published in 1983, in *The Fictionalists* (*Survivals* IV).

Burials

One day in 1947, when I was seventeen and a student at Matei Basarab School, my friend Calu[1] and I started reciting a poem by Aragon[2] in the middle of chemistry lab: "The Party gave me back the colors of France, / The Party gave me back the light of my eyes." Calu took one stanza, I took the next. Our classmates listened, stupefied, their test tubes forgotten. Like experienced political agitators, we had seized power as soon as the teacher, a cabinet member during Antonescu's regime,[3] had left the room.

We were completely in command of the situation; we had taken the class reactionaries by storm. Reciting the poem was more effective than any propaganda, more dramatic even than the slogan "Vote for the Sun."[4] I was transfigured: it was my first public performance. My voice shook as much as my body—I don't know whether from art or from politics. I was usually so nervous I'd never been able to play Chopin's *Écossaises* on the drawing-room piano for our guests. But now, in the sulfur-laden atmosphere of the classroom, among occult and scientific metamorphoses of elements governed by immutable laws, I felt transformed, in search of new valences, about to produce a new substance—happiness.

Then came Calu's turn. He seemed very sure of his performance—it was vigorous, unrefined, purposely unpoetic. (He wanted everyone to know we weren't fooling around.) While he was reciting I looked up at the door and saw the teacher come in, back from the common room. He cast us a scornful glance, his eyes grim and cold as steel. Calu jabbed me in the ribs with his elbow—I'd forgotten it was my turn again—and in that split second of confusion all the students turned, as if mesmerized, to the teacher towering above us. My stanza fell apart, and so did I.

I hung around Calu for the rest of the day, not because I wanted to explain why I'd failed but because I wanted to punish myself. Calu's silence was as contemptuous as the teacher's icy stare. Yet he accepted me; he didn't drive me away or reprimand me. At noon I followed him up to his place, though he didn't tell me what his plans were. He lived by the Vitan Water Pump, on a dead-end street not far from the Edison Cinema, the auditorium of which was an affront to the sense of smell. (I'd been there once and vowed never to return.) I sensed his fury toward me but thought I detected pity as well, a feeling the idealist in me wanted to cherish.

Calu's clay shack was one of several spread around a filthy courtyard. When we stepped in the stench hit me, turning my stomach upside down. I couldn't go any further nor could I turn back. Calu left me standing in the doorway while he went and groped for something under the bed. He found whatever it was and put it in his coat pocket; it looked like a handgun. On the way back to town, he finally broke his silence, "Your petty bourgeois fear stinks worse than my room. It makes me sick to see you scared so shitless. But ideas can be scared shitless too. You should at least learn how to deal with them: inhale some of them deeply and blow off the rest."

I felt too guilty to be offended by his words. And besides keeping up with his long strides (careful not to inhale the smell of his jacket), I tried to feel the object in his coat pocket with my elbow (though I was pretty sure he wasn't going to shoot me; I had done nothing to deserve that). I didn't succeed. All I got from him were noises, noises familiar to me from recess—ugly, violent, shameless sounds he never apologized for. He knew they didn't bother me any more; I even found them funny. Anything is better than a bullet.

Still silent, we boarded a tram at the Colonel Orero stop and, after a while, got off in front of a small graveyard next to the Belu Cemetery. Its gate, half fallen, was open. We entered the desolate place. I couldn't tell Calu (he had a harsh vibration, like a neighing, in his vocal cords; we didn't call him "The Horse" for nothing) that I'd never been in a graveyard before. I kept as close to him as possible as we made our way among the graves—few in number but crowded together—all the time waiting for him to drive me away. But that was the last thing on his mind. He knelt beside a grave at the end of a row and began digging in the earth with his ugly hands (his nails were a ghastly sight, too). There was no cross, no flowers, only a mound piled neatly and patted into place. I was so bewildered that this was all I could take in. But it made me remember something, and I clung to that memory with all my might.

The summer before I would walk twice a week from Poiana Țapului to Bușteni,[5] pulling a handcart with an empty gas container tied to it. My responsibility was to exchange it at the station next to the paper mill, across the street from a private lending library. I stumbled into that paradise of books like a sleepwalker; I'd never seen such a hoard before. The owner, a kindly soul, accompanied me to the shelves (they smelled wonderful from the perfume shop next door) and suggested I first read *The Hooligans* by Mircea Eliade,[6] a writer I knew nothing about.

For the next few days I didn't speak to anyone in my family (my sister Sappho hadn't come home from Bucharest yet). "What's the matter with you? What's wrong?" my mother and aunts kept asking, since it never occurred to them that someone could be moved to silence or to eating and walking differently by a novel. But I wouldn't explain. I had assumed Anicet's pride, his hatred for the petty bourgeois family. I looked with disdain on everything I had read before.

A week later the library owner, a semi-invalid, let me in with an ominous expression on his face and asked me to hide the book he was going to lend me: *The Return from Paradise*, the sequel to *The Hooligans*. "Why?" I inquired. He wouldn't tell me, but the way he nudged me with his elbow toward the door gave me some idea.

I read the book in the woods behind our house, crouching behind the thickest trees to avoid being seen. It was the first time I'd ever read something in secret, and in each line I tried to find the key to why the book needed hiding. My approach to reading had totally changed; I had turned into a censor right there in the midst of nature, as I shivered with cold, the birds twittering and the branches swaying above me. And yet, though not quite a layman at identifying politically offensive passages, I was unable to discover anything to be censored beyond a few erotic lines. As the only person defending the Petru Groza[7] government at home (though Calu hadn't yet taken me to sign up at the Union of Communist Youth), I clearly perceived the hero's hatred for the bourgeoisie and his family. And I knew that couldn't be politically wrong. Then what was? My father, an avid reader of Cezar Petrescu's popular novels (which had never interested me), wouldn't be able to understand my dilemma, my mother even less.

At the end of the week I went to Bușteni again, the gas container tied to the handcart and the book hidden under my shirt. On the way to town I was seized with intestinal cramps and had to rush into the woods. The whole time I was relieving myself I clutched the book to my chest for fear I might lose it. When I finally reached Bușteni, the salesgirl at the perfume shop couldn't tell me why Mr. Lăzărescu had been locked up. Was it Mr. Lăzărescu or his library that had been locked up? The woman, busy preparing a white face cream in a bowl, shrugged her shoulders. Back home, I buried the book in the woods near my house, trusting its safekeeping to the trees. My cramps forgotten, I dug the clayey earth at the roots of a tree, a dark mist enshrouding me and the rain-swept branches above. While busy with my molelike work, I imagined the white cream from the perfume shop mingling with the slimy black soil. I tore off a wide strip from the bottom of my shirt to wrap the book in. As I was patting the dirt over the grave I had the distinct impression that someone had called my name. Instinctively, I undid my pants and pretended to go, right there in the rain by the tree. Nothing spurted out of me, though, and no one appeared.

Calu took the mysterious object out of his pocket—it was enveloped in a frayed cloth—and laid it in the hole he had dug. I asked him if it was a revolver. He covered it with dirt, pressed the mound with his palms, bringing it to the level of the next grave, then rose and told me that it was a harmonica and that I should keep my mouth shut.

"Why did you bring me with you?" I asked, tired of being humiliated by him, and haunted by the vision of my memories.

"To give you something to do."

As we started down the dusty alley leading to the gate, he began abusing me again (cheerfully, as if in celebration of the burial), insulting me and the bourgeois world I came from. Before returning to the city of the living, with its streets and trams, he left me with the following idea: "If there's a God, as your family taught you—between your piano lessons—to refer to the history of your race (I was struck by his sharp perception), He'll see how I picked you up from the streets, the filthy son of a bitch that you were, with no hopes, no future, and He'll see how I brought you to my place—I don't know why, out of pity maybe—so you could find out how houses and people stink." At the gates of Heaven, he went on, Saint Peter would ask him what he had done on earth, and he would say he had brought Oscar Rohrlich[8] to the Communists, and it would take another hundred years for him to get into heaven, because that wasn't enough to recommend him.

I refused to vouchsafe a reply, feeling strong and proud in my secret. Later, on the tram, I asked him whose grave it was we had visited—his father's, his brother's? He nodded both times. When I asked what they had died of, Calu finally looked me in the face. "A bad case of politeness."

My father died of a heart attack the next year at the spring equinox. For a long time afterwards, I admit, I distinguished true revolutionaries from petty bourgeois like myself by the way their parents died and were buried (and Communists from Fascists by the way Communists could be ironic, and Fascists could not). In time I found other ways of making distinctions, but they never had the shining, subversive power of a book buried in a forest, even if buried in fear and defiance.

✿ Mircea Nedelciu (1950–)

Mircea Nedelciu studied philology at the University of Bucharest (1969–1973). A decade later he became the leader of the "Textualist" school, an offshoot of the *Junimea* Student Literary Club. The assumption behind Nedelciu's prose, stated in his *Ten Commandments*, is the co-ownership between author, text, and reader. His short stories, therefore, abound in commentaries on techniques of authorship, readership, and textual format. They are also characterized by a complex interplay between reality, what is said about that reality, and what the reader perceives. Thus Nedelciu not only treats problems of communication, but also achieves a clearer and more accurate perception of reality.

Nedelciu's works include several collections of short stories, *Adventures in an Inner Courtyard* (1979), *Amendment to the Instinct of Ownership* (1983), and *Yesterday Will Be a Day, Too* (1989). He also wrote two novels, *The Wild Raspberries* (1984) and *The Woman in Red* (1990, coauthored with Adriana Babeți and Mircea Mihăieș). *Adventures in an Inner Courtyard* (1979) earned Nedelciu the Writers' Union Prize.

"The Forbidden Story" was first published in *Amendment to the Instinct of Ownership* (1983).

The Forbidden Story

You have a quick way of thinking: you think like a twentieth- or twenty-first-century man. (I don't think a nineteenth-century reader would have been able to grasp this story, written only a century later, in 1982.) So as soon as you've read the title, you'll have guessed what one-quarter of the text is about, and your eyes will have jumped to line fifteen, if only to confirm what you've just taken in.

That's right, you've got it. Congratulations. This is a true love story, one that occurred in the seventies of the present century, a story that might reveal its uncommon beauty only if you have the patience to follow it step by step (stories usually move by steps, not leaps), a story the likes of which has not been written in many years, though it has been heard before. I myself heard it from several people, the people involved. Why should several people have been involved? You'll see. Don't be in too much of a hurry. Or, if you are, better skip to the last line. This story's been postponed before.

Anyway, he was eighteen at the time and very handsome. What was the most handsome thing about him? His eyelashes. They were very long, unusually long for a man. She, too, was eighteen, and very beautiful. What was the most beautiful thing about her? Well, everything. Her body, her eyes, her hair, her mouth, and all the other things, too. Good heavens, don't make me list them all. You can picture a beautiful girl for yourself. Her name was Maraia. Or maybe something else. But that's the way he pronounced it—Ma-rye-uh. It was probably an English pronunciation for the name that, in Romanian, is written and spelled Maria. So he didn't say Mary or Marie. It would have been too vulgar—that's for sure! Anyway, every time he mentions her, that's how he pronounces her name—Ma-rye-uh. Probably, it's a kind of code, a key to the story's events. If you don't pronounce it the right way, you won't understand a thing.

Of course, when he talked to me about her, there was a trace of nostalgia in his voice, a special kind of nostalgia. He was trying to be as straightforward and objective as he could, even a bit cynical, but he wasn't very good at it. He was struggling to hide his regret, his sadness, his fear of reopening a deep old wound.

Otherwise, he's pretty ordinary, a happy-go-lucky young man with faith in his own powers. He's got the guts to appear in public during the winter with his head shaved. He hardly ever smokes, but he has a collection of pipes at home, and if it's foggy, cold, and quiet in town, he'll phone you and suggest taking a walk in the park after midnight. He'll bring two of his precious pipes and a highly perfumed package of Dutch tobacco. He's not afraid of bureaucrats waiting in their offices for fresh victims or of women obsessed with getting married. He never lowers his voice when saying what he thinks. He knows how to make pickles, prepare exotic sauces, and, when necessary, can fix his own car. Though still a bachelor, he can play games with his friends' and relatives' children, no matter how young they are. He has season tickets for the Classic Film Series, and long ago stopped turning up his nose at films not made in America. He's a good storyteller, the kind who gets right to the point without any detours or fuss—like an outside forward shooting a goal pass to a team member.

Anyway, the two were classmates at a prestigious secondary school in Bucharest. And they were in love. Look, I don't know why I'm using the past tense. The past tense can seem like a tense of ownership in a story like this. (And in other stories as well. You tell things the way they were, and when you want to describe them the way they are, you suddenly find yourself wondering, "Why aren't things now the way they were then?" If you begin your tale in the past tense, the present will seem pale, plain, withered, and imperfect in a sense other than the grammatical. Better stick to the present tense; thus you avoid unpleasant surprises that keep you from unraveling the story step by step.)

So, Maraia and Claudio are in love. Actually, his name is Claudiu, but that doesn't sound elegant or exotic enough. These young people were, excuse me, *are*, a bit snobbish. And everybody knows that the most common form of snobbishness in Romanian society is a love of all things foreign. Snobbery of indigenous origin is almost nonexistent. Maraia has a very good friend whose name is Giulai (pronounced July. Actually, her name is Iulia. You can figure it out, can't you?). Maraia's parents are divorced and live apart. He, male Comrade Tulea, is department chief in an important state agency. She, female Comrade Tulea, works somewhere else and lives comfortably in the same house as her daughter Maraia.

(Department Chief Tulea's rise up the social ladder wouldn't be so striking if we didn't specify that he'd been orphaned at an early age and had to make it on his own. He didn't meet some of his close relatives until he was about to retire and articles about him started appearing here and there in the papers. He met his future lifelong comrade in 1950 and married her in the autumn of the same year, in a big auditorium, most likely a workers' club. There the notary public read the marriage vows just once, then shouted names, two by two, heard "I do's" echoed two by two, and declared almost the entire assembly husband and wife. The Tulea family, one of over a hundred families created in this festive environment on a single Sunday morning, first went to live in Floreasca. (A five-minute documentary would give you an idea what that part of town looked like back then.) The Tuleas' house had doorways that led from room to room like a trailer, and they shared it with other working people. Maraia was born there, holding the position of only daughter of the Tuleas as long as the family existed and even afterwards. As a matter of fact, the Tulea family fell apart just as fortune was beginning to smile on them, that is, just after they had taken up residence on the second floor of a modest detached house in a semicentral district of town. The two women, female Comrade Tulea and Miss Maraia, went on living in the house owned by male Comrade Tulea, no doubt as a condition of his keeping his job.)[1]

Several young girls, classmates of Maraia's, often gather in her room to listen to music and make small talk. But Giulai is the one who comes the most frequently. She's a real friend. Sometimes Giulai leaves her home early in the morning, half asleep, and tries not to wake up completely on the bus ride to Maraia's. Once there, she slips into bed beside her friend, snuggling into the place female Comrade Tulea left an hour before. The two girls doze on and off until nine or ten. This doesn't mean they skip school; they just arrive a little late. It also means they're the best of friends. They confide in each other, too, so Giulai knows every detail of this love story. It's good to have several variants of the story at hand, so we can compare them.

Let's first hear Claudio's variant.

Giulai is a very nice girl, but clearly the adolescent stage (of her future hysteria) is playing terrible tricks on her. She can't concentrate when she studies; she falls in love at first sight and then suffers horribly. She's curious; she wants to experience everything love has to offer, but none of the boys she's in love with is bold enough. He, Claudio, knows all of this from Maraia. When they sit together in the park, they tell each other these kinds of unimportant things.

Maraia also talks about her travels through Europe. She's been with her father on several long and interesting trips. At moments like these Claudio listens, as they say, with his mouth open. His imagination works feverishly: hotels with ocean views, discos, jazz clubs, Mediterranean or Atlantic beaches, records that haven't yet been played in Romania, metros and museums, books (or adventures from books) from a series written by someone by the name of San Antonio. After such conversations they both feel more energetic, enthusiastic, optimistic. Back home, Claudio listens to Beethoven, lifts weights, and pummels his punching bag to build both mind and body. He thinks of Maraia, picturing her among the places and things she's told him about, and feels even more in love with her. He sits down to study, only to realize that he would make more progress if Maraia were by his side. He must find a solution. In turn, Maraia thinks of Claudio when listening to music, working out, or studying alone. She quickly comes to the same conclusion: they'd get more done if they studied together.

In the meantime Giulai falls in love with a certain Mihai (or Maikl, to keep to the same pattern), and describes all the details to both of them, that

1. It really happened like this. If anything seems embellished, blame my storytelling. (Author's note, First Amendment.)

is, to Maraia and Claudio, without the slightest embarrassment. One confession leads to another: Giulai is let in on their secret and then given the task of asking, begging, persuading female Comrade Tulea to let the four of them study together.

Female Comrade Tulea is not an unreasonable woman; in fact, she comes up with stronger arguments in favor of their idea than they do. The young people will be taking the same entrance exam; Claudio is an intelligent young man (as the whole school knows); his parents are hardworking, respectable people (she has investigated the family thoroughly); he is head over heels in love with Maraia, and a year from now, if both are admitted to the university, they'll be able to get married. She agrees to think it over during the next two weeks (all this takes place at the end of August 1970), while her daughter is staying at the seaside with male Comrade Tulea.

Distraught at the prospect of being separated from Maraia for two weeks, Claudio tries to get blood from a turnip. (How? Let's see! You go home, deep in thought. Your parents haven't come back yet from their mediocre but secure jobs. You chew with disgust on some nameless item you've found in a pot in the refrigerator. Finally you hear your father unlock the door, lock it again, whistling all the while, then pause in the dining room and dial a phone number. He stops whistling while waiting for someone to answer. You chew noiselessly—you have no appetite anyway—while he's on the phone. You then hear the same tune again, this time hummed off-key. You try hard to identify the melody, and you're elated when you realize it's from his native Transylvania, which means he's in good spirits. You give him time to get to the kitchen. You greet him extrapolitely before he even sets eyes on you. You make sure he doesn't know what you have in store for him. You don't let him suspect a thing, take him completely by surprise. "Father, I need three thousand *lei*." At first he'll be so preoccupied with the motive behind your request that he'll ignore its shocking quantitative component. He'll probably suspect the worst— you've done something terrible, committed a grave error you think you can somehow rectify with three thousand *lei*. But he'll feel obliged to consider the moral and legal aspects of the issue as well. Finally he asks, "Why?" You let him sweat it out for a while. Your mouth is full; you can't answer him. He repeats the question, thinking you didn't hear it. If he panics, all the better. You wipe your mouth with the crumpled napkin and swallow hard, which frightens him even more. Anything you say after this careful bit of staging will seem a relief. "I want to go to the seaside with Maraia." Which means, "Look, I haven't broken into the school; I don't have to pay a fine; I haven't raped anyone; I haven't gotten anyone pregnant; I haven't even borrowed the money from one of your friends. I've been an obedient, mature, responsible son, and three thousand *lei* is a just reward." He'll breathe a sigh of relief, sit down at the table, and tell you, before resuming his whistling (back in the right key), "You could go to the coast on a thousand. But I haven't got that kind of money anyway." You don't say anything for a while; you toy with the food on your plate. He'll eventually realize he's offended you with his whistling. He'll stop and try to ease your suffering with gentle words that don't mean much. "Believe me, son, I haven't got it. I haven't been this broke in ages. I'm perfectly aware that you'll be finishing school soon and all your classmates have either gone or will be going to the coast. If I had that kind of money, I'd have sent you there myself; I wouldn't have waited for you to ask." Suddenly you hear the doorbell ring. You both think your mother has forgotten her keys, and you morosely go to open the door. But at the door you see the postman, who says he has a money order for your father. "How much and from whom?" you shout at the poor man bored with his afternoon shift. He puts his glasses on his nose and hands you the cardboard form. Three thousand to the *leu,* from an all-but-forgotten uncle in Transylvania, a brakeman at a railway station near Cluj. "Come in, come in," you tell the postman, motioning him to a chair by the dining room table. "Look, Dad, you've got a money order," you say to your father as you open the refrigerator door and take out a bottle of wine. Your guess is confirmed when you return to the table with the bottle and two glasses. Your father seems amazed to have received the money and fills out the form as if in a trance after a Ouija session. You feel pretty sure the money represents his most recent bet with you. The amount: three thousand *lei.* The winner: you. The postman clinks glasses with your father, downs his wine, says good-bye and departs the battlefield. You don't even look at him as you see him to the door. That is, you never take your eyes off your father. He lets you approach in silence and tenders the pile of bills. Of course, your mother must know nothing about it.[2]

The complicated story of the money is resolved about four months later.) Triumphant, Claudio leaves for the coast.

There he finds Maraia and a spacious beach, where they are allowed to go strolling all night long. Her stories are now reinforced by concrete examples: a few discos by the shore—Club 33, the Melody Nightclub, the Tavern—stay open until six in the morning; you can see Western faces; you

2. If two stories appear somewhere together, one of them has to be owned by the other. As long as they are separate, they are concurrent. (Author's note, Second Amendment.)

can water-ski; you can mingle the flavors of melons with those of exquisitely long cigarettes, etc., etc.

Male Comrade Tulea doesn't have much time for his daughter. He lets her set her own pace.

Claudio still feels overwhelmed by that summer. He'd rather not go into detail, though, as many of its pleasures have lost their mythical quality since then.

Claudio and Maraia return to Bucharest tanned, jubilant, energized. They plunge into the last year of school with a great zest for life, for studying, for overturning mountains, a zest they've never experienced since. Together they prepare for the sociology entrance exam. They pass the exam and are both admitted to the university. Female Comrade Tulea and Claudio's parents are pleased and congratulate one another for the clever way in which they have guided their children to this wonderful stage in their lives.

Now let's turn for a moment to Giulai's version of the story. She says that at the beginning she was in love with Claudio, too, only in secret. (Oh, that past tense!) She still is, though she won't admit it even now. We, the author, must infer it from the pleasure she takes in telling the story. "You must know, dear," she says, "that even *they* quarreled from time to time. They'd be upset for a couple of days and keep asking about each other. Then they'd come over to our house. I had married Maikl by then and was pregnant. I helped them make up. But one day he went to her place to apologize, and what did I find out the next day? That they'd broken up for good. And what do you think he did? Withdrew from school. She had a fit, threatened suicide, went searching for him. They never got back together."

Claudio doesn't talk about that evening until much later, and then perhaps only to justify himself—who knows? But he totally *forbids me* (the author) to mention it to anyone.

(If I ignore his wish, I should at least respect the order in which he related the events. Why should I be in a hurry to tell you how and in precisely what words the two of them put an end to a love that seemed destined for all eternity? I could, I suppose, conveniently recall that I haven't explained the story of the money that had providentially fallen from the Transylvanian sky at the end of that August. I'd better.

Claudiu's father had six brothers. Through a merciless trick of fate he was the oldest of the four still living at the time the story took place. The youngest, an inveterate rake who had tried and abandoned a few dozen jobs, was the only one who hadn't settled down yet. His brothers did not know this; they believed he was a brakeman at a small station near Cluj.

That is what he had written to them in a letter a long time ago. The only way he could see to cast off the guilt of his lie was to come to Bucharest in his own car, shower his brothers, sisters-in-law, and nephews with gifts, and then confess that he was a mere forest ranger. Suddenly a chance presented itself: an aunt who had become a Hungarian citizen during World War II, nobody knows how, and whom everyone had forgotten, had just died, and the youngest brother was the only one to hear of it. He went to Hungary and declared himself the sole heir. The local authorities, eager to resolve the case, accepted his statement and made him the heir of assets amounting to about one hundred thousand *lei*. He had transferred the money into his account in Romania, ordered the car, and sent a three-thousand-*lei* money order to each of his brothers just at the time when Claudiu was trying to leave for the coast with his girlfriend. After Claudiu had returned and started his last year of school, another one of his uncles, a man with a penchant for amateur detective work, became intrigued with his brother's sudden windfall and decided to begin an investigation. Three months later he'd dug out the whole story. He informed his brothers and asked them to return the sums received in August until the matter could be settled. The memory of the Transylvanian uncle would remain unsullied only in Claudiu's mind, and even there not for long. The day of reckoning with the two Tulea women put an end to his theory of how one can do something unusually nice for someone hundreds of kilometers away while doing a bad deed in one's own backyard.)[3]

So Claudio drops out of the university and gets a job in the Bucharest office of an international airline company (he has spoken French from childhood and learned English in school). He leads an outwardly successful life, wearing the newest styles and living in an apartment furnished according to the latest trends in interior design. He even has a car, a Ford. He is still a likable young man but has turned into a bit of a dandy, making one conquest after another. He is taking revenge on Maraia for the stories she once told him for now it is he who is travelling the world. As a matter of fact, he has all but forgotten her, thinking of her only when he considers going back to school. But there have been changes at the university: the Sociology Department no longer exists and he's no longer that keen on studying anyway. This could be his Maraia complex, especially if she got her degree and he is still pining after her. Which he isn't.

In 1981 Giulai runs into Claudio at the Zurich airport. He's on his way

3. When a story is the possessor and another story the object possessed, their moral significance need not be similar. (Author's note, Third Amendment.)

back from Lisbon, where he went for some reason or other. She, Giulai, who in the meantime has divorced Maikl and remarried (she has two beautiful children, both of them living with her and her new husband), is returning from Stockholm. She agrees to tell me about her conversation with Claudio at the Zürich airport only if I promise never to reveal it to anyone. *She forbids me even to talk about it.*

So I put off bringing it up.

"Well," says Claudio, "in 1977, right after the earthquake, I dialed Maraia's old number and Madame Tulea answered the phone. I recognized her voice. 'Yes, they're *fine,*' she said, 'just *fine.* They're at *their* place, with their *children.* But who are you?' I didn't reply. I hung up. So Maraia had married and had children. I still don't understand what made me call her. Maybe I'm sentimental in spite of myself."

And Giulai says, "He carries his feeling of failure all over Europe. At the time I said to him, 'Let's stay here, Claudio. Let's not go back!'" After she tells me this, she seems ashamed but then she almost shouts at me, "I *forbid* you to tell anyone what I've just told you!"[4]

But I'm not putting anything off any more; I'm trying to stay in the present.

Claudio says the voice of female Comrade Tulea hadn't changed at all. "It was the same voice that told me, when we last saw each other, 'Claudiu, my dear fellow, you should have told us earlier you didn't intend to marry Maraia. Then I wouldn't have talked Tulea into putting a word in for you with the Admissions Committee.' Can you imagine? That woman thought I'd been admitted to the university because she'd interceded for me with her former husband."

Was he convinced at that point that Maraia believed it too?

But why am I slipping back into the past tense?

"That very day I went and had my file withdrawn from the university." He pauses, pride struggling with near tearful memories. Pride wins. "But don't you ever tell anyone about this. I *forbid* you!"

Didn't I tell you you could skip to the last line?

LES PASSAGERS POUR LE VOL DE BUCAREST SONT PRIÉS DE SE PRÉSENTER À L'EMBARQUEMENT!

This is a forbidden story, anyway. Stop reading it, comrades! Forget the whole thing!

---

4. Is the violation of this injunction to be considered theft or fraudulent possession? (This is not an amendment—author's note.)

❧ *Cristian Teodorescu*   (1954–)

Cristian Teodorescu received his degree in Romanian language and literature from the University of Bucharest in 1980. After teaching Romanian and working as a proofreader for the *Contemporanul* magazine and editor of *România Literară*, he became assistant editor-in-chief of the newspaper *Cotidianul* (1991).

Teodorescu began his writing career in 1983, when some of his works were included in a collection of stories by young writers, all members of the *Junimea* Student Literary Club of Bucharest. His volume of short stories, *Light Director* (1985), received the Writers' Union Prize for a first work. Other works include *Mysteries of the Heart* (novel, 1988) and *Faust for Children* (1990).

"Dollinger's Motorcycle" was first published in *Happenings in the New World* (1996).

Dollinger's Motorcycle

We had moved into the apartment building just a few days before. I was afraid of the black marble staircase, the elevator cage, and the woman who crept furtively out of one of the rooms of our new apartment. The house I had known had a yard, with a water spigot and two dogs. The bed I was used to sleeping in had a certain smell, which I only realized later. Father had come home one evening, and instead of sitting down at the table and putting me on his knee so we could eat together, he had gathered me into his arms and trundled me into the cabin of a truck. Mother had come with us. She was carrying the pillows, the bedsheets, and our clothes. The cabin smelled of halvah.[1] The driver was fumbling around, his head inside the engine. While I sat alone inside the truck, the halvah smell made it so I was quiet. I was afraid of my father. When he came home, he would first beat my mother. Then it would be my turn, but only if I cried. He never hit me out of meanness, though he would clench his teeth and strike me very hard. Then he would take me in his arms and talk to himself. When he did that I was even more afraid of him. When he let me go, he would fling himself onto the bed and fall asleep. Mother would take off his boots and I would go put them out on the porch.

We arrived at the new building at nighttime. I couldn't hear any dogs barking. The streetcars were clanging in the distance. In the silence of the room where I suddenly found myself, I could hear muffled sounds coming from the walls, the ceiling, and the floor. Everything around me was new, yet everything was worn out. The cot in which Mother had placed me smelled of peepee. I was afraid of this smell. In our old house, Mother used to slap my legs in the morning and ask me, "What's this smell?"

Father woke up when it was still dark outside. After he got out of bed I could hear music in the room. I don't know when I realized that the music came from a radio. At first I thought that as Father moved around the room, the heavy smell he left behind mingled with the cheerful music of the morning. Mother would hurry into the kitchen, and he would wave his arms about, fart, and swear to himself. When the children in the apartment building got to know me, they would ask how Dollinger's little girl was. I told them I didn't know. What about Dollinger? Didn't I know how he was? He used to have a motorcycle and give rides to all the children in the building.

On Sunday Father opened Dollinger's garage. He cut the padlock, then squeezed his way inside. Ten minutes later he called me inside too. I was greeted by the sight of a motorcycle with a sidecar that stared at me with its big glass eye. Father was sitting on it. We both played on it for a while, and then Father took me in his arms and told me this was how the working class got its justice.

He ran upstairs to fetch the motorcycle keys. He left me behind to guard the garage. When he came down, he had a padlock in his hand. He opened the garage door, threw Dollinger's padlock away and replaced it with the one he had brought.

Suddenly it was silent in the courtyard. The silence was as thick as lard. The children had disappeared.

"See, son? They don't like it when the working-class people take back what rightfully belongs to them."

I had to pee. Father pointed me to the garage door next to Dollinger's.

"Good job, son! Higher! Make it go higher! 'We live in this building, *we* can't stomach those militia officers!' Move over! We'll show them!"

He swore several times as he peed.

"I wonder where that German hid his keys. Did he think he could throw me off the track?"

In the elevator Father spat at the mirror, he was so angry. Then he started to laugh. When we got back to the apartment, he went straight down the corridor to the door at the end and strode in shouting.

"Hey, woman, tell me where the motorcycle keys are!"

Mother wasn't home. I walked into the room where our own things lay heaped. I put my pillow on the floor and curled up on it. Mother had gone to visit our former neighbor, Aunt Vița. Before we moved, she used to take me with her. We would all sit in the summer kitchen. I would play on the bed with the kittens, and they would talk and take sips of plum brandy from Aunt Vița's yellow glass goblets. When we came home, Mother would be red in the face and would keep whispering to me not to tell Father where we'd been. Aunt Vița lived three houses down from us. Mother would chew parsley so her mouth wouldn't smell when she got home.

Father lifted me from my pillow and stood me up. It was dark.

"Let's take all this stuff out to the trash, son," he said, putting my pillow in my arms. He lifted the mattress on to his shoulders and tucked another pillow under his arm.

After we'd made three trips to the trash cans in back of the building, the only object left in the room was the still for making plum brandy that had been part of Mother's dowry. Father smashed it with a hammer.

"Mother's out there, getting drunk with her Vița. I've brought her to an apartment in the city and she's still drawn to her bad ways. It's all in the mind, son. You have to work with people's minds. Remember that. I'm telling you."

When Mother came home, he didn't beat her. He only slapped her once. Then he rapped her temple with his knuckles.

"You're the wife of a militia officer, woman! Get that? We've got our position to live up to. And here you are getting drunk like a tramp! Off to bed with you!"

When Father came home the next evening, he went straight to the bookshelves. He threw books from the second shelf onto the floor until he found what he was looking for. The motorcycle keys. He jingled them in front of us and flung himself onto the bed.

"Here they are, sonny! Come and get them!" He made the sound of a motorcycle with his lips, as he sat me down on his chest and handed me the keys so I could look at them.

"'*We* are engineers! *We* read books!' Well, son, that's what the books are! A façade they use to hide their wealth from the working class!"

About two weeks later Father took us for a ride on the motorcycle. He put me in the sidecar. Mother didn't want to go. Finally she sat behind him. At first Father drove slowly. The motorcycle lurched from time to time. We came to the paved streets. Mother threw her arms around Father and said in an excited voice:

"Slow down a little, Lică."

When we came back home it was nighttime. Mother's face was all red. In the elevator she arranged her hair. Once in the apartment she gave me my dinner quickly in the kitchen and sent me to bed. Then they had dinner. They came to the bedroom with a bottle. It smelled just like Aunt Vița's kitchen. Mother laughed with her hand over her mouth.

"So that's what the German did, Lică?"

"What do you think, woman? You think I play games when I ask them questions? He did it with both of them. With his wife and the one in the room there."

Mother ran away from home at the beginning of winter. It was after Father started taking her to the room at the back where Luci lived, the woman I had been afraid of at first. Now I liked her. I had two mothers, and Father took only me on the motorcycle for a ride.

After Mother ran away, the room in the back stayed empty because Luci took my mother's place. I liked her. There was something about her that reminded me of the kittens in Aunt Vița's kitchen. Now Father always took off his boots in the corridor. And before he went to bed, he would pick up a book out of the bookcase and place it by his head on the night table. When I missed my mother, I went to the room where our things from home had been. Even though they weren't there any more, it still smelled like them. The smell had made its way into the leather of the couch and the weave of the carpet. Gradually, it became my room. And when Father bought our first car, I kept the motorcycle. I rode it all through my university years. After I got married, Father and Luci moved out.

In 1991, a German woman turned up at my door. Her blue BMW filled the whole courtyard. She was about my age, and she claimed to be Dollinger's daughter. She was. Her father had died in prison. I listened to her carefully. She spoke Romanian with a slight accent. They had all been taken from their apartment in one night. She said nothing at all about Luci, as if the woman had never existed. She and her mother had been taken to the Bărăgan[2] Plain, and from there, ten years later, they had left for Germany.

I sat up drinking all night long with the German woman. We drank to her father, to a better world, even to the little cot she had left behind. I offered her the keys to the motorcycle so she could take something back home with her.

Karla now writes me a letter every month, sending them to my PO box. And when I'm at home alone, I call her. In her last letter, Karla told me she had found me a position as a computer programmer in her town and was waiting for me there. She's not bad-looking. And, after all, we did sleep in the same bed even as children.

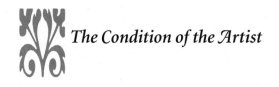

The Condition of the Artist

❈ *Sorin Titel* (1935–1985)

Sorin Titel studied Romanian language and literature at the University of Bucharest. A teacher, then an editor for the *Orizont* magazine in Timişoara, he later moved to Bucharest, where he was an editor of *România literară*, the weekly publication of the Romanian Writers' Union. His first collection of short stories, *The Tree* (1963), was followed by *Noble and Sentimental Waltzes* (1967) and *The Night of the Innocents* (1970).

Literary critics hailed Titel for his exquisite descriptions, almost photographic in detail. Yet the symbolic intent behind them is always apparent, Titel placing his characters in undefined situations that lead to a multiplicity of interpretations. His novels display the same fondness for allegory and parable as his stories, and *The Prisoner's Long Journey* (1971), reminiscent of both Kafka and Beckett, bears the influence of the French *nouveau roman*. His novel cycle, of which *Woman, Behold Your Son* (1983) is the best representative, deals with the mythology of the decline of the Habsburg monarchy. *The Bird and the Shadow* (1977), an earlier novel in the cycle, was awarded the Writers' Union Prize.

"She Wants Me to Climb the Stairs" first appeared in *The Night of the Innocents* (1970).

She Wants Me to Climb the Stairs

She is near me and she pushes me from behind; I hear her panting impatiently behind my back. "You have no choice, you have to do what I tell you," she says. Indeed, I have no choice but to obey, so I start climbing the stairs. From time to time I slip and fall. I'm not used to it; I haven't climbed such steep stairs in a long time. But she catches me in her strong manly arms. "Not like that," she says, laughing at my helplessness. "If only they can finish the roof before we get there. Then we'll have a roof over our heads," I tell her. "So it won't snow inside. We'll be warm," I add, seeing her eyes fill with distrust. Sometimes her tendency to drag me after her almost by force rouses in me a strange, unexpected resistance, and I stop and whimper and clutch the metal railing of the stairwell with both hands. Then I see her fly into a rage. I watch her biting her nails in frustration—after all, she wants us to get to the top as soon as possible. And I feel the sweat trickle in rivulets down my spine. "We have to get there," she whines behind me, "we have to get there as soon as possible." Again I grab the railing with both hands, refusing to go one step further. The cold metal, with its slippery paint, revives me a little. Suddenly she remembers her handkerchief and fumbles for it until she finds it. "Look what a nice handkerchief," she says; and indeed, the red-orange silk scarf she waves before my eyes is quite striking. Then her large, knotty hands pat my cheeks. She blindfolds me as if in jest and thus, with my eyes covered, I sit beside her on the dirty stairwell. We start gobbling down huge ham sandwiches, and although I can't see them, they make me hungrier and hungrier. Yet I feel I'm growing stronger; I could (I say this without boasting) climb to the top floor in just one breath. But then we'd be there much too soon, before they finish the roof. And I can still hear them moving around up there, above my head. "Let's go," she says. "We've eaten, we're full, we're stronger." She rises, wipes the crumbs from her mouth, then checks the knot in the handkerchief to make sure my blindfold is tight enough. I feel her hands on my neck—she's finally found a pretext for touching my body; she's discovered an excuse for stroking my hair without me scolding her. Compassionate all of a sudden, she unties my blindfold. At first, I find it hard to adjust to the light; I must be blinking comically because she bursts out laughing. She hangs the handkerchief on the railing so the perspiration can dry. "Come on, get up," she says, kindly this time. "Let me help you." She smiles gently. But my legs no longer obey me; I've hardly gotten up when I find myself rolling down the stairs, stopping only when I hit the bottom. "Does it hurt after the injection?" she asks. "Let me see if you're swollen." And she blows on the spot to make it cooler. Though bent like a pretzel, I recover quickly. Quickly enough, anyway, to realize that my arms aren't broken, that I'm in one piece. After further investigation I determine that my legs are intact too. Before long I've calmed down completely. And when I look up at her, I see her sitting there, several stairs above me, not angry, but not cheerful either; more likely, fed up with my helplessness and eager for everything to come to an end as soon as possible. She breaks into her hard, almost masculine laughter; I see her holding her stomach in an effort to control it. "Are you in one piece?" I hear her shouting from a distance, from up there at the top of the stairs. "Are you still in one piece, you poor thing?" It's my turn to laugh, no doubt infected by her good mood. "Yes, I'm fine," I reply. "If you want, we can play a game of Ping-Pong. I am, as they say, in great shape. That fall down the stairs has invigorated me." "I can hardly wait to start climbing the stairs again," she confesses. "All right," I say. "I'm fine, look— I'm perfectly fine. I've lost none of my agility. Whatever I do, as they say, I always land on my feet. I'm a kind of jack-in-the-box, that's what I am." "That's right." She smiles. "You're like a funny jack-in-the-box; you're a very good boy." And she jokingly shakes her finger at me. Her approval means a great deal to me. "I'll do it again if you like," I say. "Yes," she urges me, "please do it again." So I go through the whole business once more, but this time, to my amazement, things go differently. That is, I break an arm and fracture a leg. It takes me a while to answer her whether it's my left or right leg, but finally I shout out triumphantly, "It's my left!" "Thank goodness it's not your right," I hear her shout from the top of the stairs, just before I faint from pain. This time, I have to say, she's more compassionate than before: she bandages my broken arm and leg, carefully tying the dressings with her handkerchief to make them hold; she even helps me brush the dust from my trousers and hat. Shuffling my feet, I start climbing the stairs again. But this time I'm annoyed, almost irritated by her fussing over me. So I do my best to make our climb together difficult, if not unbearable. Whenever I catch her off guard, I hit her from behind; whenever she looks away, I strike her knees with the back of my hand. And now and then, pretending to be tired, I get down on all fours, thus forcing her to drag me along. Gradually, all this resistance on my part seems downright idiotic, even to me. So I stop clowning and decide, not without last-minute qualms, to follow her meekly and faithfully. At first our chief concern is to coordinate our movements as well as we can. If one of us happens to pass the other, we beg forgiveness, we swear we'll never do it again. For a while, everything proceeds in an orderly fashion; we're both pleased with the progress we're making up the stairs. Then, all at once, a horrible accident occurs. This time it is she who slips down the stairs, so quickly and unexpectedly that I don't even notice it. To tell the truth, I almost burst out laughing, seeing her arms up in the air, her large coarse palms stretching out to me like those of a surrendering soldier. I take the cane I've been leaning on and aim it at her—in jest, of course—the way one aims a rifle, while imitating the sound of a machine gun. But the very next moment, before I can intervene, I see her arch her back in a strange way; I had no idea she was so supple. She wants to bend over, I say to myself, to show me what she used to do in gymnastics at school. Oh, I think, she's surprisingly limber. Delighted, I watch her flex backwards, but my joy is short-lived because the show she's putting on comes to an abrupt end; her body bends as if snapped in two, and she tumbles down the stairs gracelessly. It's all so entertaining I find it hard not to laugh. She cries for help from the bottom of the stairs. But I'm still so amused at the image of her flying headfirst down the stairs like a cannonball, her legs flailing helplessly in the air, that, try as I may, I can't restrain my laughter. "Help!" she shouts. "You fool! What on earth makes you laugh like that, for no reason at all?" She lies down there, curled up in a ball, and after her first screams, which are, as I've said, insults, she sinks into silence—a bad sign. I hold my breath, straining to hear whether she's still breathing. To my horror, I can hear nothing; she's just lying there, at the bottom of the stairs, her head in her lap, like a rag doll. After a while, I admit, I'm seized with dread, if only because it'll be anything but pleasant to climb such a stinking pile of stairs all by myself. Yet I don't have the slightest desire to go down to the foot of the stairs and find out what's wrong with her. I keep thinking of the sacrifices I've made to get to where I am now, and I simply don't feel like starting all over again. So I wait for her to regain consciousness. My mixed emotions, my impatience make the wait seem endless. An unexpected sadness comes over me. "Why," I say to myself, "I'm all alone. She was the only family I had, my support in old age." I call her name again, this time making my voice sound as warm as possible, but there's no reply. She is still lying there, hunched over at the foot of the stairs. Enraged, I accuse her of making it up. "You want to frighten me," I tell her. "It's all a cruel trick, a mean attempt at revenge." But before long I hear her snoring; she has the thin snore of a little girl, the gasp of an infant. "She must have fallen into a deep sleep," I think. "It's the powerful shock she's had." Moved, I let her be. A long time passes, however, and she shows no signs of waking. Eventually I begin to worry in spite of myself. From where I am at the top of the stairs I shout to wake her up, all the while hurling reproaches at her. Amidst this shower of abuse she sits up and smiles at me, wiping her eyes like a little girl. "I must have dozed off," she says. "I got sleepy all of a sudden." Then, from up here, I watch her efforts to stand up; she collapses every time she tries to rise to her feet. "I'm afraid I've fractured my leg," she whimpers, and her words soften me against my will. Reluctantly, I climb down once more to the bottom of the stairs, driven only by my sincere wish to offer assistance. Slowly and carefully, we start our way up the stairs again. Every once in a while her pain becomes unbearable and she asks me to give her a moment of respite. We stop for a moment or two so she can regain her strength, then we continue on our way. To endure her pain more easily, she starts swallowing painkillers. Since they take effect slowly, she resorts to stronger ones. Though I ask her to stop, explaining it's bad for her weak heart, she pops sleeping pill after sleeping pill into her mouth, in a mad fury. Soon the drugs start working. Overcome by drowsiness, she closes her eyes and begins stumbling. Finally, the pills take full effect and she falls into a deep slumber. I lift her in my arms. Barely awake, she lovingly puts her arms around my neck. This makes me so happy I almost forget how hard the rest of the climb will be. At times she talks in her sleep, her words full of love for me. "So she loves me," I say to myself, overjoyed, as I head up to the top floor with her. If she has hesitated to tell me so until now, it must be because of her deep sense of modesty. But as I climb the stairs, I feel she's growing heavier, and it's some time before I realize that the woman in my arms is the Venus de Milo herself. A very strange Venus de Milo to be sure, for as I glance at her again I notice how much the Venus actually resembles her. "How beautiful she is," I think. "I'd never have imagined her so beautiful." I must handle her with the greatest care, lest I drop and break her. For she now belongs to the whole world; her picture will be in all the textbooks. An object not to be toyed with, one might say. Yet the stumps of her arms hinder my progress; the cold marble of her hips threatens me with a full blown case of rheumatism. At the same time I'm aware that the eyes of the whole world are riveted on me. My future, my fame will depend on how I carry the statue to its destination. I know this very well and, as I advance, I feel the weight of both the statue and the immense responsibility I have assumed bearing down on my shoulders.

❦ *Mircea Horia Simionescu* (1928–)

Mircea Horia Simionescu took his degree in philology from the University of Bucharest in 1963. A prolific journalist (he wrote music reviews, among other things) in the early 1970s, manager of the Romanian Opera, Simionescu came late to his literary career (1969) with a spectacular indictment of Socialist Realism, the literary dogma of the 1950s. His first work, *The Well-Tempered Innovator, I: A Dictionary of Names,* a collection of short fiction, launched him straight into Romanian postmodernism. At the same time, through his refined, erudite, and ironic writing, Simionescu broke with the tradition of ruralism and magic realism heretofore dominant in Romanian short prose. Other volumes include *The Well-Tempered Innovator, II: A General Bibliography* (1970), *After 1900, in the Afternoon* (1974), and *The Banquet* (1982). Simionescu has also written the novel *The Frock Coat* (1984). The volume *Half Plus One* (1976) earned him the Academy Prize.

The short pieces translated here, "Mateo Orga: 'Waiting'" and "Ramiro Helveto: 'Circumstances,'" were first published in *The Well-Tempered Innovator I: A Dictionary of Names* (1969).

FROM *A Dictionary of Names*

MATEO ORGA: *"Waiting"*   Except for a few details our life is one long wait. I've been waiting for Ricardo for two days. He's late coming back from the Crusade. Of course, he won't be in time even when he does get back. He owes me five dinars. I'm as healthy as a horse and my wrist, the one I injured in the battle on the Arno, no longer bothers me. My perfect health, though, worries me no end. If you somehow have a wound, a migraine, a weeping eye, or a limp—you are concerned, naturally. But you know for certain how much harm's been done. The situation is clear: you've been tested, your good and bad deeds have been weighed, and you've been punished for the bad ones with that wound, those tears, that limp. But what if there's nothing wrong with you and you enjoy the best of health? That means you haven't been judged *yet*. It means there's been a mix-up, a slip in the paperwork, a deliberate omission in the bureaucratic system of records. Then you can expect punishment to fall precisely when things are at their most productive and enjoyable. If you ask me, I'd prefer an ache in the jaw or leg. The price would be high but I'd be at peace, since I could still do a lot with the other leg or the unafflicted jaw. I'm still waiting for Ricardo. He owes me five dinars. But I'm waiting with the same impatience to fall ill. It may happen in two or three days; I'm as healthy as a horse and that means the groundwork is already laid. But some people have waited to see where they'll be struck for no less than sixty years. Poor souls! What a life! You wouldn't be able to start anything if you were in their shoes; no matter what you did, it would come under the sign of the strictly temporary.

Brother Benedict has told me not to worry. He has known people who stayed healthy until very late in life. Leaving aside the fact that most monks overembellish reality—monks are the first journalists I have met—if things were the way kindly Benedict says, the world would be a horrible place. All members of society would have an unforgivably high quotient of self-confidence and, naturally, impertinence. And nobody would get along with his brethren any longer.

If happiness came to me in the guise of tuberculosis of the bone, with a floral localization in the leg—the left leg, say—things would be just perfect. I'd have a medical certificate to keep me out of both the campaign to Pomerania and the much anticipated encounter with Philippe d'Anjou, the Bellicose.

But I'm dreaming of forbidden pleasures. Perhaps I have been forgotten for a long time and these stupid thoughts will only anger those who mete out punishments. Then, instead of what I'm expecting, I might find myself sporting a magnificent cancer. But we must admit that the order of the world is extremely unjust. Maté Rodrigo, the fisherman, who has a wretched family and is always hitting the bottle, has been blessed with a cough that has turned his face purple, down to the roots of his beard; his master has forbidden him to go out to sea, forcing the other fishermen to do his work so that his family will not starve. And that rascal of a Bruno Modi was stricken with Iscariot's Disease and now lazes around on his lordship's estate. But me, I was left with an iron constitution—me, a man with so many things to do, who at the age of forty, though in my prime, can hardly envisage beginning, let alone finishing, any of them. If there were any justice, I'd contract lockjaw and have trouble eating; I'd take food through a rubber tube or a funnel and people would be convinced that death was knocking at my door. In the meantime I could study the movement of the stars, the rising and setting of the sun and the moon. As it is, I have discovered the relationships between the stars, the growth of plants, and the actions of humankind under dreadful conditions, my perfect health always under a threat, while I was toiling at my lordship's accounts. How much more advanced my investigations might have been if only the thoughtless judge had come a few years earlier to parcel out his punishments! No doubt an incurable fracture of the leg—the left leg, say—would have come in handy, possibly accompanied by groans by far outlasting the pain. If truth be told, I'd be better off with some spectacular disease—a tumor, a flowering of flesh on the chest, throat, forehead, or between the eyes, a hideous crimson excrescence that wouldn't affect my sight but would be continually leaking pus, thus driving everyone away. Somewhere deep in the jungle I once saw a grocer who had sprouted a second head. At first his master was glad, thinking the man's intelligence had doubled. Even though this wasn't the case, the grocer still had enough of a brain to convince his fellow villagers that that little brain of his kept moving from one skull to the other. As a result, his limbs no longer knew whose commands to obey. His jerky movements proved only too well the truth of his words. The villagers left him alone. So he went out into the world and started writing poetry, or more precisely, resumed his favorite pastime. He wrote plays until old age under the pen name Shakespeare. He has been sighted in England. Has anyone heard from him lately?

Judging by my dreams, one might think I am waiting for the resurrection of the dead. Alas, I'm only waiting for Ricardo. He owes me five dinars. He'd better pay me back. No matter how stubborn he is, I'll teach him responsibility. The wretch! He hoped to dodge his problems by being stricken with palsy—he hoped his commander would send him home. He has eight children; he could have done with a bit of foaming at the mouth before the trip. He needed to go to Jerusalem as much as I need a hole in the head. Who knows what part of his body he may be breaking on some stinking hill out there in the wilderness! The poor devil, he used to like mathematics. He would do sums and multiplications to ten figures in his head. He'd better pay me back. If he'd really been stricken with palsy, I'd have canceled the debt. . . .

I know one Cristofor Luca, a man lucky by nature, who one day fell off a horse. His breastbone rammed into his shoulder, dislocating his shoulder blades and twisting his neck. Once tall and imposing, he became short and crooked. But that's exactly what he wanted. He's happy as a midget. He stays at home, cared for by his countless sons, and draws all day long. Maestro Girolamo Battista Alesse used to look at his panels and say he'd never seen such a gifted artist.

A well-carried-out fall can disfigure you in such a way that men immediately take you off their rolls and leave you alone. A broken shinbone—in the left leg, say—coupled with hip displacement, might be the solution. It remains to be seen if fluids are truly influenced by the appearance and disappearance of the planets. I was in the midst of testing the hypothesis (partially, since I had just set up the signals and was waiting for confirmation—God knows how eagerly!) when they sent me with the fleet to Alexandria to meet the satrap. By the time I got back everything had been thrown into disarray. More work, more signals, more waiting. There's a close connection, it will be seen, between the growth of plants and the disappearance of certain constellations (Orion among them) during the hot season. I've had to put off my investigations until next year. For now, I'm supposed to record the number of carts laden with food, the days spent hoeing in the field, the lord's hunting trips and the game he brings home, as well as the gifts he receives. I've noticed that the greatest injustice is done to those who work with their brains and hearts. Their needs, as far as time is concerned, are greater than those of other people. And yet, they are the ones given the most to do; nobody leaves them alone. Nobody dares to disturb the peasant sweating in the sun as he strains against the handles of his plow, not even with a simple question. But whenever people come across a scholar meditating on the purpose of man on this earth, racking his brains to find the hidden links between phenomena, travailing to compose verse, or searching the sky with his mind, they interrupt his work with all kinds of queries and pester him with all the trivia of the world. They send him from pillar to post, pursue him, torment him with drivel and wild goose chases. People take extraordinary pleasure in wresting a scholar from his books because his profession gives the impression of ease, indifference, and shirking one's duties. Even if they appreciate the fruits of his reasoning, the general opinion is that since acts of thinking and creation are spontaneous, the result of daydreaming and idleness, they must come fairly cheap. I know talented artists who are jeered at because they stare into space, their head in their hands. Their fellow-men deem it necessary to bring them out of their reverie, which is in fact the very token of intense mental labor. Thus, scholars are the most oppressed group in society, their masters forever placing demands on them. I know a Spanish writer of the highest caliber who has had to use his exquisite style to make up menus for his lord. Since his master is not so well-off as he used to be, my acquaintance keeps busy designing imaginative dinners and elaborate banquets and laying them out—but only on paper, of course. The poor creature has penned several cookbooks, admirably put together yet quite sad. Look carefully in the stewards' offices, stableboys' quarters, and in workrooms on the docks, and you'll find thousands of refined men buried under heaps of registers, men who might have left mankind brilliant works, yet what they leave behind are merely dark, grieving rows of letters and figures, forever useless.

I'm waiting for Ricardo. His wife thinks he'll be back in three years, like last time; in any event, my money's not lost. He owes me five dinars. As for me, I'm still waiting for a fever, a bout with measles, something temporary if nothing else, that will confine me to my bed for a few weeks and cut me off from the world. Everybody will shy away for fear of contagion. And during my illness, despite the murderously high fever, I'll still have time to watch the sky for Scorpio's encounter with Virgo. The laboratory is up there, above my head. I could also palpate my liver to monitor the frequency of intestinal spasms in relation to the aforementioned constellations. And if the fever subsides, I'll be able to jot down a few notes.

I repeat, this is only a temporary solution. The permanent one would be a tuberculosis of the bone, incontinence, or deformity of the leg—the left leg, say—which would take me out of active duty forever, thus freeing my mind for meditation.

I've been waiting for Ricardo for three years. It's obvious the poor chap has been delayed. But I need the money now. He owes me five dinars. The disease I'm expecting is late too. If I had more brains and gumption, I'd no longer postpone sticking my leg into the cogs of the mill so that, crippled and in pain for the rest of my life, I could finally fulfill my mission of writing a treatise on the relation between planets and the growth of plants, an idea I've been carrying around in my head for over a quarter of a century.

Galuppi, Menelaus, Parini, Alighieri, Diodor from Tripoli, Boccaccio, Prohaska, Dionis, and many others have sought similar reprieves. Unfortunately, the cogs in the mill or the teeth of the saw, the vise of the screw or the bore of the drill didn't stop in time, and ended up chopping them into bits and killing them mercilessly. Those men had talent.

Of course since their disappearance technology has made some progress. It has certainly advanced more than people's opinion of scholarly work. Today's machinery is more precise. The saw cuts exactly where the notch is made, and the leg—the left one, say—falls into the bucket. Not to mention cigarettes, whose poisonous dry smoke can in a few years (something always amusing to those observing the process) fell the strongest man (maybe seriously, maybe not), either through persistent pectoral angina or recurrent fits of coughing which, with time and a few carefully chosen activities, may end in the most sublime of casualties. (Sansoni Publishing House, Florence, 1937)

RAMIRO HELVETO: *"Circumstances"*   De Sanctis is wrong when he says Ariosto's culture was inferior to that of his contemporaries. Having studied the biography of *Orlando Furioso*'s author only superficially, he never learned about the poet's major work. A more thorough investigation would have taken him to the archives, which contain several hundred letters by Ariosto's fellow citizens. They frequently refer to his mature work, *Lucynda and the Forest,* calling it, among other things, "the most perfect conception of the human genius" (Guicciardini), "a strange, brilliant, creative, and profound piece of Italian writing" (Aretino), in short, a work that made Folegno call his elder colleague "the illustrious doctor and academician of universal suffering." As Marcel Roy put it, *"Lucynda and the Forest* is a grandiose poem; mankind will someday forget *Orlando Furioso,* which is by contrast a mere sketch, and will recognize the true genius of this work, which has all the qualities needed to transcend the centuries."

It must be mentioned that this outstanding epic was never copied or reproduced, nor did anyone ever think of publishing it. The manuscript existed in one copy only; Ariosto read it to his friends many times and destroyed it a few hours before his death.

Thus the only book that might have shown us the astonishing breadth of Ariosto's culture—its universality, its solidity—disappeared without a trace. Here follow the circumstances of the disappearance, which R. Helveto, a literary historian, described after working assiduously on it for over thirty years.

When Ariosto started writing *Lucynda and the Forest,* he was already well known for several minor works, among them the mediocre epic poem *Orlando Furioso,* an account of knightly exploits compiled from similar French and Spanish epics. After filling more than two thousand pages of manuscript, he realized it would take him another fifteen years of dogged work to finish the poem. To test his stamina and see if the rhymes worked, he began reading the manuscript to his friends, the only witnesses to this miraculous piece of literature.

His friends praised him, confident that Ariosto had finally found the path best suited to his artistic temperament and his as yet untapped potential. They mentioned his work to other friends, who were not exactly men of letters but who nevertheless meant well. Thus began the evil that would eventually lead to the disappearance of a rare and brilliant masterpiece from the face of the earth.

It happened like this: after the first reading, Giani Monaco, enraptured, paid a visit to Cardinal Marucci and spoke warmly of the poet's talent. At the time Marucci was preoccupied with a scandal going on in an abbey in Vercelli, where a novice had killed one of her fellow sisters over a disagreement. Marucci needed a well-educated ambassador, able to describe the case and defend the cause of the Church before the podestà, who had been greatly affected by the affair. Ariosto seemed just the right man for the job, the kind of man the cardinal had been searching for since the incident had come to light. Ariosto was hurriedly summoned and told all the details. At first he refused, claiming such a task was beyond him. Then, having no recourse, he accepted the assignment. He spent several weeks in Vercelli, but was unable to understand what had transpired or shed any light on the case. Afterwards he visited the cardinal, making a deplorable impression on him and coming off like an idiot. Eventually the case was closed, after the young murderess put an end to her days.

In the meantime the mayor of Genoa, hearing of Ariosto's genius from another of the poet's friends, assigned him a new mission. The mayor wished to purchase several fishing vessels from Spain, and the Spanish shipowners were eager to sell them, but there were bids from Greece and Poland as well. Only a man of sharp wit could thwart all the plotting and conniving that kept raising the prices. The mayor asked for Ariosto's help because he had heard good things about him. He gave the poet full authority but hinted that failure would cost him his freedom. Ariosto went to Spain and carried out lengthy negotiations. The fishing vessels were perfect and would have made a splendid acquisition, but he lost out to the Greeks, who cunningly offered a better price.

When he returned, Ariosto had to live up to his part of the bargain, so he went to prison. And if he served only one year out of the three imposed by the irate mayor of Genoa, it was due to the good offices of the condottiere Geraldi of Orvieto. The cannon makers in Geraldi's workshop had long been laboring on a large-caliber cherrywood cannon that would fire repeatedly, but had so far been unable to make the mechanism work. They had just managed—with the greatest difficulty—to construct the barrel, wheels, and cannonball. An astute mind was needed to see the enterprise through. Geraldi appealed to Ariosto. At first the poet declined, claiming that whatever skill he had lay within the realm of poetry; eventually, however, he gave in, reluctantly putting his genius at the condottiere's service. He toiled day and night for several months, in the heat of the foundry and amidst the chaos of the carpentry, but failed to solve the puzzle of the cannon. He was fortunate enough to escape unpunished by his patron, who had threatened him with castration in the event of failure. But as luck would have it, Geraldi lost his legs in a battle, and so Ariosto was able to make his getaway.

Having no means of subsistence whatsoever, Ariosto agreed to write a five-hundred-stanza poem for the chancellor of the University of Padua, to be recited on the fiftieth anniversary of the institution, which had been established for the sons of officers unsuccessful in war. He lauded the initiative in inspired verse, hailing the undermining of academic education as an act of justice that would form the basis for tomorrow's Italy. He took the modest sum offered him and was on his way before the ceremony he had honored with his talent actually took place.

On the road to Verona the poet was detained by the soldiers of an Arab who had made his fortune in Mantua. The Arab had learned of Ariosto's art from a friend, who had recited a few of his verses from memory. The Arab had been delighted. He lavished great honors on the poet, promised him a considerable salary, and entrusted his map room to him, asking only that he put it in order and add to it. Since he could not obtain any reliable cartographical sketches from the sailors, Ariosto was allowed to receive travelers, from whose accounts he was to compile the required maps (the Arab was preparing to conquer Asia Minor and India in the coming years). The poet spent two years listening to endless tales of hundreds of strangers. He made up maps of all kinds, to all scales, in all styles and colors, with only one drawback: they were extravagantly inaccurate. This soon became obvious: the Arab set off on his expedition to Asia and, following Ariosto's directions, reached Marseille. The poet was punished severely (at the time, a beating with the rod was the preferred form of chastisement), then banished.

By chance Ariosto found himself in front of the post office in Siena, the most important center for letter distribution in all Italy. His initial refusal to sort letters was to no avail, because the post office was controlled by the military, and Ariosto had been recommended by the supreme commander himself. For a year he skillfully sorted and classified domestic and foreign letters, distinguishing himself for his diligence, as he often worked long after midnight. For the first time he was able to save some money from his pay so that, with a loan from the Postal Credit Union, he could have a two-bedroom apartment built in one of Siena's better neighborhoods. At the end of his three-year probation, when he could finally see himself clear, a complaint about a delayed parcel shattered his career. He was dismissed, his apartment was confiscated, and he was forced to pay damages that by far exceeded his meager savings.

This time it was a letter from Rome that saved him. The new pope, a prelate of Portuguese descent, had just heard from a Galician friend about the writer's extraordinary talent. He received Ariosto and had a long discussion with him about the form and content of his manuscript. Then His Holiness confided his thoughts to his visitor: his counselors, the pastors of souls in Mondolia and Franconia, had alerted him to the existence of a dangerous sect that was threatening the unity and harmony of his flock. He asked the poet to spend a few years among the group to discover their intentions and report on them. Ariosto demurred, insisting he had first to finish his epic, since the poem was still only a sketch, an outline. The Holy Father sympathized, but the problem he wished the poet to address was, of course, much more important. The situation would grow increasingly serious if the Church failed to halt the sect's attempts to convert true believers. He spoke warmly of the trust the Council had in Ariosto, the most enlightened poet of modern Italy. He pointed out that the poem could not hope to save more than ten or fifteen strays, while the action Ariosto was asked to participate in would save thousands upon thousands of God's innocents. The poet agreed and packed his cases. His work went well in Mondolia, even garnering him the Grand Blue Ribbon, but in Franconia he encountered resistance. The Franconians, sect members and nonmembers alike, quickly realized he was eavesdropping on them and prying into their business. They intercepted his reports written in invisible ink. They beat him. The pope recalled him, admonished him, and had him thrown in prison.

Ariosto was on the verge of being sentenced to death when the emperor of Southern Germany, a great lover of poetry, ransomed him. One of the writer's friends, apparently Bembo, had told him of Ariosto's genius. The emperor brought the poet to his court, heaped praise upon him, and appointed him assistant curator of his private library. The head curator was a Dutchman, one Van den Vande, a fastidious and exacting man, whose ambitious project was to copy all the famous works in the world: manuscripts, pictures, and statues. Ariosto could not avoid the preordained activity—though to complete it would have taken at least two hundred years—and so for three years from morning till night tirelessly transcribed treatises on poetry, military subjects, gardening, embroidery, drawn work, astronomy, cooking, trade, and finances. He fell gravely ill, used his sickness as an excuse, and returned to Florence. There he rented a room from a diamond cutter, tried to keep his presence in the southern city of light a secret, and joyfully resumed work on his great poem. But the fifteen years necessary to complete the last cycle had already elapsed. He succumbed to his illness.

He thought it would be wrong to leave an unfinished work to the mankind he had loved despite everything, an illusion of splendors still unformed. From his deathbed he threw his manuscript, page by page, into the fire. After carrying out this proud and ambitious act, immensely beautiful in its ethic, he died.

Thus was lost forever the epic poem *Lucynda and the Forest*, whose verses might have made humanity an infinitely richer creation than it is today.

᙭᙭᙭ Ov. S. Crohmălniceanu (1921–)

Ov. S. Crohmălniceanu graduated from the Polytechnical Institute of Bucharest in 1947, then switched to the study of literature. For many years a professor in the Department of Romanian Language and Literature at the University of Bucharest, Crohmălniceanu is the author of *Romanian Literature Between the Two World Wars* (vol. I, 1967; II, 1974; III, 1975), a landmark of postwar literary criticism. In the 1980s, Crohmălniceanu played an important role in the development of the *Junimea* Student Literary Club at the University of Bucharest.

Although Crohmălniceanu turned to prose writing rather late in his career, his collections *Extraordinary Tales* (1980) and *More Extraordinary Tales* (1986) established him as one of the best authors of science fiction in Romania, an author with a tendency toward the ludic and the parodic. His publications also include several volumes of literary criticism: *Literary Reviews 1954–1956* (1957), *Tudor Arghezi. A Monograph* (1960), *Romanian Literature and Expressionism* (1971), and *Our Daily Bread* (1981). The last two works received Writers' Union Prizes.

"A Chapter of Literary History" was first published in *Extraordinary Tales* (1980).

A Chapter of Literary History

Not long after literature-writing machines started rolling off the assembly line and operating at maximum capacity, it was observed that literary critics had begun to disappear on a daily basis. The phenomenon had an immediate cause, easily perceivable: the profession of literary critic had become for all intents impossible to maintain. No one was able to read even the smallest fraction of the books being published. According to rough estimates (the history of this particular point in time was reconstructed much later, and concrete data are still vague, based as they are on indirect sources), a machine could compose a poem in less than two seconds. A novel under three hundred pages took eighteen minutes to write. Inexplicably, however, the time required to write a play amounted to nearly an hour. The machines worked without interruption for about ninety days, then had to stop for an overhaul. As a result, 10^{12} volumes appeared on bookshelves every year in Lima alone, and publishers' profits skyrocketed. Literary historians were the first to relinquish their mission. Unable to examine the great majority of books in print, they found the reason for their work reduced to the absurd. No matter how many efforts they made, they could not read even 0.0001% of the machines' literary output. Soon after, newspaper columnists laid down their arms. Even if they deliberately quit selecting books according to their importance (there was no way of knowing whether, among the countless unread volumes, they might be overlooking some major works), they acknowledged as insurmountable one question of principle: if the machines were to perform the type of work for which they had been programmed, they would have to dispense with all critical objections. The literary commentator's calling was, first and foremost, to examine the extent to which an author had accomplished his or her artistic intention. But since the machines never strayed one iota from their program, they created only masterpieces. Thus any assessment became *ab initio* superfluous. Even the most eccentric of readers' tastes had been predicted in the original statistical calculations. Surprises were no longer possible.

Since the critics' demobilization threatened to strip literary life of all color, someone came up with the idea of having a number of bad books programmed, just for the sake of comparison. Otherwise, there would be no way of telling a masterpiece from something mediocre. But once the project was carried out, it became apparent that the vicious circle could not be broken. The machines designed to write worthless books also performed their task unfailingly. The resultant texts were flawless in their mediocrity or stupidity, thus automatically acquiring an inestimable aesthetic value. Then a highly respected philosopher put forward the theory that—since machines could only create perfect works in response to their programming—literary criticism was indeed doomed to disappear. The philosopher's reasoning was rather unclear, wandering about in the mists of metaphysics, but his conclusion was strong and impressive and quickly gained almost unanimous approval. The last of the critics died in his library of brain congestion one morning in May, literally buried under a mountain of books (he had been reading at the rate of three pages per hour, for twenty-six hours nonstop).

Still, no one could conceive of literature without critical analysis. And so the day arrived when it was considered necessary to build machines for judging books. From the outset, however, the designers came up against a major hurdle: what kind of programming were they to give them? First, they had to solve the problem of basic information. The machine-critics had to be able to read all the output of the machine-authors and classify it according to genres, species, themes, subjects, and artistic formulas. The designers began by planning summary bulletins to help orient the reader. For this task, electronic brains were assembled, which, once started up and hooked in to the literature-writing machines, began producing a steady stream of book lists. The results, unfortunately, proved disappointing. The bulletins were virtually unusable, having so many pages no one could read them through. Obviously, additional machines would have to be designed in order to read all of the lists and proceed to a further selection. But what criteria should be used? After much debate, they returned to analytical criticism. The designers encountered great difficulties in creating programs for their new machines. The critical theories in fashion during the period of literary apprenticeship (the age in which books had been written by humans) led, one after the other, to unexpected effects. Existentialist criticism in electronic shape clashed with the paradox of machine-produced literature. Was it the genuine expression of human experiences? Yes and no. The works existentialist critics set out to discuss did express life experiences (the programs contained so many possibilities that results were utterly unpredictable, thus mimicking the ineffable flutterings of human existence), but the machines themselves remained heaps of filaments, levers, and interconnected wires that entered into a state of inertia the moment a single button was pushed. Psychoanalytic criticism aroused controversy as usual, because its deductions extended not only to the subconscious motives of its designers but also to those of the managers of the industrial enterprises supplying the electronic brains meant to engender literary works. The newspapers of the time even recorded a few spectacular trials: the head of a large financial corporation found himself accused of experiencing the incestuous drives described in the 12,604th *Antigone* (a play conceived by a machine constructed by a firm associated with his bank). The defendant claimed he hadn't even heard of the original play, but his plea met with serious theoretical objections.

For a while the machines programmed on a theological basis enjoyed some degree of success. They were identified with the human beings of times past into whom God the Designer had breathed the grace of creation. The Church protested, however, and the analogy was denounced as diabolical. The only system that met with any real approval was the one that returned to an earlier view of the critical act of interpretation: that of a condensed reconstruction of the essential elements of literature, one that pointed out the virtual possibilities left unexplored by the author. Literary work was to remain a spiritual stimulant for the scholar, challenging him to produce an infinite number of new poetic interpretations. Subsequently, the machine-critics began to extrapolate artistic intentions. From one novel they generated several thousand; from one poem, entire cycles; from one play, millions of superior variants. Literary production flourished as never before. Everyone seemed satisfied, but in a few years people noticed that the machine-authors had started to show signs of irritation. Dissonant elements kept turning up at the end of their works, as if on purpose. A disorder of self-annihilation or, as some historians termed it, "aesthetic suicide," emerged. At one point the novel, play, or poem would veer off with equal mastery in a diametrically opposite direction from the one declared at the beginning, utterly obliterating the work's original artistic intention.

And so, once again, critical works stopped appearing. The machines in charge of writing them kept turning out novels, short stories, poems, and plays, while advertising agencies, no longer able to insert even a single book review in the newspapers, found themselves on the verge of bankruptcy. Then someone had a revolutionary idea that solved the problem for good. The two types of machines were plugged into the same circuit. The electronic brains of writers and critics were thus obliged to consume one another's output: the former frantically started passing judgments on the works produced by the latter. An astounding reversal ensued. Whereas the machine-critics had displayed a secret bent for creative writing, the machine-writers now revealed a previously hidden passion for literary criticism. And since, thanks to this innovative idea, all of the above occurred with devouring violence within a closed circle, people were able to go about their business undisturbed.

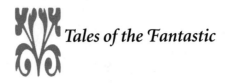 *Tales of the Fantastic*

⛉ *Ana Blandiana* (1942–)

A graduate of the University of Cluj (philology, 1967), Ana Blandiana served as an editor for *Viaţa studenţească* and *Amfiteatru,* two national student magazines (1968–1974). Active as both poet and prose writer, she published her first poems in *Tribuna* magazine in 1959. In 1964 her collection of verse entitled *First Person Plural* was hailed for its candor in conveying impressions and sensations. In her later volumes, however, Blandiana became increasingly concerned with ethical and moral questions. In 1984, for instance, she published four poems in *Amfiteatru,* decrying her nation's passivity. The issue was immediately suppressed, but continued to circulate in Samizdat. Her book of poetry for children, *Events on My Street,* was perceived as a satire on the authorities, and she was forbidden to publish until 1989, just prior to Ceauşescu's fall from power. Today Blandiana is one of the leaders of the Civic Alliance, an organization working to restore Romania's civil society.

Blandiana's prose works include a collection of essays, *The Quality of Witness* (1970), two volumes of fantastical tales, *The Four Seasons* (1977) and *Projects for the Past* (1982), and a novel, *A Drawerful of Applause* (1992). Many of Blandiana's works have received national and international awards.

"The Phantom Church" was first published in *Projects for the Past* (1982).

The Phantom Church

There are so many kinds of fantasy it is no wonder that some of them may pass for reality. Sometimes reality itself arrogantly extends its borders and the overlapping zones remain ambiguous, uncertain of status for years, decades, even centuries. And then—who knows how, perhaps simply through the natural erosion of time—either the fantastic or the real blurs and slips to the other side, astonished it could ever have appeared otherwise. Of course neither the trickling of reality into the molds of fantasy nor fantasy's invasion of the real can have overly serious consequences for anyone trained to see beyond appearances; the mere occurrence of an event cannot remove it from the bounds of the imaginary, any more than fantasy's shading of an incident is sufficient to oust it from the realm of actuality. Since Creation, a line has been drawn between the real and the unreal, and transgressing it signifies a desire to test its strength rather than an intention to defy it, in the same way that taking a drug means not so much underestimating its effects as being willing to experience them. Most of the time the real and the unreal coexist in parallel spheres, independent of and even indifferent to one another. Yet in the rare moments when they do come together, their union brings forth a mutual revelation: having passed through reality, an element of the fantastic returns to the imaginary world strengthened by the authority of the test, while an element of the objective universe that joins fantasy becomes charged with a new significance capable of transforming the existence from which it escaped, if only for a moment.

The extraordinary journey of the wooden church that began in the village of Subpiatră[1] in the Transylvanian Mountains of Bihor in the late eighteenth century, more precisely in the winter of 1778, is one of those occurrences which, though having actually taken place, belong by nature to the domain of fantasy. Yet having passed through reality, even if under the sign of the miraculous, they bring to the imaginary world a prestige all the more undeniable for being unnecessary.

The story, which began as verifiable history, is as follows.

The serfs of Subpiatră, having no legal right to construct a church for themselves, decided to bring to their village a church already built. Such an unusual idea might never have crossed their minds had there not been an abandoned wooden church some ten kilometers away in Lugoşu de Jos, a village of free peasants who had managed to build themselves a new stone church. The idea of hauling a church ten kilometers—from the valley of the Crişul Repede River to the Carpathian Mountains—as well as setting it up hundreds of meters higher, complete with porch, spire, roof, vestibule, nave, altar, benches, icon screen, and even icons, may today seem an exclusively literary idea, a clever symbol not to be taken seriously (and thus an aberration). At the time, however—it was before the peasant uprising led by Horea[2]—the people about to revolt might well have deemed it possible. The legend, though detailed, does not say whether or not the villagers of

Subpiatră voiced any doubts about the feasibility of the move at the outset. It merely describes the negotiations for purchasing the church, the difficulties encountered in raising the money, and the fashioning—more toilsome than the move itself—of a an immense saw, as long as the church was wide, to sever the building from the place where it had been erected more than a century before.

For that is how the church was wrested from its foundations of thick logs, thrust into the ground like deep roots: it was felled with the saw as if it were a tree, hewn down at its base like one of the countless fir trees—crisscrossed and pegged together—that had brought the church to life so many years before. It was not in fact difficult to cut, as the saw's teeth passed gently through the wood; it was only hard to keep it standing, the thin arrow of the spire pointing up and the porch pillars supporting the infinitely high roof. The age-old skill of loggers had to be called upon for the twenty pair of oxen, yoked in an elaborate web on three sides of the church, to extricate it from its foundation and make it slide evenly, centimeter by centimeter, without toppling. The journey, or more precisely, the first part of it, took almost a year. They could advance no more than a few meters a day, and only on days when the ground was dry. After careful planning, they decided to avoid the winding roads and go instead straight across the slopes and woods, opening new trails and clearing whole forests. The weighty frame of the church, plowing through the dust, dug deep and wide furrows into the ground, leaving behind scars visible even today on the ancient face of the land. In time the trail became a road, a highway even (a strange kind of highway, one gouged into the earth, with inexplicably high banks). Covered with asphalt now, it still bears the name (a name absurd to anyone unfamiliar with the story) of the Church's Furrow. Today you can reach Subpiatră from Lugoşu de Jos either by the Lane—the old country road that no one uses any more, where grass grows idyllically in the deep ruts made over the centuries—or by the Church's Furrow, the asphalt highway, which is much shorter and steeper and cuts the forest in two.

In that year of 1778 spring had come early, Easter too, and by Saint George's Day the earth was dry and covered with lush grass. The serfs began hauling the church on the patron saint's name day, April 23. Though advancing only a few meters a day, they managed to bring it out of the cemetery by Ascension Day, and by Whitsunday they had reached the higher end of the village. The church moved more easily than they had dared to hope, and they dragged it carefully, lest the bottom of the porch, with its wide swath of carvings one handbreadth above the saw cut, should wear off. They were in no hurry; they knew it was no use reaching the Criş River before the frosts of winter: only over the hard-frozen riverbed could they hope to make the church glide like a sled.

But there were long summer months until then, months in which the church progressed without swaying, scarcely betraying its motion, so slowly and imperceptibly did it inch forward. But for the yawning furrow left behind and the teams of oxen tangled in their yokes and ropes and brought to their knees with the effort, one might have said, glancing at the cross barely stirring on the horizon, that the church was ascending the mountain by itself. This impression grew even stronger when the church entered the woods and proceeded along the deforested path, only its eerily thin spire still visible both from the village below, now left behind, and the village above, not yet reached. The steeple thrust up above the tops of the fir trees, not like an object resisting the laws of gravity but like a creature growing from the earth, floating above the peaks of the other firs, unadorned with crosses.

Consequently, though no one forgot how hard the labor was (and how could they when they had all taken part in it?), the more the weeks and months passed, the more people thought of the church's progress as something of a miracle. Thus, on major holidays, streams of believers from neighboring villages—or perhaps merely curious onlookers—would converge on the church. Smaller groups, like envoys on reconnaissance missions, came from the other side of the mountain. It would have been hard to say whether those who came from afar were paying homage to the miraculous relocation of the church or to the human effort that had made it possible. Be that as it may, the fame of the church making its way from one village to another burgeoned, its legend gradually taking shape, though nothing out of the ordinary had yet happened. Whenever a holiday caught the church on the road, it would come to a halt, and the priest—his chestnut beard flying in the wind, his voice reverberating from tree to tree—would perform the service on the porch stairs, bystanders swelling the ranks of the moving team. By August 15, the Day of Our Lady, the church had reached a clearing in the hills, where shepherds' gatherings and festivities had taken place for centuries. The large bright meadow looked like an elegant anteroom, its flooring the short, coarse, brushy grass of Alpine pastures. Not until they saw the crowds surround the church (and overflow into the forest, since even the wide meadow could not contain all of them, as they stood there respectfully in their bright clothes) did the peasants from Subpiatră really begin to believe in the miracle of the move. They looked at Father Nicola, the priest who had started it all, with new eyes, full of astonishment and awe. Thus everything that followed not only failed to surprise anyone but even seemed expected, as if predestined by forces beyond human control.

The church reached the Criş River at the onset of winter, as planned. They now had to wait for the river to freeze over so they could slide it across to the opposite bank and haul it up the mountain through the thick, soft snow. By Saint George's Day the next spring the church would have finished its course, ending its journey at its future home. But that year the snows may have come early, falling deeply and deceptively; perhaps, since everything had gone so well until then, the men had started to rely on miracles rather than on doing their duty; or perhaps they wanted to push the church within the village borders by Christmas. In any case, they did not wait for the Criş to freeze over. The ice had not had time to thicken between the nervous restlessness of the water and the pacifying sleep of the snow. It held up as the dozens of teams of oxen, their yokes adorned with fir twigs and colored woolen threads, crossed over, but then, with a prolonged, ominous sound, as if gnashing against its own powerlessness, it cracked, at first invisibly, then split and broke apart, causing the church to go down erratically, tilting it to one side and finally depositing it majestically, under the terrified gaze of the crowd, on the gravelly riverbed. For a few long moments the sharp spire continued to sway, like a bent branch beating the air, fighting to regain its place. Then the flowing water surrounded the church with unconditional acceptance, as if it were an island suddenly submerging. The water in fact barely covered two of the three steps of the porch, and the topmost row of carvings could still be seen, its flowery motif coiling like a plaited rope. Having reached the other bank, the oxen strained to look behind them, not comprehending why they were no longer being goaded and sensing they should not move. A few men, roused from their stupor as from a heavy sleep, rushed to unyoke the beasts. The slightest mishap could topple everything. It was getting dark; they would have to wait until morning.

But by the next day the church seemed to have taken root, as if it had been built there from the beginning. After a night of hard frost, the hardest of the winter, the ice had sealed it in completely, clasping it jealously like a gift it refused to give back. As nothing could be done until spring, the parish celebrated Christmas and Epiphany right there, in the middle of the Criş, the voice of Father Nicola rising in tune with the water pounding below the ice, stronger than the howling winds and the snowstorms. Thus he stood on the porch all winter, in raging wind or blizzard, officiating to the crowds gathered on the frozen surface. Meanwhile the church's renown continued to grow, its fall through the ice, though unexpected and unforeseen, soon being interpreted as a new sign of its extraordinary destiny.

Father Nicola was the only person not carried away by the miracle that seemed more and more in control of the move. Instead he acted as a cautious steward, closely overseeing the details of his charge and continually repairing one thing or another with such unusual skill that his parishioners soon exaggerated it in their eagerness to make it part of the miracle. All that winter he worked on the church's floor, replacing it with long, carefully planed boards that he joined together almost seamlessly. He worked alone, requesting no help yet never saying no when a bystander offered to fetch some tool he needed.

For there were always spectators—after the initial astonishment and timorous questions about the priest's daily visits to the church had worn off, after the first expedition had surged through the snow to see what was going on—sometimes only a few, sometimes more, but all of them striving to discern some hidden meaning in the priest's strenuous labor and uncommon skill. They had no doubt (at least this was the conclusion they had reached in the village, where they talked of nothing else) that the priest knew something they could not yet fathom, that there was an order to things they could not yet grasp. Otherwise, why would Father Nicola be working in the biting cold, trudging for hours through waist-high drifts, some days not even returning home but sleeping on the bare floor of the church, wrapped only in his homespun woolen cloak? True, there were those who said, albeit guardedly, that since the priest had no family or household, he might be restless in the village, while his work on the church trapped in the ice would occupy his time and make him feel less lonely. Of course, no one paid any heed to such an absurd explanation. The mystery taking shape before their eyes could no longer be separated from the tall, slightly bent figure of the priest.

Once he had finished the new floor, Father Nicola set to carving the altar screen, an altar screen such as had never been seen before. Then came the benches with notched patterns and high backs, like thrones for voivodes.[3] When he asked the women to weave piles of strong white linen cloth, the villagers took it as a sign that the repairs were coming to an end and that the priest was certain the church would be raised from the riverbed in the spring. The women thought the linen was to serve as altar cloths and window drapings, and they wove eagerly and diligently, not surprised by the priest's request. Later, much later, when tidings of their church reached them from foreign lands, tidings so fantastic they surpassed the realm of human imagination, the cloth was seen in a different light and the priest's request interpreted as proof of his prescience.

By the time the ice started to thaw, at a frantic pace, the women had finished weaving the cloth and brought it to the church. The way the ice melted that year has been retold by the people of Subpiatră for the past two hundred years, and although there have been no eyewitnesses for a long time now, the villagers still relate it in the minutest detail, as if each narrator had actually been there. So great is the number of details and so rapid their proliferation that, in time, as you listen to the storytellers, you begin to wonder whether there ever were any eyewitnesses, whether the whole extraordinary tale of the church is not merely unfolding before the transfixed eyes of the storyteller each time he retells it, as if he were under the spell of his own vision. But such is not the case. The peasants' account is reinforced by place names dating back two hundred years: the ford of the Criş, for example, is called the Ice Hole of the Church. The excess of local color at this point in the story stems from the fact that, though real, the event had none of the dimensions of reality. And though certain of their truth, people sense how unbelievable it sounds when they relate it and start piling up details, trying to evince a reality the very details deny.

In fact, there was nothing unusual about the way the ice melted that year. Spring had given fair warning, and long before the ice began to thaw the church had been anchored with plaited ropes that coiled around the sturdy fir trees on the banks or were tied to posts laboriously pounded into the snowy ground. Once the thawing began the oxen would replace the posts; they would pull the church off the river bottom as soon as the spring torrents loosened it from its miry place of rest. For weeks that moment had been carefully watched and waited for. Men took turns keeping vigil on the banks, and Father Nicola never left the church, day or night. The women looked after him, bringing him pots of stew and slices of *mămăligă*,[4] which they would find barely touched a day or two later when they came to bring more. During those last few days Father Nicola grew more and more silent, seized by an anxiety far greater than they would have expected. His long beard flowing wildly, he seemed consumed by a terror known only to himself. The villagers—especially the women—hovered around him, awed by a suffering they could not comprehend but which they promptly associated with the miracle, calling it after the fact a premonition or even a preparatory ritual.

For several days the layer of ice had been thinning, growing transparent, and the sun, emerging from time to time from among the fluffy clouds, shone its rays here and there on the river, turning cracks into ice holes. Finally, the water spilled over the surface of the ice, gushing up as from a spring. Overnight it froze again, but the frail, hurried freeze only proved that the cold had lost its power, that these were its death throes. The morning before, the water had begun lapping against the sides of the church, and twice the church had swayed slightly. Less than an hour before the ice finally broke, Father Nicola came out on the church porch and shouted at the sentries on the banks to come to him, at the same time urging the women about to set off in the boats to bring him food that they should stay where they were. His voice sounded harsh and strong above his wind-whipped beard; his eyes impatiently searched upriver. The men clambered into the boats, seized in turn by the urgency of his summons.

That was the last the women saw of their husbands before everything sank into confusion: the boats striking against ice floes as the men hurried to reach the priest, who was still staring anxiously and restlessly upriver. No one ever found out what Father Nicola told the twelve men he had called to his side. The women waited on the bank—patiently at first, then apprehensively—as they gazed at the water swelling up like dough. Now the ice was pouring down in chunks that screeched wildly and rebelliously, smashing into one another and leaping into the air like huge glossy fish, only to crash down again ominously. When the women finally screamed out to their husbands, it was too late. The roar of the river was stronger than their voices. In the space of the one hour the men had been in the river, everything had changed. Crying and shouting at the top of their lungs, deafened by their own wailing and the mad whirling of the waters, the women never knew whether the men had chosen not to answer or whether they had not heard the answers the men had shouted to them. This is the most debated point in the story, the moment that is open to the most diverse interpretations, the juncture at which the narrators have to declare their position, either trying to grasp the facts or boasting that those facts are incomprehensible, as if the nobility of the epic were in direct proportion to its mystery. And this moment of decision is, quite naturally, followed by the moment of truth, the dénouement.

Seeing the church tilt slightly to one side, then turn upright, then list almost playfully to the other side, the women ceased weeping. Mute, they kept their eyes riveted on the steeple, which swung like the clapper of an overturned bell, as if trying to cry out to the walls of sky and water imprisoning it, then changing its mind before making itself heard. For a moment there seemed to be a pause in the river's tumultuous clamor, and in the unnatural, suspended vacuum of silence one could hear a long, searing shriek, as if all the fir trees sacrificed in the body of the church had heaved a deep moan, a single note, almost human, of pain. The very next moment the ice swelled up to the sky with a thundering roar, releasing the church and sending it viciously downriver. For an instant the steeple made an astonishing bow, almost touching the water, and the sides of the porch were exposed indecently. But just when all hope seemed lost the spire miraculously righted itself again, as if brought round by the steady hand of a helmsman. The church, standing straight as a frigate, its mast perfectly vertical, started snaking down the pebbly surface of the waters. The ropes that had held it in place stretched to their fullest to keep it back, then gave way, uncoiling gracefully from the posts and trees and turning the church loose. On this point all narrators agree: the ropes uncoiled effortlessly, as if of their own volition, and whether this is explained away vaguely, as due to the driving force of the ice, or stated proudly, as part of the miracle, nobody overlooks the moment when the ropes let go of the church. Astounded beyond terror, the women watched the church grow smaller and smaller as it proceeded downriver. At times, through the din of the torrents and the thawing of the ice, they thought they could make out voices, voices that could only belong to the men inside. And though what they heard could only be cries of despair or pleas for help, the women stubbornly insisted, themselves amazed at their words, that the sounds coming from within the church and echoing down the water were songs, that the men sailing off were singing horas.[5]

On this bewildering note (which would have been impossible to accept had the storytellers themselves not presented it as incredible and thereby, paradoxically, made it seem unequivocally believable) the historically verifiable account (down to the most outlandish detail) of the church of Subpiatră comes to an end. Everything I have related so far was seen by eyewitnesses and retold by their children, grandchildren, and great-grandchildren. The proofs are in evidence to this day—the bare foundation of the church still visible in the old cemetery of Lugoşu de Jos, the deep ruts in the road called the Church's Furrow, the place that goes by the name of the Ice Hole of the Church, the unnaturally deep ford at the narrow headwaters of the Criş, where even now a child will sometimes drown. Everything I have related so far actually took place. All the rest is hope—a dream belonging not to me but to the villagers who were both the heroes and the bards of the events. And if I can reproduce all the richness of detail of their story, it will be because of my fascination—from the beginning—with the absence of boundaries between the real and the imaginary. Reality flowed into dream, according to God knows what mysterious laws, as unexpectedly and dramatically as gall can seep into the bloodstream.

At first, the sensation that something was terribly wrong overcame even the feeling of sorrow—not so much because the misfortune appeared incomprehensible as because it seemed so intentional. The sense of the miraculous that had filled the village with its euphoria went through a crisis of confidence; people started to give interpretations, mundane and harmful to all concerned, of facts that up to then had required no interpreting. A strange reversal occurred: as long as everything had been unquestionably real, the outcome of their own work, they had considered it fantastic, but the moment things went out of control and took a turn for the fantastic, they analyzed them, as if suspecting a fraud. Father Nicola's expectant glance upriver, his summons to the men on the bank, and especially the strange singing coming from the church—all these led them to believe that the events had been somehow foreordained. Things were complicated even further by the ropes uncoiling of their own will (though what if they had been cut?) and by the church sailing confidently down the river (heading where?), ambiguities that cast a shadow over the grief of the village mourning its lost men. The peasants' sorrow mingled incongruously with doubt, anger, and curiosity, feelings that together formed a fertile terrain, rich in omens, for the dream that was to follow.

In the spring of 1779, five years before the great peasant uprising led by Horea, soldiers of the emperor in Vienna, together with agents of the Hungarian landowners, were combing the villages of the western Carpathians in search of that notorious agitator *(ille famosus agitator)*. Eventually they reached Subpiatră. I cannot claim that the inhabitants of Subpiatră had never heard of Horea or were ignorant of the exaggerated tales—verging on legend—about him, but they believed they had never seen him, and it was only that spring that they heard the facts about him, facts they later mulled over in secret gatherings.

The emperor's men were looking for a certain Nicola Ursu, nicknamed Horea, a builder of churches and a skillful singer from the village of Albac. They asked the people of Subpiatră if Horea had paid them a visit and offered to build them a church or address grievances to the emperor on their behalf, if he had sung for them or urged them to revolt. Strangely, as if by unspoken agreement, the villagers said nothing, either about the extra-ordinary journey of their church or about Father Nicola. Only after the soldiers had left did they begin to put the facts together (amazed at their own reaction, which they could only attribute to the miracle they had been honoring for over a year), and came to the conclusion—by a swift, firm shift in their collective psyche—that Father Nicola was none other than Nicola Ursu from Albac, the man called Horea. They reached this conclusion with evident, almost radiant, relief, as if it suddenly made everything logical and clear.

Soon thereafter news began pouring into the village. The more incredible it was, the more promptly and enthusiastically it was reported. First it was rumored that a church had been seen cruising like a ship down the Criş River, its sails, fastened to a steeple-mast, billowing in the wind. Then they heard that Horea had set off to see the emperor with the people's petitions. That settled the matter. The women recalled the linen they had woven at Father Nicola's behest and were proud to have been involved in so daring an adventure. Facts fell into place and took on a design that—it was increasingly obvious—had long before been masterminded by Father Nicola. The priest's name, which everyone now accepted as Horea, was pronounced with true conspiratorial pleasure, both as a sign of the mystery that united them all and as a token of the undeniable importance that secret had conferred on them. After weeping for many days and many nights, the women whose husbands had been called to the church were now respected and looked upon—by virtue of their suffering—as equal participants in the expedition. None of the villagers doubted that their church had been chosen from the start for the journey which, from the Criş down the Tisa, from the Tisa down the Danube, was to take the delegation of mountain peasants to the emperor in Vienna. Of course, the miraculous transformation of a church into a ship and its miraculous advance down the thin thread of water lost none of their significance by joining forces with the true wonder that was the birth of a leader. The miracle no longer required separate acceptance: if you believed in Horea's strength, you took everything about his acts or existence for granted, without any possibility of doubt or need for proof.

The legends from Subpiatră do not say whether the men who left with the church ever returned after Horea, back from Vienna, urged the people to revolt, but the documents of the uprising do mention an unusually large number of rebels from this particular village in the western Carpathians following their leader to the bitter end in the terrible winter of 1785. When it was all over, the peasants of Subpiatră, the few that were left, returned in silence, as if awakened from a dream they had taken for reality and continued to believe in, while choosing to view reality as a harsh and incomprehensible slumber. Reports of the executions in Alba Iulia found the villagers locked in an impenetrable silence, gazing on the outside world with an unwavering, untrusting eye from behind bolted doors and drawn-up bridges. And though they never spoke, they seemed to say, "Your attempts to frighten us are in vain. We know that everything is only part of this bad dream. Reality is otherwise; we have just returned from it. And things are quite different there." Only when they were alone—beyond the ultimate wall, the wall of silence that shielded them from themselves—did they shut their eyes, daring to face the deep and slippery place where doubt lived, chained and gagged, but still babbling on and on, "Which is the true reality?"

And just when too much time had elapsed for doubt to lie hidden any longer, just when, in its deep and slippery vault doubt had grown stealthily and threatened to break its chains at any moment, to erupt in the rotting silence of uncertainty, a rumor came from the other reality, hard to believe yet impossible not to accept, and started the debate all over again. A man journeying back to the Romanian Lands from the great sea had come upon the church floating down the Danube, its sail joined to a cross-topped mast, and he spoke of the event with awe, not knowing it was their church. He had seen it clearly one evening as it floated gently on the lazy surface of the water, and described not only the porch with its notched pillars and carved panels running like a twisted rope around the base of the church but also the candles burning inside as if on Easter morn.[6] He had seen no one, the traveler hastened to add, seized with a wonder akin to dread, nor would he have expected to. The scene was so tranquil and serene that the church might have seemed deserted had it not been for the deep manly voices singing secular music, not hymns but haunting strains filled with anxiety, which made sense only later, when he realized what he was hearing from the unseen men in the church lit up as for Easter was a *hora*.

After the stranger left (never suspecting the turmoil he had wrought in the souls of his listeners, who accepted his story greedily, as those denied hope always accept the miraculous), the news he had brought so molded the spirit of that mountain hamlet that even now, two centuries later, it is utterly different from its neighboring villages. A quiet but stubborn pride—its source the deep mystery that could not be disclosed but that illuminated everything from within—lends to this day a defiant and enigmatic grace to the women, a secret vigor to the men. Even now, when the days of the revolt are lost in the mists of history and the church's voyage is but a legend recounted to tourists, the inhabitants of Subpiatră (forest rangers, workers in the furniture factory, commuters to the towns of Ştei or Beiuş, hurried passengers crowding into dusty, rickety buses, people for whom history exists only in long-forgotten schoolbooks and on the television screen that they doze in front of) have a secret of their own that shows in their laconic words and penetrating gaze: "That's right, everything is as you see it—not very good and nothing to be done about it. But it doesn't really matter. There's another reality in which things are completely different." Obviously, the villagers themselves are unaware of their uniqueness; they would be the first to express surprise at what I have just said, just as they would be amazed if I mentioned the touch of unmistakable defiance, absent in other country people, that characterizes their gestures, words, and demeanor. To me it is evident that, unbeknownst to them, some of the shock of unquestioningly accepting the miracle as part of their existence— everyday reality thus becoming a mere deviation, a secondary projection, easy to ignore—has transformed the very core of their being. The people who (smiling ironically, their emotion barely surfacing) tell the story of the strange traveler and its influence on the psychology of their village at the end of the eighteenth century show the unconditional acceptance of the tale in their own psyche and behavior. I have always been fascinated by the impossibility of establishing facts in an absolute manner, the sensation that anything, no matter how simple and indisputable, can acquire (as it basks in the bright light of that unconscious, bewildering defiance) complex connotations, contradictory interpretations, new meanings. Throughout their long history, tragic and devoid of hope, flowing down paradisiacal valleys topped by fairy-tale peaks, the villagers' absurd yet profoundly optimistic belief that miracles do exist ultimately made miracles occur over and over again.

I was a child when I first heard about the church floating down the river, saving its heroes from martyrdom and the people's faith from disbelief. It happened one summer many years ago, when I was accompanying my father—a passionate hiker—on one of those treks that delighted my early years. Everything I learned then is still intact and intangible within me, crowned by misty haloes of wonder and uncertainty. When I went back to Subpiatră as an adult, I feared that nothing would be left of the tale that had so charmed my childhood: it might have all been just a flower blossoming on the threshold of sleep, a perfect fruit ripening in the orchard of dreams. It would not have been the first time I discovered how utterly incongruent the images in my memory were to reality.

Aware of my tendency (which I concealed and cherished like a vice) to let fantasy mingle illicitly with the truths surrounding it and take on their hues and shapes so that no alien glance, no matter how profound, could distinguish between them, I passed through adolescence with a persistent feeling of guilt, a lasting fear that I might be found out. The less I could tell the difference between fantasy and reality, the greater my guilt became. Before going to bed at night or while painfully trying to take a nap during the long afternoons, I would review the day's occurrences in my mind, correcting their shameful or embarrassing aspects so that, as I recast them for filing in my memory, the central character, me, gained in intelligence, kindness, and daring, without losing credence. Then I would finally fall asleep, whereupon everything took a definite shape in its subtly revised version. Aftr a while I would forget the original, though a dim glow of guilt remained, a guilt that I carried throughout my childhood and that sometimes envelops me even now.

To my surprise, however, the beautiful tale did not exist solely in my mind: as an adult prepared to accept even the most prosaic of accounts, I came across the story almost word for word among the recitations offered to tourists by the inhabitants of Subpiatră. I relished revisiting the tale, whose improbability had given it the courage (or prudence) to arm itself with so many proofs of its veracity. I relished driving along the Church's Furrow and bathing (together with West German hikers pausing for a rest) in the Ice Hole of the Church. These topographical traces, like markers on the road to the Surreal, strengthened my feelings of certainty. It was as if my own private experiences gained credibility by being linked to the truthfulness of the events. But no matter how much the storytellers' personalities caught my attention and my own recollections colored the story's fantastic outline, I still believed only in the spirit, not the letter, of the account. I was moved, yes, but with admiration for its mysterious and timeless naïveté. The adult's nostalgic superiority surrounds even the final episode of the journey of the church of Subpiatră, with its confusing interplay between real and unreal, possible and impossible.

A few years ago, during a very mild September, I traveled to the Danube Delta to write about its magnificence for a foreign tourist magazine. But what impressed me most, more than the unsurpassed strength of its waters and land and the unrivaled beauty of its birds and fish, which I described for the benefit of septuagenarian American women and tottering Scandinavian men (so they would gratefully spend their currency in Romanian hotels, restaurants, and fisheries), were the residents of this swampy terrain, halfway between water and dry land. Bearded and taciturn, they kept themselves aloof from civilization as well as history, obeying mysterious laws that rarely coincided with those of the uncaring world around them and many times vehemently opposed them. In those villages, so stable in their beliefs, though lying on land so unstable, my wordless queries were unable to break the people's tight-lipped silence, a silence like a door slammed in my face.

One morning, well before dawn (in fact, just after two o'clock, when the moon had set), I went fishing with the crew of the Timofteanu family, father, sons, and sons-in-law. They seemed indifferent to my presence, with the almost insulting indifference that closed communities display toward strangers. Yet I could not say that their silence bothered me. I was grateful to them for accepting me among them; I could not ask for more. They talked among themselves without paying me the slightest heed, totally unconcerned about having excluded me. As far as I could make out, there was something troubling them, some cause for anxiety I was ignorant of. But something—I don't know what—made me sense it was of a mysterious nature, out of the ordinary even for them, perhaps supernatural.

"Stepan saw it," one of them remarked. "He swears he saw it. And he hadn't touched a drop of vodka for two days."

"He was dead drunk last night," another voice rejoined, distrustful, withdrawn.

"True, but he got drunk afterwards. He swears by everything sacred," insisted the first, as if something vital to them all were tied up with Stepan's credibility.

"God, who'd have thought it!" said a third voice, bursting into laughter. But he said nothing more, his mirth ending abruptly.

My back turned to them, I stood looking at the Danube, its waters a quivering mirror for the setting moon. I was trying to guess what it was all about. It was like a game. Their fears had no power over me.

"Victor saw it too," the old man said, breaking the long silence. I could tell it was his voice by its hollow hoarseness and by the deferential quiet that followed. But it was not merely respect for the old man that had made the others listen to him in awe. His words had disturbed them profoundly. If Victor had seen what Stepan had, then everything was suddenly different; the event had taken on a much greater significance.

"When was it?" one of them asked.

"Last night."

There seemed to be nothing more to say. The ensuing pause was so long that I involuntarily turned my head to see what was going on. They were all staring down the river, scrutinizing the vast expanse of water. Some stood erect; others were bent forward, though they could have seen nothing even if there had been something to see: the moon had set and the stars that were still visible, though brighter now, were too feeble to illuminate the night.

"We'd better go back," someone said. No one answered, and the suggestion remained suspended in a night that was growing thinner, more apprehensive. The weather was calm; clearly it was not a storm that had given them cause for alarm. And since I was a mere spectator, unable to take part in their drama, I could only stand back and watch, the heightened suspense enhancing the value of the performance.

"Did they hear it too?" somebody else queried, then quickly added: "Did Victor hear it too?" And since no response came I guessed that someone had nodded or shaken his head.

"What were they singing?" a voice close to me whispered, one I had not heard before.

"What they always sing," the old man answered, almost with a snarl.

There was no way I could find out what they meant, and that both annoyed and excited me. I felt involved in a great adventure, yet I hoped I would never have to discover the reason for their mute, anxious terror. I only wanted to take back with me, unaltered, their restless silence, like a gift that the universe, its mysteries parceled out in trivial realities, sometimes decides to offer us. This did not happen, but the solution to the puzzle exceeded by far my need for the miraculous.

Day had not yet broken, but vague contours loomed in the darkness of the disintegrating night. The dim outlines of the riverbanks looked strangely expressive. The air smelled saltier, felt colder; we were approaching the sea. No one had said a word for over an hour; only the engine whirred at times, like a teased, maddened cat. Then, all of a sudden, someone turned off the engine and the men started rowing. In the eerie stillness, interrupted only by the rhythmic splish-splash of the oars as they rose in the gray air and sank eagerly back into the water, we heard the song. At first I paid no heed to it; I thought it might be a transistor radio left on in the boat. Maybe I didn't really think about it at all: a song from nowhere is just another banal reality, one that no longer registers in our dulled minds. It was the unnatural tension I felt behind me, the oars pausing oddly in midair, that made me listen more intently. The singing rose in an uncanny crescendo, as if someone were turning up the volume, slowly but steadily, on an invisible radio. In an instant I became aware that the sound couldn't possibly be coming from anywhere near me. Nobody was singing, nothing was playing in our boat, and there was no other boat either up- or downstream.

"There she is," I heard the old man say, almost in a whisper, yet clearly, over the rising song. What surprised me was not so much his tone, in which awe verging on joy had replaced terror, but the use of the feminine to describe a reality that had nothing feminine about it. The song we were hearing (though it may have been just a tune, since it was hard to say whether there were words in its tumultuous waves) was sung by deep male voices in a pitch so low that it sounded like a murmur weirdly amplified by night and wind. I turned and stared at the fishermen. By now it was light enough for me to distinguish their features. Their faces were more than half covered by untrimmed beards, and matted hair grazed their bushy eyebrows, but their eyes burned from beneath the rebellious mass of hair with a brightness that stood out against the dull thatch. The expression in the men's eyes, as they strained to see what they could only hear, was one of intense expectancy, as if they knew what was about to happen yet did not fear it in the least. By now I could tell that the mysterious "she" did not refer to the song we were hearing, which was only secondary in importance, but to what was about to be revealed, to what they shuddered yet waited impatiently to see. Our boat had been slowly making its way down the Danube, drifting along with the current, when all at once it veered sharply around a bend in the river. As I stood gazing upstream I suddenly knew that the curve in the river's course had disclosed something. The fishermen's eyes widened, lighting up with a mixture of elation and dread. But there was joy in their dread, if that can be believed—a dread almost relieved that it could finally be expressed. I realized that at long last they had seen "her," and I turned to see for myself.

It must have been four o'clock by then, and the atmosphere, halfway between day and night, was oppressive, uncertain. Yet under the smooth gray sky and in the pearly, fluorescent dawn the view had broadened considerably. The river's banks had spread out, and in the distance, where sky and water merged, the sea seemed to be breathing deeply, like a beast not yet roused from its slumber. There, where landscape ended and dream began, a church rose above the waters, silhouetted against the horizon. It looked so familiar to me that at first I was neither surprised nor frightened, and my gaze subconsciously traveled beyond it. Only seconds later did it strike me that this church from the western Carpathians, with its carved porch and slender spire, did not belong here, at the mouth of the Danube, in the gentle caress of the morning sea breeze. And the moment I realized it, the story came back to me. I cannot say if the windows were lit by the rising sun or by burning tapers, but in the grayish morn the dark silhouette of the church swaying on the waves seemed to glow from inside, as on holy days, with a joyful fire that yet did not consume it. And the dancing flames formed the very image of the *hora*, the dance whose melody had swept over us, the more disquieting as not a soul could be seen in the church.

And I knew at once it was the church from Subpiatră. I stared as we approached it at unusually high speed (had the water accelerated its course all of a sudden, or did it merely seem faster because the church itself was getting closer?) as if I had seen her before, as if I knew her well. Now she was revealing herself to me, as if I were a long-lost relative, one of her own. Even when I realized she did not belong there (no matter how strange it might seem), I still wasn't surprised. It was as if I had expected the apparition, as if I, too, had always believed the story of the church's journey. In the meantime she had pulled up alongside us, her advance raising waves so high that they lifted and lowered our boat like a walnut shell. The song could still be heard, dizzyingly, maddeningly, a *hora* sung in perfect rhythm, suggesting the syncopated movements of the dance. Yet her festively lit interior was empty. When she passed us, so near I could have reached out and touched her, she looked incredibly tall. I leaned back to see her top. To my astonishment, an immense sail towered above the porch, billowing in the wind. It may have been too far away for me to see before, or it may not have unfurled until she started upriver. For without a doubt the church was heading upstream, fast enough for her progress to be seen with the naked eye, her bulk stirring up ever greater waves in the resistant waters, waves forcing our boat in toward shore. As she glided along her steeple swayed almost imperceptibly, and once or twice it tilted so much it made the whole church list precariously. Then we caught a glimpse of the ancient base of the church, now covered with moss and barnacles, deep down in the water. I don't know why this indecent display of the innermost parts of the being that the church of Subpiatră had become for me troubled me more than her very presence. For while her advance up the river was clearly a miracle, those old beams, furry with moss, were a telling detail that forced me to consider everything in a logical sequence. The image of the smooth mountain wood strangely overgrown with algae and shells kept bothering me until I remembered the logs that the church (felled like a living tree) had been cut from, far away in Lugoșu de Jos, logs blanketed in moss as thick as lamb's wool. And once I connected the two, I suddenly grasped the concrete nature of the facts. One thing was certain: there was nothing subjective about the church's passage alongside our boat. Its laborious progress, with its steeple turned mast, gave no hint of the ethereal or intangible. It was real, utterly real. And it was only such indisputable reality that would be able to enter the realm of the supernatural.

Once the church had passed us, my companions seemed exhausted and confused, as if having received a message they didn't know what to do with and whose meaning was beyond them. I sat down facing them, certain that the trial by fire of this apparition had overcome the abyss of silence that had made us feel we belonged to different species. To be honest, the most astonishing part had not been the appearance of the church itself—that was familiar, something I had long known—but its significance for this colorless world, so far removed from my own. It astounded me not so much that they had seen the church as that she seemed to belong to their universe, possess an importance I could not grasp. Moreover, I could not fathom how much of the church's true story was known here in the Danube Delta, how much had remained unchanged within the changed conditions of the community's spirit. I had trouble imagining the Timofteanu crew talking about Horea or having even a vague idea about the village in the western Carpathians to which their phantom rightfully belonged. For I only had to look into the fishermen's somber eyes to understand that they had seen a ghost, a ghost whose ominous significance was clear to them. Surprisingly, when I asked them about it, they spoke of it simply, with no reticence, as if by having seen the floating church together we had somehow become related, as if I had become part of their universe and they were amazed that I too had been vouchsafed the vision.

Some time later I returned to the western Carpathians as if to a spring, eager to tell about the distant places its waters had reached. The villagers of Subpiatră were stupefied to hear that their miraculous church was known as the Dead Church at the mouth of the Danube. What distinguished their place of worship from all others in the eyes of these mountain peasants was its intense, even supernatural vitality: the sailing church was not only alive, incredibly alive, she was a savior of life. While for the Danube fishermen she was a phantom, inhabited by corpses and presaging death, for the people of Subpiatră she was a denial of death, counteracting, annulling the rebels' execution on Hanging Forks Hill in Alba Iulia. I hastened to tell them what I had seen, certain that it would please them and reconfirm their belief in the miracle. But I discovered that my account saddened them: what they needed was not so much outside confirmation as acknowledgment of their own truth.

One warm evening that smelled of smoke, milk fresh from the cow, and *mămăligă* (a smell that remains for me the most ineffable definition of the Romanian village—as long as it exists, the village itself exists, no matter how "commuterized" its inhabitants may have become), I was sitting on the porch of the parish house in Subpiatră, talking with the young priest, just out of seminary, who, with his long blond hair, thick beard, and checked shirt, and rolled-up sleeves, looked more like a nonconformist artist than a cleric. He had been born in the very house where he was now master, and was following his father into the pulpit.[7] His decision had been sudden and unexpected, as he had almost finished his degree in architecture. His father, the village priest for over forty years, was also the son of the village priest. (Such dynasties were once quite common in Transylvania, but few have survived to the present.) I had known the young priest since childhood—we were about the same age—and I remember even today the prestige he gained in my eyes when, the day after I heard the story of the church, he took me to visit the places that proved its reality: the furrow, the ford, the cut-off foundation. I never forgot it, and ever since I have considered myself related to him by virtue of the tale.

"What is life to some is death to others. It's very natural," the young priest said, his gaze fixed on the village church, perched high on a hill and surrounded by a churchyard where the sun was decorously setting among the crosses. "The revolt that brings death in its wake and thus leads to immortality—that is, to life—is open to both interpretations, without changing any facts or distorting any meanings."

His words sounded both bewildering and familiar. Maybe I had heard them before or thought of them myself. Yet I sensed that the story of the church was more complicated than his summary made it out to be. The church taken by the waters was the sign of the uprising's defeat, and at the same time, of its profound, though barely perceivable, victory. All its meanings were gathered forever in the elliptical, inflexible line of the legend; the rest was ideology. I followed the young man's gaze. His little wooden church stood out against the reddish dusk, incredibly graceful and fragile, its tall pillars carved masterfully, its dagger-thin steeple topped by a cross that softened the sharpness, its notched swath of wood winding around it like a tightly knotted rope. It looked exactly as I had always pictured the other one.

"I've never asked you," I said to my friend, using that casual conversational tone one resumes at the end of serious discussions to signal that they are over, "I've always meant to ask you—when was the present village church built?"

"It wasn't built," he replied matter-of-factly, though slightly startled by my question. "It was brought here."

I turned to him, at first not understanding his meaning, then not daring to pursue my thought. He looked at me, almost amused at my confusion, yet puzzled as well and curious to know what I was thinking.

"This is the church," he said smiling. And only then did he express his astonishment. "Didn't they ever tell you how the story ended?"

❧ *Dumitru Țepeneag* (1937–)

Dumitru Țepeneag took a degree in education, then turned his attention to literature. In the late 1960s, together with the poet Leonid Dimov, he initiated the literary trend of "aesthetic oneirism, "which attempted to use dreams as a creative principle, not psychoanalytically or surrealistically, but semantically, as in the paintings of the artists Yves Tanguy, René Magritte, and Giorgio De Chirico. Țepeneag experimented with this principle in his three volumes of short stories published in Romania, *Exercises* (1966), *Cold* (1967), and *Waiting* (1971).

In 1971, Țepeneag happened to be in Paris when Ceaușescu launched his own "cultural revolution" patterned on the Chinese model; Țepeneag's articles and interviews published in *Le Monde* and the *New York Times* warned against the dangers of Stalinist revivalism in Romanian culture. Consequently, his volume *Waiting* was withdrawn from Romanian bookstores and his Romanian citizenship revoked.

In France Țepeneag served as editor of *Cahiers de l'est,* a journal for East European writers in exile. He also published fiction: *Exercises in Waiting* (1972), *Arpeggios* (1973), *The Hourglass Word* (1984), and *The Train-Station Novel* (1985). After the fall of Ceaușescu in 1989, *The Futile Art of Running* (1991) and *A Romanian in Paris* (1993) came out in Bucharest.

"The Accident" first appeared in *Waiting* (1971).

The Accident

They heard the whirring of a plane outside and Uncle Leu said excuse me, just a second, and went to the window, one hand clutching his long razor, the other smeared with lather. Irritated at not seeing the plane, he drew the grimy curtains. The whirring persisted. Where could it be, he wondered. Excuse me, I'll be right with you. Mihalache, who had also stopped working, lifted his scissors up to his ear and twirled them in the air a few times.

Meaning, of course, that Uncle Leu must be crazy. The others laughed as if it were a joke, the whirring faded into the distance, and Uncle Leu returned to his chair in the barber shop, panting and red in the face. I saw it. It was way up there. . . .

Did you really see it, Uncle Leu? I did, he said, wiping the lather from his hand with a towel. Then he sharpened his razor against the strop hanging from the wall. The customer, one cheek shaven, the other covered with foam, mumbled something—it wasn't clear what—and Uncle Leu apologized again, soaping his face once more. After that he took two steps back as if to admire his work.

Lică started to talk about planes. The French had built a very large one; God knew how many seats it had. And it was incredibly fast, one thousand kilometers an hour, I swear it's the truth. No, Mihalache contradicted him, not the French, the Americans. Isn't that right, Uncle Leu? But Uncle Leu was not in the mood for talking; his thoughts were elsewhere. He scratched his head with the nail of his pinkie. His hair was gray at the temples, with another two silver streaks on the crown of his head. He couldn't hide them. He looked at himself in the mirror. His mustache was still jet black, glossy, stiff with brilliantine, undyed. It wasn't his problem if they thought otherwise.

Have you flown this month, Uncle Leu? He didn't answer. He had to be careful as he wielded his razor near the man's throat. Why did they keep pestering him? They asked just because they thought he liked to talk about it. But they knew very well—all of them in the barbershop did—that once a month Uncle Leu would take a day off and catch a plane to a city as far away as possible. One summer he had been to Budapest on a plane so huge you didn't even know you were flying. And every time he would tell them what had gone on during the flight—whether there had been air pockets, something wrong with the engine, a stopover, or some other interesting detail. Still they didn't need to chatter about it all the time, did they? He had his customer bend over the sink while he rinsed off his face. Eau de cologne? Rubbing alcohol? He fanned him with the bib, combed his hair with care, even gentleness. How young he is! And how much he looks like that other one! An astonishing resemblance. Now that the man was shaven, Uncle Leu could see it better. The young man rose to leave, and Uncle Leu felt his cheeks redden when his customer slipped a tip into his pocket.

Mihalache was the only person he talked to at length whenever they played backgammon. To him he confessed how much better the small air-

planes were—the smaller the better. You didn't even feel you were flying in
the big ones. You sat in an armchair as if at the theater and looked through
the round window at the sky or clouds as motionless as lather sheep. But
for the muffled whir of the engines you'd think that it was all a fake. That
the plane was standing still. What do you mean, still? Like this, as if suspended from a cable. Who knows? You've got some ideas all right, Mihalache would say, shaking the dice in his hand like a craps shooter.

They didn't play in the shop. Mihalache would come to his place. He
was younger, a bachelor. You're so lucky, damn you! And Uncle Leu would
laugh heartily and pour them glasses of cheap brandy. Cheers! And after he
drank he would wipe his mouth and mustache with the back of his hand
and smack his lips contentedly. Out of Mihalache's fist the dice would spin
endlessly. What a pro! Mihalache would smile. Aha! Gotcha! Now, Uncle
Leu, go find yourself a newspaper so you won't get bored. Uncle Leu would
slap his knees, pour himself another glassful, and swallow it in one gulp.

Don't you ever get dizzy? Don't you ever feel like throwing up? Uncle
Leu would smile, rolling the dice in his big red palm. Why don't you try it
yourself? Mihalache knew his companion liked him to act surprised. And
maybe he really was surprised. He bent over the backgammon board, one
arm raised with clenched fist, so that he wouldn't drop the dice. What for?
You won't get me up there in that contraption. And the dice would rattle
cheerfully. Uncle Leu would smile, superior. You're afraid, that's it! No, I'm
not! I just don't want to fly. What on earth are trains for? Why shouldn't I
go by train? I can look out the window at plains, mountains, rivers. . . .
What's the hurry?

Sprawled on the flower-patterned ottoman, Mişu the tomcat slept
peacefully, unperturbed by the rattling of the dice. Still smiling, Uncle Leu
played on absentmindedly. A car rushed down the street. A dog started
barking; his cry was taken up by others. Soon it was a noisy pack. Startled,
the ducks in the backyard quacked loudly. Uncle Leu went to the window,
then came back. What are you doing? Aren't you playing any more? He
picked up the dice and hurled them across the polished wood of the
backgammon board. He made a bad move. He slapped his knee with his
palm, but you could tell he didn't really care. What's wrong, Uncle Leu?
Mihalache stared at his friend critically, his hands on his hips. There was a
button missing from Uncle Leu's shirt, and his collar was dirty. His barber's
smock was never any too clean either.

Uncle Leu was sharpening his razor, but his thoughts were elsewhere.

He had been sharpening it for about five minutes; his movements, repeated thousands of times, were utterly mechanical. There was only one customer in the barbershop, and Mihalache was trimming his hair. It was hot. The driver had turned on only two lights; the others had been broken by slingshots. Uncle Leu swore, though the car was long gone. There was a silence, an unusual, unnatural silence. Even the dogs had stopped barking. A customer came into the barbershop and went up to his chair. Is it taken? No. Please, sit down. He tested the razor against the width of his thumb. He still had to sharpen the other side. You've ruined that razor, Lică cried, laughing stupidly. Uncle Leu made no reply. The customer sat down in the chair and stretched out his legs. He was tired. He glanced at himself in the mirror. A large head, with sparse, slightly russet, hair. A round face that looked quite young, though covered with a reddish stubble. He leaned his neck against the leather pillow mounted on the chair back and closed his eyes with a low moan. The beard, right? The young man nodded, yes, lowering his chin several times. He clasped his hands across his stomach. . . . The dogs hadn't barked. There was no one in the street. He hadn't seen the car.

Poor Uncle Leu! Mihalache thought to himself. He caught sight of a small, round spot of blood just under the shirt's soiled collar. He said nothing and tossed the dice. Six-six. You're lucky, Uncle Leu murmured dreamily, and lost another game. The bedcover was sadly worn, shredded by the claws of the tomcat, who lay asleep on the bed purring thinly. It's your turn, said Mihalache. Uncle Leu picked up the dice, shook them, and threw them so hard that one of them rolled across the carpet. Mihalache bent down to pick it up and accidentally bumped his head against the backgammon board. The pieces slid from their places, scattering all over the board. Mihalache was flushed with effort and frustration, and rightly so; he had been winning. I won't play any more if you don't concentrate. I just won't! Uncle Leu kept his calm but remained as absentminded as ever. They went on playing. It was hot, and the drink had made them dizzy. Both made mistake after mistake. The car had sped by, vanishing around the corner. Or had there been a car? Who knows? What could he have done? He gazed at Mihalache, at his bulbous nose. What would he have done in my place? The car had raced along crazily. The windows had rattled, the headlights had lit up the room as bright as day. They were a car's headlights, he was sure of that.

He had finished shaving one cheek when he heard the plane. To hell with it! But the whirring grew louder and louder. He couldn't help himself.

Excuse me, just a second, he said, bending over the ear of the customer, who seemed to be asleep. He dashed to the window, the razor in one hand, the other one smeared with lather. He couldn't see the plane. He hesitated for a moment, then pushed the door handle, went down the three steps, and ran across the backyard, almost losing his slippers. There was no one in the street. The car had turned down an alley and could no longer be seen. A body lay motionless in the middle of the road. Uncle Leu took a few more steps in the direction he thought the car had gone—he had seen its headlights flash across the room—and swore. What would Mihalache have done in his place?

What are you looking at me for? It's your turn! Come on, you're going to win this time! Uncle Leu was not himself. Lately, he's been worse than usual. Mihalache had also stopped working; he raised his scissors to his ear and twirled them, making snipping motions all the while. Meaning, he's crazy. Lică laughed, the others joining in as if it were all a joke. The plane's whir faded away, and Uncle Leu came back in panting, his razor in one hand, the other one smeared with lather. They all stopped talking and looked at him.

Did you see it, Uncle Leu? Lică asked, breaking the awkward silence. Yes, I did. He wiped his hand on a towel and began sharpening his razor on the strop. They all knew how much Uncle Leu liked planes, but this was too much. What are you doing? Why aren't you playing? And Mihalache shook the dice in the hollow of his palm.

Uncle Leu lived in a long low house somewhere near the edge of town. He had two rooms and a kitchen; the rest of the house was occupied by other tenants. The yard was unpaved, and when his wife was alive they had planted flowers. In the back of the yard there was a water spigot, and next to it an elderly apricot tree that had begun to wither. Ducks waddled nearby, quacking, and a few geese honked. Nobody knew for certain who they belonged to—perhaps to the other tenants or maybe the neighbors—since they roamed freely from one yard to another, squeezing through the pickets of the fence. On Sundays, especially in the summer, Mihalache would drop by and they would play backgammon. Mihalache was younger than Uncle Leu and was incredibly lucky with the dice. You're cheating! The hell I am! You'd better concentrate on the game. Do you think it's only luck? Uncle Leu took another gulp straight from the bottle. Mihalache pretended not to notice and tossed the dice, which spun around on the table several times, whirring like a plane. Up there. Way up there. Where it's blue and tranquil. Below, clouds like mountains covered with ice and snow. More beautiful than real mountains. Giant sheep, as white as foam. Or maybe an old man's hair, hanging between earth and sky. . . . Didn't you ever get dizzy? He shook his head and gazed at Mihalache, smiling gently. Why don't you try it? It's great to fly, to know that there are countless small beings below you, as small as ants, and you are up there, you close your eyes, and you have wings. . . . But didn't you say that you can't feel much in a plane? That's true. Only in the small ones you do. And sometimes not even in them. . . . Then Mihalache would lose his temper and declare that he didn't get it. Devil take him if he understood! What was the use of risking your life when you could take the train? It was more convenient and less expensive. You could look out the window, admire the scenery, mountains, fields. . . . What's the hurry?

Uncle Leu lathered the customer's cheek again. The man seemed to be sleeping. Motionless, his face turned upward, his hands crossed over his stomach, he looked like a corpse. Uncle Leu walked up to him, taking small hesitant steps and shuffling his slippers. He was young, almost a child, and had wings. Big white wings. He bent over but could see no bloodstains. Not a drop. Maybe they'd thrown him out of the car after they'd beaten him up. Or maybe it wasn't a car at all; maybe he'd simply gotten tired and had fallen down from up above onto the dark cobbled street. Have you flown this month, Uncle Leu? He made no response. Why did they keep pestering him? What did they want from him? The beard was particularly bristly under the chin and around the Adam's apple, where it seemed to grow in all directions. He had to be careful. What would Mihalache have done in his place? Maybe he wouldn't have gone out in the street after midnight wearing only his longjohns and slippers. He would have rolled over and gone back to sleep. But he wasn't sleeping. That's it. He just couldn't fall asleep. He had played backgammon with Mihalache all afternoon, and those wretched dice kept rattling in his ears. He tossed and turned in the bedclothes, inadvertently kicking Mişu the tomcat, who meowed and moved away, trying to avoid his master's feet. Uncle Leu couldn't fall asleep although he had tried everything. He thought of the first time he had flown on a plane, the night before takeoff, his fear they wouldn't let him on the plane at the last moment. What are you doing here? It had been a small pleasure craft. Small planes are the best. On the big ones you don't even know you're flying. You sit in your armchair, you fasten your seat belt, which most of the time he forgot to do, and look out the window at the motionless clouds, like mountains covered with snow and mist. But for the muffled whir of the engines you'd think that. . . . Did you ever throw up? No. He was never dizzy, never nauseated. He was born to fly. He smiled. Then Mihalache would get even more upset, his face all red. What's the point? It's foolishness!

Silence. Under the blanket, Mişu snored on evenly, curled up in a ball at his feet. Suddenly the engine roared and the wheels careened madly over the cobbled pavement. He couldn't help it. The headlights of the car—like a plane taking off—lit up the room. He hurled the blankets aside. Startled, Mişu gave a yowl. He put on his slippers and rushed to the door, pushed down the door handle, and in no time was out in the street, cursing. The car had disappeared. Murderers! Beasts! He took a few more steps in the direction in which he thought the big black car had gone, that is, to the left. Then he turned and saw the white body lying on the ground. The wings were long, much longer than the arms. He patted them gingerly. Soft white fluff, like goose or swan's down. He glanced around, saw no one, then bent over, grabbed the young boy under the arms, and started to drag him along, the wings flapping helplessly. Maybe he's not dead yet. Maybe he'll come to. There was no one in sight. The street smelled of lilies and carnations. It was quiet, unnaturally quiet. The only noise was the shuffling of his slippers over the cobblestones, on the small tufts of grass in the yard, up the stairs. The three stairsteps, the click of the door handle. The wings were too wide for the door; they jammed against the doorframe. He had to twist the body to one side. It wasn't heavy, and it was still warm. He felt its warmth through the thin silk shirt with the large lace collar. Suddenly he was seized by fear. He started to jerk and shove the body of the winged being he was dragging into his house, without really knowing why. Maybe he would be all right. Maybe he had only fainted. . . .

Mihalache crossed his arms over his chest and glanced at Uncle Leu, studying him closely. It wasn't scorn; it was concern, and, of course, curiosity. His dirty collar, the bloodstain, his shirt gaping open, a button missing. Poor Uncle Leu! Still he said nothing and cast the dice again. Uncle Leu cast them too, but so clumsily that they rolled onto the floor, one sliding under the bed, the other God knows where, maybe on the carpet or under the chair. Mihalache bent over to look for them. Forget them, said Uncle Leu. To hell with them! Let's stop playing. He got down on all fours next to Mihalache, who was lying on his stomach and had thrust an arm under the bed. Forget them, Uncle Leu shouted. Startled and confused, Mihalache turned his head. Under the bed his fingers had encountered something soft and fluffy. Was there a goose under the bed? Uncle Leu grabbed him by the other arm and jerked him away. Leave them there, leave them alone. Mihalache withdrew his arm and got up without a word, leaning his weight against a chair. As he rose, his hip struck the tin backgammon board that lay precariously balanced on a kitchen stool. The board overturned and the pieces scattered all over the room.

The young man had a big head, russet hair, a round pale face. He was handsome, with wings much longer than his arms, wings with which he flew above the city, alone in the blue, rarefied air of the heights. What could he do? He went to the window. The street was as quiet and deserted as before. For a moment he thought of calling the police. But was he really dead? And who would believe him? They would torment him with all kinds of questions. They might even beat him. He took the body in his arms and lifted it onto his bed. He gently stroked the blue velvet trousers and the patent leather shoes with long pointed toes. Maybe he will open his eyes. He pulled a chair near the bed and sat down, deep in thought. Something had to be done, that was clear. But what? The young man had thin lips and a pale face. Maybe something inside him had broken when he smashed against the pavement. Like a wristwatch that falls onto cement— you can kiss it good-bye. There was no use calling the police or shouting for help. What good would that do? He turned him on his stomach. His wings were too large for the bed.

He went into the barbershop, panting, his face red, his hair tousled. He had obviously come at a run. Everyone stared at him curiously. Mihalache had also stopped working. He raised his scissors to his ear and twirled them in the air several times. Meaning, he's crazy. The others laughed as if it were a joke. From his corner, Lică grinned and said, You've been flying, Uncle Leu! You've been flying, haven't you? Yes, I have. And they laughed again. Ha, ha, ha. Look at Uncle Leu, up above the city, way up there, making wider and wider circles, floating smoothly, like a hawk, like an eagle. Like a lion, even, with large white swan's wings, way up there. . . .

☭☭ *Ioan Petru Culianu* (1950–1991)

Ioan Petru Culianu received his degree in Italian language and literature from the University of Bucharest in 1972 and left Romania that same year. In 1975 he obtained a doctorate in the history of religion from the Catholic University of Milan, and in 1987 earned a second doctoral degree from the University of Paris–Sorbonne in letters and human science. After teaching at the University of Groningen in Holland, he served as visiting professor at the University of Chicago (1986–1988). Later he became full professor of history and philosophy of religion in the same department as his mentor, Mircea Eliade. In 1991 Culianu's career was cut short by assassination under circumstances that are still unclear.

A true cosmopolitan, Culianu wrote and published in Italian, French, and English. His best-known works in the field of religion are *Iter in silvis: Essays and Other Studies* (1981), *Eros and Magic in the Renaissance* (1984), and *Gnosticism and Modern Thought: Hans Jonas* (1985). Culianu also wrote a monograph on Eliade, published in Italy in 1978. His fictional works include short stories—*The Emerald Collection* (1989) and *The Diaphanous Parchment* (1993)—and the novel *Hesperus* (1993).

"The Secret of the Emerald Disk" first appeared in Romanian in *The Diaphanous Parchment* (1993).

The Secret of the Emerald Disk

Smaragdus lapis est preciosus, unus ex XII.

Auget opes.
Auxiliatur eis qui scrutantur abdita.
Lapidarium, Bodleian Library

Grobok suspected that all those letters inscribed on the green disk he had purchased the day before in Lea's antique shop (Lea[1] was

Gottfried's young wife) belonged to no known alphabet. Then Lea herself called him, telling him that an expert had come to her shop and that they could finally get a professional opinion on the inscription without having to pay for it. The expert was a thin, nervous young man who smoked cigars and could barely conceal his interest in the red-headed Lea. He confirmed that the markings were not the letters of an alphabet. "This object is no doubt a recent copy, synthetically produced, of an emerald disk dating from the first centuries of Christianity," he declared. "In those times people believed they could invoke spirits and demons with the help of sounds, gestures, and drawings. As you can see, the disk is perforated. They used to insert a thin strip of leather into the hole and, by some action, make the disk rotate. As it whirled it emitted a kind of hiss. The figures carved on it are thought to act upon a familiar spirit; in fact, they represent that spirit's name." The expert stayed for a while, joking ambiguously with Lea. At one point he remarked to Grobok, "They called it a *strophalos.*"

Before he left, the expert inquired casually how much Grobok had paid for the disk. The price had been modest, but Grobok was sure that Lea had paid no money for it. "Listen," the expert told him, "if you hadn't bought it from Lea, I'd have said you paid more than it was worth. But since the museum is planning to organize an exhibit of magic objects, I can offer you double that price." No matter how synthetic the disk might have been, however, it had roused Grobok's curiosity. Besides, he didn't need the money. He politely declined. The expert asked to see the disk one last time. By now he was by the door and had already said good-bye to Lea. He weighed the disk in his hand, stared off in the distance, pursed his lips, and doubled his previous offer. "That's as high as I can go, and believe me, it's five times its value." Whether that was true or not, it was four times more than Grobok had paid. And although he again rejected the specialist's proposal without the slightest hesitation, he was vaguely intrigued.

The next day it was already dark when someone tapped at Grobok's window. It was Lea, bringing him one of her numerous presents: two glasses of Bohemian crystal and a bottle of wine to fill them. "Gottfried had to go to England unexpectedly to look at some furniture, so I'm on my own for a few days, and you are the most likable person around. You're like a brother to me." Lea was a well-built woman, that was for damn sure; so attractive he had to keep reminding himself of his friendship for Gottfried to keep from stroking her russet hair, her arms, her hips outlined in green tights. Today, he noticed, she was elegantly dressed, carefully made up, and smelled like the breeze. It was terribly hot in the apartment, and he felt a strong taste of sea salt in his mouth. He thanked Lea for the crystal glasses, uncorked the thirteen-year-old bottle of Chianti, and filled the glasses to the brim. Since Lea hadn't had dinner yet, he invited her out to a Chinese restaurant. Then they went back to his place and chatted until two in the morning. Although Lea's remarks about her loneliness and Gottfried's shortcomings could have been interpreted as a veiled encouragement, Grobok feigned deafness and deliberately thought of something else. In the doorway Lea hugged him warmly, stepped out, then turned to him again. "I've forgotten something," she said. "Are you sure you don't want to sell that disk? It's not really worth that much, you know. But I've had a crazy customer who's offered me a thousand florins for it. He's into magic or something. I'll give you nine hundred and keep a hundred for myself." That was nine times what he had paid her for it. Yet once more he refused politely.

All night long he dreamed of Lea, so much so that the next day he was horribly edgy and performed badly at his job. He had scarcely arrived home when Lea showed up at the door. "I've bought two delicious *babi pangang* and I've got one more bottle of that thirteen-year-old Chianti. Come on over for dinner." This time, by nine o'clock he found Lea's mouth pressing spasmodically against his, and until nine o'clock the next morning their bodies incessantly sought each other. It was unbearably hot, and he felt a salty sea breeze in his nostrils. "From the first day I saw you," she told Grobok, "I was irresistibly attracted to you. It's fate. You can't fight it." He dressed quickly, phoned his secretary to tell her he'd be late, and promised Lea he would return as soon as he could. "Look," she said, "we're friends, right? So I'm going to let you in on a good business deal. My crazy customer came back yesterday and offered me two thousand florins for the disk. I'll take five hundred, and give you the other fifteen. What do you say?" Grobok promised to think it over, but Lea, drawing him to her in an élan of passion, urged him to make up his mind then and there. "Give me the key, and I'll pick it up myself. The customer will be in at noon." "I'll bring it to you tonight," he lied. "Unfortunately, I took it to work yesterday to show it to a colleague." "Oh, all right, go to work then, but come and have dinner with me at six."

Intrigued once more, Grobok stopped off at his place and picked up the disk. Why was he now being offered twenty times the amount he had paid for it? What value could it have? The translucent green object looked somewhat like an emerald. But an emerald of that size, if it existed, would undoubtedly be worth 4 million. Since he found it hard to imagine that so many people had failed to recognize the object for what it really was, he decided there must in fact be some crazy customer out there who wanted to buy it for its supposed magical properties. He decided to relinquish it for love of the fair Lea. In fact, he was still thinking of her when, just before three o'clock, the expert dropped by to see him at work. "You know," he said, "I've just been by Lea's. She told me that you've got the disk here in your office and that you're going to take it to her place tonight so she can sell it for two thousand florins. Well, I've managed to get three thousand from my museum, and I've agreed with Lea to purchase it from you at that price. I've got the money with me." Grobok accepted the new offer, but not before phoning Lea to see if she had indeed given her consent. She confirmed the arrangement. But, she told him, in the meantime the crazy customer had increased his offer to five thousand florins, and she of course preferred to sell to the highest bidder. If the expert paid more, so much the better. "You're crucifying me," the expert said when he heard the news. "I'll give you six thousand, and not a florin more. Come on now, give me the disk." But he only had three thousand with him, and Lea shouted in the receiver to Grobok not to let go of the disk before he had the whole amount in his hands. The expert departed to procure the money.

Half an hour later, Lea called Grobok again. The crazy customer's offer had risen to ten thousand. She implored Grobok to bring her the disk quickly, before the expert arrived at her office; otherwise she would have a lot of explaining to do. On the bus, Grobok decided to keep half of the money and give the rest to fair Lea. The bus ride should have taken ten minutes; yet, after the ten minutes had elapsed he noticed that he was alone on the bus, and that the bus was taking an unusual route. "Isn't this bus number five?" he asked the driver. "Yes, it is. But I told you I'm taking it to the depot, didn't I?" Grobok didn't remember hearing him say this, but since the bus had stopped by then, he got off. Not only had they returned to the depot, they were inside it, and it was pitch dark. The driver snatched Grobok's briefcase without a word and took out the green disk. Stupefied, Grobok stood staring in a corner while the fake driver took off his shoes, unfastened his belt, and inserted it in the hole of the *strophalos*. He twirled the disk slowly, but soon it began whirling on its own, making a sibilant hiss and spreading a green brilliance which suddenly became dazzling. A form emerged, leonine in appearance, and the hiss turned into a fearsome roar. The driver tried to run away, but a salty wind arose and the green lion rushed after him. The man collapsed on the ground, writhing, and his whole body stiffened. Then all at once everything returned to normal. His heart pounding, Grobok recovered the disk, made for the door, and somehow found his way back to town. He headed straight for Lea's shop, where she was waiting for him impatiently.

When Grobok told her what had happened, Lea expressed her concern. "You know," she said, "I didn't want to frighten you, but the disk, whose value as an antique object I haven't been able to confirm, seems to have some peculiar qualities." She took Grobok by the hand and led him down a spiral staircase into the cellar. There she pressed an invisible button, which made part of the wall turn, revealing a secret chamber. Grobok tasted the salty sea in his mouth and nostrils and suddenly felt extremely hot. On the ground lay Gottfried's stiff body, yet there were no traces of decay visible. "You see," Lea went on, "I surprised him using the disk in exactly the same way as your phony bus driver. A green form emerged that looked like a lion, and this is the result. Gottfried has been lifeless since then, but he doesn't smell dead. Naturally, I wanted to get rid of the disk after that, so I sold it to you for a hundred florins. Then I wanted it back, but in the meantime I figured out a thing or two. I got you involved in this because I love you. I've loved you since I first laid eyes on you." Grobok confessed he too had been madly in love with Lea, but his friendship for Gottfried had prevented him both from approaching her and acknowledging his love to himself. "We have no time to lose," Lea insisted. "The expert will soon come to claim the disk, but there's the other man too, who is much stronger. And I've been playing him off against the expert. Because I didn't intend to sell the *strophalos* to anyone but you." They left Gottfried neither dead nor alive in the secret chamber and climbed back up to the shop. Anxious, Grobok inquired where the green disk had come from. "I'll tell you another time," Lea whispered, pointing to the opaque pane of the shop door, where they could see the expert's silhouette. The next moment the doorbell rang. "Quickly, out through the back," she urged Grobok. But there was a giant of a man standing in the backyard. He was about fifty, with thick eyebrows and the look of a man who takes things very seriously. He grabbed Lea and flung her like a sack over his left shoulder. When Grobok made a move of protest, the giant punched him so hard that Grobok crashed through the green pane of the back door. "The *strophalos!*" Lea screamed. "Make it sing!" Then she disappeared, borne off by the giant.

Hearing the commotion, the expert had come running into the yard, and now threatened Grobok with a dagger. "Give me the disk!" he ordered, while Grobok, still dazed from the blow, could hardly make out what he was saying. "Give me the disk!" the expert shouted again. But Grobok noticed that the expert's hands were trembling and that he had not come any nearer. "I wonder," he answered calmly, "why you find this disk so valuable." "I'll explain as soon as I have it," replied the expert. Grobok gave him the disk. The expert went through the same motions as the phony bus driver. He took off his shoes, undid his belt, passed it through the hole in the disk, and slowly twirled the disk around.

"I have some expertise as an antique dealer," the expert confessed. "This disk is a slab of pure emerald, with magic seals notched into it over eleven centuries ago. It is worth more than anything I have ever seen in my life. Unfortunately, it cannot be sold because it was stolen from Rome in 1963. It's said to be one of the famous disks belonging to Julian the Theurgus, and it invokes a demon, a woman of incredible beauty. It's my misfortune to have met this woman and fallen in love with her. Only if I own the emerald disk will she belong to me. All I have to do is make it sing."

In the meantime the disk had begun to hiss quietly and emanate its green brilliance. Then everything proceeded exactly as before. The leonine form emerged and hurled itself, roaring, at the expert. The expert tried to flee but fell stiffly to the ground beside the now inert disk.

Grobok picked up the emerald disk with its strange markings. It began vibrating but remained opaque. Then he recalled Lea's last words, "Make the disk sing!" Clearly, that was his last chance, though the idea of confronting the green lion terrified him.

I've got nothing to lose, he told himself, taking off his shoes and doing exactly as he had seen it done before. The disk started to hiss and spread its green glow, which remained suspended in the air like an amorphous emerald cloud. Lea's silhouette emerged slowly, descending to him on an emerald ray and accompanied by a warm, salty breeze. "It's about time," she said, pressing her lips against his. Grobok embraced her cautiously. But she was the same creature he had caressed the night before, warm and supple. Only her delicate extremities were cold. "I don't seem twelve hundred years old, do I?" she asked. She seemed the youngest creature in the world, and, with her untidy russet curls she looked vaguely like a lion.

Grobok said nothing. He understood. She would take on a frightening appearance to scare away all those who tried to use the *strophalos* to conquer her forever. And when it came right down to it, he couldn't have cared less who the phony driver and the fifty-year-old giant were. The disk belonged to him, and with it, Lea as well, though he had no idea why she had ultimately chosen him, a timid, silent admirer.

The leonine demon took Grobok by the hand and pulled him up the stairs to the shop.

Before they left, Grobok picked up the green disk. "Tell me," he asked, "is it worth 4 million florins?" "It's worth more, much more," Lea replied, as the emerald disk began to vibrate slowly, lighting up the whole room with its brilliance.

Suddenly Grobok felt an incredible heat overcome him, and the taste of sea salt filled his nose and mouth.

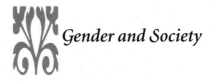 Gender and Society

❧ *Mircea Eliade*   (1907–1986)

Though best known as a historian of religion and mythology, Mircea Eliade was also a prolific author of novels, essays, and short stories. After receiving a master's degree in philosophy at the University of Bucharest (1928), Eliade studied philosophy and religion in Calcutta with Professor Surendranath Dasgupta and subsequently obtained a doctorate in philosophy (Bucharest, 1933). In 1940–1945 Eliade served as cultural attaché for the Romanian Legations in London and Lisbon. After teaching at the University of Bucharest (1933–1940) and the École des Hautes Études of Paris (1945–1956), he was offered a full professorship at the University of Chicago (1957), where he remained until his death in 1986. Eliade wrote over thirty volumes and twelve hundred articles on topics such as yoga, shamanism, initiation, alchemy, and the significance and structures of religion and myth.

As a prose writer, Eliade led the young generation of Romanian authors prior to World War II, especially after the publication of his novel *Maitreyi* (1933), the story of a dual erotic act—seduction and initiation—set in an exotic Indian background. After the war Eliade was banned from publication in Romania as a defector and scholar of religion. He continued to publish in France and the United States, contributing to the development of the literature of the fantastic. His fiction works—among them the novel *Night of St. John* (1971; English translation, *The Forbidden Forest,* 1978) as well as the novellas "Miss Christina" (1936), "At the Gypsies'" (1963), and "On Mântuleasa Street" (1968)—have been widely translated.

Other literary works published before the war and Eliade's departure from Romania include *Isabel and the Devil's Waters* (1930), *India* and *The Return from Paradise* (1934), *The Hooligans* and *Construction Site* (1935), and *Marriage in Heaven* (1938).

In the late 1960s, Romania lifted the ban on some of Eliade's works; in the early 1990s, both his literary and religious writings were published extensively.

"The Captain's Daughter" was written in 1955 and first published in *Stories* (1963).

The Captain's Daughter

As usual, they had gathered on the edge of the ravine to look at the trains passing by one another. As soon as the express train bound for Braşov left the station, it would pass by the commuter train, slowly making its way from Băicoi. Both would give long, simultaneous whistles, then Năsosu[1] would call out:

"Listen for the echo!"

But they didn't all hear it, nor did they hear it all the time. That evening they knew the express train hadn't yet arrived at the station, so they stood waiting. There were only a few minutes left. The wait seemed long, and no one was in a mood to talk. The sun had not yet set in the hills, but in the valley it was already dark. The Prahova River had lost its silvery sheen, taking on the violet hues of deep and evil waters.

"It's coming!" Năsosu announced suddenly.

They heard quick steps behind them, as of someone running down the path. Then a girl called out in a hoarse voice, as if from far away:

"Brânduş, the captain's orderly is here."

A boy of twelve or thirteen, freckled and ruddy, with hair as stiff as a brush, turned his head in boredom. His eyes were large, black, and unusually deep.

"Stay a while," Năsosu urged him. "The train's about to leave the station."

The boy stood undecided for a moment. Then he shrugged his shoulders, spat, and, thrusting his hands into his trouser pockets, began sauntering down the path. When he came to the road, he heard the whistle of the engines and stopped to listen. But the echo didn't reach him.

The orderly was waiting for him on the bench in front of the house. When he saw the boy, he pulled his cap to the back of his head and smiled.

"Come on, master, hurry up, or the captain will be angry!"

But the boy didn't quicken his step. Hands in his pockets, he strode on calmly, staring ahead. The soldier hastily adjusted his cap and set off after the boy. The two walked on, about ten paces apart, along the trail by the road lined with tufts of chamomile and small, dusty wormwood bushes. When they reached the villa with the chimes on the balcony, the orderly turned to the boy.

"Are you afraid?"

"Me?" Brânduş sneered. He shrugged his shoulders and spat again.

"Then hurry up. The captain's waiting!"

Again the boy failed to quicken his steps. The orderly gave up and began walking slowly beside him. After a while he put his hand up to adjust his cap and whispered:

"Double-quick. The captain's seen us."

The captain was waiting for them in front of the gate, in his shirtsleeves, smoking furiously. He was a middle-aged man, small, thickset, with legs that seemed too short for his body. His face was round, his eyebrows sparse, and the little hair he had was gathered and plastered to his forehead, as if he were attempting to make himself look severe, even ferocious.

"Valentin," he shouted over his shoulder to his son, "you can go and change now."

When Brânduş entered the courtyard, a swarthy boy with black hair combed straight back came running from the veranda to meet him. He was wearing swimming trunks and carried two pairs of boxing gloves. Brânduş paid no attention to him but made straight for the water spigot at the far end of the courtyard, pulling his shirttails out of his trousers as he went. He folded his shirt with great care and laid it on the tree stump next to the spigot. With the same smooth, measured gestures, he took off his sandals and leisurely wiped his feet on the grass. Then he turned up the cuffs of his short trousers as high as they would go.

"Come on now, hurry up, young man," the captain shouted. "It'll be dark soon!"

The captain had already fitted a pair of gloves on Valentin's hands and now stood waiting, impatiently slapping the other pair against his hand. Brânduş approached him, smiling, and held out his hands in a dramatic gesture, as if expecting to be handcuffed. The orderly watched the preparations with curiosity.

"On your honor!" the captain's voice boomed. "Approach each other, look your opponent in the eye, and shake hands like gentlemen."

As the boys were walking toward each other with stiff, clumsy steps, glaring at each other and trying not to blink, the captain's voice burst forth again, almost choked with nervousness:

"Have your words ready! Enunciate them clearly, and don't stutter!"

The boys now stood face to face. They grasped each other's gloved hands with great difficulty and shook them carefully several times for fear their gloves might slip before the next command came.

"Say your words!" the captain went on, more nervous than ever. "Listen to my commands and give your challenges!"

"Vir-tu-o-so!" Valentin said slowly, stressing each syllable. "Hafiz!"

"Stop!" The captain raised his right hand and took a step toward the boys. "What was the word I gave you?"

"Virtuoso," Valentin said, cowed. "Virtuoso and Hafiz were my words."

"Who's that? I've never heard of him before," the captain interjected.

"He's a Persian poet," Valentin replied.

"How do you know about him?"

"Agrippina told me."

"Oh, well," the captain shook his head. "Start over. Three steps back, then forward. Say your words and give your challenges. One, two, three!"

"Virtuoso! Hafiz!" Valentin called out as clearly as he could.

He waited a few moments, then, bewildered, turned his head to his father. Brânduş had not said a word. He had merely lifted his gloved hands to his mouth, probably to conceal an enigmatic smile.

"Come on, young man. Say your word!" the captain shouted. "Say something! Say a word, any word! That's the rule! Come on, speak up, what the devil's wrong? Can't you talk?"

"No, I can't," Brânduş whispered after a long pause. "I can't say my word. It's a secret."

Brânduş knew what would happen next. Every evening the captain would come to him, put his hand on his shoulder, and plead with him. He would challenge his pride by calling him uneducated, vulgar, and uncouth. Eventually, exasperated, he would withdraw a few steps and yell at him: "Then do it without your word! Go!" This time however, the captain did not insist. He smiled purposefully and looked at his son Valentin.

"Do as I say," he told the boy.

He stepped back, smiling mysteriously, and waited, anticipating Brânduş's surprise. But the boy seemed to be staring at him scornfully, and the captain shouted at them:

"Go at each other! Just do it!"

Brânduş started off as usual, leading with his head and not bothering to protect his face, his fists raised high, his gloves like two small cannonballs or dumbbells. Valentin waited for him tensely, his knees stiff. He jabbed Brânduş with both fists, in rapid succession but not very hard. Brânduş did not flinch. He stood smiling, his look challenging the boy.

"Go on!" the captain shouted again. "Go at it!"

Valentin took a step back and, when Brânduş approached him, punched him full force in the mouth.

"Defend yourself!" the captain admonished. "Keep your guard up!"

But Brânduş went on smiling, his fists raised above his shoulders, his head tilted back, as if awaiting an order that was late in coming. Enraged, Valentin began pummeling him faster and faster, all the while grinding his teeth and panting.

"Your guard! Keep your guard up!" the captain shouted, annoyed. "Take your time, Valentin. Remember what I told you. Brânduş, defend yourself."

Valentin stood motionless for a few moments, his fists clenched, ready to strike. Breathing heavily, he stared at Brânduş, who was still smiling. Suddenly, as if finally receiving his order, Brânduş stretched his arms out to his sides, held them there for a moment, then raised them, dropped them to his sides, and brought them straight out in front of him.

"Brânduş, obey the rules, or I'll stop the match," the captain threatened.

Again Valentin charged at the boy, hitting him randomly, sometimes with both fists at once. Incensed, the captain jumped between them and separated them. He grabbed Brânduş by the hand and pulled him aside by the water spigot.

"Listen, Brânduş," he began, his voice low, as if holding back tears. "Have you forgotten our agreement? What are you trying to do, make fools of me and my family?" He put his hands on the boy's shoulders and forced him to look him in the eye. "Listen here. Listen to me. I'm doing this for your own good. I want to mold you for life, for the life we live today. You have to understand once and for all that in boxing, as in all other sports, you must abide by the rules of the game. Is that clear?"

"Yes, Captain," Brânduş replied in a grave voice, looking meekly up at the man.

Encouraged by the boy's submissiveness, the captain continued, his tone almost intimate. "It's in your best interest, but you'll also make me happy. I've told you before I have this soft spot. I like to be a coach and referee. But not just for anyone. For my children. I'm not sure if you know it or not, but I've modified the rules of the game for you. I've made them more suitable for gentlemen. The orders 'Get ready!' and 'Give your challenge!' are my own inventions. Do you understand?"

"Yes, Captain," Brânduş repeated, his tone as grave as before.

"Good." The captain patted Brânduş on the shoulder. "Now let me see how you do."

But as soon as Valentin resumed his attack, Brânduş dropped his guard. He merely dodged the blows by drawing back, jumping aside, or holding out both arms to keep his opponent at bay.

The captain gazed at the match in dismay. Suddenly he noticed some small boys hanging on the garden fence. Without turning his head, he motioned to his orderly.

"Marin, fetch the riding crop."

The orderly picked up the crop and hurried out the gate. The children fled toward the church, hooting loudly. The orderly spat, amused, pulled his cap to the back of his head and returned to his post. Now and then he turned to look at the fight.

"His nose is bleeding!" he said to himself, spitting as far as he could.

His thumbs under his suspenders, the captain stared in exasperation, almost in despair, as his son punched the other boy wildly. As indifferent as at the start of the match, Brânduş smiled between blows, though his face was covered with blood. From time to time he held out both arms to shield himself from his opponent so he could spit out the blood streaming from his nose.

"Stop!" the captain said after a while. "Enough for today."

Pale, his teeth clenched, almost trembling with fright, Valentin gazed at Brânduş's blood-spattered face. Agitated, the captain removed his son's gloves.

"Go and wash up, both of you." His voice was bitter.

Brânduş put his face under the spigot and let the water course over his eyes, his mouth, his nose. Now and again he stepped aside and spat out the blood trickling into his mouth. The captain came up to him.

"I'll give you one hundred *lei* for today, though you don't deserve it," he muttered, slipping the banknote into the boy's palm. "I'm doing this to encourage you. But if you don't obey the rules of the game next time, you won't get more than fifty. And if you keep on being stubborn and refusing to fight, I'll have to find somebody else. Is that clear?"

"Yes, Captain," said Brânduş, gazing at the captain with compassion and respect. He did not dare wipe away the blood that was still trickling from his nose.

The captain seemed to want to say more but changed his mind and walked away, ill at ease. Valentin joined Brânduş at the water spigot and they took turns washing. Brânduş kept his head underneath the faucet as long as he could, while Valentin filled his cupped hands with water and dashed it over his face, arms, and chest.

"The missus and the young ladies are coming, Captain!" the orderly shouted from the street.

Bored, the captain fumbled for the watch he had hidden in the small pocket behind his belt before the match had begun.

"Run and bring me my tunic," he snapped at the orderly. Then, trying to sound indifferent, he urged the boys, "Hurry up and finish so the ladies won't see you. They mustn't see blood. They're too sensitive."

Brânduş had dressed in silence and was now smoothing down his damp hair with the back of his hand. When his eyes met Valentin's, he smiled with unexpected gentleness and came closer to the boy.

"Is Agrippina your sister?" he whispered. "She's the one who had to be put back a year, isn't she?"

Valentin froze, his cheeks red, his shirt limp in his hand.

"That's not true," he said with an effort, after a long pause.

"She was too put back a year," Brânduş repeated, with the same gentle smile.

Then, without another word, he headed for the little gate in back of the garden. Smiling, he opened it and passed through it slowly, his hands in his pockets. He pretended not to notice the group of boys trailing him. Their derisive shouts followed him at a distance.

"He licked him good! He punched him right in the nose!"

Recognizing Năsosu's voice in the chorus, Brânduş brightened. He stopped several times to spit into the ditch, trying to rid himself of the taste of blood that lingered in his mouth. He slowed his pace, hoping to hear Năsosu's voice again. There were two more sentences that always followed, "The captain's son pounded him like a walnut! He slapped the sparks right out of his eyes!" Brânduş loved that last remark, and smiled with secret satisfaction whenever he heard it. Năsosu had also said once: "Valentin struck him a glancing blow and stunned him!" He had liked the words, though he had not really understood what they meant. But Năsosu hadn't said that for a long time.

After passing the villa with the little bells, Brânduş no longer heard the boys voices behind him. He didn't turn to look. He strolled along, hands in pockets, stopping to spit into the ditch from time to time. The only noise was that of crickets chirping in the grass. Suddenly he knew why the shouting had stopped. He felt rather than heard the orderly's steps thudding hurriedly behind him.

"You, there, young man!"

Brânduș stopped and turned his head slowly. The orderly caught up with him.

"The captain wants you to wait for him," he said, taking Brânduș by the arm. "Wait for him here. He'll be with you right away."

"Let me go!" cried Brânduș, trying to wrest his arm from the orderly's grasp.

"No, young man. His orders are . . ."

"Let me go. I won't run away," Brânduș cut in. "I know what the captain wants. Let me go."

"No, I won't, young man," said the orderly, shaking his head.

They waited in silence by the side of the road. Finally the captain appeared. He was striding toward them, his short legs pumping. He stared intently ahead, as if not seeing them. Then he stopped abruptly and took a deep breath.

"Marin," he said to the orderly, "go back home and tell the mistress not to worry. I'll be back in a quarter of an hour."

When the orderly had left, the captain took a step toward Brânduș.

"Who told you Agrippina was put back a year?" he whispered. "For one thing, it's not true. It's slander. But who told you?"

"Nobody told me," Brânduș declared evenly. "I just said so. I knew it wasn't true, but I said it to see what Valentin would do. . . ."

"Brânduș," the captain broke in, "you're a nasty little brat. You play the fool just so you can make a laughingstock of me and my household. But don't think I'm going to put up with these insults and accusations from a little snotnose like you. First of all, how can you imagine that I, Captain Lopată,[2] believe that you came up with this nonsense about my daughter being put back a year, just like that, out of the blue? Tell me! How did you come up with that? And why are you standing there like an idiot?" Brânduș stood as if rooted to the spot, utterly silent, his eyes riveted to the captain's face. "Speak up! Answer me!"

"I was trying to think of what to say," Brânduș began, his voice grave, "and you interrupted me."

The captain grabbed the boy by the arms and shook him violently. Suddenly they heard voices on the road, probably a group of people coming out of a house. Reluctantly, the captain let the boy go.

"I speak to you as a friend," he went on, lowering his voice again. "You must trust me. Don't be afraid. I won't harm you."

"I'm not afraid," Brânduş replied. "But I don't know how to explain it to you. If you want to understand me, you must know my secret. And that's what I was thinking of when you interrupted me. How can I tell you my secret?"

The captain stared at the boy as if trying to read his thoughts. Two young couples approached them, talking loudly.

"I have secrets too," the captain blurted out. There was a sudden warmth in his voice. "But they're connected, you see. I don't know if you noticed, but during the game this evening there was a secret between Valentin and me. I'd just taught him how to deliver a left-hand jab followed by a strong punch with his right, so he'd knock you out. But, you see, my secret was connected to the game."

The captain lit a cigarette. He inhaled the smoke avidly. The couples walked past them, still engaged in conversation.

"That's how it is with secrets," the captain resumed when the group was out of earshot. "They're always connected. But what can your secrets have to do with Agrippina? What made you say that Agrippina was put back a year? Have you told this to anyone else?"

"No, I haven't, because I knew it wasn't true. I was only joking. I wanted to see how Valentin would react. If he'd become angry and jumped on me, we'd have been able to fight for real, without gloves."

"Aha!" the captain exclaimed. "I see what you mean. You wanted to find a way—a means of challenging Valentin, of provoking him."

"That's right."

"You were trying to insult him."

"Yes, I was."

"But how dare you insult my family, you backwoods little snot from Breaza?" the captain burst out, his rage mounting. "What if someone in the street had heard you? Tomorrow all the people of importance in town would have thought that Agrippina was put back a year."

"They wouldn't have heard me," Brânduş defended himself. "I spoke very softly, so only Valentin could hear."

"You were angry with him because he beat you at boxing."

"That's right."

For a while the only sound was that of crickets chirping in the grass. Agitated and confused, the captain scratched his neck.

"You have an evil streak in you," he said at last. "You are a strange, wicked child. When you have your gloves on, you refuse to defend yourself. You let Valentin beat you till you're bloody, and then, when I, the referee, declare the game's over, you insult my family and want to fight with your fists, like a common street urchin."

Brânduş looked at him steadily and kept his silence.

"But what I don't see, you little bastard, is how you of all people could come up with something like this. How could Agrippina, who's an educated young woman, have been put back a year? Why on earth couldn't you have thought of something else?"

He paused for a moment, then, enraged, raised his arm threateningly.

"Don't you ever say this again. Don't you dare. I'll beat the crap out of you. I'll whip you till you're flat as a pancake. Flat as a pancake. Do you hear me?"

The next day at sunset Brânduş did not stop as usual at the ravine's edge to watch the trains cross. Instead he continued down the road. After a while he set out on a sloping trail that forked off the road. His hands in his trouser pockets, his thoughts far away, he walked on, leisurely but steadily, as was his habit. Reaching a clearing, he sat down on the grass. Tourists had been there before him; the place was littered with newspapers and greasy pieces of wax paper. Brânduş gazed at them intently, as if trying to fix them in his memory. When the sun had sunk behind the trees, he stood up abruptly and returned to the path, heading for the pastures near town, where they had just finished mowing the hay. Suddenly he heard someone call him.

"Oh, little boy!"

He turned his head. A few steps behind him a young girl was beckoning him to wait for her. She was blonde and pale, tall and skinny, with unusually long arms. When she came near him, Brânduş noticed she had eyes of such light blue they seemed faded. Her mouth had a curious shape, the lower lip long, thin, and delicate, the upper lip full and heavy. It made her look like some rare exotic fish. She was dressed strangely too; her dress, of an indefinite pink-yellowish hue, seemed much too short, while the sleeves looked much too long. Brânduş gazed at her, unperturbed, then smiled and walked on. The girl quickened her pace. Before long she caught up with him and seized him by the arm.

"I'm Agrippina," she said. "I've been wanting to meet you." She dropped his arm and looked him straight in the eye, with a combination of pity and scorn. "I know that Valentin beats you at boxing every night. He makes you all bloody, and then the captain gives you sixty *lei*."

"He gave me a hundred yesterday," Brânduş cut in, smiling to himself.

"He gives you sixty or a hundred and then sends you on home," Agrippina continued. "I've been wanting to meet you in person, to see what kind of a specimen you are. If you don't understand all the words I'm using, by the way, please let me know. Raise your hand, like they do in school. I'll stop and explain what they mean, in plain language, so you can understand."

"You were put back a year," Brânduş said suddenly.

The girl looked at him searchingly, then smiled. "You guessed right," she murmured. "And that's exactly why I wanted to meet you. I wanted to know how you guessed. This is a family secret. It's not personal. I don't care if people find out about my personal secrets. The whole town of Buzău knows I've been in love three times, but that it's only now for real. My fiancé is far away, far both in time and space. So you must be thinking he's a man who died a long time ago. A man?" she cried out, all at once serious, as if she were on the stage, trying to change her inflection. "Just a man? Oh, no, little boy. A poet, a genius, a Lucifer. That's the man I chose. And that's why it's only now that I'm truly in love. Everyone in town knows that. It's no family secret, like my school record. But how did you find out?" Her voice returned to the harsh, clipped tones girls sometimes use when addressing each other in the street. "Do you know someone in Buzău? Has one of your friends there written to you?"

"No," Brânduş replied.

"Then let me tell you. This summer we had planned to go to the spa in Călimăneşti the way we do every year, but one week before we were suppose to leave Mother changed our travel plans because Călimăneşti is full of tourists from Buzău, and the family honor was threatened. You don't know my mother," she added. "What a pity you don't read real books, little boy—poetry and novels, I mean. My mother is like a character straight from a novel. My father, the captain, he's like one too, in his own way. First, he's a victim of his family, maybe even of society itself. He didn't want to become an officer. He didn't want to be our father either. He didn't want to get married—or more to the point, he didn't want to marry Mother. I found that out when I was five. It's not as if it were a secret. Mother would tell him this every Sunday after dinner, while Father was making the coffee.

She doesn't any more," she went on, lowering her tone confidentially. "She stopped telling him long ago, because she's had something else to cast up to him for years now. She keeps reminding him that he failed the major's exam three times, that he'll retire and be pensioned as a captain, that he'll grow old and die as a captain. But these are all family secrets. I shouldn't be telling you any of them. You'll no doubt repeat them, and tomorrow all Prahova Valley will know about them."

"No, I won't," Brânduş answered quickly. "If they're secrets, I won't tell anybody."

Agrippina looked at him, a glimmer of admiration in her eyes.

"What a shame you don't read real books," she repeated. "You're like Valentin, or Eleonora, our sister. Both of them are at the top of their class."

"No, I'm not." Brânduş shrugged his shoulders. "I've never been at the top of my class. I don't have the memory for it." He turned his head and spat.

Agrippina took Brânduş by the arm and pulled him after her.

"Let's sit on the grass," she said. "You probably don't know what the word 'bucolic' means, but we happen to be in a bucolic setting. Or, if you like big words, you could even say Arcadian. You should learn to enjoy words, Brânduş," she went on, regret and irony mingling in her voice. "You should love them. You should try to enrich your vocabulary all the time." Then, without giving him a chance to speak, she asked, "How did you guess I had been put back a year?"

Brânduş shrugged his shoulders, as if embarrassed or confused.

"I can't tell you. It's a secret."

The girl fell into a reverie.

"I like you, Brânduş," she said after a pause. "If you were five or six years older, seventeen, like me, I might fall in love with you. I like it that you can keep secrets though you have a short memory. But later on you must be sure to be a little crazy, to go a bit mad. When you're eighteen, tall and handsome and strong as all eighteen-year-old boys are, I'd like to know that you had a pair of invisible wings on your shoulders, the unnatural, fatal shadow of madness. Then you'll wander through the world with a melancholy forehead and disheveled hair, your temples bare and your eyes half-closed. . . ."

Her words tumbled out more and more frantically. She gestured wildly, clasping her hands, throwing them in the air, pressing them to her knees. She glanced at her hands furtively as if afraid they might start trembling on their own.

"Oh, Brânduş, how handsome you're going to be some day!" She pushed her knuckles into the grass. "But you must also have the wings of madness. You must be ironic, you must be demonic. You must insult people and challenge them to duels. You must break engagements with women who are too rich, too beautiful, and too foolish. I don't ever want to hear that you have fallen in love with girls who are foolish or girls who have been at the top of their class. Ask them questions before you make love to them. Philosophy. Vocabulary. Poetry. Poetry most of all. Ask them. Draw it out of them. 'My dear, do you like Rilke? Do you like Hölderlin?' And if they don't answer, don't kiss them." She smiled, yet she seemed overcome by sadness. "Though you'll probably be as clumsy and boring as the others. You'll cry when you fall in love and remain a pure Byronic romantic. You'll do crazy things only when you're drunk. It'll be horrible. Madness, in the plural, with a direct object. A collectively conditioned madness."

She stopped, tired and disappointed. She gazed at him without seeing him.

"I know what you're thinking," Brânduş said after a moment. "I told Valentin what my tomcat used to do, and you must have decided I was crazy. But that's just another secret of mine." He smiled.

Agrippina turned to him with a slight frown. "I don't know what you mean."

"Valentin must have told you about my tomcat," Brânduş went on calmly. "He must have repeated what I told the boys one evening, as we were coming down the hill. But he didn't understand because I didn't tell them everything. He must have thought that what I told them was happening then. I have a tomcat now, too, you see. His name is Vasile too. But that was my secret. I didn't tell them that the story happened when I was a child. I was five at the time."

"I still don't follow you," Agrippina interjected. "Tell me what you mean. Don't be shy. You're not in an exam."

"I'm not being shy. I just thought you might have heard it from Valentin. I was sure he'd told you the story about the tomcat and that was why you were talking about madness a few minutes ago. Because you might think I wasn't in my right mind to have seen the tomcat putting his paws into the big laundry cauldron and drawing out the clothes, one by one."

"Brânduş," Agrippina chided him, "you should think what you want to say before you speak. Express yourself clearly, in short sentences. Be grammatical. Subject, predicate, and whatever follows. I'm not sure what parts of speech they are," she added, as if in parentheses. "I've never really liked grammar. But you're a boy. You're preparing to confront the world with the wings of madness fluttering on your shoulders. You must be clear, impeccably grammatical, or your madness will be all for nothing."

"If you keep interrupting me, I won't be able to explain anything," Brânduş told her. "So Valentin hasn't said anything to you about my tomcat."

"What tomcat?"

"When I was five," Brânduş began slowly, stressing each word, "I once saw my tomcat Vasile come through the window and jump onto the top of the stove. There was a big cauldron full of laundry boiling on it. I saw Vasile thrust his paw into the scalding water and pull the clothes out, one by one. I told the boys about it. I told them some other things too. Like how Vasile used to climb up the chimney and jump down the flue into the kitchen, brushing his head against the glowing coals. He wasn't afraid of the fire. His eyes would spark, and he would spit over the coals."

"Little boy, you're a wonder. An extraordinary case." Agrippina grasped Brânduş's arm and pulled him gently toward her. "You live in a world of folklore."

Brânduş pulled his arm away. "You're not listening to me. I told you it was my secret. Everything I used to tell the boys happened when I was five. But they thought I was talking about something that had just happened. Maybe that's why they thought I was crazy. But I don't care." He shrugged his shoulders. "I know what I know."

Agrippina cast him a piercing glance, as if trying to read his thoughts. Then she gazed up at the mountain with a melancholy smile.

"It's a shame you interrupted me," she said in a low voice, as if talking to herself. "I was inspired. I could have told you the most extraordinary things. I could have told you myths and legends, revealed to you the meaning of your very existence, rooted as it is in fable. It doesn't matter that you can't understand me now. Later, when you turn eighteen, you'll remember meeting a fair damsel such as you'd never seen before. You'll remember me, Agrippina, and then you'll understand."

Dusk had fallen. Now and then Brânduş glanced up at the mountain. Agrippina tucked her legs under her and pulled her skirt down over her knees.

"What a shame," she repeated sadly. "You came so close to hearing a revelation and you stopped up your ears. You refused to hear it."

"I've been speaking clearly," Brânduş retorted. "But you haven't been listening to me. I've told you that it all happened when I was five years old. Now even more wonderful things are happening to me. But I can't talk to you about them. All the things that are happening to me and to me alone are my secrets. I can't tell them to anyone."

"You're amazing," Agrippina burst out, resting her clasped arms on her knees. "I thought the only adventure you'd remember in your whole life would be meeting me. I've been waiting a long time to let you in on this surprise—by meeting me you could pull yourself away from the common horde, escape the humdrum routine of everyday existence. I've been watching you from afar for the past two weeks, sniffing you out and trying to understand what you're made of. Every night I'd question Valentin about you. I'd prowl around without you seeing me so that I could get to know who you are, find out why you don't defend yourself when you box, why you let Valentin beat you up every night and then take money from the captain. You had some secret I couldn't fathom. You concealed a mystery just as I do. That's why you fascinated me. You were like a fairy-tale hero. You deserved to meet Agrippina and have a fairy-tale adventure. Because, little boy," she cried out, suddenly impassioned, "I'm not the person you think I am. I'm utterly different from the other girls you see. I'm inspired. I'm someone such as has never been seen before. And then last night, out of the blue, you told Valentin. . . . It's infuriating that I can't figure out how you guessed I was put back a year. Tell me the truth. Did someone from Buzău write to you?"

Brânduș made no attempt to answer her. He went on staring at her, his thoughts elsewhere.

"You can't imagine how spoiled I was in school, what a prodigy I was. I knew all the poets in the world. At eight I could recite *La chute d'un ange* by heart. They used to call me Iulia Hașdeu.[3] And then something happened, Brânduș." She gripped his arm again. "*It* happened. Nobody knows about it. And even if they did know, they wouldn't understand. It can't be put into words. You'll understand later what I mean by *it*. It's a real mystery. It was revealed to me alone, and only by an act of grace. It was a gift. Of course, I was punished for it. They put me back a year, and all of Buzău found out about it. But they only found out about the punishment. Because the real cause, the cause of it all, the *it*, is incomprehensible to the others. And that's what infuriates me. I still can't understand how you guessed it, if you really did, and you didn't just find out from someone in Buzău. Tell the truth. Did someone write about it to you?"

Brânduş glanced once more at the mountain. "It's getting late. I've got to go."

"Oh, Brânduş," Agrippina said in an altered tone. "Later on in life, when I write down all the novels and stories I have in my head, I'll write a story about the two of us. The way we're sitting in the grass now, at nightfall, and how you're afraid and looking furtively at the forest."

Brânduş smiled. "I'm not afraid."

"Please don't interrupt me. I'm trying to tell you something," Agrippina said severely. "You're not aware of it, but you're afraid. And when it gets totally dark, you'll be paralyzed with fear. You'll beg me with your eyes to let you go home."

"That's not true," Brânduş cut in.

"But I won't let you go. I'll make you stay here till midnight. Because you see, Brânduş, in the story I'll be writing I'm a wicked girl, a kind of witch. I like to torture boys from the country. I'm even more cruel when I'm in town. In town I write anonymous letters. I write them because I'm envious of girls who are rich and beautiful, girls who get along well with boys. In this short story, you see, I, Agrippina, the captain's daughter, am in love with love. I love it with all my heart."

She stopped abruptly, exhausted, and wiped her brow.

"I've written a whole series, dozens and dozens of novels and stories, but only in my mind. The series is called 'The Captain's Daughter.' That's me, Agrippina, daughter of Captain Lopată. I've written them in all sorts of styles. And in each of them I'm different. I no longer look like the girl in the previous story. I change, yet I remain the same. Agrippina. I wrote the first short story in the romantic style, à la Pushkin. It begins like this: 'In 193— —a strange family moved to the town of X. They lived on Principatele Unite Street, next to the public gardens. Before long the family acquired a certain renown. Who were they? They were the family of Captain Lopată. . . .'"

"It's getting late. I've got to go," Brânduş repeated, standing up.

"Don't go," Agrippina insisted, rising quickly and grasping his arm. "I wrote this story a long time ago. I've composed over a hundred others since then. But I didn't put them on paper, as my first literature teacher advised me. For you, though, I'll write a fantasy story. Because you have to admit that something truly out of a fairy tale is happening to us. We're both living an extraordinary adventure. You had, and still have, a secret. I've been trying with all my might to decipher it. And suddenly you, a little boy from the country, a boy shod in dirty sandals, stumble upon the most sinister secret of Captain Lopată's family. But I'll get my revenge, Brânduş. In my story I'll torture you. I'll frighten you. I'll hiss like the witches in Macbeth. 'A lizard's tail! Ha, ha, ha! Adder's tongue! Ha, ha, ha!' You're afraid of me, aren't you? All by ourselves, here in the forest. A ghost, a vampire, could appear at any time. . . .'"

"I'm not afraid," Brânduş replied. "But I have to go. It's late."

"Why do you have to go?" Agrippina brought her face closer to his. "Do you really think I'm a witch? Am I so ugly and wicked? Are you afraid of me? Answer me. Are you afraid of me?"

"No, I'm not."

"Aren't you afraid of my big, greedy frog's mouth? Aren't you afraid of my long, sharp teeth? These teeth, so ugly, so eager to tear you to pieces, so ready to crush you and gobble you up, piece by piece? Tell me. Aren't you afraid of me?"

"No. But I have to go."

"Then it's even worse!" Agrippina exclaimed, a hint of terror in her voice. "You're not afraid of me. You feel sorry for me. You're ashamed to stay with me at night because I'm ugly. Tell me the truth. I'm ugly, aren't I? Like all those stupid boys, you probably like beautiful girls. And I'm ugly. My legs are terribly thin. I'm not attractive to boys. I'm like a scarecrow. I know, I know, little boy. I'm horribly ugly. But there's one thing I do have, something that not even the most beautiful girl in the world has. I have the blood of both a fairy-tale princess and a witch flowing in my veins. Maybe that's my destiny. To be ugly, so that stupid people run away from me. But my true love will recognize me. The boy who will kiss me some day will never forget me. He will see at once who I truly am: a fairy turned into a cinder-girl. If you were a few years older, you'd kiss me and the scales would fall from your eyes, and you'd see me for who I really am. The fairy of all fairies, the wonder of wonders. I'd teach you how to love me, how to hold me in your arms, and I'd show you the stars, one after another, as only I know how. And I'd reveal the poets of the world to you. I'd teach you rare, unknown words. Brânduş," she cried out in anguish, tightening her grip on the boy's arm and drawing him close, "I'd teach you how to pronounce words of Persian and Greek, words rare and hard like precious stones."

"Let me go," Brânduş repeated, trying to rise once more.

"I'd teach you how to say 'apodictic, choeforic, shalimar'—"

"Let me go!" Brânduş's voice was serious, almost threatening. He jerked himself free and jumped to his feet. "You've been talking for an hour. You keep repeating words like all girls do. Lots of words. Words that make no sense. Women's words. Stop saying them to me. It's useless. I don't want to learn them. I don't need them. I know what I know. I don't need anything else."

Brânduş gazed at Agrippina as she sat at his feet in the grass, her dress too short, her head buried in her lap. He smiled.

"You thought I was looking up at the forest because it made me scared. But it was only because it's getting dark and I have another three hours ahead of me. I'll be staying up in the mountains overnight. The moon won't come out until after midnight, and I want to be up there on the peak to see it rise. You said I was scared," he said, hurt, and spat contemptuously. "If I'd been scared, I wouldn't have let Valentin beat me up like that. I would've knocked him down with one good punch. But I wanted to prove to him and his father that I'm not afraid of pain. That I can stand anything he gives me. That he could whip me and I still wouldn't show it. I'm trying to make myself tough. I'm learning how to face adversity. I'm always preparing myself. I'm not like the others, you see. I'm a foundling. So I'll never be ordinary. Some day I'll become famous, more famous even than Alexander the Great. One day I'll rule the world. I know what I know. That's why I don't do what the others do. I sleep in the mountains at night, and I'm not afraid. I climb trees without the birds being aware of it. And some day I'll be able to slide down the ravine without hurting myself. I'm a foundling. I don't have ordinary parents like everyone else."

"Oh, Brânduş, Your Highness!" Agrippina burst out, gripping his knees. "You may have the blood of kings in your veins!"

"You can make fun of me all you want," Brânduş replied, still smiling. "But I won't get angry. I'm used to people's insults and cruelty. I don't let it get to me. But I don't try to make believe and act cheerful either, like everyone else does."

"Your Highness!" Agrippina cried again, with pathos in her voice. "Let me touch you. Let me kiss your hands. I want to be able to say I've touched an emperor's son."

"You never stop talking," Brânduş broke in. "You talk too much. That's why boys stay away from you. You throw so much gibberish at them they run away. They can't follow what you're saying, so they think you're making fun of them. And they start avoiding you. That's how it must have been with all of them. They run from you because you say too many things and you use too many beautiful words on them."

He stopped and looked at her with pity. Agrippina let go of his knees; her hands trailed wearily in the grass. She did not look up.

"Cry. Go ahead, cry," Brânduş went on. "You're a girl. You can cry. You don't need to feel ashamed. It's different with me. For one thing, I'm a boy, and boy's don't cry. And then I'm a foundling. I'm not like the others. I'm going now," he added after a short pause. "I've got a three-hour walk ahead of me. Good night."

He started up the trail. He heard her sob, but didn't turn his head. He went on his way as usual, deep in thought, his step light and steady, his hands in his pockets.

Täsch, July 1955

❧ *Gabriela Adameşteanu* (1942–)

A graduate in Romanian language and literature from the University of Bucharest (1965), Gabriela Adameşteanu made her debut in 1971 in the *Luceafărul* literary magazine. Her first novel, *Every Day an Equal Road* (1975), received the Writers' Union Prize for a first work. Adameşteanu worked as an editor for several publishers from 1968 to 1989 and since 1990 has been editor-in-chief of *22*, a weekly magazine issued by a group of former dissidents and oppositionists concerned with Romania's cultural and political rebirth.

Adameşteanu's short stories and novels (especially the novel *A Wasted Morning,* 1983) do not glorify the "achievements" of Communism; on the contrary, they expose the dreariness and hopelessness of everyday existence through photographic realism. By singling out and laying bare ordinary moments in people's lives, Adameşteanu reveals the absurdity of a police state.

Adameşteanu's short stories have been collected in *Give Yourself a Holiday* (1979) and *Spring and Summer* (1989), in which "A Common Path" first appeared.

A Common Path

"You getting off at the next stop too? Maybe you can help me then. . . . Maybe you can take her in your arms so she won't fall down the steps. . . ."

A broad round face, a small nose. Reassuring wrinkles. Not a trace of makeup. Here and there, a few broken blood vessels. Wisps of blond hair struggling out from under a wool cap.

"What have you done to yourself? Open your eyes! Why do you keep stumbling? You wouldn't sleep where they'd let us, now you'll have to sleep in the station! But even there they won't let you! She didn't want to go to bed in a strange place. I've been dragging her all over the place since noon. 'Cause he's thrown us out! Kicked us out and bolted the door. What do you want? A piece of pie? Here, take them both!"

A brown fake-fur coat, slightly faded, slightly worn. Broad, flat shoes. Old legs, swollen by cellulite, plodding along.

"A lady gave them to me at noon. I know her from the vegetable shop. I was so ashamed, but finally I went up to her and said, 'Please, ma'am, give me something for the child to eat.' And she gave me these little pies. What could I do? I had no choice. I went to her and said, 'Give me something for the child. He's thrown us out and bolted the door.'"

March: a fresh caressing breeze. The air so transparent that the pastel hues of the sky dissolve above the two-story houses. Chimneys still exhaling serene white smoke.

"He charged at the child, tried to hit her with the grill! Why wasn't there anything hot to eat? he yelled. But there was! There was borscht, there were pork steaks. What more did he want? Why wasn't the meat grilled? He went after her like he was going to kill her! So he'd have one child less to support. He's got another little girl, you know, in the Children's Home."

The child walks beside us, nibbling at the homemade pie. Large blue eyes, broad cheeks, teeny tiny nose. Wisps of blond hair struggling out from under a wool cap. Plain, clean clothes.

"Maybe he's unbolted the door by now. But if he hasn't, I wonder where we're going to go. There's my father, of course, but he's old, he's got heart trouble. If he sees me coming to him like this, something may happen to him, God forbid. And you know how friends desert you when you're down. Besides, this is how it was yesterday, this is how it was the day before, and this is how it is today. He's destroyed me. He starts drinking the moment he gets to work and then anything sets him off! At least I've had a job for the last four days. I used to work as a secretary in a school, but they laid me off, so for a while I had no job at all. Now I've found one again. A good one, and close. I can take her to kindergarten, drop her off, and pick her up later. And the teacher and the aides all love her so much! They're so good to her! Me, everybody loves me. I'm friendly by nature, see. I talk to everyone the way I'm talking to you. At the kindergarten they treat me like one of the family. They really love me. I had the child when I was forty, went through hell to have her! I still get bladder infections."

The spires of a church, round, heavy, sedate, like the tranquil air of Sundays. The black outlines of trees, their crowns more full now that they're painted starkly, branch by branch, on the warm screen of the sky, than when they had leaves.

"I keep wondering what I'll do if I find the door bolted. 'Cause I can't go back to my apartment. You see, I've got a place of my own, one room. But the lady's there. She's a good woman, I have to say. And she's paid for it, she has the right to be left alone. I rented it out last summer. She gave me ten thousand *lei*. And I did go to my father a few months ago, when the same thing happened. He kicked me out. I'm not legally married to the man, see. Besides, I'm not stylish enough for him, not chic enough. How can you be chic when you're broke? You're young, but I'm forty-five years old. I've had phlebitis, and I put on a lot of weight when I had to stay in bed all that time. My leg swelled up this big, as big as a bucket! But men want you to be fixed up nice all the time. And since my bout of phlebitis, I couldn't do it any more. You know what I'm talking about—you're a woman. So I don't see why I should have to put up with so much from him! I'm not married, I don't take money from him, I don't live with him. You're a woman—you know what I mean. He brings me nothing but grief. Nothing but grief!"

A misshapen crane is trying to turn the corner. The muddy tracks advance, retreat, advance again hesitantly. With its long ladder like an immense, awkward, quivering neck, a hook swaying at its end, it looks like one of those heavy, tiny-brained reptiles "condemned to disappear because of slow reflexes."

"He goes to work and drinks. He goes to work every blessed day! Yes, ma'am. Sundays, too. He goes because he loves it. His job is his only love. He's never missed a day. And all he does after work is drink. He's destroyed me! Men can bring you so much grief you hardly recognize yourself! Sometimes I get to the point where I hate the child myself."

She smiles. Her broad blond face, her small nose, her skin red from the cold and the broken blood vessels.

"Yes, I'm headed this way too. We've been living here since August. No, not in the private apartments, with the VIPs. I told you that everyone loves me. I had to go from one office to another, but in the end the young lady did write my name on his lease. Yes, even though I'm not married to him. And I've got a good job now, still in education. Why, I can go in as late as nine if I feel like it! And leave as early as twelve! They're very good to me. And it's close. I drop her off in the morning and pick her up at noon. But wouldn't you know it, no sooner do I start working than he asks me for money. If I go to work one morning he'll ask me for money that very night! What can I do? I borrow three hundred *lei*, say, from someone like you. But the money isn't mine, see? Which means I'll have to pay it back. But I borrow it anyway and give it to him, just to make him happy. And all for nothing! Why, you ask? Because he's found somebody else, that's why! Since I had phlebitis, I couldn't do it any more—you know what I mean. So he started fooling around with the girl's nanny! Thirty-eight, all spruced up too. Look, there's the building. We live on the second floor, see that window? With the balcony and the TV antenna.

A balcony filled with neat lines of laundry: several men's shirts, a pair of flannel pajamas, a dress. Wide and buttoned down the front: the dress of a fat, busy woman. The windows dark, the lights turned off.

"See," the little girl calls out, "the balcony with the TV antenna."

"I've got the keys, but what's the use if the door's bolted? And I can't go back to the other place either. I didn't get married 'cause I didn't want to lose the apartment. It was like a premonition. I have to say, she's basically kind. Whenever I drop by she gives me cakes or stuffed cabbage rolls. I told you, I get along with everybody. The young lady who wrote my name on his lease, for instance. He's a real big shot and if I went to complain, I could get him in trouble. But since I'm not his wife, what can I do? If we were legally married, I could go to his boss and tell him everything! But since we're not. . . . That man over there, see him? He's the building manager. He's in charge of our wing. I thought of going to him and telling him what happened, but I changed my mind. Why? Because they always stick together."

"Good evening."

A young man. An ordinary face, dark, rather long. Just before he turns the corner, the little girl shouts, a little too loudly and cheerfully:

"He's bolted the door on us!"

"Really?" the man replies. "He has?"

He turns to face them. Slightly embarrassed, his chin in his muffler, he smiles as if having heard good news. He nods a greeting and disappears around the corner.

"Here, the balcony with the TV antenna. But if it's still bolted, where can we go? My father's a math teacher. 'It serves you right,' he says, 'taking up with the likes of him.' All my friends are educated, you see. Teachers. I used to have them over when I wasn't working. I'd tell them their fortunes in the coffee cups.[1] I asked them to come so they'd bring things and he'd be happy. They'd bring Kent cigarettes or clothes for the child. I'd tell him the gifts were for my fortune-telling. I tried so hard to make things work. Know what I mean? Let's go in. Let's wave to the lady from the balcony. If the door's open, you'll see us on the balcony. If it isn't, you'll still see us, 'cause we'll come back out. We'll have to; we have no place to go. Where are we going to sleep tonight? We'll sleep outside!"

She smiles serenely and walks toward the door of the building, holding the little girl by the hand.

"If the door's bolted, we'll sleep outside," cries the little girl.

A hoarse, colorless voice. Too loud.

❧ *Gheorghe Crăciun* (1950–)

A graduate of the University of Bucharest (Romanian and English, 1973), Gheorghe Crăciun began writing while a student, and a member of the *Junimea* Student Literary Club. A teacher of Romanian after graduation, since 1992 Crăciun has been an associate professor of literary criticism and theory at the University of Brașov.

One of the three foremost representatives of the 1980s generation of writers (together with Mircea Nedelciu and Mircea Cărtărescu), Crăciun made his literary debut in 1982, with *Original Documents, Notarized Copies,* a work characterized by narrative experimentation and intertextuality. His dissatisfaction with traditional rhetorical and poetical frameworks and interest in postmodernist techniques like pastiche and parody is even more evident in *Composition with Unequal Parallels* (1988), neither a novel nor entirely a collection of short stories, in which his characters converge in a common narrative universe. Crăciun has also written a novel, *The Beautiful Woman Without a Body* (1993).

"Gravity and Collapse" first appeared in *Composition with Unequal Parallels* (1988).

Gravity and Collapse

The couple threw words back and forth to each other at the tempo of a lively French air. They were discussing household matters, calmly, *allegro ma non troppo.*

Sunk deep in his armchair, coffee cup in front of him, newspaper on his lap, the husband studied the palm of his hand through the curved lens of his glasses. He knew his destiny. Why was he looking? Perhaps he was just bored.

A smell of frying onions wafted in from the kitchen.

He went on speaking, twirling his glasses in his hand, holding them up to the light with a pensive, resigned look. He blinked several times.

Yes, of course, the gas bill. No, he wouldn't forget again. He'd find time tomorrow. And the rubber seal for the pressure cooker—well, didn't she know? There were none to be had anywhere in town! Not even in the warehouses. The light bulb in the entrance hall was burned out. Okay, he'd make a note of it. He'd buy ten lightbulbs, word of honor. Boots for the children, with winter coming? Wasn't it a bit early for that? He didn't know, he was only the father! Of course it mattered! What did she mean by that? Okay, okay. It was clear. It's no use. Of course. He'd go downtown tomorrow to see what there was. Of course he'd get good ones! The best quality, water-resistant. Aha! the vacuum cleaner! To hell with it! It's broken down five times in the last three years anyway! He'd toss it out next payday, *danke!* True, they were living on a shoestring, but he'd get a new one. Maybe a Buran, that'd work for sure. (Oh God, what a fate! What a dreary existence! Who could have imagined this eight years ago?) Yes, he understood. He'd go to the market too. Salad greens and vegetables. And anything else that looks good. He won't forget the potatoes. No, that's too much. Not everything at once. He'll do what he can and only what he can, dear lady. He doesn't have thirteen hands, fourteen feet. He's not a beast of burden or a robot. What's wrong with her? Feeling superior is she? Yes, she cooks and washes and sweeps and irons and teaches at the Continuing Education School (as if the five hundred *lei* you earn there makes a difference). Like any other woman. That's life, darling. Or do you want me to do all of that too?

He stood up furiously and strode around the room, a lit cigarette in his mouth. The smell of cooking oil annoyed him. In fact, the whole kitchen got on his nerves. What a fate he'd chosen! What a life he'd fallen into! He felt completely drained. He was fed up, up to here. He'd had enough. He was sick of it. He couldn't stand it any longer. Rolling up a newspaper, he swatted at the flies as they buzzed about the room, viciously kicked aside a shoe in his way, slammed the closet door shut, hurled a sweater from the table onto the bed. He halted momentarily when his eyes fell on the record player.

Caught off guard, he paused a moment. He rushed over to the record pile, picked one up, hesitated, then put on a Corelli. He sat down again. What was the use? What can you do when you're in such a state? What can you listen to or read? You think music will calm you down? Oh, come on! Get serious! It depends on the circumstances. Everything does. His life is tied to someone else's, it depends on hers. A nothing, that's what he is. A nothing. Defeated, he threw his head back and sank again into the deep armchair. He closed his eyes slowly, massaging his eyelids temples veins. A good thing she'd finally shut up. If she hadn't, he'd really have given it to her! Why didn't she keep her mouth shut and just do her work? Grin and bear it! She's a woman. He'd had enough.

Whenever they talked about household matters, *allegro grazioso*, she did the talking; he listened, remembered, then lost his temper. Then they'd switch.

A modest family, psychologically unequal, a submissive woman, or at least submissive enough to please an irritable, impulsive, and lackadaisical husband, always burdened by household matters. With a lot of care and effort—through sheer willpower really—the woman is beautiful, tired, chic. She hasn't yet resigned herself to being a housewife. She tries to cope, struggles, overcomes obstacles. She can be persuasive when she has to. She can also quarrel. She doesn't need to now. Their life is ordinary, matter-of-fact, devoid of mystery. The couple is realistic; they have no secrets, as obvious from the above.

At that moment the vegetable stew began to bubble, and the smell permeating the room became milder, more promising.

Five minutes later there was a knock at the door.

(In the meantime, Dionisie, the rebel anarchist, our proud husband on the threshold of a fit, sinks into his armchair with a newspaper on his knees, trying to accept things, compromise, regain his composure. He calms down—at least to the extent possible at home—by breathing deeply and thinking peaceful thoughts to a tranquil background of classical music. His eyes fall by happy chance on a short, subtle, and poignant article in the paper, an interview with a man of culture. He skips to the final paragraph, a quotation from von Humboldt: the way a man accepts his destiny is more important than the destiny itself. He memorizes it immediately; his own sense of purpose in life is wanting. He is pleased by this revelation. He will ponder it seriously, doggedly, until it transforms him. There are sentences that enlighten the most beknighted and instinctive creatures; this was one of them. He stands up, turns the record over, glances at his wife Sena assembling the parts of the mixer for the fruit mousse. He stares at her calmly, limpidly, says nothing, and sinks down once more into the oppressive leaden smell. He reads a little more, but he feels things are all right, that she too. . . .)

The two friends come in holding a bouquet of flowers and a box of chocolates, carrying with them the warm scented breeze of the last days of summer.

The atmosphere in the little house changes abruptly, as if in a melodrama.

The couple becomes warm, relaxed. The husband stops reading; the wife comes out of the kitchen. They turn into model hosts, happy to receive their guests. Thrilled, in fact! They speak excitedly, suddenly animated, *vivace maestoso*. We're delighted! Early music is everything—for him, for her. The husband encourages his guests' vague claims of musical knowledge. Yes, of course. Telemann, Vivaldi, Pergolesi, Scarlatti. So what if they get names and works confused? So what if they make a blunder here and there, thinking that Puccini. . . ? Saying that Boccherini. . . ? Yes, of course, music calms you down. It's ennobling, it elevates the spirit.

A dish of fruit preserves[1] makes its appearance, together with the requisite glasses of cold water. The lacy doily on the silver tray. Drooping from the heat, weary from work, the guests welcome the coolness of the mineral water. Teo in fact will not refuse a drop of cognac; she, Dania, is not permitted any. From this point on, their visit reveals its purpose, point by point, step by step, detail by detail.

They've come to see their friends. They've missed them, they've been intending to drop by for a long time. They don't have too many friends. Well, nowadays people you used to be close to, you can't even recognize any more! It's as if they've gone crazy. They only think of their own interests. The car, the house, the furniture, the children. They've turned ferociously egotistical. They set themselves apart. Their friendships are based only on mutual advantage. There are some who act as if they didn't even know you. Just like that! Overnight! You remember Traian? We were friends in school. Well, I'm trying to get an apartment, approvals, intercessions, appointments, traipsing back and forth. I came across him at the People's Council. I didn't know he was working there. I couldn't believe it. He was all dressed up, suit and tie, briefcase in hand. A field inspector. You know what that means? You don't even have to be a crook to line your pockets when you're a field inspector! You can be an idiot! The bribes just keep rolling in! I was overjoyed when I saw him. This is my lucky day, I thought. But boy was I wrong! The guy's a stiff! He goes around with his nose in the air, talks as if he had a stick up his ass! After three minutes I saw it was going nowhere, so I gave up. He didn't have to say a word. There was no need to. He'd changed completely, know what I mean? He was afraid that I might. . . . I realized it immediately so I pretended I was in a rush, some emergency. I was so embarrassed. Know what I mean, Dio? I couldn't believe it!

The two men sit together talking. And their consorts?

It's not hard to figure out what Sena and Dania are doing. What do two women of different ages, with similar jobs and identical lives, do when circumstances throw them together? The boy is still sleeping. Dania wanted to see him, but Sena wouldn't let her. He's a sensitive child who wakes up at the slightest noise. The large kitchen, furnished in white and red, becomes their center of interaction. Chatter, women's stories, that sort of thing.

It's a drama. A small one, but a drama nevertheless. Because their existence is fragile. Teo's an engineer; he makes good money. She can't complain. It's enough. He pays child support. He doesn't see that slut he was married to any more. He sends her the money regularly. And the boy is almost grown up. Last time he promised him a bicycle, and he'll keep his word. After all, Teo is a man of character. A gentleman. He loves his son dearly. He talks to him on the phone all the time. But this divorce is one big headache. His ex makes his life hell. Putting him off, delaying everything. Actually, the two of them met once. But then she had behaved like a lady. Still, Dania read it in her eyes, saw the woman's hatred for her, felt her jealousy. She couldn't stand seeing Dania and Teo get along so well, make such a perfect couple. Sena herself is quite aware—and so is Dionisie—that they've been in love for two years. And now, of course—well, she just didn't expect it at all. She knows her body. It's like a clock. Thirty days exactly. But this time . . . Trouble comes when it damn well pleases, not when you're prepared. They're going to have a baby! Isn't it awful? If they'd been married, of course . . . But now they're a bundle of nerves. And she's not feeling well at all. She can't go on this way. Her breasts hurt. She keeps fainting, losing her balance. And the dreams she has! It's impossible!

. . . I dreamed I was giving birth. And the child was horribly beautiful. Like in the pictures, almost inhuman. The child walked, sang, ate, had teeth, talked to me. I don't remember what he said. He came out with curly blond hair. The child had wings. It was horrid. The dream was terrible. I woke up drenched in sweat. He had feathers on his wings. Really, I swear. The wings didn't grow from his shoulders, as you might expect; they sprouted from his elbows. I touched the feathers. They were delicate, utterly artificial. They looked like nothing I'd ever seen before. And I tried to compare him to a bird, an animal, a swan, perhaps. Some meaning. Some similar softness. I was wondering what he would turn into. Yes, thick, puffy wings, with feathers sticking out of the skin like hairs. I was terrified. I feared for his life, for his future. You see, I don't believe in God. I could never deal with the idea of divinity. I was ashamed. I told myself I'd have to hide the child's wings. I could already imagine a coat with large sleeves, a loose coat made just for him. I was ashamed. But not for a moment did I bring God into it. I'm scared, you see. I'm a heathen. I don't have the ability to believe in God. But I do believe in something else. For instance, five days ago, Teo was sick in bed with the flu, so I went out to get a prescription filled for him. You know that church—the Holy Trinity? I think that's what they call it. The one in the center of town. I had to wait for an hour. There were some drops they had to prepare. But I'd left home with a splitting headache. Well, I ended up in the church, I still don't know how. Maybe it was instinct. And I could hear his voice right next to me. A ruddy-faced priest with white hair and gray eyes. It was only much later that I saw the loudspeaker. But I never saw the microphone. And I kept wondering where they'd hidden it. There had to have been one, I was sure of it. And at the end there was a great rush. They all thronged up to him eagerly. They approached the priest, kissed his crucifix. But he didn't say a word. He only looked at them. I watched him carefully. And suddenly—can you imagine—I was there, right in front of him. I don't know what drew me to him. He didn't say anything to anyone; he just made the sign of the cross. But to me he said , "God be with you." He didn't look at me, he didn't even blink. And I froze. He'd seen through me. When I came out, I felt dazed but relieved somehow. Light, almost. And the headache was completely gone. It was as if somebody had taken it out of my head. I have a terrible subconscious. But I haven't finished telling about my dream. I was with Teo and "him". We were walking down a path bordered by bushes. We stopped in a garden to plant potatoes. It was drizzling, and the child's wings were wet and dirty. I wanted to take him in my arms, but he was crying. There were big marble pedestals in front of us with statues coming to life and falling off. Sad statues of men with long, white beards. They'd make a few gestures, start to liquefy, then fall into the sea. The sea was very green and clear and still. The child cried when he saw it. I woke up, as I said, drenched in sweat, dazed. And all day long I was terrified, with a visceral, unspeakable terror, the terror of a hunted, cornered animal. I didn't dare tell Teo. You're the first person I've said anything to.

She too is overtired, her cheeks red and glowing, a few beads of perspiration on her chin and forehead. She smooths back her hair, black as jet and glossy as a record. She has large green eyes. She stares at us, waiting for our decision. We've had our cognac, and Teo has told me everything. He's asked us for help. For her, Sena, to go and speak to her uncle. To ask him to intercede on their behalf. So they can get on with the divorce. Sena can do it, Teo is sure. And Sena doesn't hesitate. She agrees quickly, she'll be happy to help, her pleasure clear and serene. She'll talk to her uncle, a good man and very close to her. Influential, competent, kindly. Known in all the courts and held in awe. The pregnancy has started to show. It's always the worst in the first few months: the nausea, the dizziness, the violent reactions to strong smells. You can't toy with nature. With the woman in yourself or the future mother. You stick it out, you bear it as long as you can. But people don't wait. They see you, they talk. You get into the maw of the world, and there's no escape. Because Dania is distant, reserved. She has no friends at the office. Her boss can't stomach her. Her colleagues, all old and married, can hardly wait to start the rumors going. She dresses differently from them, behaves differently. She isn't used to talking about herself, giving away confidences, voicing her thoughts and secrets. Nobody knows where she lives, what she has in her house, what she does in her spare time, who she's with. So it's clear. She's immoral. She has to be. That's their verdict. There were earnest men around, men who were well regarded and had good job prospects, and she'd had nothing to do with any of them. She'd turned them down brutally, leaving no room for doubt. It was shocking. Her boss tried something too, and got slapped on both cheeks. So this is the last thing she needs! And time is running out.

Then there's the child. Let's not forget about him! You can't leave him alone in the house, on his own! He's not used to it. Otherwise, he's sociable, friendly. A good child. But somebody has to stay with him. And she's tired. Dania's tired all the time now. Your legs get swollen, it's hard to walk. When you breathe there's a knot in your throat. When you bend over, you feel exhausted, you lose your balance. Your muscles are rigid, your breasts have grown; they're fuller, more beautiful. Your body's preparing itself, working in secret. But your state of mind is miserable. A weariness that comes from inside, from the nerves, from the silent flesh that is changing, thickening. Hard to believe. And you're afraid. The chaos inside you, in your soul! The depression! There's no use putting it off. She'll try to catch some rest while the boy is sleeping. What a pretty child! I can hardly wait to see him and play with him! I'll tell him a story! The last time? Yes, a month ago, when you came to visit. Has he grown taller since then? She pats her forehead with her handkerchief, presses on her breasts with her free hand. It's so warm. So warm in here.

The air is hot, heavy, as if the entire day were pouring out its sultriness, like a load of liquid balloons. The evening draws to a close.

Such is the reality of the fiction. Now Dania becomes the main character. Perhaps we should round out her portrait. Let's proceed.

Psychologists are familiar with a typology established by Ernest Kretschmer called the schizo-cyclo syndrome. To fill in the questionnaire: complementary with the man Teo, the woman Dania has a cyclothymic disposition. Contrary to the syndrome, however, she is not corpulent. Quite the opposite. She's a well-built woman, with beautiful legs, an oval face, and the body of a dancer. Lissome. Flexible in her relationship with her mate. More precisely, spontaneous and generous. Open, altruistic, friendly. Cheerful and lively. Often infantile, with small bouts of melancholy. It must also be admitted that she has trouble concentrating. Her thoughts and reactions are less than tidy. She likes to dream, but her dreams are concrete. Memories nostalgia regrets reveries. But she's a free spirit. She loves with passion; she is sensual. She is dazzlingly warm, faithful. A perfect woman, we'd venture to say. A syntonic type, adaptable. Teo, who's an introvert, should be delighted with this quality of hers. Teo is a bear; capricious, self-centered. Who else could put up with a man like him? Dania is patient. She has no secrets, no mysteries. She bombards Teo with news novelties convictions beliefs opinions observations. Her study is a zoo. A miniature bestiary. She tells him everything. She forgives nothing. And she cannot stomach her colleagues, the old nags. It's a hostile environment she can't stand and therefore rejects. If she were to join their game, she'd feel older and as mean and as petty as they. She herself imposed the distance and difference between them. But among her own kind she is different. She's talkative, expansive, yet calm. A honey of a girl. A real sugar pie. Likable, desired, coveted. You turn your head when she walks by, even if you're with your wife.

The truth is, something else had happened (Teo confessed one day after they had begun living together) that evening in the street near the brasserie. Apparently it had been his last outing with his wife. They were going to an engagement party for one of his cousins, Lică. They had to go; they couldn't get out of it. They were family. The party was extremely successful. No stiff expressions, nothing overly formal. A very youthful atmosphere. The girl was a university student. Her colleagues and friends were there. Well-chosen music. The older people in one room, the young people in another. Very simple: according to generation. Teo told her in detail what the party had been like. His wife, Fanny, had felt a passionate need for movement, for dancing. She'd told him so before they left home. Then it became obvious. First she cornered a young man, a dark-haired university student, and lured him into a trite conversation. Then she turned her back on him dumped him and let a muscular blond man, who was quite tipsy, flirt with her. She bounced around with him for a full hour. In point of fact, she was a good dancer. But people had noticed and started poking each other in the ribs. The couple then agreed to do an exhibition dance for the crowd. It was spectacular. No other couple could match them, the way they kept to the demented tempo of the rock music, the explosive rhythm of the drums. Teo had no such passion for dancing. He moved heavily, stiffly, though elegantly. He lacked agility, motivation. He danced with the contentment of the man at home with the ordinary conventions of modern life, its rigorous amusements. He was well aware that everybody knew that the woman being seduced in the middle of a rock'n'roll dance was his wife. Yet this was not what bothered him. It was her independence that bothered him, and for the umpteenth time. It drove him wild with frustration. The libertine independence of the flashy woman. It made him sick. Over time he had come to understand that the only thing they had in common was extreme vanity and the pride of the mortal who stands up to life. During a break in the dance he had told her so. He no longer cared if she stayed there or left with him. She threw on her coat, furious he had spoiled her evening, and hurriedly caught up with him in the street. Night was falling.

Dania had been returning from the market, strolling along slowly as if out for a walk. A lazy, dreamy step. She was ineffably charmed by the street scene. She felt detached relaxed. She couldn't hear what the two were saying to each other, but it was clear they were quarreling. She stared at them, surprised amused her thoughts elsewhere totally unconcerned. She took a few steps forward, then turned her head. Just like that. For no reason whatsoever. At that moment her plastic bag full of tomatoes broke. At the same instant he turned away from his crazy wife bored annoyed, and bumped against Dania. He was suddenly aware that a beautiful woman had been following them. A split second of surprise-reproach-seduction-dizziness. What ensued was droll, even ridiculous: the man stunned by the presence of the woman, the woman amused by his confusion, trying to pick up the tomatoes. Their hands met, their heads bumped together. The small red dusty spheres lay scattered all over the ground. The scene was still so vivid in her mind it was hard to believe. She saw not only him but the entire scene with an exaggerated slowness. She saw a small coin buried in the asphalt, a sheet of blue paper wadded up, a shard of broken glass glittering, and the fine, soft gray dust (she must have been mistaken. Dust is always ugly). And a narrow crimson petal of a flower. Her muscles remember how she bent over, her breast recalls how his knee brushed against it. She saw once more his brown shoes with the lyre insignia, their dull gloss. His tan suit, his tie. She saw his face, sought his eyes, his uplifted eyelids. This part was misty. Something was getting lost, was melting. But she felt the heat of his hand acutely. She felt her skin tingle at the touch of his palm. And she saw the four large fleshy tomatoes enveloped in dust. One had split, and a yellowish juice stained his finger, his ring. Dania found herself across from a silly man offering his assistance, a little stiff in this unusual posture, startled, awkward, almost frightened, but so straightforward, so Idon't-knowwhat, so serious and likable, so grave and yet so comical, that she almost burst out laughing.

It's eight o'clock. We're back, we go into the courtyard. The blue of the evening light clings to the wall. Deep contentment marks the steps of these problematic, problem-ridden people. They're satisfied. Teo's nerves are no longer on edge. He's less anxious, more hopeful. More confident. He's been assured of real help, a prompt intercession on his behalf. Sena's uncle, Marian Calomfir, the magistrate, will study the dossier, make some suggestions, speed up the resolution of the housing problem. He hopes that in a month, a month at the most, light will be shed on the matter, a decision will be made. He should tell her the good news, calm her down. The hazy mineral evening light trickles down the walls in azure tones.

There was no warning. No one had had the slightest foreboding, the slightest suspicion. Her face is white; she's having trouble breathing. Her body tenses relaxes, her breasts heave. Her face contorts. The bed is rumpled, the coverlet has fallen off, the pillows are flattened. Her mouth twists to one side, her forehead is covered with sweat. Her eyelids tremble vibrate scream. Teo is terrified the way a man is when he sees something repeat itself. He kneels, strokes her arms. She's had palpitations before. But not like these. She whispers this between her teeth, between lips clenched in pain. Twice she faints, comes to, rubs herself with vinegar, asks for a lemon, and eats a slice. She thinks it's over. But now her heart. She mutters babbles incoherently, struggling to master her pain. She closes her eyes, clutches the pillow in her fists. She's on the verge of another fainting fit. Teo is speechless, a man in agony, on the brink of collapse but not yet weeping. We can't ask him to make a decision; he can't think. It's up to me and Sena. But nothing like this has ever happened to us. This hampers us, slows us down. We want to help her, and we're wasting time. A handkerchief dipped in water. Or vinegar. A sedative. Hurried, baffled gestures. We vacillate between words and action. Crowded around Dania, asking questions or keeping quiet. She no longer sees us. She gasps deeply, murmurs something, starts trembling. Now she cannot even voice her cries of pain. Her body shakes all over. Teo holds her white hand and futilely asks what's wrong. Mechanically, absurdly. Frozen. Her body convulses, as if heralding her death. Her body vibrates with agony. She clenches her jaw, twists wildly. Her torment is almost fascinating. I'm frozen too. I can't make sense of it. I don't understand what I'm seeing. I hear sounds. They don't suggest pain to me, nor do they imply loss of consciousness. They overwhelm me, sweep over me like a siren's song, like an urge to sleep, to dream, to plunge into the abyss.

Then Sena shouts, screams, curses. We both deserve her curses. Because we can't come to a decision. We're like two limp dishrags. Dummies, men of straw. Two milksops. Dionisie the slug and Teohar the sloth. She goes out, slamming the door, and runs to the telephone. Roused from our torpor by this cold shower, we stare each other in the face. Ashamed and contrite. Chastened. That is, aware. That was it, of course: the telephone. Call an ambulance! We should have done that at the start! But we lost our heads. That's what the hospital and ambulances are for, I tell Teo. Someone should examine her; that's what she needs! And what will be, will be. Nothing to be ashamed of. It could have been worse. Let's not panic. After all, she's pregnant. You can't play around with two lives. A doctor is a doctor; he'll know what to do. Maybe she should be hospitalized. Maybe some medication. An exam, at least you'll know what's wrong, what to expect. Meanwhile Dania is lying on the bed, breathing deeply. Her convulsions are weaker now; her cheeks seem to have regained their color. She comes to, hears us, speaks.

This is how it ends.

It wasn't a doctor who came after all. It was only a nurse. She herself set me straight when she got out of the car and heard my simple greeting. I waited for her in the street; I saw her into the courtyard. I told her to mind the stairs. I took her elbow, gently, amiably, helping her up the stairs in the darkness. She was talkative, I realized. Blonde hair, glasses. She had a sterile charm, nothing more. She liked to talk, she was sensitive to words. I tried to be witty, to use a detached, jocular tone. I couldn't tell her right away that she had come for nothing.

It was clear, though, the moment we walked into the room. I was afraid she would think we were God knows what. Dania was standing there, combing her hair. There was nothing for her to do. But they quickly told her what had happened, embroidering the story well. Dania herself went into everything she thought she knew about her fainting fits. They were passing spells, normal for her, according to some doctor. And we hadn't known. We panicked. Like anyone would have. Though we needn't have worried. Teo chimes in, backs her up. They're going to a doctor tomorrow, just in case. I understand what's going on. Their joint effort has one purpose only: avoiding hospitalization. Avoiding it now. And the nurse listens, nods, smiles amiably, adds a few words of her own, contradicts one of their claims. She inserts an important detail. She knows what she's talking about; this is her field! They go too far. Too much pathos. I'm sure she thinks so too. So I'm not surprised when she asks a question. She wonders if there was any blood. And if . . . They look at her astonished, almost furious. How could she even suspect . . . ! They know the law, Dania responds in a clear, cutting voice. Teo reinforces her words. Their solidarity unites them. They rush to speak, resoundingly declaring they want this child. Their voices are heated. They want it no matter what, at any price. They're fighting to keep it. It never even occurred to them. How could she say such a thing? What a horrible joke! It's just that the two of them haven't got everything worked out yet. They're doing the best they can. Life is complicated, you know! It's not a novel you can open or close at whatever page you want! Life doesn't shelter you, doesn't spare you. Have you ever read Hemingway? Have you? Do you by any chance speak English? There's a line I'd like to quote you. "Man can be defeated but never destroyed." Now how would you say that in Romanian? *Omul.* . . . Remember this, ma'am! And the show goes on for another five minutes. Teo was dreadful.

During the entire scene the nurse sat on a chair with her coat on, asking no more questions, keeping her glasses on, refusing all offers of coffee and cigarettes, and shifting a sheet of paper from one hand to the other. It was an official form, a document to account for her visit. She didn't seem annoyed in the least. She merely got up brusquely, interrupted Teo in mid-sentence, and asked him to write that he had refused treatment and to sign the paper.

I remember the wide scrawl of his signature, like the final act.

❧❧ *Mircea Cărtărescu* (1956–)

Mircea Cărtărescu took his degree in Romanian language and literature from the University of Bucharest in 1980. A schoolteacher in the early 1980s, he now teaches at the University of Bucharest. A leader of the 1980s generation of writers, Cărtărescu is an important representative of Romanian postmodernism. His short stories, collected in the volume *The Dream* (partially censored before 1989), illustrate a commitment to the literary techniques of biographism, stylistic synchronism, and the blending of poetry, prose, and literary criticism. His first volume of poetry, *Lighthouses, Shopwindows, Photographs* (1980), received the Writers' Union Prize for a first work. Cărtărescu's short fiction has been translated into several languages. Other works include volumes of poetry—*Everything* (1985), *The Levant* (1990)—and the novel *Travesty* (1994).

"The Game" was first published in *The Dream* (1989).

The Game

I dream enormously, in demented colors. I experience sensations in my dreams that I never experience in real life. I have jotted down hundreds of dreams in the past ten years, some of which return convulsively, over and over, dragging me down the same humiliating paths of shame, hatred, and loneliness. Some say that a writer loses a reader with each dream retold, that in a story dreams are convenient, if boring, and obsolete methods of *mise-en-abîme*. It is rare for a dream to be meaningful to other people. Writers may also counterfeit or invent dreams to give shape to and highlight the diffuse reality of a story, just as one will place the cap of a pen in the middle of a page of distorted scribbling to glimpse the outline of a naked woman. And since I want to begin this story with a dream, I'm just trying to protect myself from the automatic accusation of laziness and naïveté.

I am, as you know, an occasional writer of fiction. I write only for you, my friends, and for myself. My real occupation is dull, but I enjoy it and know its tricks. The tricks of writing, however, don't impress me. From your Sunday meeting, which I've been attending for the past year or so, I have learned a lot about the techniques that make a story work, but I've been afraid I won't have very much to say. As a matter of fact, until the night I dreamed the dream I'm about to tell you, I was convinced there was nothing in my life worth shedding light upon. So I won't try a *mise-en-abîme;* I'll just start at the beginning. I believe that, both in life and literature, the beginning sets the tone. In madness too. I remember how the mental ramblings of a former friend began. One evening he came to my one-room apartment in a very agitated state and started to tell me, with unusual coherence, what had happened to him an hour before. "I took the streetcar to go and see an acquaintance. It was so cold outside that the windows of the car were steamed up. Sitting in front of me was a woman dressed like a peasant, in a dirty brown windbreaker and a green kerchief. I didn't notice her until she raised a hand, gloved in coarse cloth, to wipe off part of the steamed-up window. I looked out through the clear spot she had made on the glass as the tram entered a tunnel. Suddenly the spot was pitch black, in start contrast to the icy white of the rest of the window. The black patch looked like a perfect reproduction of Goethe's profile in the famous Chinese silhouette. It had everything: the straight nose beneath the slanting forehead, the wig ending in a pigtail, the firm lips, the rounded chin. . . ."

To make a long story short, let me tell you my dream. About two months ago I dreamed I was shut up in a jar, of all places, but a jar that seemed to be carved out of rock crystal. I turned round and round in the jar, which shimmered with rainbows from time to time, and gazed with contentment at the fluid, flickering world outside. A bird came waddling up toward the jar from some distant mountains, and the closer it got, the wider and more arched its image became on the curved walls of the jar. When it got very close, I saw its huge almond-shaped eye spread out as if under a magnifying glass; suddenly it enveloped me. I buried my face in my hands with a terrible feeling of shame and pleasure. When I looked up again, I saw the thin contour of a door in the wildly sparkling wall of the jar. I rushed to the door, dreading it might be open. It wasn't: an enormous padlock, as soft as flesh, hung at the door. I breathed a sigh of relief. Then I saw a little girl coming down the path that began in the mountains and ended outside my door. As she approached the door—her braids tied with big bows, her small mouth moist—I could tell she was a well-behaved child. The walls of the jar were now as straight and clear as glass. All of a sudden I felt an inexplicable fear, a terror such as I had never experienced. The little girl walked up to the door and began to knock on the thick crystal with her small, ivory fists. Frightened, I hurled myself to the ground and started writhing, but I never took my eyes off of her. When she grasped the padlock, I felt my heart explode, my gut tear open. The little girl broke off the padlock and, her hand smeared with blood, pushed the heavy quartz door open. She stood petrified on the threshold with an expression no words can describe. And then I found myself outside, looking at the scene from behind the girl, on my way up the path to the faraway mountains. I could now see an ever broader expanse within the massive ice or glass or crystal walls of the jar. The jar itself was no longer a jar at all but a huge castle, a heavy structure with cornices and plaster, moldings and gargoyles, skylights and balconies, crenellations, watchtowers and rain gutters, all made up of the same cold, transparent material. I saw myself on the ground in the midst of the thousand rooms with translucent walls. The girl stood framed in the wide-open door, and behind her, from the entrance to the castle to the chamber in the center, I could see a hundred doors standing open, their padlocks stained with blood.

I woke up with an odd feeling that nagged at me all morning, but I didn't remember the dream until after lunch, first as a flash of pure emotion in the pit of my stomach, then at school—while I was listening to my students' lessons—like unintelligible, recurrent stabs of pain. It was only the next day that I was able to reconstruct what I've told you so far. I don't know why. I even have the feeling that I've forgotten some of it in the meantime. Yes, it strikes me as I write that I knew what gestures the little girl made and what words she said, but I seem no longer able to focus on them. I hope I'll remember them as the story unfolds.

After I jotted down the dream, I tried to psychoanalyze it as usual. I began randomly, attempting to recall any detail I could link to one point or another. After two hours of daydreaming over my coffee cup, my eyes fixed on the plastic butterfly stuck to its side (a scarlet butterfly with two spots on its wings like huge blue eyes rimmed with gold, and a body like a disgustingly smooth worm), I spontaneously scribbled the following entry into my diary: "In my dreams, a little girl jumps out of her bed, walks to the window and, her cheek glued to the pane, gazes at the sun setting over the pink and yellow houses. She turns to look at her bedroom, which is as red as blood, and coils up again under the wet bedsheet. As I dream, something approaches my immobile body, takes my head in its hands, and takes a bite from it as from a translucent fruit. I open my eyes but don't dare move. Then I jump out of bed and go to the window. I look out: the sky is filled with stars." And as if having uttered a sacred formula, I started putting bits and pieces together. I couldn't remember all of them, but I did recall that the story of the jar had originated in a telephone conversation with my former girlfriend, that is, when she told me she had bought a pair of hamsters and kept them in a jar lined with wood shavings.

Then my earliest memory came to me: I was two, and lived with my parents on Silistra Street. The owner of the house, a man named Catana, had given me a little bell. To this day I remember with perfect clarity how I walked out of the yard in my little boots and waded into a large puddle in the street. I dropped the bell into the muddy water, and although I groped all over the puddle's bottom, I couldn't find it. I can still recall how puzzled I was. This made me realize I should have set the dream even further back in my past. I concentrated on the little girl, on her braids tied with enormous bows of starched white linen. I thought she looked like one of the peasant women painted by the Dutch masters, women who wore large, richly embroidered veils on their heads. I thought of the sheets of holland linen on which the superbly arched nudes of Ingres reclined, and suddenly my memory blossomed: the little girl's name was Iolanda. Then the glass door to Stairwell One—so hard to open—appeared before my eyes, the Dâmbovița flour mill, my toy watches with their crude, gaudy coloring, and the view of Bucharest from the rooftop terrace with red and green neon lights flashing on and off at night. In a state of sheer exaltation and in a matter of minutes I had dug out of my memory all these things I thought I'd forgotten, realizing that this period in my life contained all that was authentic and perhaps a bit unusual about myself. I don't know how that perfect, ivory-colored globe had survived until now, stashed away beneath the gray layers of my existence as a bored, unmarried school teacher whose life goes on solely because he was born. But I felt very happy to have found some interesting things to relate from my own experience. I'm thinking less of writing a story than a sort of memoir, a brief and sincere chronicle of the most (in fact, the only) strange period of my life. And the hero, though only about seven years old "at the time the action took place," deserves to be described, since he forever affected the fate, albeit subconsciously, at least in my case), of all the children playing behind the apartment building on Ştefan cel Mare Boulevard.

The building was eight stories high, and there is a parking lot behind it now, where cars shiver side by side in the winter's frost. When we moved in twenty-one years ago, my mother had just come out of the maternity hospital where she'd had my sister. I remember how, in the middle of a bare white room where the blinding white spring sunlight came in through a curtainless window, my mother sat on a chair and breast-fed her baby. The top of my head barely came up to the kitchen sink, whose enamel was so chipped at the bottom that the dark stain looked like a reproduction of the continent of Africa with its great deserts and rivers.

The apartment building was in the final stages of completion. At one end it abutted on an edifice that always troubled me because of its turrets and crenellations and infinite vistas (which I later rediscovered in De Chirico). At the back of the building, opposite the mill (another medieval edifice, of a sinister scarlet hue), there was still rusty scaffolding standing by the wall. The ground in front of the scaffolding was torn up by sewage ditches, which in some places were over two meters deep. This was our playground. Separated from the mill yard by a concrete wall, it was a different world, dirty and mysterious, full of hiding places, where we, seven or eight boys aged five to twelve, roamed and reigned every morning, armed with blue and pink water pistols we'd bought for two *lei* at the "Red Riding Hood" toy shop, situated at the time in the Obor Market, the veritable old Obor, which always smelled of the gasoline they used for waxing parquet floors.

Our gang had a hierarchy based strictly on physical strength, that is, who could beat up whom. I remember some of its members: Vova and Paul Smirnoff (how surprised I was later to learn about the vodka of the same name); Mimi and Lumpă (I don't know what their last name was); Luță; Dan from Stairwell Three; Marconi and his brother "Chinezu"; Luci; Marian (or Marțianu, or Marțaganu, or Țaganu, or Țacu), who married a candy salesgirl two years ago; Jean, from the seventh floor; Sandu, my next-door neighbor; and Nicușor, the boy from the stairwell adjoining ours. Each boy was interesting in his own way. Paul ate tar and sucked butterflies' abdomens, claiming they contained honey. His brother Vova was shy and quiet, but had a mania for telling everyone about the Titanic, which, he said, was taller than three apartment buildings stacked on top of each other and had a thousand propellers. Mimi had a pet hedgehog and collected foreign cigarette packages, some of them made of thin plastic. He was the biggest and could beat up any one of us. That's why, though he was as dark-skinned as a gypsy, he was our leader. His brother Lumpă, however, was as weak and helpless as Mimi was strong. Lumpă was swarthy too, snot-nosed, and whined constantly about things, which is why we called him "Symphony in C Major." He must have been about four at the time and was probably retarded, since he could mumble only a few words. Luci, whose nickname was "Luciosu," just as mine was "Mirciosu," was my best friend. I followed him everywhere, listening to his stories about horses galloping in silk-draped arenas and wearing flower-print cashmere slippers over their hooves. Luţă was grim and brooding; when his older brother finished secondary school, he climbed up to the roof and threw himself onto the asphalt below. I was in my room folding paper saltcellars when I saw his big body falling, making strange flapping movements. Then I heard the thud and looked out the window. Dressed in his school uniform, Luţă's brother lay on the sidewalk by a Russian Pobeda car, his noble profile outlined by a slowly widening stain of cheerful scarlet.

The gang had other members too, of course, but they were less important or memorable. There was the little boy from Stairwell Six who had had polio and whose leg was encased in a complex metal contraption like the one Eminescu's sister Harieta[1] must have worn. His grandmother brought him out behind the building, where he watched us play Witchy. (No one ever paid any attention to him.) By the way, I almost left out Dan, Crazy Dan, whom Mimi had nicknamed Mendebil.[2] To this day I have no idea where he picked up such an odd name or how it came into his thick mind. Dan used to sit astride the banister bordering the rooftop terrace (which the rest of us didn't dare even approach) and shout down to us from the height of eight stories, making wild gestures and pretending he was falling.

The little girls our age were not included in the gang, of course. They spent their playtime drawing innumerable landscapes on the pavement with blue, yellow, and cyclamen-pink chalk or pieces of red brick. They played their games of Handkerchief, Prince Charming, Give a Kiss, Patty-Cake, Patty-Cake, and Precious-Stone-Like-Unto-None. I'll mention a few of them: Viorica, the daughter of the deaf-mute couple, the only one in her family who could speak, though she used sign language with her parents; Mona, Dan's sister, a psychopath just like him, with small yellow eyes glaring with hatred, the only girl allowed to play Witchy with us boys; Fiordalis, the daughter of a Greek family named Zorzon; Marinela, to whom Jean used to sing "blonde hair, high in the air," to the tune of "Marina"; and finally Iolanda, the girl who appeared in my dream.

But enough about them. These fragrant colorful little clouds are merely picturesque, and I don't want to bore you with picturesque stories. Background—that's what we all were for the little boy who came and changed something in us, or at least left his mark on all of us. It's hard to explain. He couldn't even beat up Lumpă, yet for a while even Mimi obeyed and followed him. Everything I've said so far has been nothing but a prelude to this story, but it's worth going through it, even if it comes from a teacher used to repeating things over and over again: every composition must have an introduction indicating time, place, and characters, as well as a body and a conclusion. I've strung out my introduction a little; I have yet to come to the body. But first I must show what our pastimes were before the "main character" moved into our apartment building.

Most of us hardly ever strayed beyond the area behind our building. Pressed against the *Pionierul* Bakery, as if growing out of it, stood a gnarled old horse-chestnut tree, its large hollow filled with cement. A long rusty nail jutted out crookedly from its ant-ridden bark. Sandu, Luci, and I used it as a step when climbing into the tree, where we felt as much at home as the old people in Truman Capote's story "The Grass Harp." Up where the branches forked there was another hollow, and there we rested our feet. Early that summer we had found a cache of Chinese plastic pencil sharpeners there, a treasure trove of pastel colors that took our breath away. There were more than fifty, in the shapes of all sorts of gentle animals—bushytailed squirrels, white rabbits, rocking-chair horses, Disneylike deer, and tiny blue-eyed frogs. There were red and green rockets as well, translucent pink barrels, tortoises and giraffes that moved their heads and tails. The night before there had been nothing there, and we arrived early in the morning. No one but us prowled around the tree during the following days either. We concluded the pencil sharpeners must have grown there, opening like a fairy-tale blossom on the tree, the way cactuses or bamboo trees blossom once every hundred years. Yet a stern, unforgiving steel blade lay concealed beneath each rabbit, beneath even the most benign-looking deer. We took them home with us.

There in the chestnut tree we would sit and confer among ourselves like wise old Indians. When Luci got bored with his horse stories—after heaping the creatures with all that heavy silk and ruby-studded brocade he ran out of things to invent (he claimed he really kept such horses in the country)—and when Sandu, who would never become a mathematician, had irritated us with the absurd statement that he had an arithmetic book where they used letters instead of numbers to do addition, subtraction, multiplication, and division, and after I had sworn that I had seen a ghost once, we would pass on to serious matters. Did that short word written on concrete walls or scrawled on the tar wrapping of sewage pipes really mean that all grownups. . . ? That's what I thought of during the long, agonizing afternoons when I had to take a nap. The red-gold light would slowly fill my bedroom, bouncing off the glossy wardrobe door and falling on my cheek. I would lie in bed with my eyes open and gaze through the window at the bright fairy-tale clouds rolling along whimsically in the summer sky. Sometimes I got up stealthily from under the starched sheets, sharp as glass but light as paper, and went to the window. I could see the skyline of Bucharest motionless under the clouds, stretching to the horizon, first a cluster of old houses with gutter pipes and casement windows, with skylights and massive oaken doors, then big gray buildings with countless windows, then the high-rise in the center, with its Gallus chemical ad like a big blue ball on its roof, the Victoria Department Store, the Fire Watchtower on the extreme left, the arches of the apartment buildings along Ştefan cel Mare Boulevard, and, in the distance, the power plant, its huge chimneys spewing out thick threads of steam. All this I glimpsed through the rustling leaves of poplar and hornbeam trees, whose canopies of clear emerald or dark green surged here and there between the buildings. I never felt like going to sleep. I would quickly jump back into bed at the slightest creaking noise, knowing it was my father, his head wrapped in a stocking, coming to see if I was still awake.

Our games were cruel sometimes, even barbaric. All day long we would chase one another through the maze of sewage canals. We reached them from points known only to ourselves, stepping along tar-covered pipes and over huge spigots, the smell of earth, of worms and larvae, of fresh tar and putty permeating our nostrils, mingling with our very blood. It maddened us. Armed with water pistols, masked with pieces of corrugated cardboard from the furniture warehouse (we colored the masks at home, making them as frightening as possible with grinning fangs, goggling eyes, and puffed-out nostrils), we would run down the twisting canals, the slices of sky above us growing darker and darker. When, rounding a corner, we came face to face with the enemy, we would roar and charge at each other, scraping ourselves and tearing our shirts and undershirts. I don't remember who came up with the game we called Witchy, but we played it for years and never tired of it. (We were still playing it in eighth grade.) It was a combination of tamer games: Cops and Robbers, Hawk and Doves, Prison Warden: Be On Guard. In the beginning there was only one witchy, whom we chose by counting. She was the only one allowed to wear a mask and carry a stick stripped of its bark. The witchy would count, facing the wall, and then rush through the canals in search of victims. We could leave the canal but were not permitted to escape to the stairwells of the nearby buildings or jump over the fence to the mill yard. The witchy would hunt us through the evil-smelling tunnels, and when she managed to touch someone with her switch she would let out a horrible scream. The victim had to freeze. The witchy would drag him to her lair, where she would pound him on the head a set number of times. Thus initiated, the victim would himself turn into a witchy. He would put on a mask and the chase would continue. At dusk, when the first stars shone in the still-blue sky above the huge mill towers, there was generally only one survivor left, hounded by a horde of witchies emitting sinister cries. The residents dreaded that moment and threw potatoes or carrots at us from their balconies. The cleaning women came out and threatened us with their brooms. But to no avail. The witchies would not rest until they had caught the last victim, a little child who, seeing that it wasn't for fun any more, would be seized with panic. (At night it was terrifying enough to be confronted with one masked witchy, let alone a whole host of them.) The last one to be captured was carried to the nearest stairwell, where the others made faces at him and pretended they were going to eat him up, until our exasperated mothers came and dragged us home.

When we didn't feel like playing Witchy or erasing with the flimsy soles of our tennis shoes the blue houses, yellow trees, and green mothers the little girls drew on the pavement (just to hear them cry and run indoors), our gang would sit together on the curb and tell stories or play alphabet games with film titles. I remember Marțiganu telling about an adventure in the mill yard. "I jumped the fence by the house with the skull and crossbones on it. I got to the mill. A miller saw me. Other millers came and I fled. They threw stones at me, but I dodged them. When they ran out of stones they took out their pistols, but they didn't hit me. Then they started using machine guns. When they aimed high, I crouched down. When they aimed at my legs, I jumped up. They rolled out their cannons, but I kept ahead of them. They chased me with tanks, but I kept running. They sent bombers after me, but I made it to the fence and jumped over it right here, where the gate is." He would say it all so seriously we almost believed him. Hardly anyone dared whisper "Oh, sure." When we played the alphabet game, everybody knew what films went with what letter. *A Sometime Friend* was followed by *A Sometime Thief,* and the third had to be *Agatha, Stop Your Crimes.* The first movie for B was always *Babette Goes to War.* When one of us ran out of titles, the others would prompt teasingly, "Say *The Iron Ship,*" and when that boy finally said *"The Iron Ship,"* he would be told disdainfully, "There's no such movie."

One day a mother and her little boy moved into a second-floor apartment off Stairwell Three. I had just turned seven and would be starting school in the fall (Vova Smirnoff was in the third grade and Mimi was in the fourth—he had been put back a year). The new boy was about my age and at first I didn't notice him. But his mother was extraordinary, totally different from the other mothers, who washed and scrubbed all day long. She was so tall you could hardly see her face; it was lost high up in the blue of the sky. Tall, thin, and dreamy, she glided among the pieces of furniture on the first floor landing, giving instructions to the moving men who were dragging hemp ropes to and fro. I never saw her wear any color but deep red. Even her housedress was made of red satin. She had black hair, and her face always seemed to have a bluish tinge to it, with highlights of pink and ivory. The child sat aloof in an old armchair whose large flower pattern made him seem even smaller than he was. He was thin and frail, with an intent and dejected look about him. For a moment we abandoned our tunnels and went over to him. We asked if he was moving in and if that towering woman was his mother. Where was his father? "Daddy's a carpenter," he said, as if that answered the question. He stared at us and gave one-word replies, so finally we left him alone. He told us his name, which we promptly forgot. It was Ion or Vasile, something ordinary like that. We dove back down like devils into our tunnels and began playing Witchy again.

The next day the little boy came up to us. His clothes were very clean. He wore "lederhosies" (as my mother used to call them), short bouffant yellow pants with suspenders. He didn't say a word. We asked him to join us down in the tunnels, but he refused. He would only watch us from above. Having a spectator made us lose all interest in our games. He watched the little girls with equal avidity, which made us despise him. He even asked Mona, of all people, for a piece of purple chalk. Mona, never one for polite conversation, turned her backside, clad in tan pants, to him and slapped it. "Why don't you kiss this instead?" The boy gazed at her indifferently and walked away. Every day for about a week I saw him talk with the little boy who'd had polio. He explained all kinds of things to him, occasionally scratching drawings on the pavement with chalk brought from home or making gestures that I would now call ritualistic. At times he seemed to be brushing off invisible cobwebs; at others he pointed to the sky and smiled enigmatically. In the mist-enshrouded evenings we would watch the two of them from our tunnels, our faces shielded by our cardboard masks. As the twilight mist changed from purple to brown hues, the metallic glint of the orthopedic brace worn by the polio victim and the sibyl-like gestures of the new boy grew stranger and stranger. We could make nothing of them. They went home earlier than we did, leaving behind crooked circles and other geometrical figures on the bluish asphalt. We erased them furiously.

The new boy was trying to impress us; we concluded he was a show-off and decided, by choice or by chance, to force him into a confrontation. If he joined us, fine. If he didn't, even better, since we felt the need for a real enemy. We had tried once before to define ourselves as heroes and had failed miserably. We had gathered behind the building and in the raw, saffron light of a bonfire of television boxes had armed ourselves with thin planks from the furniture warehouse. Then, in complete silence, we set off to attack the children living over the Circus Lane flower shop. Masked and screaming at the top of our lungs, we charged from behind the building, routing the children playing foot tennis and kickball. Shrieking, the little girls rushed inside. We took only one prisoner, a tiny child no taller than Lumpǎ, whom Crazy Dan and Paul were trying to make eat a caterpillar, when all at once three or four fathers in their undershirts emerged from the building. At the terrifying sight of adult males with hairy arms and chests, we dropped the little boy and raced down the street. Since the newcomer had no father (at least none had appeared so far), he seemed a manageable enemy.

One morning we surrounded him cautiously, as the senators surrounded Caesar, and dragged him to the sewage tunnels. We were going to make him a witchy. He dug in his heels and thrashed about fiercely. From up close his face looked totally different from that of any child we'd ever seen. His hair was chestnut colored, slightly wavy, with golden highlights reflecting from each curl, and puffed out on top, as if teased in a reddish cobweb. He had bangs, and his thin eyebrows arched above his half-closed oval eyes. The halves of his violet irises shone through the lashless, black-tinged lids. The circles under his eyes were somewhat darker than the delicate copper tinge of his cheeks. His nose was long and thin, but straight, the groove underneath the sharply outlined nostrils unusually deep. He kept his lips firmly shut, almost never showing his teeth, though occasionally his moist mouth would open in a smile, a mixture of cunning, sarcasm, and genuine kindness. Now, however, as we carried him down into the tunnel, his face showed extreme concentration. It wore us out just to look at him. I was holding him by his left arm when, at the edge of the tunnel, his struggling suddenly increased. He thrust his narrow chest forward, as if trying to push it through his shirt, while tensing his shoulders with such strength that we let him go and, startled, backed away from him. For a moment he continued to flail about, twisting his back as if he would break it. Then, with a groan, he slowly dropped to his knees, large tears falling from his eyes. The rest of us fled to Stairwell Three and climbed up to the roof, from where we looked down at the boy's mother, her red pleats and flounces flying as she ran out from the building's entryway. She gathered the boy in her arms and, still running, disappeared into the building.

I went home. After lunch I was again subjected to the torture of the afternoon nap: I could never sleep. The most agonizing thing was that I had no clock, so I never knew when my two hours were up, the two hours of lying in the bed I had come to hate, in the summer's dry heat. Through the window I watched the shimmering blue clouds spin past endlessly, as if brushed away by the tops of the poplar trees. Later I went back to our playground and found the gang reassembled. The boys were gaping up at something that was apparently quite shocking but that I couldn't see from where I was behind the building. "Hey, Mirciosu! Come here," they yelled at me. "Come see Mendebil the Second! This one's even crazier than Mendebil!" Even Mimi and Vova, who were older than the rest and not so easily impressed, seemed hypnotized. Luță, the boy with the dark face and no eyebrows, stood by. Nicușor, plump and wearing fancy clothes and John Lennon glasses, craned his double chin forward with the astonished, irritated expression of the nearsighted. I went up to them, then stopped short.

Near the scarlet walls of the Dâmbovița Mill and beyond the concrete barrier looms the Pionierul Bakery, an old building with a zigzagging roof and round windows with flour chutes coming out of them. Lumpă would stand astride the barrier all day, waiting for the workers to send him for cigarettes or newspapers. In exchange they gave him golden-brown buns or hot rolls, which the snaggletoothed little gypsy would gnaw on for hours, saliva dribbling from his mouth. The bakery's brick chimney was taller than our apartment building; it rose, heavy and rust red, to the clouds through the oval coins of the acacia leaves. I had never examined it up close, but now I could make out a fire escape, as thin as if etched by a pen nib, that ran the length of the chimney and was surrounded by protective metal rings, which made it look like a huge trachea. Three-quarters of the way up, about level with our building's seventh floor, there was a yellow blotch. It was the new boy who, in his yellow *spielhosen,* was slowly and carefully climbing to the top of the chimney. His thin torso, covered by a flowery short-sleeved shirt, was barely one-fourth of the width of the chimney. The residents, alarmed, had poured out onto the balconies crowded with television aerials and pickle jars and were shouting to him to come down. But Mendebil (because that's what we ended up calling him, Dan being left only with the nickname "Crazy") kept climbing, rung by rung. When he reached the top, he clutched the rim of the chimney, hoisted himself onto it, and squatted there for a few moments. The screams of the women on the balconies grew louder, and a couple of bakery workers in white coats and aprons ran across the yard toward the foot of the chimney. As if to defy his spectators, Mendebil rose hesitantly until he stood erect, thin as a nail, at that dizzying height. He glanced up, then waved down, probably to us, and began descending the metal steps, passing through all the rings of the fire escape until he disappeared into the foliage of the acacia tree. A short while later we saw him through the diamond-shaped openings of the concrete barrier. He clambered with difficulty over the wall and jumped into our midst. His cheeks were red, but the rest of his face was yellow. He fixed his gaze on Mimi and said, "I don't like to play Witchy."

Some of my prose-writing friends, for whom I've been trying to write this story for several days, may no longer be paying attention. I may seem to have strayed onto the beaten (or overbeaten) path of the child-hero who sacrifices himself for a noble cause. Mendebil, as I knew him, did have something of that archetype in him. But, as I hope will become clear, he was not in the same league as the Scouts of the Cherry Blossom or Nemecek of Pál Street.[3] His actions and words, which I remember with a suspicious clarity though they have lain for twenty-odd years in the multicolored mists of my subconscious, had nothing childish about them. Rather, they seemed compelling fantasies that caught us, slowly but surely, in their net. I should add that I dreamed of him last night, that I saw his face distinctly, which is why I could describe him so minutely a few pages ago. Yet I wonder if Mendebil really looked the way I saw him in my dream. In any case, I'm haunted by his eyes, dark lined as if bordered with eyeliner, and his ambivalent expression, firm and gentle at the same time.

From then on we let ourselves be swayed by Mendebil's charm. Next morning we didn't go to the tunnels at all, though the smell of the earth enticed us. We surrounded him instead and listened to his stories. He told us (as I know now) the legends of the Round Table, Charlemagne and Arthur, tales of cruel pagans and a sword that had a name. Then he started on "The Brave Man in the Tiger's Skin" but stopped halfway. That wasn't a good place for telling stories, he said. The dirty ditches, the mounds of earth, and the putty-smeared pipes disturbed his concentration. "I know a better place," he said with a smile, and took us there. It was Stairwell One.

Stairwell One could be reached only by an extremely dark and narrow corridor jammed between our building and the research institute next door. Up to then, during the two months we'd all been living there, we hadn't been curious enough to explore the lugubrious passageway. But now we followed Mendebil in single file, brushing against the whitewashed walls for about twenty meters, the length of the corridor. Finally we came out into a courtyard bordered on three sides by our building and the institute and on the fourth by the concrete wall of the mill, acacia leaves and twigs poking through its crevices. It was a small yard, paved with asphalt, very clean compared with the back of our apartment building. On one side was the glass door to Stairwell One; on the other, high stairs led to a small platform enclosed in stone, ending at the bricked-in door of the institute. We called these stone steps "The Bridge." Against the wall stood a block of concrete topped by a slightly dented metal basin. We never found out what it was for. We called it "The Throne." One last peculiarity of Stairwell One was the huge transformer with curved pipes and a concrete façade which, as I recall, was always covered with Mendebil's large, colored-chalk handwriting. The transformer must have been broken, since it stood there abandoned for a long time.

This was our playground for about a month. We thought only of Mendebil's stories, which we awaited day after day. When he didn't feel like telling one, we played kickball, told jokes, traded soccer stories. He didn't take much part in these activities, which we accepted as normal. We had quickly come to realize that the boy, though younger than most of us, was ahead of us in ways we hadn't even considered. At home we drove our parents wild with "Mendebil's done this, Mendebil's done that. . . ." Gradually he started talking about things other than knights and swords from his concrete and metal throne. Sometimes, as if dreaming, he would interrupt a story and in an altered voice, firm and hard, impossible to contradict, come out with ideas so bizarre we simply couldn't grasp them.

This is what I want to talk about. I shudder to realize I can remember words I didn't understand at the time, words I thought I'd forgotten as soon as they'd been uttered. Some of Mendebil's strange "theories" contradicted outright what our parents had told us or what we had heard on the "Windrose" science radio program or on the "TV Encyclopedia" show. But the boy made his ideas attractive, meaningful. I don't know how—perhaps through his mere presence, his voice and gestures, to say nothing of the words themselves having something otherworldly about them. Only one thing I have ever read compares in spirit with what he used to tell us: the description of the haven of the blessed in Plato's *Phaedo*. Anyway, to give you an idea of what I mean, let me jot down a list of what few theories I still remember, ideas he expounded during the blazing red evenings or cool blue mornings we spent near the shiny yellow walls of Stairwell One.

1. In my head, under the arch of my skull, there is a little man who looks just like me. He has the same features, the same clothes. Whatever he does, I do. When he eats, I eat. When he sleeps and dreams, I too sleep and have the same dreams. When he moves his right hand, I move mine. He's my puppeteer.

But the arch of the sky is only the skull of a huge child, who also looks just like me. He too has the same features, the same clothes. Whatever I do, he does too. When I eat, he eats. If I sleep and dream, he too sleeps and has the same dream. I have only to move my right hand to make him move his. I am his puppeteer.

The world around us is the same for me and for him. Both my puppeteer and my puppet are surrounded by a Luță, a Lumpă, and a Mimi, and by all of you. And they are just like you. That beer cap down there exists both in the teeny-weeny world of my puppeteer and in the gigantic world of my puppet. Because everything is the same.

But inside my puppeteer is another puppeteer, who sits in his skull, looking like me. And there's another one even smaller inside him, and so on, ad infinitum. And my puppet moves another puppet, a much bigger one. And there's a puppet living in its skull too, which that puppet handles. And so it goes, ad infinitum. And their world is the same as ours.

Even I don't know which of them I am. Right now, as I'm speaking to you, there's an infinite line of puppets and puppeteers somewhere, speaking to an endless line of children, using the same words I am.

2. The earth is an animal that thinks and lives, only its will is much stronger than ours, glued as we are to it. Birds and butterflies have an even stronger will; that's why they can fly. As for us, we can become as light as air if we try hard enough. (Mendebil once demonstrated this theory. He crouched in the hall of Stairwell One, his arms clasped around his knees, and threw his head back. He squeezed his eyes shut and tensed himself so hard that we were terrified. His face became inhuman. He shuddered, his lips tight, his cheeks bulging like sacks furrowed by blue veins. Then Marţiganu and Vova, standing on either side of him, raised him up to the ceiling with only one finger. We tossed him around for about fifteen minutes, a living ball, curled in fetal position, as light as a balloon.)

3. Women do not mate with men. They carry a cell in their stomachs, and when they reach the right age they need to give birth. So they start the "birth" stages, which are: a flea comes out of the cell, a bug comes out of the flea, a frog comes out of the bug. Then a mouse comes out of the frog, a hedgehog out of the mouse, a rabbit out of the hedgehog, a cat out of the rabbit, a dog out of the cat, a monkey out of the dog, and a human out of the monkey. Women can stop the process at any stage. Some women give birth to frogs, others to cats. But most of them want children. They could give birth to creatures far more wonderful than children, because the birth stages do not end with humans. ("I've seen a creature like that," Mendebil said in conclusion.)

4. Not all humans are the same. There are four kinds: those who haven't been born, those who are living, those who are dead, and those who have neither been born nor are living or dead. These last ones are the stars. (This very short sentence was one of the last Mendebil uttered before his fall from power. I can still see the scene before my eyes. It was about nine in the evening, and we were waiting for our parents to call us in from the balconies. So deep were the shadows of the night that we couldn't even see the whites of each other's eyes. The sky shone indigo above the mill. A red star twinkled in the distance, the star on top of the Scânteia[4] Publishing Complex. It was as if Mendebil had had a premonition, because we had never sensed so much suffering, longing, and nostalgia in his voice as at the moment when he suddenly raised his hand and pointed to the star-dotted patch of sky above the chimneys.)

5. (He uttered the following sentence after overhearing an argument

between Paul and Nicuşor. The two boys had just come out into the yard, waving some paper flags, both red and Romanian tricolor. "My father's brought me ten flags from the parade," Paul said.[5] "*My* father's brought me fifty," said Nicuşor. "Well, my father's brought me five hundred," Paul retorted. "And mine's brought me a million," Nicuşor countered. "My father's brought me a billion flags from the parade," Paul went on. "And mine's brought me a zillion," Nicuşor returned. "My father's brought me five million hundred zillions," Paul declared. "Well, my father's brought me an infinity," Nicuşor replied. "And mine's brought me a million infinities," Paul rejoined. "That's impossible. My father told me that infinity's the largest number. There's nothing bigger.") There is in fact more than one infinity. There's an infinity of infinities. Along this line ten centimeters long there's an infinity of points, but along a line one meter long, there are more. I call one particular infinity The Bull, because I've got this purse around my neck that has a bull embroidered on it. And I believe I have an infinity in my purse, a whole universe in which there are several worlds like ours. But what is this purse compared with me, who's made out of an infinity of points? It's a smaller infinity. And this apartment building—it's a bigger infinity than I am. In the whole world there are only bigger or smaller infinities. A chair is one infinity, a carnation's another, this piece of chalk is yet another. Infinities crowding into each other, eating each other up. But there's an infinity that includes all the other infinities. I picture it as an endless herd of bulls.

6. When you die, you walk along a very long road. It goes up and up. You walk and walk and little by little your features change. Your nose and ears sink into the flesh of your face like the muscle of an oyster. Your fingers sink into the flesh of your palm and your arms are swallowed up by your shoulders. Your legs sink into your hips and you can't walk any more. You float along walls of red brick, leaving your shadow behind like an elongated disk. You are so round you become transparent and you can see on all sides around you. As long as we're alive, we can only see things as if through the slot of a mailbox. But when we die, we see on all sides, through our skin. As we float through the air, the fleshy red brick walls getting closer and closer, we come to a place that's round like a circle. In the middle there's a cell, because we're inside a mother's belly. We enter the cell and look through the eyes of all the creatures as the birth stages unfold—the eyes of the flea, the bug, the frog, the mouse, the hedgehog, the rabbit, the cat, the dog, the monkey, the man—and, if we're lucky, we get to look through the eyes of

the wonderful creatures that come after man. A dead man looks at you through my eyes.

7. (Actually the seventh point is not a "theory" at all but a few lines Mendebil wrote in big letters, in different colors of chalk, on the smooth, slightly slanting concrete surface of the transformer in the corner of the inner courtyard. Maybe he'd woken up early one morning so he could write them. We discovered them unexpectedly in midsummer some three weeks after Mendebil had moved into our building, and they became a thorn in our side. He had told us nothing about the deed. After making sure we had all read the lines, he climbed onto his metal chair and went on with the story he'd begun the evening before, "The Stories of Asian Peoples.")

WE SHALL NOT MAKE FUN OF LUMPĂ

WE SHALL NOT TORTURE ANIMALS

WE SHALL NOT TEASE GIRLS

WE SHALL NOT PLAY WITCHY

WE SHALL NOT GET DIRTY

WE SHALL NOT USE BAD WORDS

WE SHALL NOT LIE

WE SHALL NOT TATTLE ON ONE ANOTHER

WE SHALL NOT QUARREL

WE SHALL NOT FIGHT

(The moment we saw these words, we felt we had to take them seriously. There was something in us that made us want to obey them. For two or three weeks we did none of the things Mendebil had prohibited.)

I don't remember other similar "theories"—I'm only using the term for lack of a better one—but just about all of them were in the spirit of the ones above. We were fascinated because they were so much a part of Mendebil's character. You should have heard him speak, seen him gesticulate. You would have felt the charm, the terror, the melancholy of those evenings. It was as if we were watching a strange film, in browns and grays, against the maroon background of the mill and the blackish green of the acacia leaves. In the middle of some story or other, about Arabs and galleons, he would pause and prepare us, wrapped up as we were in the harsh perfume of the tale, for the revelation.

We spent a whole month that summer gathered around Mendebil. We did nothing without asking him first, and our parents, though surprised at how clean our shirts and undershirts had become, viewed our dependence with a jaundiced eye, as day by day we grew more abject. "What's that child doing to you, darling? He's got you all under his spell." But all we cared about was The Brave Man in the Tiger's Skin, Ruslan and Ludmila,[6] Tristan, and other heroes from Mendebil's stories. The little girls forgot about singing "The Stone Bridge," abandoned their tangled drawings of green women with blue legs in orange houses, and gathered around the concrete and iron throne, sobbing when the stories had a sad ending. Even Mona stopped turning her back on Mendebil and started looking at him, her eyes two green slits, with less hatred than at the other children. Iolanda was the closest to him, and we saw them quite often chatting together. She had huge bows in her pigtails and addressed everybody, even her dolls and cats, as "my dear." Once she had tossed red barberries at an enormous spider hanging immobile in its cobweb between two trees, and when the black bunch of claws and legs tried to escape to the edge of the web, she cried, "Where are you going, my dear?" Yet Mendebil maintained a certain reserve in his sporadic relations with the girls, which was more than we did anyway, since we never spoke to them at all. Naturally, from time to time we would play soccer or table soccer with buttons or bring out the chessmen. But they were no longer our main interests. And whenever we played, Mendebil would go find the little crippled boy and have long conversations with him.

About five or six months ago, in February, I took a stroll through town on my day off from school. I had just come out of the Mihail Sadoveanu Bookstore and was passing by the Cyclops Garage when a violet flame suddenly shot through my stomach, an unbearable memory. I had glanced at the little display window to the right of the garage (which reeked of tar) and as I gazed at the selection of cigarette lighters, the sight of one of them, the kind you throw away after the butane's gone, made me stop short. Like Proust's madeleine, this ordinary object had a color that brought back a strong emotion from the period I've been telling you about. Of an odd purplish pink, streaked with yellowish half-moons, it had a soft and fleshy opalescence in its slightly curved plastic surface. It was the same color as my cheap watch, the one I had bought that summer, the first of the twenty-one summers I lived in the building on Ştefan cel Mare Avenue.

I distinctly remember that afternoon when a man in a red-checked shirt came sneaking along the corridor that linked Stairwell One to the rest of the apartments and, creeping like a caterpillar between the two buildings, almost got caught on the gas meter. He finally emerged—panting as if after a strenuous climb and wiping the whitewash from his elbows—and called out to us, pulling something out of his pocket as he spoke. I can't recall his face, no matter how hard I try; I can see only a white balloon. But the things he displayed in his open palms I can picture down to the last detail: the cellophane-wrapped chewing gum tablets, yellow or cream-colored, with raised drawings on the packages; the tin watches covered in gold foil, with multicolored plastic bands; and the pastel-hued whirligigs, with their two-winged propellers twirling around twisted wires and whizzing in circles up to the sky. We gathered around him and asked how much each object cost, then scattered to our apartments to get the money. For fifty *bani* I bought a watch that had a strange purplish pink strap. Mendebil bought a colored propeller. Then he watched the man as he crawled back through the narrow slit of the corridor. His eyes half-closed as if in a dream, Mendebil stared rather vacantly at the base of the two gilt-colored wires twisting around each other, when suddenly the wings started rotating all by themselves, spinning faster and faster up the wires and rising a meter high into the air, where they went on whirling for several minutes. The boy looked on, but his mind seemed to be elsewhere.

Before he left, the man in the red-checked shirt had shown us one last thing, holding it gently and stroking it from time to time. We drew in closely. It was a black fountain pen. On one side there was a rectangular window through which you could see a woman in a black one-piece bathing suit. If you held the pen with its nib up, what at first looked like the black top turned out to be a liquid that descended slowly, revealing first the woman's breasts, then the rest of her body, until she was completely naked, as we had never seen or imagined a woman. "It's 25 *lei*," the man told us chuckling. "A little out of your league."

At about nine o'clock that night, after most of the boys had gone home, Luci and I went behind the building and climbed the old chestnut tree in which we had found the pencil sharpeners. For some fifteen minutes we talked about the peddler's visit, all the while glancing at our golden-tin watches by the pale neon lights of the mill yard. Luci had just started on another tale of horses bedecked with cloth of gold, when I saw Mendebil step out slowly, tentatively, from the stairwell and head for the sewage tunnels. We couldn't believe our eyes when we saw him step gingerly into one of them. We craned our necks so hard we nearly fell out of the tree. There he was, walking to and fro in the dirty labyrinth and making strange gestures that reminded us of Witchy. At one point he took something out of his breast pocket and pulled it over his face. As he came closer we could see it was a watercolor mask, by far more terrifying (with its teeth bared menacingly) than anything we had ever invented for Witchy. It was about ten o'clock when Mendebil came out of the ditch and went back into the building.

(Let me interrupt the story here for a moment. From time to time I have felt the need to come up for air, but never so much as now. Maybe I've been trying too long to keep my head and floating hair under the gelatinous waters of that summer, and now my eyes are stinging with the golden light of the water's reflections. But there's another reason for my shortness of breath, a more profound one. I'm no longer so sure I want to read this story at the writers' meeting. There's too little literature in it and too much of something else. I've been writing for over two weeks now, and I'm beginning to feel the need to jot down things that would have no place in the "chronicle" I mentioned earlier. Simply put, I can see how the act of writing is changing me as a person. If I don't write, be it at school or in my leisure time, I feel and behave like someone hallucinating. I haven't been able to grade this week's papers because pale images keep erupting on the glossy surface of my brain, images that torment me even when my students are reciting their lessons. I've also been having bad dreams, so bad I can't talk about them. And it all came to a head—or at least I hope it did—last night, when I was awakened by a steady loud noise. On the desk at the foot of my bed, in the dark, my typewriter was typing all by itself. I got up mechanically, turned on the light, and leaned over to see the patten advancing across the page, with a clatter of keys and ringing of bells. I read what was written there. The invisible fingers had tapped out my story from the beginning; they had arrived at the dream about the glass jar and were now at the sentence, "When I looked up again, I saw the thin contour of a door in the wildly sparkling wall of the jar." As I read, I was overwhelmed with awe at a prophecy fulfilled. It grew to infinity, accompanied by an unbearable golden-yellow buzzing in my temples. I felt as if my skull were dissolving in flames of terror. Only then did I fully wake up, and even so, as the bluish night faded into morning, I wasn't sure if I hadn't passed into another dream. Anyway, if I continue to write this, it's only on impulse and only for myself.)

After the peddler's visit, the harmony in our gang slowly disintegrated. Mimi, Lumpă, Luță, and Marțiganu listened with only one ear to Mendebil's stories, and Mendebil himself, as we soon came to notice, had started to neglect his audience. He still sat on his throne of concrete but no longer said anything new, starting in on the knights of the Round Table all over again. He stopped frequently, unable to recall any words for minutes at a time. He would stare vacantly at the wall, and in the awkward silence we could hear the truck engines' whir as wheat was being unloaded in the mill yard. But only Luci and I sensed that something was really wrong. Every afternoon, awake in my bed of torture, I would look at the bright motionless clouds and ponder what I had seen that night: Mendebil, a cardboard mask over his innocent face, wandering through the maze of dirty, noisome tunnels as if playing Witchy all by himself.

Summer was coming to an end. It must have been early September (I recall my parents scrambling to get me a satchel and supplies for my first year in school). One evening, Mendebil had been going on and on about Ruslan and Ludmila when suddenly he uttered those words I still cherish: "Humans come in four kinds: those who haven't been born, those who are living, those who are dead, and those who have neither been born nor are living or dead. The last kind are the stars." Then, as many times before, he gestured to the stars above the mill's high towers, as if on the verge of vaulting himself toward them. As we walked home down the narrow corridor, I asked him what he meant. He was silent until we reached the back of the building, but there, looking down at the ditches, he said he didn't know. He asked me to come and see him the next day; his mother had no idea what to get him for school and wanted to know what my parents had bought me.

At nine o'clock the next morning I was there. His mother was wearing a scarlet housedress and seemed dizzyingly tall, but she talked like my mother, like all the other mothers in the neighborhood. She brought us a plateful of apple strudel and let us "play" in Ionel's, or maybe Vasilică's, or George's room (I don't remember what she called Mendebil). He had a surprising number of toys in his room, most of them in pieces. You couldn't find a whole toy car anywhere. The body of a tiny ambulance lay abandoned in one corner; the engine and gears had been discarded in another. A tin frog lay belly up, the spring inside gushing out like a shiny intestine. A triggerless rifle had been thrown under a chair with a lacquered pink back. The shelves were lined with books (though not so many as I had expected), most of them thin, with large lettering, like the ones young schoolchildren use. I no longer remember what we talked about, but let me get to the point: as soon as Mendebil left the room for a few minutes, I pulled several books off a shelf and saw something fall onto the polished ledge below. I'd never been so astonished, not even when I saw Mendebil in the sewage canal. Hidden behind the books was the black pen with the woman on it. I replaced it carefully, and when Mendebil came back, I told him hurriedly that I had to go. As I rebuckled my sandals in the hall (his mother had asked me to take off my shoes when I arrived), I glanced once again at the mother and son standing in the doorway, he with his arm circled lovingly around her waist, she with her hand resting on his shoulder, towering and misty in her red satin housedress. They both wore the same smile, a smile that could mean so many things, cunning, sarcasm, or simply kindness. Both had lashless eyes, delicately bordered in black. I was deeply troubled. Outside I ran into Luci and told him what I'd seen. I couldn't figure out when Mendebil had bought the lurid pen; the peddler hadn't been back to our building since we'd first seen him three or four days before. Even now I have no idea how he got hold of the pen.

Oh, God, if I could only describe the image that hangs on, alive and painful, in my memory! Maybe then I could get rid of it. But even if I tried, would I really want to? Or is it that I just wish to see it more clearly, again and again, each second of my life? It's only now that I've reached—whether I'm ready for it or not—the high point of this "chronicle." I don't care if it seems unlikely; I'm writing for myself, and I did see what I'm about to relate. It still makes me shiver, so maybe it's the translucent egg I've been hatching all unawares for twenty-one years. Who knows what monstrous chick may emerge from it? But I won't think about it any more; all I need now is the strength to describe the scene "realistically," though it almost seems beyond me.

Mendebil had started to act crazy. Or at least that's what most of our gang thought, since we couldn't account for his embarrassingly long speeches now filled with gibberish, for his aimless wandering in his yellow *spielhosen* along the dirty walls of Stairwell One. He hardly ever told his Oriental tales any more, and even "The Wooden Cup and the Clay Cup" or "The Genie in the Bottle" he would leave unfinished. He stared for hours at a time at the whimsical drawings the girls made. He even began talking to the girls. Iolanda, the girl with the huge hair bows, had become Mendebil's "intimate adviser" and confessor (or so we thought), replacing the crippled boy with the nickel-plated leg braces. Mendebil would talk to her all the time, his expressive arms describing strange arcs in the air. The evening before his fall from grace, Iolanda at his feet and all of us around him, he told us the most beautiful story we had ever heard. It was almost group hypnosis: we stayed until ten o'clock, when we could no longer see each other's faces, until all that remained in the world was the square of dark blue sky, streaked over by the stars powdering the Milky Way. It was "The Tale of the Eleven Swans." The boy's voice rose and fell, enveloping us, until we were wild with grief. The little mute girl knitting nettle garments for her brothers who had turned into royal birds, their flight across the churning green sea, the boy left with a swan's wing—it had all been familiar to us for a long time. He was only reinforcing the story in our souls. When he stopped, we could hear the streetcars going down Ştefan cel Mare Avenue, rumbling in the stillness of the night.

The next day was to be the last. In the cold light I got together with Luci and Sandu and climbed into the horse-chestnut tree laden with large prickly fruit. All morning long we peeled the pods off the glossy nuts. It was then that Sandu found (I remember his cry of surprise) a heavy, glittering crystal under one of the thorny green pods. It looked like a glass egg, and light twisted through it strangely. It's a bad sign, I thought, when a chestnut tree grows this kind of fruit.

Just before noon—Mendebil hadn't yet come down to Stairwell One, and everyone was listless—we thought of an old game, one we'd played before Witchy, called Explorers. Halfway down the building wall there was a tin-plated door studded with rivets and painted gray. It was the entrance to the inner sanctum of the basement. We opened the door carefully so it wouldn't creak and started down the metal steps of the spiral staircase, avoiding the tar-slathered walls lined with electrical panels. The farther down we went, the darker it got. Finally we reached a long, narrow room smelling of putty and rust-soaked hemp. Pipes of various sizes sprouted from the walls and curved around the corners like tangled entrails, covered with sprockets and manometers. A light creeping through a tiny barred window near the ceiling gleamed dully on the damp cement floor. We stared in fascination at the pipes. Some were thicker than we were, others as thin as fingers and infinitely long. We crossed the room in silence and opened another metal door, which led to the boiler room. The dozens of pipes had pierced the wall and were now embedded in immense metal bellies, scarlet in color and girdled with rivets as big as fists, like iron pigs lying on cement platforms. Here and there manometers with black numbers and green glass covers glinted threateningly. We felt we were inside the temple of powerful and inscrutable gods. Once past the potbellied monsters, we tiptoed to the furthest room, a tiny chamber deep within the bowels of the building. It was the domain of the maintenance man. Its door was also made of metal, and had a small window. We peered through the glass, raising ourselves up as high as we could. Then we froze.

The room was traversed by a broad beam of light coming from a barred window near the ceiling. There was a luminous steam around the trail of light, and in its brightness we saw something we would never have thought we would see. Two naked children stood facing each other in the small bare room. The light filtered through the boy's hair and delicately outlined the girl's ankles and feet on the rough cement. The children were incredibly beautiful. They appeared very blond in the golden haze, the boy's hair glowing with russet and gold curls, his face lit up by his black-bordered eyes. The groove under his nostrils seemed deeper than ever. A strange, inexplicable smile kindled his tightly pressed lips. His slender body, the muscles framed by curving yellow lines, the frail ribs visible, the thin, firm legs, was like a finely traced, disquieting silhouette. The girl, shorter, her braids caught up in white satin bows, her bangs curling on her forehead, smiled awkwardly as she gazed into his eyes, the way I have since seen all naked women smile. There was almost no difference between their bodies. Their clothes lay in oddly neat heaps on the cement floor. They looked at each other with no definable feeling, their faces wearing inhuman expressions, like those of statues, or maybe even colder. When the girl raised her hand and touched the boy's shoulder with her fingertips, Sandu jerked away from the window and raced back through the boiler room. Terrified, Luci and I followed him. Even now, when I remember the scene in that room, I shiver and sob. Even now I can hear Iolanda's scream of terror when she heard our feet pounding on the cement, a scream that shattered my eardrums as it reverberated amidst the boilers and the pipes and pursued us to the outside door.

We ran until we reached Stairwell One, a deserted place at that time of day. We couldn't look at each other. We couldn't do anything. Luci shook as if in the throes of a fit, and in fact he came down with fever the next day. At noon we went to our apartments. All through my afternoon nap I babbled incoherently, my head buried under the sheets. All I could see was the two frail bodies facing each other in the solitude of the maintenance room. I could make no sense of it, none. Why had Mendebil changed so suddenly, so completely, after the peddler's visit? But I couldn't even formulate questions any more. Sandu reacted differently; he was furious, indignant. In the evening, when the old gang gathered outside Stairwell One, he recounted the whole story, even expanded on it. From the way he talked, Mendebil had led us all on with his idiotic prattle, but now he had shown his true colors. Vova and his brother rushed to the transformer and wiped off with their palms the sentences which Mendebil had written in colored chalk, which we by turns had since reinforced several times. Mimi was triumphant. He climbed up on Mendebil's throne and from there—big, potbellied and swarthy—led the debate over what Mendebil's punishment should be. Of course he wasn't able to come up with anything beyond "Let's really give it to him." Marțiganu suggested we play Witchy again, since we hadn't for a long time. We rushed behind the building and descended once more into the grimy ditches, taking in the beloved smells of earth and caterpillars and milky chrysalides, and with them the pungent scent of fear. We put on our cardboard masks, reverting to devils and monsters, giants and dragons and savages, and began chasing one another through the maze of canals.

Mendebil showed up at about eight o'clock. We could hardly believe our eyes when we saw him approaching the ditch. We thought he would stay locked in his room for a week at least, and his daring to confront us seemed like a slap in the face. We stopped playing and turned our grinning masks up at him. He tried to say something, but Paul picked up a ball of dirt and threw it at him, hitting him hard in the leg. Jean did likewise, and Mendebil fled to Stairwell One amid a shower of dirt clods. We dashed after him, shouting, our faces covered by the masks, our pockets filled with clumps of dirt. Rushing out of the narrow corridor, we gathered in the middle of the inner courtyard. There was no way he could escape us there. We couldn't find him at first, but finally caught sight of him hiding behind the stone walls of The Bridge, crouching in the dark on the small platform that led to the bricked-in door. We screamed and began hurling more dirt clods at him, but he yelled even louder and fought back like a demon. In the neon light of the mill yard we could see that he too was wearing a mask, his terrifying watercolor mask. Dirt hit him from all sides, though he was protected by the stone enclosure, high up on the platform, while we were out in the open on the ground. He hurled the dirt back for a long time, maybe an hour, until at last a clod hit him hard on the head. In the twilight we saw him slowly sag to his knees, his body arching backwards, and start to jerk violently. We came close, but he didn't seem to see us. Tears streamed down his cheeks; he groaned and howled amid spasms that contorted his body into impossible positions. We were so frightened that Luță ran to Stairwell Three and rang the doorbell to Mendebil's apartment. From our hiding place behind Stairwell One we saw the woman in red rush out and take the tormented child in her arms. She could hardly squeeze him through the narrow corridor that connected the stairwells.

And that's how everything ended. Mendebil's mother must have sent him to his grandparents or a boarding school or somewhere. We never saw him again. The next day it started to rain in small, freezing drops, and the area behind the building turned into a swamp, impossible to play in. School began about a week later and, by the time it was summer again, our gang had dissolved. Twenty-odd anonymous years followed. I finished secondary school, military service, the university. And here I am, part of the Establishment. But for three months now, since the dream with the jar of hamsters, I have felt like a different person. I can't stand it any more. Night after night I have bad dreams, so bad I don't dare log them in my journal. I feel something coming on, a smell of poisoned ice that makes me shiver. Sometimes, in the afternoon, I sob nervously, without tears. I have a feeling of imminent disintegration. I had one such fit just yesterday, after describing the scene in the maintenance room. What will happen, now that I've finished this tale that sprang up so miraculously from my memory? Will I start wandering aimlessly down the street, go into shops and restaurants, create a disturbance in movie theaters by telling Mendebil's story out loud? Because I feel I haven't told it all. Because I can't help screaming at the top of my lungs this truth that is mine and only mine. Because I can't hold in my sorrow any longer. I just can't. No, I won't be reading this at the writers' meeting. For these pages aren't really literature; they're a horrifying prophecy. I'll take them and read them on the streets in a snowstorm, by the light of the shop windows, on streetcars. I'll find people who'll understand and follow me, and we'll go searching all over town for Mendebil, and at last we'll find him. And we'll know it's him, and we'll understand him, and we'll cry and sing together. And Mendebil, wrapped in rays of light, sending out bolts of blue lightning, will lift up his arms and ascend, illuminating the city as if it were day, up to and beyond the stars. And we'll be left behind, like white ashes, becoming ever more pure. . . . I can't go on.

This morning, as I was looking for tape to mend a book cover, I came across these typed pages, which, by the look of them, are more than two years old. They were lying on top of the wardrobe, underneath some laminated pictures. I read them and couldn't help jotting down on the last page how surprised I was. They were written on my "Erika" typewriter, no doubt about that, and they refer to a definite period in my childhood; I recognized some of the facts mentioned in the "chronicle." I did live in the apartment building on Ştefan cel Mare Avenue; the mill, Stairwell One, all parts of the scenery are real and exist even today. All, that is, except for the underground heating complex; our building never had boilers in the basement. The children are real too. I remember their names. Some I still run into. But the whole story about Mendebil seems absurd. There never was a child wise beyond his years living in our building. Vova Smirnoff is an engineer now. Lumpă clears tables at the Athênéé Palace restaurant; I often see him there. Sandu's an engineer too, Marţiganu's doing something somewhere, and Nicuşor is my friend, Nicolae Iliescu. But what's become of Mendebil? Where on earth does this story come from? I should read it again, but I'm afraid to. There's something sinister about it. I can't make up my mind what to do with it. I don't want to throw it out, but I don't want to stumble upon it again. I'd better put it away somewhere, find a place where it can stay forever and not, like so much else (thanks to my wife's masterful touch), be tossed out with the newspapers.

Voices of the City

ᕈᚠᕈ Ion Băieşu (1933–1992)

After studies at the Mihai Eminescu School of Literature and at the University of Bucharest (philology), Ion Băieşu worked for a time as editor-in-chief of the student magazine *Amfiteatru* (1965–1968) while pursuing his career as a prose writer and dramatist. Băieşu's sketches, short stories, and satirical articles—*The Night of Love* (1962), *People with a Sense of Humor* (1964), and *They Suffered Together* (1965)—are among the best examples of Romanian irony: humorous, occasionally absurdist, rich in vivid characters and dialogue. Băieşu is also known for his social comedies, some of them gathered in *In Search of Lost Meaning* (1979) and for a series of skits for television, *Love Is a Really Big Thing* (1967), that satirized the "wooden language" of Communist propaganda. Băieşu won many literary awards, including three Writers' Union Prizes. Among Băieşu's last publications are the novel *The Scales* (1985), and a selection of sketches and stories, *The Accelerator* (1990).

"Death and the Major" first appeared in *They Suffered Together* (1965).

Death and the Major

Major Tache reported to the head of his department, Colonel Ştefănescu, and informed him that the difficulties concerning his vacation in Sinaia[1] had been resolved. He thanked the colonel heartily for his help.

"So you're going after all?" The colonel's voice was glum.

"I am," replied the major, trying to look as if he badly needed the trip.

"Leaving today?"

"If possible."

The colonel was silent for a moment, and the major knew why. He was needed at the office.

"All right, you can go," the colonel said finally, chagrined that Tache hadn't offered to stay. "Are things really that bad?"

"I'm on the verge of a nervous breakdown. I haven't slept in ten days. I'm climbing the walls."

"Oh, all right, go then. Just make sure you come back ready for work."

Major Tache headed for the door, then turned. He rummaged in his pockets for a slip of paper, found it, and handed it to the colonel.

"By the way, Comrade Colonel, what do you make of this bad joke?"

The colonel held up the paper. "Best regards and see you soon. Death."

"What's this?"

"I got it in the mail."

"Here or at home?"

"At home."

The colonel frowned. "Who would do such an idiotic thing? Bică, maybe?"

"It's his style all right, but he won't admit to it."

"Has your wife seen it?"

"Unfortunately, she has," Tache said dolefully. "I hid the first two letters, but she found the third one."

"So you've received three of these?"

"Yes, and I'd really appreciate it if you could convince whoever's doing this to stop it. Every night my wife has nightmares that I'm being assassinated. She almost came to see you about it herself."

The colonel buzzed his secretary and asked for Major Bică to be sent in. Bică appeared almost instantly. He was very short, blond, and fat, with ruddy cheeks that seemed to laugh all by themselves. The colonel stared at him severely for a few moments.

"Comrade Major Bică, I'd like you to keep your jokes in check from now on. Some are good and we appreciate them, but others are downright stupid, if not evil."

Bică attempted a smile. "Which of my jokes are you referring to, Comrade Colonel?"

"This one." The colonel handed him the slip of paper.

Bică read it and frowned. "I didn't write this, Comrade Colonel."

"We've known each other for a long time, Bică."

Bică tried to look grave. "I give you my word of honor that—"

"Bică, I want you to think about what I've just said."

"Yes, sir."

The two majors walked out into the corridor. Bică took Tache by the shoulders. "Tache, do you really believe I did this?"

"I thought it might be you. But I couldn't be sure."

"I find this very upsetting."

"Well, don't. It's not that important."

Tache went straight home. On the way, he pondered how he could tell his wife about his trip without making her angry. She was tired, worn out, probably even more than he was. But they had no one to leave the baby with. And there was no way they could rest if they took it along: it was only eight months old and it cried all the time. Should he tell her he was going on an assignment for two weeks? No, that was out of the question. He'd only been home five days since the last mission, and that one had lasted a whole month.

Tache entered the house with a sheepish look on his face. His wife shot him a piercing glance and knew at once he was planning to go away again. She always found out about his trips by the expression on his face. Sometimes she could even tell how many days he'd be gone.

"You're off again, aren't you?" She slammed the door behind him, a gesture that always signaled a struggle ahead.

Tache tried to keep his cool. He followed his wife into the baby's room. "Won't you just listen to what I have to say?"

"I'm listening."

"The doctor told me that my nervous breakdown wasn't caused by pressures at work."

"So?"

"He thinks it's been brought on by stress at home."

"How should your doctor know anything about your stress at home?"

"He suggested it, and I confirmed it. You're a wonderful wife and an exceptional mother. There's only one problem: you hate it when I go away."

"You know, you're right. I do hate it when you go away. How would you like to be left on your own for a whole month? How would you like to be wakened at all hours of the night and have to wash diapers all day long? How would you like to have to do all the cooking and the shopping and have nobody around to talk to? Just how would you like that?"

"It's not my fault that nature made you a woman. Besides, I don't go away on pleasure trips."

"Whatever made you go after those epaulets anyway?"

"If you haven't figured that out by now, there's no use explaining it again. You're just being spiteful. You're always after me about this. One of these days, I swear, I won't put up with it anymore. I'll . . . I'll. . . ."

Tache stopped short of specifying what "he'd . . . do." Instead he went into the next room and started packing his suitcase. He was certain his wife would join him eventually and give him the opportunity to make up with her. But she never came. When he was ready to leave, he went into the kitchen to say good-bye. She responded curtly, without turning her head.

"Have a good trip."

Tache arrived at Sinaia in the evening. After securing a single room at the reservations desk (by slipping a generous tip inside his ID), he proceeded to the telephone office, where he placed a call to Bucharest. Hearing his wife's affectionate "hello" at the other end of the line, he knew that she had calmed down, something she always did as soon as he was out of town.

"How are you, darling? Did you have a good trip?"

Tache sighed with relief. "I'm fine. And I've got a nice room."

"So you were telling the truth. You really are on vacation, aren't you?"

"Of course I am. What's new? How's Bimbirică?" Bimbirică was the code name for their child.

"Fine, happy, eating like a horse."

"Great. Anything else? How are things with you?"

"Oh, all right. Nothing unusual."

Tache knew his wife so well (as she knew him) that he realized at once that something unusual had in fact happened.

"Come on, tell me," he urged her.

"It's nothing. Don't worry about it."

"You're the one who's always worrying. Come on, out with it."

"I don't want to upset you."

Tache sensed her hesitation.

"You've received another one of those letters," she finally blurted, her voice thick with anger or maybe tears.

Tache burst out laughing. "You're kidding, aren't you?"

"No, I'm not."

"Damn that Bică! He's a first-class idiot."

"What's Bică got to do with it?" she asked, puzzled.

"Oh, didn't I tell you? I guess not. I found out he's the one that's been writing those letters. He's been sending them to everyone in the department. The typist turned him in. Know what he was trying to do? See if we recognized that the letters had been typed on our own typewriters! Can you imagine?"

"I think it's a very bad joke. You tell him I never want to see him again. And he's no longer welcome in our home."

As soon as he hung up the phone, Tache thought of one immediate danger: his wife running into Bică. He made a preliminary analysis of the problem on his way back to the villa. Clearly the letters had not been sent by Bică. He'd sensed that from the start. Bică's great talent lay in pulling legs, not fighting crimes. (He could have been a great circus entertainer or vaudeville comedian, but he didn't want to change jobs.) That was why Bică was the most popular officer in the department, the one invited to all the birthday parties, name day dinners, weddings, and anniversaries. But he was also the officer who had unintentionally caused two people to faint (once when he informed a police captain, falsely of course, that the captain had been appointed military attaché in Washington, and another time when a colleague thought he had won a sports lottery prize, in a contest Bică had fixed). None of his friends had been spared his pranks. (In fact, most office jokes were played on Bică, since he enjoyed them the most.) He would even imitate the voices of his superiors and those of a number of famous actors. But never, not even in the most outrageous or "irresponsible" of his jokes (as Colonel Ştefănescu had labeled them), had Bică dared make fun of an officer at the expense of his family, that is, play tricks that might have adversely affected the wives or children of his colleagues and friends. Tache knew this very well. So it was clear to him that Bică couldn't have been the one to write the letters. His suspicions now centered on the one remaining alternative: the Cega affair. Was it possible that the toughest criminals he had ever dealt with had somehow resurfaced?

Tache took a sleeping pill, but he couldn't fall asleep. He went out and strolled around for an hour. The whole time he tried to think of something else, but the death threats kept flashing through his mind. It was crazy, ridiculous even, yet he couldn't shake a feeling of dread.

When he returned to the villa, the cleaning woman stopped him on the way to his room. Putting her finger to her temple and thinking deeply for a few seconds, she finally recalled what she wanted to tell him. A man had asked about him.

"Who was it?"

"A comrade. He's staying here too. Room 14."

"What did he want to know?"

"He asked if you were staying here and in what room."

"What else?"

"He asked if there was a vacant room next to yours. But there wasn't, so I gave him Room 14. I thought he was a friend of yours."

"What's his name?"

The woman looked in the register. "Silviu Constantinescu, Bucharest."

Tache went up to the second floor and listened in at the door to Room 14. He could see that the lights were on and could hear noises coming from inside. He tapped at the door. After a pause, it opened.

"Good evening," said Tache.

"Good evening," the man at the door replied. He was young, very thin, and blond. His eyes were a cheerful blue. He seemed in good spirits.

"I'm sorry to trouble you, but I was informed you had inquired about me."

"Really? Who said so?" the blond man asked evenly, with a sly, impertinent smile.

"The cleaning woman."

"She must have mistaken me for someone else."

He tried to withdraw, but Tache stuck his foot in the doorway. "Isn't your name Constantinescu?"

"Yes, it is."

"Then there's no mistake. She told me that a person who registered as Silviu Constantinescu had asked about me."

"I'm Silviu Constantinescu, but I don't know you, and I never asked about you."

Tache apologized and left. He went downstairs and questioned the woman again, thoroughly this time, until he was convinced there had been no mistake. He returned to his room, took another sleeping pill, got into bed, and slept like a log until nine o'clock the next morning. The cleaning woman woke him up with a discreet knock.

"Comrade Tache," she whispered in a conspiratorial tone, "the man's moved next door to you. He's in Room 3. He asked for it the moment it was vacant."

"I hope he's happy there," murmured Tache drowsily.

"I only told you because you asked about him. And he asked about you too."

"All right. Thank you."

Tache dismissed her, annoyed at having been disturbed. He got dressed and walked down to the cafeteria. It was in another villa, a few hundred meters away. On the way, he wondered if the cleaning woman had passed along the information on her own or because his new next-door neighbor had asked her to. He also wondered if he should let things develop by themselves or help them along. He always liked to be one step ahead of his opponents, first baffling, then panicking them. His boss had described his energetic and unpredictable style as "aggressive"; once he even criticized Tache in a meeting for his "adventurism." Colonel Ştefănescu detested the spirit of adventure some of his younger colleagues displayed, demanding cool-headed, "scientific" work from them. "There is no place for risk taking in criminology," he would say. "If you wish to pursue that path, you should become criminals yourselves, or detective story writers." Most of the time, these hints and accusations were directed at Tache, since he had his own oftentimes eccentric way of doing things. Tache had joined the police force out of sheer love of the profession, a love he had cultivated since child-hood; he had even given up his assistant professorship at the Faculty of Law to become an officer. For many years he had dreamed of becoming a daring, invincible commissar, who looked danger in the face and solved cases with speed and efficiency. ("There are high-risk jobs, and there are risk-free jobs. People are free to choose whichever they want," he liked to say, viewing himself as a cross between a wise Sherlock Holmes and a dig-nified, muscular cowboy.) Because of these secret beliefs—and despite his boss's reprimands—Tache followed his own course in all assignments, extending the range of investigation far beyond what was required of him, bringing forward new elements and making greater-than-usual physical and intellectual efforts to achieve his aim. In their last conversation, the colonel had given him another warning.

"I'm afraid you'll end up writing detective stories, Tache. You don't intend to stop those cheap heroics of yours, do you?"

Once again Tache decided not to waste any time, so he set to work right away. (His best ideas always came when he was doing something.) First he had to establish whether the fellow who called himself Constantinescu was indeed after something or whether the cleaning woman had somehow mixed things up.

Entering the dining room, he noticed the blond man seated at a table. Although there were several empty tables nearby, Tache asked if he could join him.

"Certainly," the blond man replied, his sallow lips set in a bland smile.

"The cleaning woman tells me we're neighbors now."

"Are you in Room 2?"

"Yes."

"Then you're right; we are neighbors. I've moved into 3. It's brighter."

"You prefer bright rooms, do you?"

"I certainly do."

The blond man was smiling, but Tache didn't know whether it was simply a reflex or whether the man had noticed the irony in his tone.

"It's good we're neighbors," Tache said. "We can help each other out if need be."

"Right. Don't hesitate to knock if you need something, even if it's late."

In the course of their conversation they learned each other's reasons for going on vacation; coincidentally, both were suffering from nervous breakdowns. Two more disclosures followed: both claimed to be accountants (Tache always introduced himself as an accountant), and both were fond of backgammon.

"How about a game?" the blond man suggested.

"Why not?"

After breakfast they played ten games. The blond man won them all. To Tache's surprise, the man rolled six sixes in a row.

"Where did you learn to roll like that?" Tache asked.

"In Grant district. I grew up with dice in my hand."

Before noon Tache paid a visit to the local police station and conferred for an hour with the police chief. That same day a drunk got into a street brawl with Tache's neighbor. An officer who happened to be patrolling the area took them both down to the station. Two hours later Tache had another chat with the chief, who reported, "He may be one of ours, Comrade Major."

"What makes you think that?"

"He's too sure of himself. Besides, he looks just like Gane, one of our district lieutenants."

"Let's find out."

They placed a telephone call to the district headquarters.

"Can I speak with Lieutenant Gane, please?" asked Tache.

"Who's calling?"

"Major Tache."

"Comrade Lieutenant Gane is on assignment."

"In town?"

"No, out of town."

Tache wondered if Colonel Ştefănescu, wishing to ease his conscience, had had the district office send someone out to keep an eye on him. He found the action unnecessary and offensive. He considered phoning headquarters, but that entailed the risk of being recalled or told not to do anything on his own. He walked back to his villa lost in thought.

He found a telegram thrust under the door and tore it open nervously. It read, "Greetings. See you soon. Death." It was postmarked Bucharest. Dumbfounded, he crumpled the note and threw it onto the table. What could these repeated threats mean?

At one o'clock sharp he knocked at Room 3. The blond man opened the door with the same sallow smile.

"Shall we have another game?" Tache inquired.

"Yes. Let's."

At some point during the game Tache remarked casually, "I've got a feeling you're losing, Comrade Lieutenant."

The blond man made no reply, which either meant that he hadn't noticed or that he'd intentionally ignored the statement.

Eager to determine once and for all whether the blond man was or was not Lieutenant Gane from the district headquarters, Tache followed him around town all afternoon. At one point, the man went into the telephone exchange. Tache entered through the back door, showed his ID to the supervisor, and listened in on the phone call. The voice on the Bucharest end of the line was a man's, hoarse or trying to sound hoarse.

"Everything's fine, Uncle," said the blond man.

"Did you get the room all right?"

"Yes. Villa 2, Room 3."

"Is it quiet?" the hoarse voice demanded.

"Yes, it is. You can come."

"Fine. I'll be there. You can expect me on the ten o'clock train."

"Great. Good-bye, Uncle."

Preoccupied, Tache ambled down the street. He was less intrigued by the conversation he had just overheard than by the recollection that, at the train station in Bucharest, he had glimpsed a face that now seemed to belong to the blond man.

At ten o'clock the next morning he went to the station and positioned himself behind the newspaper kiosk. The train came in and went but the blond man didn't show up. Tache quickly took a taxi to the next station, on the outskirts of the city, where morning and afternoon commuter trains stopped. He arrived just as the train did. Sure enough, the blond man was standing at one end of the platform. He briskly stepped forward into the crowd of people coming off the train and took the arm of a little old man, white-haired but spry. Tache tailed them all the way back to the villa. Then he returned to the telephone exchange and had another conversation with the district police.

"Has Comrade Lieutenant Gane returned from his assignment?" he asked. "I'm a relative."

"Yes, he has, but he's not in the office at the moment."

"Thank you."

Tache pondered a while, then had the operator dial another number, Colonel Ştefănescu's private extension. Should he tell him or not? If he did, would the colonel order him back? "No doubt he will," he said to himself, and a moment later canceled the call. He walked back to the villa and knocked at Room 3. The blond man opened the door promptly.

"Well, hello there, neighbor!" he cried cheerfully. "Come on in!"

The old man he had met at the station was with him. "Let me introduce my uncle," he went on. The uncle bore a striking resemblance to the blond man. The same sallow smile lit up his face.

"We were just having a game of backgammon," the blond man said. "Will you join us?"

Tache sat down. He noticed the older man had the same amazing skill at throwing dice. Later they had dinner together and then beer at a bistro, where they chatted amicably for a while. The two men were jovial but not boisterous, friendly but not intrusive. "Nothing of interest here," Tache said to himself, disappointed. "The best thing I can do is lock myself in my room and go to sleep."

One afternoon, a group of children from the town of C——, on their way to the river for a swim, discovered a green plastic suitcase in the hollow of a willow tree. They opened it and found the corpse of an eight-year-old girl inside. She had been visiting her grandmother the day she disappeared.

Major Tache, accompanied by three assistant detectives, went to the scene of the murder on the day the body was found. After a careful examination of the evidence he stayed on in the town, focusing his investigation on the suitcase. His preliminary findings quickly led him to believe that there was a safe built into a wall of the house, a safe the little girl's grandmother knew nothing about but the murderers did. They had entered the house while she was at church, ripped open the wall, and cracked the safe, from which they had most likely taken some valuables. The little girl had stumbled upon the evildoers while they were breaking in, and they had choked her to death. They hid the corpse in the garden (the grounds around the house were neglected and overgrown with weeds), and in the evening they took it away in the suitcase, abandoning it in the hollow of the willow tree by the river.

At least this was how Tache envisioned the scenario after his initial inspection. It remained to be seen whether his assumptions were correct or not. He found out that there was only one shop in town that sold plastic suitcases. He went and questioned the salesgirl thoroughly. Who had she sold a green suitcase to in the past few days? The girl couldn't remember. She had sold several. Tache kept pressing, engaging her in conversation for hours at a time.

"Think it over carefully. Reconstruct what happened every time you sold a suitcase. Try and remember what the people who bought them looked like. Were they short or tall? Young or old? Blond or dark-haired?"

After a week of effort, the salesgirl remembered. She had sold a green suitcase to a short man, neither old nor young. Tache asked the girl and her parents to tell their acquaintances that he and the girl had become engaged. Thus they were able to stroll through town eight hours a day, the girl's mission to observe each passerby closely. Two weeks later she hesitantly identified the purchaser as a man crossing the main square. That very day Tache entered the suspect's apartment while he was at work and found the receipt for the suitcase in one of his coats. Then he proceeded to the suspect's office and waited for him to leave work. When the man came out, Tache whispered mysteriously in his ear, hoping to make him think he was one of his group.

"See you in the park at seven. The third bench on the right."

At seven the man appeared. The ensuing conversation was brief but enlightening.

"They're on our trail," Tache said in a low voice. "Be careful who you talk to."

"I don't talk to anybody."

"Make sure you've covered all your tracks."

"I have."

"You sure you didn't leave the receipt in your pocket?"

"I don't remember. I'll look."

Arrested the next day, the man who had purchased the green suitcase told Tache everything he knew. A man from Bucharest he had met in prison had hired him for three thousand *lei* to help crack a safe. He wasn't sure what the man's real name was (the man had introduced himself as Nelu), nor did he know the name of the man who had actually broken open the safe.

Accompanied by several experts, Tache returned to the scene of the crime. It soon became clear that the marks of strong blows on the safe had been made to lead the authorities off the track: the safe had been opened by normal means, by a key or some other device. Tache knew for certain there were only two men in the country who could open a safe without leaving a scratch. Since one of them was in prison, Tache returned to Bucharest to contact the other. He went directly to the Pantelimon district and knocked on the door of Uncle Solomonică, alias "Cega."[2] The file on Cega, which Tache had reviewed several times, could form the basis for the romanticized biography of one of the most notorious burglars of the thirties. In his youth Cega had worked the great capitals of the world side by side with Florică Florescu, superstar of large-scale bank robberies. When the war came along, Uncle Solomonică, aka Cega, had retired from his trade and gone home to his children and grandchildren.

When Tache came face to face with Cega for the first time, he was startled to see a seventy-year-old man who got around with the aid of a cane and a grandchild. Tache took the old man to headquarters and had a long talk with him.

"Where might you have been on the fourteenth of the month, my dear man?" Tache asked jovially.

"The fourteenth of what month?"

"You know perfectly well."

"Oh, the fourteenth!" Cega exclaimed. "The fourteenth was a Friday, Saint Dmitri's Day. I went to a memorial dinner."

"Let's not waste our time," Tache urged. "I can produce someone in a minute who'll say otherwise."

The man who had purchased the green suitcase was brought in. He recognized Cega at once. Suddenly Uncle Solomonică became reasonable.

"Look, sonny," he said soberly, "I've dealt with all kinds of police chiefs in my life. Before you were even born I'd busted open two banks and put holes in more than one policeman's guts. You don't mind me calling you sonny?"

"Of course not. You could be my grandfather."

"Right. So I'll be frank with you. I'll lay my cards on the table, you do the same. I'll defend my interests, you do your job. Here's the story. A guy named Moarcăş—you don't know him, he used to own flour mills and oil presses—skipped the country in '45 in a private plane. I don't know what his plans were, but he left behind all his liquid assets—gold and silver coins and jewelry worth about 2 million *lei*—for his wife to take to him later. His wife couldn't get out of the country, so she put the coins and jewels into three boxes, hid the boxes in a safe, and built the safe into a wall. Well, she died a few years after that, and then Moarcăş died, abroad, and only a nephew was left. He was living abroad too, but when he got wind of the hidden treasure, he decided to come as a tourist. He asked a retired burglar if he knew anyone in Romania who might help him, and the burglar said, 'Look, mister, if you need to crack a safe in a minute and a half, Uncle Solomonică, alias Cega, is your man. He and Florică Florescu could open a safe with a safety pin.' So Moarcăş's nephew comes to Bucharest and looks up a relative of his, who asks around the Pantelimon district and finds me. 'Here's how things stand,' he says. 'There's a safe we've lost the key to. We have some family heirlooms in it. How much will you charge to open it?' And I say, 'I'm sorry, mister, but I don't do that anymore. I'm an old man. What's past is past. I've got children and grandchildren; I keep my nose clean. Why should I look for trouble at my age?' 'Don't worry, mister,' he says. 'Just open the safe and you'll get ten thousand *lei.*' 'Look,' I say, 'I wouldn't do it for a hundred thousand *lei.*' So the man goes away. But the next day he's back with twenty thousand. My youngest son was listening at the door, and when he heard the amount he told his brothers and their wives, and they get together and start hammering at me, 'Ask for twenty-five, Dad. We need the money.' So I gave in and went. I got into a car, drove to the town of C——, met two men I'd never seen before, and went into a house. They broke down a wall, took out the safe, and I opened it. That's all. They grabbed some boxes, and we left. When I got back to Bucharest, the man gave me fifteen thousand *lei,* since he'd given me the other ten in advance. That was it. Now, what is. . . ."

"Wait a minute," Tache interrupted. "That's not all. There's something else."

"What?"

"You haven't told me the most important thing."

"I don't know anything more."

"Oh yes you do. What happened with the girl?"

"Oh, the girl," Solomonică said ruefully. "One of those idiots grabbed her by the throat to keep her from screaming and choked her to death. I had nothing to do with it."

"I believe you," said Tache. "What about the boxes?"

"I don't know anything about the boxes either. They didn't interest me. The man who drove me to Bucharest took them. There were three of them."

"Will you help me nail him?"

"Why not? You ought to know, though, that the boxes are here in

Bucharest. Moarcăş's nephew was going to come pick them up in September."

Tache and Uncle Solomonică strolled through Bucharest for three days, trying to find the car that had taken the old man to the town of C——. They finally found it in an auto wrecking lot. They took down the name of the person who had sold it. He, in turn, had purchased it from a cousin of his, a man by the name of Emilian Prunache who, he said, had moved with his job to somewhere in Suceava County. He didn't remember what job it was or where it was located. Tache searched for Prunache for a week both in Suceava County and throughout the province of Moldavia, but without any luck. Tired and frustrated, he went back to Solomonică for advice.

"Where could he be? I can't find him anywhere."

"Maybe he's in prison for something else."

The old man was right. Afraid he might be pursued, Prunache had found a most efficient way to protect himself. He committed a minor crime and was sentenced to three months in jail, a place where he felt safe and sound. The first time they questioned him, he told them where two of the boxes were. He had given the third to a person who had to keep it until someone came and gave a password. Unfortunately, he had lost track of that person, whose name he had never known, and who had been recommended to him by the nephew of the woman who had hidden the treasure in the wall. Later, Prunache admitted to having inadvertently killed the little girl.

Tache located the first two boxes, but the third remained a mystery. However, in his final conversation with Solomonică, Tache found himself struggling over a totally different issue, the issue of duty versus honor. It wasn't just that he liked Uncle Solomonică and somehow respected him (true, the old man was a criminal, but hardly an ordinary one); it was that Solomonică had in fact helped him untangle the case by telling the truth from the start and by directing him to Prunache, the principal culprit. And in exchange for all this, Solomonică wanted a deal.

"You can see to it that I get off with only a year or two so I'm eligible for the next amnesty. Charge me with robbery but not with being an accomplice to the murder."

"How can I do that?" demanded Tache. "According to the law, you're guilty of shielding a murder suspect."

"I'll get the other two to say I wasn't present when the girl was killed."

Tache scratched his head in dismay. "It's not that easy. They've already testified you were there."

"So what? As long as the case is still under investigation, you can find a way out. I don't have to tell you what to do."

"What do you mean, 'find a way out'?"

"I mean, they can enter a new statement in the file saying I wasn't a witness to the murder, and the old statement can be lost. That's all."

"I really don't know if I can promise you that."

"See this? See my white hair? My name is Solomonică, but I'm known as Cega, remember? I'm seventy years and two months old, I've cracked forty-eight safes and knocked off eight guys in uniform. That was my piece of the action. I don't know how much longer I'm going to live, but I want to die in my own bed. That's why I stayed out of it for over twenty years. I've treated you squarely, helped you out, and if you don't treat me squarely in return, if you don't do as I ask, well—I won't leave this world with my hands empty. In other words, I'll pay you back. Think it over, and be a man, not a weasel."

Tache pored over Solomonică's file for five days and five nights, but he froze every time he thought of doing the old man the favor he had requested. He certainly wasn't dangerous, and he was going to die in a few years anyway. Yet helping him meant falsifying evidence, and Tache, after mulling it over, realized he was incapable of doing such a thing. He told no one about his conversations with Solomonică or about his own torment and finally handed the file over to the prosecutor with the indictment, "Burglary, complicity to murder."

A few weeks later Solomonică was sentenced to five years in prison. Haunted by the old man's face and words, Tache went to the trial full of remorse for his unjust treatment of the old burglar, unjust even though it was by standards outside his professional ethic. In the courtroom, Solomonică looked straight at Tache when the sentence was pronounced. Tache met the old man's glance. An exchange of many nuances ensued: accusation and defense, a tremulous smile and bitter scorn.

The death threats started two weeks after the trial.

The three men came out of the bistro and went for a leisurely stroll before retiring to bed.

"I'd like to go up the mountain tomorrow," said the elderly man. "It'll be a good day for hiking."

"Fine, let's go." The blond man turned to Tache. "Will you join us?"

"Sounds tempting. But right now I'm going to bed. Beer always makes me sleepy."

Tache returned to the villa while his neighbors continued their stroll. He entered Room 3 through the balcony and quickly rummaged through the men's luggage. Then, satisfied, he went to bed.

The next morning the two men knocked at his door to ask if he was still interested in hiking up the mountain.

"Yes, I am," Tache said, "though I don't really have the right gear. I'll be coming empty-handed."

They set off. The day dawned clear and sunny. The trails were crowded with tourists; the woods resounded with their shouts. The blond man walked in front, the elderly man followed, and Tache brought up the rear. At one point the blond man started a conversation with three young girls who seemed willing to join them on their hike. But the elderly man opposed the diversion. When the trail forked, he turned to the right and called the other two after him. "Come this way. It's cooler."

The trail he had chosen was less traveled. There were no hikers either ahead of or behind them. When they reached a clearing, the blond man proposed a rest stop. He was tired.

"Let's walk a little further and then stop," said the elderly man, crossing over to the northern slope of the mountain, where there was still shade.

The blond man brought out a bottle of rum and each of them took a sip.

"Do you like rum, Comrade Major?" the elderly man asked.

Tache laughed. "How do you know I'm a major?"

"Well, we know a thing or two," the elderly man replied, laughing too. "We're not that stupid."

"Only a thing or two? No more?"

The blond man cast a glance at his companion, waiting for a sign of consent. It did not come. "We know enough," he said anyway.

The elderly man took another swig of rum, then put the bottle back into the knapsack. "Comrade Major," he said, "we'd like to have a serious talk with you. This place seems appropriate, since it's quiet and secluded. Can we start?"

"By all means."

"You worked on a case involving a man named Solomonică, alias Cega. Right?"

"Right."

"He sent us."

Tache lit a cigarette. "Does he have something to say to me?"

"Yes, he does."

"What, if I may ask?"

"Haven't you been getting his letters?"

"Yes, I have."

"Then he's told you everything he has to say."

The elderly man and his companion also lit cigarettes. All three smoked in silence for a few moments.

"You may not believe me," Tache said finally, "but I swear I don't know what you're talking about."

The blond man laughed shortly; that is, he raised the corners of his upper lip for a few fractions of a second. "Oh, yes, you do. You're not that stupid."

"Be polite to the Comrade Major," the elderly man said, poking his companion in the ribs.

Tache laughed and leaned back comfortably against a nearby stump.

"I'm sorry, but there's nothing to laugh about." The elderly man's face showed genuine regret.

"Maybe not, but right now I don't know what's going on, so I feel like laughing. Isn't that allowed?" Tache asked.

"Of course it is. Only it might make me angry."

"And if it does?"

"It wouldn't be to your advantage."

"Wouldn't it now? What do you mean by that?"

"I'm quite serious."

Sprawled out on the grass, Tache kept smiling. He leaned against the stump as if on a chaise lounge. "You're both very kind. Very kind indeed."

"What do you mean, 'very kind'?" The blond man frowned, barely able to keep his temper in check.

"You're trying very hard to convince me you mean business. You want to scare me. You sure you're not kidding?"

"Kidding? About what?" the blond man asked, puzzled.

"Leave him alone," said the elderly man. "Can't you see he's pulling our leg? Go take his gun."

Tache put his hands up. "I don't have one."

"Search him anyway."

Tache offered no resistance. When the blond man rejoined his companion, the elderly man turned to Tache. "Listen, you bastard! You think I brought you here so you could laugh at me? You goddamn dirty bastard!"

Tache stared straight at him and stubbed his cigarette out against the stump. "Brother," he said, his words heavy with emphasis, "don't swear at me. I'd rather have someone slap me than curse at me. Don't try it again."

The elderly man stared back at him in surprise.

"I mean it," Tache went on. "If you want to say something to me, say it politely."

"Don't forget who started all this," the blond man said defensively.

"It doesn't matter who started it. Did I swear at you?"

"No, but you were making fucking fools out of us."

"That's different. It's one thing to poke fun and something else to curse."

"Okay," the blond man agreed. "We'll stop."

"Then let's go back to the beginning. You're here on behalf of Uncle Solomonică. What does he want?"

"This," the elderly man said, taking a gun out of his pocket. "He told me to put a hole in your gut."

Tache's eyebrows rose in mock astonishment. "What's gotten into him?"

"Nothing," the blond man replied, his tone just as mocking.

"How come he asked you to do it?" Tache said, his voice earnest.

"We met in prison. We were getting out just as he was going in."

"Had you known each other before?"

"Yes. For over forty years," the elderly man replied. "We were in the same line of work."

"Here at home?"

"Yes. I never left like he did. I stayed. He taught me everything I know."

"What did he tell you when you got out?"

"He said, 'There's this guy named Tache I want you to plug for me.' That was the last thing he said."

"That makes sense," Tache admitted. "The last time we talked, he said he had an unpleasant surprise in store for me if I didn't help him out. I would have if I could, but I couldn't."

"He said you could have," the blond man replied.

"Well, he was wrong."

A silence fell over the three men. They all lit cigarettes again. In the distance, beyond the mountain ridge, people were hoooting and laughing, but the voices moved farther and farther away, fading into the woods.

"Did you take him seriously?"

The two didn't respond.

"Do you really intend to kill me?" the major went on.

"What do you think we followed you for?" the blond man asked in a bored voice. "To see what color eyes you have?"

"So you do?" Tache repeated.

"You don't expect us to take pity on you, do you?"

Tache grimaced. "No, but I just can't believe it."

"Why not?" the elderly man asked.

"I can't imagine you taking out that gun and shooting me. I just can't picture it. Did I do you or even Solomonică so much harm that I deserve to die? Are you so indebted to him that you carry out his orders blindly? I don't get it. It's not that I'm afraid of death. It just doesn't make sense. It's not logical."

The elderly man stared at Tache once more, spat, and said, "I'm telling you. It's what Uncle Solomonică swore me to do: put a bullet in your gut. But maybe we could strike a deal."

"All right. Let's strike a deal."

"Only if you're willing."

"I have no choice."

"We'll let you go if you give us the password."

"What password?"

"The password Prunache used when he handed over the third box."

Tache's face brightened. "Wait a minute. I want to be clear about this. What will you do with the password if I give it to you?"

"That's our business."

"No, it's not," Tache countered. "Tell me. What are you planning to do? I'm not hiding anything from you."

"We know there's one more box containing a thousand gold coins and some jewelry."

"It must be the biggest part of the goods."

"I don't know for sure."

"Well? Go on."

"Well," the elderly man went on, "since we knew about the box, we tracked it down. We found the person who has it, but she won't give it to us without the password, even if we kill her, and we don't want bloodshed. Prunache knows it, but he's in jail somewhere and we can't find him. You talked to him, so you must know it too."

"What about Solomonică? Did he know where the box was?"

"No, he didn't, but he told us how to track it down, and we did. Now we need the password and you've got it."

"That's right, I've got it," Tache admitted. "What happens if I give it to you?"

"You stay alive and we go our separate ways."

"All right," Tache said. "I'll give you the password, even though I'm well aware that this whole thing, from the notes you sent to the chat we're having, is a setup. You're trying to trick me."

"May my wife and children die if I'm lying!" the elderly man cried. "Solomonică was dead serious when he asked us to bump you off."

"Okay. It doesn't really matter. I'll give you the password. Don't forget it now. 'We're from Service and Maintenance. We've come for the furniture.' There. Do what you can with it."

"Don't mess with us," threatened the blond man, starting to scribble down the password in a notebook. The elderly man slapped his pen away.

"I'm not messing with you," Tache assured him.

The elderly man didn't seem satisfied. "You're not going to butt in, are you?" he asked anxiously.

"What do you mean, 'butt in'?"

"I mean, you might try to tail us and get your hands on the box before we do or take it away from us."

Tache smiled ingratiatingly. "What do you expect? Of course I'm going to tail you, try to catch you, and take the box."

The blond man seemed more struck by Tache's words than his companion was. "You are?" he asked, stunned.

"Of course I am."

"But why?"

"Just because. You think you can just take the box while I stand guard for you? Not me. We all have our jobs to do."

"Uncle Solomonică was right to want you out of the way," the blond man said scornfully. "You really are a bastard."

"Well, that's your opinion. You're entitled to it."

"We should have shot you from behind and not bothered to talk to you."

"Cut the crap, will you? First of all, you didn't come here to kill me; you came for the password—you want that box. Second, I'm not going to lie to you. It wouldn't be right. So I'm giving you notice that I'm going to follow you. Would you rather I'd lied?"

The blond man still looked surprised.

"But why do you want to hurt us? We're doing you a favor."

"There's no point in trying to explain. You wouldn't understand."

"Hmph!" the elderly man said thoughtfully. "We don't seem to understand each other at all."

"Sorry."

"Besides," the blond man added, "what makes you so sure you'll catch us?"

"I'm not sure, but I'll do my best. I may not catch you when you're going after the box, but I'll get you eventually."

"How?" the blond man asked again.

"Forget it!" his companion interjected. "That's the last thing you need to worry about. He'll find a way."

"In that case," the blond man said, reddening, "let's simplify things."

He took the gun out of his pocket and pointed it at Tache's chest. The elderly man tried to stop him, but before he could wrest the gun from his hand, the blond man had discharged all six bullets into Tache. Tache's eyes opened wide, then he doubled over and fell backwards. The ground was covered with oak and maple leaves, yellow and brown, and his body slipped downhill on them as if on a slide, making a soft *whoosh* as it went. Petrified, the two men stared at the body, and when it stopped several yards away against a tree, the older man asked the younger one, "Why did you shoot, you idiot?"

"I lost my temper," the blond man said apologetically.

"Well, don't let it happen next time, damn you, or you'll regret it."

And they both disappeared into the woods.

"We're from Service and Maintenance. We've come for the furniture," the blond man said casually. But the old woman didn't hear him.

"Come inside! I can't hear you," she shouted.

Once inside, the blond man spoke directly in her ear. "We're from Service and Maintenance. We've come for the furniture."

"Well, it's about time. I was afraid to keep it here any longer. Here! Take it! And to hell with you!"

The old woman led the blond man into the kitchen and then into a dark closet smelling of sour cabbage. "Reach into that barrel," she said.

The blond man thrust his arm up to the elbow into the barrel and brought out a rectangular box wrapped in a sheet of plastic. Back in the hallway, he slipped the box into a shopping bag.

"What's in it?" the old woman inquired. "Can't you tell me that at least?"

"I have no idea," the blond man replied. "Some papers, I think."

"Well, don't you ever come here again with that kind of stuff. I won't let you in!"

"Fine, ma'am, fine. Much obliged. Good-bye."

"Good-bye."

The blond man went out into the street and, without looking right or left, headed for the tram stop. There he hesitated for a moment or two, then set off purposefully down a side street and entered a bistro. The elderly man was waiting for him at a table at the back of the room. The blond man sat down and put the shopping bag under the table. There was a third chair at the table, unoccupied. Suddenly someone asked, "Is this chair taken?"

"Yes."

The man who had asked sat down anyway. The blond man stared at him, his eyes wide with terror. Then his lips started to twitch, his face contorted, and he toppled off his chair in a faint. The elderly man hurried to help him up, slapping his face several times. The blond man came to, but he still looked dazed.

"Have some water," said Tache, holding a glass to his lips. But the blond man continued to look at him dumbfounded.

"Let's go," Tache urged. "If you keep staring at me, you'll faint again."

He took the shopping bag from underneath the table and got up. A plainclothesman motioned to the two men to get up. In the street Tache positioned himself between them.

"Why were you so surprised to see me?" he asked.

"I wasn't," the elderly man replied.

"I noticed you weren't. Why not?"

"I don't surprise easily."

"But didn't you think I was dead?"

"No," the elderly man said, sullenly. "On the train I realized you'd replaced the bullets in our guns with blanks."

"A good thing too. Otherwise your idiot friend here would've killed me."

"I don't know what's wrong with him. Sometimes he just can't control himself. I think he's got a screw loose."

The three of them walked on, side by side, as if on a stroll. The plainclothesman followed.

"If that idiot hadn't fired, we might have struck our deal," the elderly man said hesitantly.

"I don't think so."

"But if it hadn't been for us, you wouldn't have found the box in a month of Sundays."

"I'd have found it eventually."

"No, you wouldn't. We came across it by accident. We could've grabbed it, but the old woman wouldn't give it up without the password. Over her dead body, she said. And we didn't want bloodshed."

"All right."

"Uncle Solomonică said it was full of gold bracelets, earrings, and diamonds. They'd hidden it so well the devil himself couldn't have found it. They'd lost track of it themselves."

"They got scared. That's why they lost it."

"Does it have three keys with it?" the elderly man asked.

"Yes, it does."

"I think there are some gold ingots in there too."

"Stop drooling," Tache said laughing. The elderly man laughed too.

"I hope you're not too mad at us," he said as they parted company.

"No, you're all right."

Tache left the two men at the police station and went straight home. From the street he could hear the baby crying, and from the quality of the wails he could tell it was having its bath.

"How come you're back so soon?" his wife asked, startled, seeing Tache at the door.

"I missed you. That's all," he said cheerfully. He kissed her on the neck and the baby on its stomach, tickling it. The child squealed in delight.

"I'm so glad you're back," his wife told him later, after the infant had dropped off to sleep. They were lying in bed, arms entwined. "I missed you so."

"I missed you too," he whispered in her ear.

"Did you ever think of me?" she asked, her anger forgotten.

"I did."

"Do you still love me?"

"I do."

"A lot?"

"A lot."

"Last night I dreamed about you again. I dream about you all the time."

"That's not unusual. Would you rather dream about somebody else?"

"Do you dream about me?"

"Don't blow in my ear. It tickles."

"Are you planning to go away again?"

"I don't know. I'll see."

"Please don't."

"I'm sleepy. Let's stop talking."

"All right."

She fell asleep at once, but Tache, though exhausted, remained wide awake.

"What's the matter?" she asked after a while, feeling him toss and turn in the bed.

"I don't know. I keep dozing off and waking up again."

"Stop going over things in your mind."

"I'm trying to, but I can't."

"Did something happen to you?"

"No, nothing."

"Then relax."

Just before midnight he took two sleeping pills. He slept until seven, but woke up tired and morose. He washed and shaved without his usual whistling and singing.

"I don't know what's wrong with me," he told his wife at eight o'clock as he was leaving for work. "I'm not feeling well."

"Neither am I."

As soon as he got to his office, Tache read the sports paper. Then he called Colonel Ştefănescu.

"Comrade Colonel, shall I come to your office to open the box?"

"No, don't. I'm due to report to Comrade General. Ask Bică to help you. If he can't, open it yourself and write it up."

"What if I steal a bracelet or a ring?"

"Go ahead. But be sure to give it to your wife."

"Are you implying I have a mistress?"

"Cut it out, please. I have no time for jokes." The colonel hung up.

Tache dialed another number. "Bică, can you come to my office? It'll take half an hour at the most."

"No, I can't. I'm just starting an interrogation."

"Ten minutes then. A quick inventory."

"Don't you get it? I don't have time. How much clearer do I have to be?"

Tache hung up and took the box out of a filing cabinet. It was made of wrought metal and had curved sides. The owner's monogram, "C. D.," was engraved on the lid, and the key was fastened to the handle with a strip of wire. Tache inserted the key into the lock slowly, carefully, and turned it gently. The lock creaked, then yielded. At that instant an explosion racked the building.

❧ Răzvan Petrescu (1956–)

Răzvan Petrescu began a career as a doctor (1982) but after a few years turned to his real love, literature. After serving as editor for the magazines *Amfiteatru* and *Cuvântul,* he moved to the Litera Publishing House, and since the beginning of 1995 has been editor of the All Publishing House. Petrescu's stories first appeared in a collective volume, *Debut '86.* His volume of short prose, *The Summer Garden* (1989), was awarded the Liviu Rebreanu Prize. Petrescu is also a playwright, and his book of plays *The Farce* (1994) won the Dramatists' Union Prize. Other titles by Petrescu include a collection of short fiction, *The Eclipse* (1993), and a collection of plays, *Spring at the Tavern* (1994).

"Diary of an Apartment Dweller (February–June 1990)" first appeared in *The Eclipse* (1993).

Diary of an Apartment Dweller
(February–June 1990)

I live at number 9 Mirajului[1] Street, in an old, gray, well-kept apartment building. Rats seldom find their way in, but there are cockroaches, the red kind, that crawl up the pipes. I live on the tenth floor, in an apartment with two rooms, a kitchen, a bathroom, and a storage room. The windows are large, and I have a beautiful view. I can see the streetcar tracks, the people waiting at the stop, the bridge, the park with its stunted trees, the lake, and the buildings on the opposite shore, which every morning are bathed in the light of the sunrise. Most of my neighbors like the view. They are quiet, contemplative people with serious occupations. We live together harmoniously.

For some time, however, a strange epidemic has befallen our apartment building. It all began one morning in February. I was going down the stairs, thinking of the project I had to turn in, when suddenly I heard an unusual noise that in a few seconds enveloped the stairwell. It was a plaintive kind of song, monotonous, melancholy, as it spiraled upward. I descended quickly, two steps at a time, my hand gripping the banister. The tune grew louder and louder. On the ground floor I saw a crowd of people holding lit tapers, a tall thin priest, wreaths, and a brand-new coffin with brass handles. Apartment number 1. So Panait, the writer, had passed on. No point in getting upset about it, I thought. The man had been quite advanced in years, and he had secured a name for himself that would long outlive him. Still, I was saddened. He was the first person to die in our wing of the building.

A few days later, four to be precise, I heard the mournful chant again. I put on my slippers and went out into the corridor. Driven by curiosity, I climbed down several flights of stairs. No, there was no doubt about it. Apostol, the bookseller, had passed away. A man of great learning. My God, what a commotion! They were shrieking like banshees. I climbed back up to my apartment and turned on the television. Then the radio. Then I ate an omelette.

When Lola Baltag, the violinist, died, I felt sick to my stomach. Probably an attack of indigestion. I remembered how beautifully she used to play Bach's Concerto for Violin and Orchestra. And Mozart's Seventh Concerto. Or the Ave Maria. It must have been a virus, something like that. I listened carefully to the radio reports, the telephone calls, the voices of my friends. But there was nothing special in any of them. Everything was just as before; life went on as usual. Just in case, I purchased four packets of antidiarrhea tablets. And a record of Lola playing.

Five days later Baciu, the architect, was carried out, to the tune of a brass band, into the small but elegant cemetery in our neighborhood. The instruments glittered, the people followed slowly behind the open funeral car. The third floor had been cleaned out.

At the next residents' meeting, I rose and took the floor. I brought up the subject—a brief speech—but no one listened to me. No one, that is, except for a man in a worker's cap, who glared at me. Immediately after I finished they passed on to serious issues, voting as in times past.[2] The area in front of the building was to be converted into a children's playground. Children should have a place to play, after all! I said nothing and silently prayed I had been mistaken. Maybe I was seeing things more bleakly than they were. I hoped to God it was true.

Two days later Fulga, the engineer, only twenty-eight years old, and

Ganea, the great historian, who was sixty (which in fact he would have been had he lived till June), retired with pomp and circumstance from social life. They both had yellow faces and smelled strongly of perfume. There was no room to pass on the stairwells, so crowded were they with friends, relatives, co-workers, guests, and neighbors. The memorial dinner lasted well into the night. Speeches, testimonials, hiccups, toasts, Verdi arias, the Requiem, sobs, the Beatles, the Requiem, shrieks, the stamping of feet, bottles hurled out the window in memory of the deceased, the Requiem, tears, vomiting, laughter. That night I took a sleeping pill.

When I woke up the next morning another one had gone. I almost tripped over the wooden cross someone had negligently left leaning against the wall. Without meaning to, I read the words on the ribbon: *We Work, We Do Not Die.* They sounded beautiful. A heavy smell wafted from the apartment with the black-bordered door. So Almaş the pharmacist was gone too. But not before transmitting the disease, or whatever it was, to his wife, a tall woman who followed him down the same path shortly thereafter. The priest (who was becoming plumper all the time) headed the procession, complete with banners and other trappings. There were few mourners, but the ones who showed up were very well dressed.

From Saturday on, the number of deaths soared. Not even children were spared. The coffin makers gave up carving the ornate flowers usually found on the wooden coffin lids, delivering them bare and unpolished instead. The fifth floor, the seventh, a return to the sixth for the only tenant left—a woman attorney. The eighth floor, the ninth. Worse than during the earthquake. What could be done about it? There was no mention of anything unusual in the newspapers. I went on gazing at the sunrise every morning, as if I expected an answer to emerge from the little red sun. One day I wrote in my diary, "The little red sun looks like the pupil of an eye." Crăciun, an eye doctor, Manoilă, an editor, and Axenie, a chemistry teacher, could no longer share these wonderful dawns with me. At most they could glimpse the darkness. Again the sounds of funeral marches enveloped the building.

Nowhere else in the city were people dying at this rate. I wrote exposés; I sent letters to magazines, to government agencies, to the president himself. In the meantime the gas pressure went down, the hot water was cut off, and the lights started to flicker.[3] I received neatly typed, beautifully written responses to my complaints, advising me not to worry, to keep my mind on my job, and to find myself a girlfriend if possible. So I gave up. I would get used to the flowers, the incense, the smell of death, the glaring headlights, the tooting horns, the black armbands (I wore one too), the tears, and the priest's voice, more hoarse than ever, chanting the service. He had become quite obese and very talkative. Once I made the mistake of asking him if he was sure there was an afterlife. He glanced at me, stared up at the stars (it was nighttime, halfway through a funeral dinner for a poet), and belched. Of course there was an afterlife, he told me, annoyed. I apologized, but to no avail. He turned his back on me and has completely ignored me ever since. Days passed. I would glimpse them in the morning, dripping from that reddish pupil. Or sometimes purple. One by one. The epidemic went on.

At eight o'clock on Monday morning three citizens dressed in white showed up at the door. The Government Control Board, I thought to myself, feeling hopeful again. The three of them asked for information in friendly tones, poking here and there into corners. They checked every-thing; they scribbled in their little notebooks with gray covers;[4] they searched, fumbled through things, tapped against the walls. In less than an hour they acquired a veritable halo of professionalism. Then they left, assuring me they would be back.

On Wednesday, within an interval of a few hours, two families of actors took their final exits. Then came Badea the sculptor, along with his mother, an impressionist painter, and Ene and Paraschiv, the opera singers. By all accounts, the *coliva*[5] they served was delicious. Many cars, even more umbrellas. It was pouring.

Hardly had the last group of mourners disappeared around the corner of the building than the wailing began anew. This time it was from the Gutenberg family, on the ninth floor. I had once listened to their wun-derkind playing the flute at the Philharmonic. They placed the flute by his side in the coffin. Then I saw them loading their belongings onto a big truck. I dressed and went out to visit a friend. When I came back in the evening, I was surprised how loudly my footsteps echoed on the stairs. No doubt the empty apartments acted as resonance chambers, like the bodies of violins without any strings. On the eighth floor I ran into the building manager, a well-known literary critic. He was leaning against the banister in his pajamas, smoking a cigarette. "Have the Gutenbergs moved out, Mr. Pană?" I asked him. He gazed at me wearily. He was pale, unshaven, his hair uncombed. "Yes, they have, in a way." He smiled, crushed the stub of his cigarette under the heel of his slipper, and went back to his apartment.

Since yesterday our building has been deserted. If you pound on the walls with your fist, they resound with emptiness even though the apartments are still full of things. No one has had the time to remove anything. A deep, thought-provoking silence reigns. If I wanted to, I could roam freely through the furnished rooms and take a leisurely look at the pictures, books, knickknacks, mirrors, family albums. I could smell the eaux de cologne and perfumes. I could roll around on the fringed Persian carpets. I could play with the fringes, cut them, tear them off. I could light the chandeliers, lamps, and night-lights. I could try on shirts, socks, underwear, suits. I could put on lipstick, play instruments, declaim theatrical roles. I could throw pillows, weep amidst unfamiliar objects, open doors and drawers, listen to records, eat shrimp and caviar, drink cognac or champagne, sleep in any bed, listen to the clink of porcelain in glass cabinets, break a crystal glass as I pass from one apartment to another, silhouetted at times by the dim light of the street lamps.

I lock the door and draw the chain across. I throw myself onto the bed, snuggle under the quilt, and try to think of something pleasant. A beach, perhaps. A deserted beach with gulls pecking in the sand. When you come too near they hop away, almost unafraid. One of them has lost a leg. It shrieks sharply. Yet its shriek cannot drown out the singing, the tune that keeps ringing in my ears. . . . An aspirin. A glass of water. The TV set isn't working. Neither is the radio. The electricity must have been cut off, because the night lamp won't go on. I have the feeling I'm all alone amidst echoes that fade even as they emerge from the core of the building. The building is being swallowed by a spongy white silence. I look up. The windowpane is frozen. How strange.

When I came out of the building this morning I bumped up against a tall wire fence. My briefcase fell from my hand. The street, with its trees, leaves, and garbage cans, seemed enveloped in mist, as if I were seeing it through unfocused binoculars, their lenses clogged with lint. Panting, I rushed back up to my apartment.

A beam of light shines at the top of the window. A small rainbow. It fades away. I go to the window and look out. The view is different. Either my vantage point has changed or the building has sunk at least one floor. I fill a glass with water. I gulp it down. The water has an unpleasant taste. I look at the glass, then back at the window.

Everything creaks, cracks, snaps. My head aches terribly. As if I had a ball of ice in there, behind my forehead.

Ion Manolescu (1968–)

The youngest writer in this anthology, Ion Manolescu cofounded the Literary Circle of Bucharest in 1990, one year before he graduated from the Department of Romanian Language and Literature at the University of Bucharest. At present, he is on the faculty of the same institution. His prose is based on a technique he calls "phantasmatic," which connects literature to pop art forms, such as advertisements, comic strips, and video clips. Manolescu's first volume, *Happenings in Our Little Town* (1993), creates fictive universe in a vaguely North American setting, onto which he superimposes aspects of everyday life during the final years of Ceauşescu's dictatorship.

"Paraphernalia" was first published in *Happenings in Our Little Town* (1993).

Paraphernalia

After the tree in her yard was cut down, Mrs. Robinson went a little batty. At least that's what most of the residents of the little town thought when they passed by her house and cast bored glances at her front door. Seated on the tall porch steps, her chin resting on her hands in the manner of one of her illustrious ancestors,[1] Mrs. Robinson would spend a few hours every day, just after sunrise, staring with blank, tear-filled eyes at the stump in the yard. Of course, as Mr. Tippelton informed us during the meetings in the town hall yard, one would expect a woman with such a *Mater Dolorosa* posture to be either watching over her pots in the kitchen or trying to remember where she had left her darling child playing (in the street or in the neighbor's apple tree?). But, the omniscient mayor continued, grinning, when a woman does little else besides woolgathering (a very popular habit in the town, as a matter of fact), it means that the lights are flickering but there's nobody home. So it should come as no surprise that, while glancing furtively at Mrs. Robinson's porch, the residents of

Gas City² adopted their mayor's opinion of her. The woman had simply gone off her rocker.

Mrs. Robinson had another peculiar habit: she told fortunes by reading cards. First she would tell her own future, then would do the same for other residents, who, driven either by curiosity or disregard for the mayor's opinion (there were a few of that kind), were eager to find out how they would fare in their love lives, or how many years it would take for them to replace Saunderson the policeman. These encounters, full of astounding revelations, followed a simple and well-established pattern: after finishing her tear-filled meditation on the chilly porch steps, Mrs. Robinson would lay a red velvet coverlet on a wooden table in the yard. She would then bring out a few decks of cards and shuffle them amidst bowls of burning oil and four or five wax figurines with sharp noses and bulging eyes. Next she would tie five to six gaudy scarves, each a different color, halfway up the legs of the table and wait for them to start fluttering in the breeze. If there was no wind, the customer would be sent home with threats of such a horrible fate that even the most hardened criminal would not protest, return, or ask for his money back. If the scarves flapped wildly, however, Mrs. Robinson would take the cards in her greasy palms and, asking her guest to sit in the chair opposite her, would hurriedly lay out the lime-green cardboard rectangles among the array of ancient odds and ends. Oftentimes the citizens in quest of a future less dusty and boring than any they could imagine for themselves were astonished by the cool breeze that blew across the table, making the scarves whip about tautly like menacing flames, while the trees in the street stood motionless and limp and the houses drooped in the summer heat. The inhabitants of the little town found it just as difficult to explain the purpose of the lilac-colored wax figurines, which looked for all the world like the cones that topped Dick Donovan's multistoried cake creations. Nobody could find a use for the thin knitting needles either, with their pointed tips and bulbous ends that bored through the necks of the immobile statuettes. In any case, once seated in the velvet-upholstered chair whose long arms seemed about to seize you in their embrace, you'd lose all desire to ask inappropriate questions. Indeed, you would remain stock-still, your eyes fastened on the large, grimy cards.

"This is psychedelic sabotage!" the mayor protested one sultry summer afternoon. He was repeating the exact same words that Ted Grant had murmured in his ear as they stood at the foot of the cherry tree where about fifty sweating residents had gathered. (Mr. Grant had a book with a fine leather binding tucked under his arm; he had been leafing through it before Mr. Tippelton arrived.) Strangely enough, the mayor's words had a demobilizing effect: instead of nodding approval or rising to the challenge as usual, the people shook their heads in disbelief and departed one by one, eyes downcast. Mr. Grant and Mr. Tippelton were left to themselves by the cherry tree, dumbfounded and goggle-eyed.

After this Mrs. Robinson's reputation grew, not so much because of the mayor's failure to be convincing or because of her ever-more-frequent sessions with the Ouija board (in which the fretful movements of the little glass turned upside down and pressed by the palm and the waltzing trance-state writing played important roles) but because of an occurrence related by Bill's bearded neighbor, a young man called Smither.

Smither, as everybody knew, suffered from a disease as widespread among teenagers as it was embarrassing for grownups. His face was spattered with black and red dots which, with the passage of time, and despite their owner's efforts at growing a beard to hide them, kept multiplying and swelling up in an unpleasant manner. In short, in only a few years Smither had developed the appearance of a toad that had accidentally stumbled into a beehive. Naturally, under such conditions, receiving the delicate kiss of a Lola or Kim had become unlikely. This to the dismay of the aforesaid Smither, whose misery was so great that he longed either to put a plastic bag over his head or lay himself down across the railroad tracks. It seemed that he had even attempted the latter solution once. However, a few hours after he had thrust his neck onto the rusty tracks outside the station, an old woman passed by and, realizing his intentions, informed him in a sweet, reedy voice, "There hasn't been a train in two years, young man."

The extraordinary event happened one evening when, running down from the north end of town where Mrs. Robinson's house was, Smither tripped over a log left by some good-for-nothing in the middle of the road and fell, head first, into a heap of dirt right in front of the *Roasted Haunch* Restaurant. When he got up amidst the chuckles of the tipsy patrons, Bill's wretched young neighbor displayed a face smoother than the coin Mr. Grant sat polishing at the counter. The smirking stopped abruptly. The people lazing in the pub for another glass, who had never paid the slightest heed to Smither before, surrounded him, crowding the entrance. The last to arrive was the pub owner himself, who, at the sight of Smither's face, begrimed yet no longer bearing the usual disfiguring pustules, bent down and picked up a handful of dirt. "Could there be something therapeutic in this?" he exclaimed. Smither dusted himself off, not daring to swear (who knows why), then, seated on the lowest and most worn-down wooden step of the Roasted Haunch, began spinning out his tale.

"My God, I can hardly believe it myself." Smither patted his smooth cheeks with his left hand, while he lifted the pint of beer offered him with the right. "I went out for my evening walk, as usual. For a stroll, really, since my legs are so feeble I can hardly get around on them. It was after the blasted sun had gone down, because I don't like sweating like an ox any more than I like putting my face on display. I was heading toward the edge of town, thinking I could maybe avoid some of the dust, when who should I see but Mrs. Robinson, with a black mongrel on a leash. I hadn't seen her much in that part of town, so I started following her. A person can't help being curious. . . . She walked on for a while and I followed her, keeping my distance so she couldn't see me, but not loitering so far behind that I might lose sight of her. Suddenly she stopped. I hid behind a tree and noticed her cross herself three times. Then she started digging around a weed with a stick or a hoe. She was mumbling something, but I couldn't hear her very well. You see, I still had the cotton in my ears that I had put in at home. Well, she dug and dug, and when she was done, she tied the mutt to the weed with the leash. 'Damn,' I said to myself, 'what's going on here?' The lady teased the dog with a piece of bread or meat, then tossed it in the air. As the dog jumped for it, he pulled the weed out. At that moment, I swear, I thought I was losing my mind and would croak right there on the spot. There was such an awful roar I almost fell on my back into the ditch. I put my hands over my ears and threw myself on the ground behind the tree. When I got up the lady was gone, but the dog was lying there on the ground as if struck by lightning." Smither paused, took a few more gulps of beer, and went on with his story.

"I started back home and I walked and walked until I got to the lady's house. I had almost passed her house when I saw a light on in her yard, and the lady motioned to me to come in. To tell the truth, I was scared to death and I said to myself, 'You're in for it now, old boy, she's on to you!' But it wasn't like that at all. The lady sat me down at a table crowded with oils and cards and asked me if I didn't want to get rid of that nasty stuff on my face. Of course, I answered, relieved to have gotten off so lightly, but still leery. 'Well then,' the lady said, 'take this ointment' (and she held out a round jar, like ladies use when they paint up their cheeks and eyes) 'and rub it on, but only when you get home. If you open the jar before you get home, you'll look worse than you do now, and woe will befall you. Is that clear?' 'Of course it's clear,' I said, and I dropped some money on the table. After I left I could hardly keep myself from opening the bottle, but I remembered the lady's warning and those scarves of hers that were fluttering so hard. So I didn't look inside it until I got home. As soon as I closed the door I opened the jar and smeared the stuff all over my face. It felt like liquid grease. I used it all up, just to be sure, but I still didn't believe it would do any good. What if it was a joke or something, I thought. I went into the bathroom and turned on the light and smiled at myself in the mirror. And what do you know! My face was as smooth as a well-trodden path! I left the house and started running as fast as I could to the lady's house to thank her. Only she'd turned off all the lights and the gate was locked. So I ran here, since I knew you folks would still be around at this hour. . . ."

Smither's story had several unexpected results. For one thing, the citizens gathering in front of the Roasted Haunch kept touching his face in disbelief. For another, Mrs. Robinson's prestige rose immensely overnight; she became a local heroine. Surprisingly, however, it was Mr. Tippelton who suffered the most significant consequences of the event occurring that fateful summer night. And not just him.

A few weeks after Smither's miraculous change of face (as the citizens of the town called it), on an ordinary evening in Gas City—the town only had ordinary evenings, with the trees smelling of gasoline and the streets buried in pitch darkness, the mayor and his followers (a team made up of Grant, Donovan, and another two men), summoned their courage and resolved to visit Mrs. Robinson in her yard. Their decision was puzzling because lately the mayor had been advising the residents—close friends or mere acquaintances—to stay home at night, since it was not safe to go out. "At night," he would say, "darkness, dust, and haze combine to form a kind of fog that hangs between trees and fences like a thick cobweb. This heavy mist envelops you like a net, blinding and smothering you. Sometimes it even demands to see your identity card. Only if you've gone through it can you understand that nocturnal goings-out are fraught with all kinds of hidden perils, practically impossible to avoid." In describing these episodes, Mr. Tippelton would wax melodramatic and waggle a finger at the potentially imprudent interlocutor. It was hard not to heed his words.

After passing through the unseen dangers which the mayor had predicted with such clairvoyance, the members of the team led by Mr. Tippelton, spruced up and dressed in their Sunday best, arrived at Mrs. Robinson's house. She asked them into the yard; they entered one by one, each waiting at the gate until the one before him had left. Mr. Tippelton was the last to go in. Slightly ill at ease, he sat down at the table covered with the velvet cloth.

"What's the matter?" Mrs. Robinson inquired, staring through the mayor as if he were made of glass. The mayor swallowed hard, then told his story. Mrs. Robinson listened silently for a few minutes, and when the mayor had finished, leisurely shuffled the deck of cards. The wax figurines, glittering in the light of the greasy flames dancing in the cups on the table, glared at the mayor with evil popping eyes. Suddenly Mrs. Robinson stopped dealing the cards and, gazing up toward the garden, asked the mayor a startling question. "What do you see there?" Mr. Tippelton cast a hurried glance in the direction she had indicated and, seeing nothing besides the usual Gas City summer sky, with the multitude of stars that had been blinking uninterruptedly since he had become mayor of the town, answered, the little finger of his right hand digging into his chin, "What's there to see? A large room with video games. A universal flipper . . ." Mrs. Robinson smiled, gathered up her cards and colored scarves, and patted the mayor on the shoulder, "You don't need to have your fortune told." Then she took her things into the house and turned out the lights.

After the visit to Mrs. Robinson's that evening, several small unpleasant accidents befell the mayor's team. Dick Donovan lost his recipes for cakes and cookies. Ted Grant lost all the hair on his legs while unsightly tufts appeared on the tops of his ears. The other two men awoke with horrible toothaches, though neither one had any recollection of having had such a problem before. Only Mr. Tippelton remained unaffected by such misfortunes. Understandably, the citizens of Gas City wondered why this should be so.

And there's no easy answer. In any case, no one dares tell Mrs. Robinson she's off her rocker, and no one dares spy on her either. Those who have, however—and there aren't too many of them—claim to have seen Mr. Tippelton working busily in her garden. Of course, this is only a rumor. Rumor also has it that the mayor of Gas City might resign—which seems quite unlikely—and that a wedding between Mrs. Robinson and Mr. Tippelton may be forthcoming. Of course, this last bit of gossip borders on the ridiculous and the citizens who put it forward can't help smiling when they mention it.

As for Donovan, Grant, and the other two, all we know is this: they are awaiting the mayor's orders before they dare show their faces out in the world again.

Notes to the Stories
Sources

❧ Notes to the Stories

Fănuş Neagu, "Beyond the Sands"

1. Most Romanians are Eastern Orthodox Christians. In the Romanian Orthodox Church, the cantor assists the priest in the service by singing.

2. The *toaca* is a long piece of wood or metal which is rhythmically beaten with one or two small hammers to announce the beginning of a religious service (or certain parts of it) in Romanian Orthodox churches or monasteries.

Nicolae Velea, "Carefree"

1. *Duminică* means Sunday in Romanian. It is sometimes given as a name to children born on that day of the week. People born on Sundays and holidays are thought to be lucky.

2. *Leu* in Romanian means lion. It is also the word for the principal Romanian currency. One *leu* (plural: *lei*) is subdivided into one hundred *bani*.

3. *Militia* replaced the *police* under Communism, following the Soviet model. The term *police* was allegedly associated with capitalist brutality and repression.

4. The campaign for literacy in the late 1940s and early 1950s was part of the Communist drive to "raise the cultural standards of the population."

Petru Dumitriu, "The Best-Cared-For Horses"

1. The Saxons (*Saşi,* in Romanian) are an ethnic minority of German origin who arrived in southern Transylvania at the end of the twelfth century. They received land and exemptions from taxes in return for military defense of the border with Wallachia against various migratory peoples.

2. Under Communism, the functions of prewar Romanian town halls were carried out by administrative units called People's Councils.

3. Făgăraş and Aiud were two of the countless prisons where Romanian citizens (prewar politicians, priests, intellectuals, farmers, etc.) were imprisoned by the hundreds of thousands during the years of Communist terror (late 1940s through late 1950s).

Dumitru Radu Popescu, "The Tin Can"

1. Ion Fieraru means "John the Ironsmith" in Romanian; János Kovács has the same meaning in Hungarian.

2. During World War II, northwestern Transylvania was ceded to Hungary as a result of the Diktat of Vienna of 1940. The "new rule" is the rule of the Hungarian government.

3. *Lupu* means wolf in Romanian; *Farkas* is the same in Hungarian.

4. *Pengö* is an old Hungarian currency.

5. *Palinca* is double-distilled Transylvanian fruit brandy.

Radu Cosaşu, "Burials"

1. *Calu* is a nickname that means "horse."

2. Louis Aragon (1897–1982), a French dadaist and surrealist writer, became a Communist in 1927. Some of his writings depicted life from a Marxist point of view.

3. Ion Antonescu (1882–1946), a controversial political figure, was Romania's premier from 1940 to 1944 and led Romania into World War II on the German side. He was tried for war crimes, sentenced, and executed in 1946.

4. "Vote for the Sun" (with its overtones of "enlightenment") was the slogan of the Communist Party in the elections of 1946.

5. Poiana Ţapului and Buşteni are mountain resorts located 133 and 135 kilometers north of Bucharest.

6. Mircea Eliade, one of the world's foremost historians of religion and mythology, did not return to Romania after World War II. His books were banned because of his "defection," because he was considered a decadent bourgeois, and because of his interest in religion, which was actively opposed by the new Russian-imposed regime.

7. On March 6, 1945, the first so-called democratic and popular government in Romania was established under the leadership of Petru Groza. Groza's government undertook the first measures against capitalism.

8. Oscar Rohrlich is the author's real name. Radu Cosaşu is his pen name.

Cristian Teodorescu, "Dollinger's Motorcycle"

1. Halvah, a Middle Eastern sweet made from crushed sesame seeds and honey, is very popular in Romania. (The Romanian halvah, however, is made from crushed sunflower seeds and honey.)

2. The Bărăgan Plain is the northeastern part of the Danube Plain, where numerous so-called enemies of the people, including ethnic Germans, were deported in the late 1940s and early 1950s.

Ana Blandiana, "The Phantom Church"

1. *Subpiatră* in Romanian means "under the stone."

2. Romanian serfs in eighteenth-century Transylvania were cruelly oppressed by their (primarily) Hungarian overlords, who required the serfs to work four days a week on their lands and hand over a tithe of their harvests, as well as other gifts. Serfs were restricted in their dress and forbidden to carry weapons. They were also forced to perform chores for the state administration, and paid heavy taxes. Desperate, many emigrated east to Moldavia or south to Wallachia.

Vasile Nicola Ursu, a priest from the village of Albac, also known as Horea, attempted to intercede on behalf of the peasants, making four trips to Vienna to petition Emperor Joseph II (1780–1790) of Austro-Hungary. The emperor tried to pass measures to improve the Romanian serfs' working conditions, but his attempts met with resistance on the part of the Transylvanian landowners.

The revolt of 1784 was the strongest manifestation of the anger of Transylvanian serfs against their overlords. They demanded that the landowners leave their estates and seek employment at the court of the emperor or in the cities and that land would then be divided among the peasants. They also sought the abolishment of the nobility, demanding that they pay taxes like the rest of the population. The rebellion was led by Vasile Nicola Ursu, known as Horea; by Ion Oargă, known as Cloşca; and by Marcu Giurgiu, known as Crişan. The serfs attacked, burned and demolished many landowners' estates, and occupied several cities. The uprising was finally put down by the emperor's army. The three leaders were caught and imprisoned in the city of Alba Iulia. Horea and Cloşca were publicly broken on the wheel; Crişan committed suicide in his prison cell.

3. Voivodes were the rulers of the medieval Romanian states.

4. *Mămăligă* (polenta), or corn meal mush, is a traditional Romanian food. It is usually eaten in place of bread in the countryside, often with farmer's cheese and sour cream.

5. The *hora* is a typical Romanian folk dance, performed in a circle with the dancers holding hands. It is a joyous part of every village celebration.

6. Easter service in the Romanian Orthodox Church begins on Saturday night, Easter Eve, and ends early on Sunday morning. At midnight, as the resurrection of Christ is proclaimed, the congregation lights candles and intones "Christ has risen."

7. In the Eastern Orthodox Church, priests are allowed to marry and raise families.

Ioan Petru Culianu, "The Secret of the Emerald Disk"

1. *Lea* is a coined word, a possible feminine form of *leu,* Romanian for lion.

Mircea Eliade, "The Captain's Daughter"

1. *Năsosu* means "big-nosed." It is the boy's nickname.

2. *Lopată* means "shovel" or "spade."

3. Iulia Haşdeu (1869–1888), a precocious Romanian poetess, could read at age three, spoke French, German, and English at eight, and finished secondary school at eleven.

Gabriela Adameşteanu, "A Common Path"

1. Romanians drink Turkish coffee, made of finely ground coffee beans boiled in water and not filtered. The dregs sink to the bottom of the cups, which are then overturned so that fortunes can be read in the shapes outlined on the inside of the cup.

Gheorghe Crăciun, "Gravity and Collaspe"

1. When people drop by for a visit between meals, it is the custom to serve them with one or two teaspoonfuls of fruit preserves on a saucer accompanied by a glass of cold water.

Mircea Cărtărescu, "The Game"

1. Mihai Eminescu (1850–1889) is considered Romania's greatest poet. His sister Harieta (?1854–1889), was physically disabled and could walk only with the help of two metal "contraptions." When Mihai Eminescu became seriously ill, Harieta looked after him despite her own frail health.

2. *Mendebil* can be loosely translated as "mentally disabled."

3. They are fictional child heroes, popular with Romanian children.

4. *Scânteia* means spark, i.e., the light of Communism. The red star on top of the building also symbolizes Communism.

5. On May Day, Communist countries celebrated International Workers' Day, usually with mass parades, where participants carried national and Communist Party flags, portraits of Communist leaders, and Communist slogans.

6. *Ruslan and Ludmila* is a fairy romance in verse by the Russian author Aleksandr Pushkin (1799–1837).

Ion Băieşu, "Death and the Major"

1. Sinaia is a popular mountain resort 127 kilometers north of Bucharest.

2. *Cega* means sterlet, a small sturgeon from the Danube.

Răzvan Petrescu, "Diary of an Apartment Dweller (February–June 1990)"

1. *Mirajului* means "mirage."

2. Under Communism, each apartment building was run by a collective of tenants. Members would vote on issues pertaining to the building. Sometimes decisions were political rather than practical.

3. These are the same privations as those of the 1980s, when Romanians suffered repeatedly from fuel shortages and power outages, especially during the winter months.

4. Officials surrounding former dictator Ceauşescu were known for scribbling down every word he said.

5. *Coliva* is a special dish of boiled wheat kernels mixed with sugar or honey and ground walnuts and decorated with candies and powdered sugar. It is given away as alms to the participants in the funeral service and offered again in annual commemorative services for the deceased.

Ion Manolescu, "Paraphernalia"

1. The famous statue of the *Thinker of Hamangia* is one of the oldest terra-cotta figurines found on Romanian territory, dating from 5,500 to 2,500 B.C. The statue represents a man in a sitting position, resting his elbows on his knees and his head in his hands.

2. The name of the town, Gas City, is in English in the original, as are the names of the characters (Tippelton, Robinson, Saunderson, etc.).

❊❊❊ Sources

The stories listed below were translated and included in this anthology with the written permission of the authors. They first appeared in Romanian in the following volumes:

Adameşteanu, Gabriela. "Drum comun." *Vară-primăvară*. Bucharest: Cartea Românească, 1989.

Băieşu, Ion. "Maiorul şi moartea." *Sufereau împreună*. Bucharest: Editura pentru literatură, 1965.

Blandiana, Ana. "Biserica fantomă." *Proiecte de trecut*. Bucharest: Cartea Românească, 1982.

Cărtărescu, Mircea. "Jocul." *Visul*. Bucharest: Cartea Românească, 1989.

Cosaşu, Radu. "Inmormântări." *Ficţionarii*. Bucharest: Cartea Românească, 1983.

Crăciun, Gheorghe. "Gravitaţie, colaps." *Compunere cu paralele inegale*. Bucharest: Cartea Românească, 1988.

Crohmălniceanu, Ov. S. "Un capitol de istorie literară." *Istorii insolite*. Bucharest: Cartea Românească, 1980.

Culianu, Ioan Petru. "Enigma discului de smaragd." *Pergamentul diafan*. Bucharest: Nemira, 1993.

Dumitriu, Petru. "Caii cei mai bine îngrijiţi." *Revista scriitorilor români*, no. 1. Munich, 1962.

Eliade, Mircea. "Fata căpitanului." *Nuvele*. Madrid: Destin, 1963.

Manolescu, Ion. "Paraphernalia." *Intâmplări din orăşelul nostru*. Bucharest: Cartea Românească, 1993.

Neagu, Fănuş. "Dincolo de nisipuri." *Dincolo de nisipuri*. Bucharest: Editura pentru literatură, 1962.

Nedelciu, Mircea. "Povestirea eludată." *Amendament la instinctul proprietăţii*. Bucharest: Eminescu, 1983.

Petrescu, Răzvan. "Jurnalul unui locatar (februarie–iunie 1990)." *Eclipsa*. Bucharest: Cartea Românească, 1993.

Popescu, Dumitru Radu. "Cutia de conserve." *Fuga*. Bucharest: Editura de stat pentru literatură şi artă, 1958.

Simionescu, Mircea Horia. "Mateo Orga: 'In aşteptare.'" "Ramiro Helveto: 'Circumstanţe.'" *Ingeniosul bine temperat (I). Dicţionar onomastic*. Bucharest: Editura pentru literatură, 1969.

Teodorescu, Cristian. "Motocicleta lui Dollinger." *Intâmplări din lumea nouă*. Bucharest: Rao, 1996.

Titel, Sorin. "Ea vrea să urc scările." *Noaptea inocenților.* Bucharest: Eminescu, 1970.

Țepeneag, Dumitru. "Accidentul." *Așteptare.* Bucharest: Cartea Românească, 1971.

Velea, Nicolae. "In treacăt." *Opt povestiri.* Bucharest: Editura pentru literatură, 1963.

Voiculescu, Vasile. "Ultimul Berevoi." *Ultimul Berevoi. Povestiri II.* Bucharest: Editura pentru literatură, 1966.